TRAIL OF
EVIL
TAU CETI AGENDA SERIES

Baen Books Fiction by Travis S. Taylor

The Tau Ceti Agenda Series
One Day on Mars
The Tau Ceti Agenda
One Good Soldier
Trail of Evil

Warp Speed Series
Warp Speed
The Quantum Connection

with John Ringo:
Vorpal Blade
Manxome Foe
Claws That Catch

Von Neumann's War

with Les Johnson:
Back to the Moon

Baen Books Nonfiction by Travis S. Taylor

New American Space Plan
The Science Behind The Secret
Alien Invasion: How to Defend Earth (with Bob Boan)

TAU CETI AGENDA SERIES

✧ ✧ ✧

TRAVIS S. TAYLOR

TRAIL OF EVIL

A Baen Book

Baen Publishing Enterprises
P.O. Box 1403
Riverdale, NY 10471
www.baen.com

ISBN: 978-1-4767-8031-3

Cover art by Kurt Miller

First Baen printing, April 2015

Distributed by Simon & Schuster
1230 Avenue of the Americas
New York, NY 10020

Library of Congress Cataloging-in-Publication Data

Taylor, Travis S.
Trail of evil / Travis S Taylor.
pages ; cm. -- (Tau ceti agenda ; 4)
"A Baen Books Original."
ISBN 978-1-4767-8031-3 (hardcover)

1. Space warfare--Fiction. 2. Artificial intelligence--Fiction. I. Title.
PS3620.A98T73 2015
813'.6--dc23

2014043653

Printed in the United States of America

10 9 8 7 6 5 4 3 2 1

This book is dedicated to the organizations like Hope for the Warrior and the Wounded Warriors Project. Our great superheroes go off to battle to protect our freedoms, and some of them make the ultimate sacrifice and give their lives. Some of the superheroes make extreme sacrifices that are as devastating, suffering severe injuries that disrupt the rest of their lives and their family's lives. My heart goes out to those brave soldiers and their brave families. I wish you the best in recovery and happiness. If it were not for the seemingly tireless organizations like Hope for the Warrior, some of these great heroes wouldn't have the wherewithal to recover and live their lives in peace. Help these projects out any way you can. And pray for our soldiers.

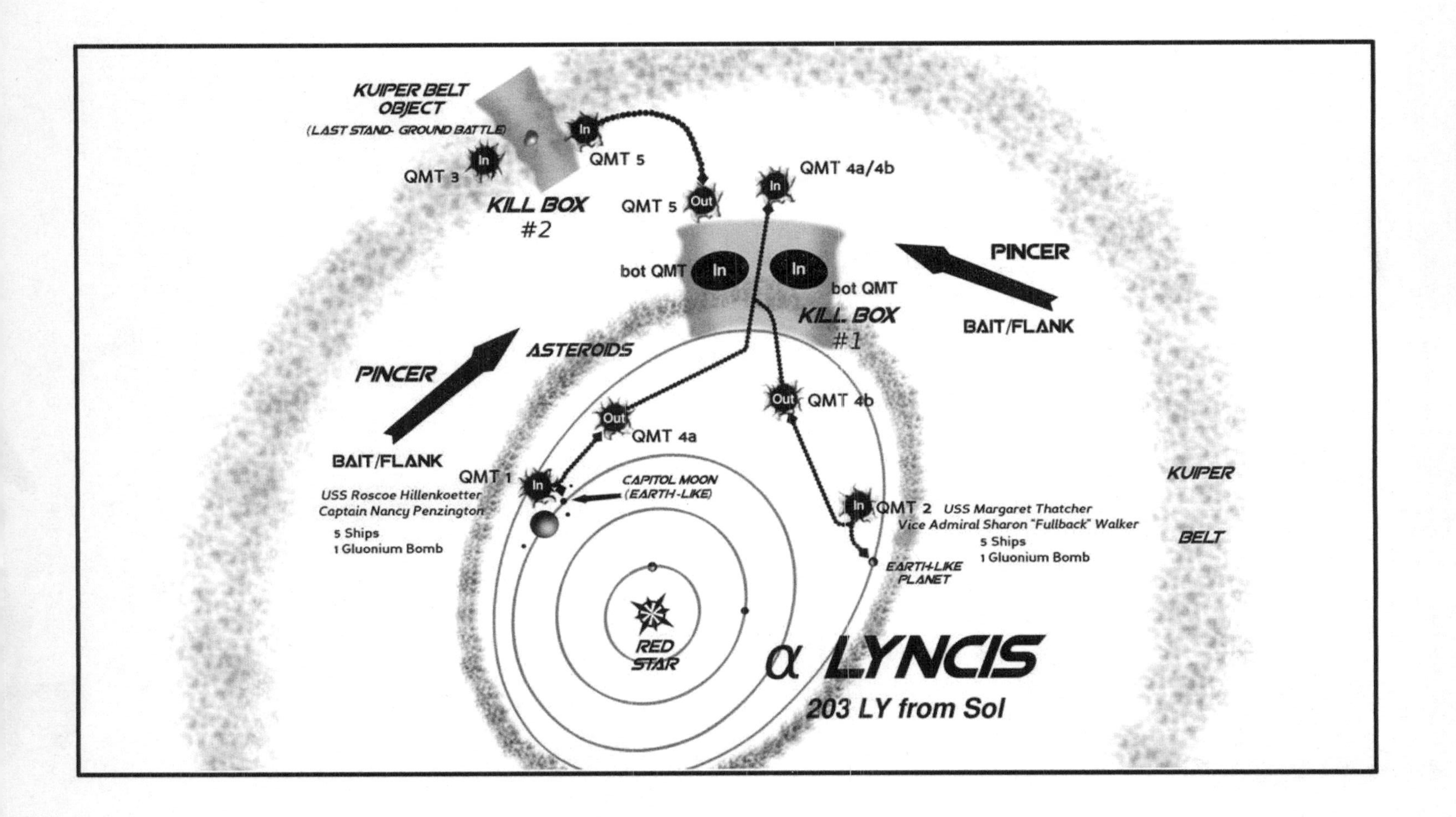
KUIPER BELT
OBJECT
(LAST STAND- GROUND BATTLE)
QMT 3
In
In
QMT 5
KILL BOX
#2
QMT 5
Out
In
QMT 4a/4b
bot QMT
In
In
bot QMT
KILL BOX
#1
PINCER
BAIT/FLANK
ASTEROIDS
PINCER
BAIT/FLANK
Out
QMT 4a
Out
QMT 4b
QMT 1
In
USS Roscoe Hillenkoetter
Captain Nancy Penzington
5 Ships
1 Gluonium Bomb
CAPITOL MOON
(EARTH-LIKE)
In
QMT 2 USS Margaret Thatcher
Vice Admiral Sharon "Fullback" Walker
5 Ships
1 Gluonium Bomb
EARTH-LIKE
PLANET
KUIPER
BELT
RED
STAR
α LYNCIS
203 LY from Sol

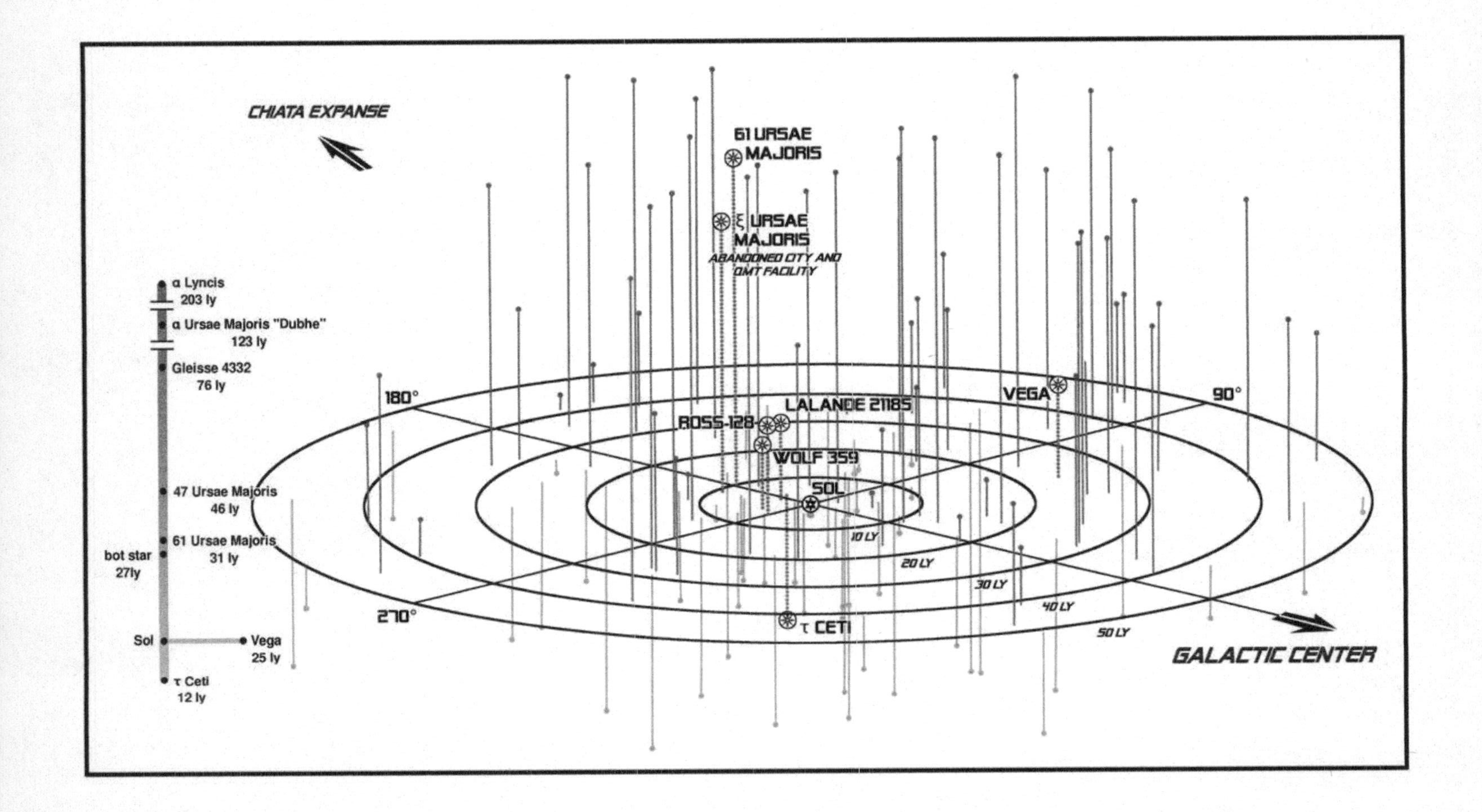
CHIATA EXPANSE
61 URSAE MAJORIS
ξ URSAE MAJORIS
ABANDONED CITY AND
OMT FACILITY
α Lyncis
203 ly
α Ursae Majoris "Dubhe"
123 ly
Gleisse 4332
76 ly
47 Ursae Majoris
46 ly
61 Ursae Majoris
31 ly
bot star
27ly
Sol
Vega
25 ly
τ Ceti
12 ly
180°
90°
270°
LALANDE 21185
ROSS-128
WOLF 359
SOL
VEGA
τ CETI
10 LY
20 LY
30 LY
40 LY
50 LY
GALACTIC CENTER

TRAIL OF
EVIL
TAU CETI AGENDA SERIES

Prologue

June 15, 2398 AD
Washington D.C., the White House
Monday, 9:45 AM, Earth Eastern Standard Time

"Mr. President, it has been more than four years since the Separatist War ended and two years' since I left office," Alexander Moore told his predecessor. Moore knew that his former vice president wasn't likely to win the election coming up in two years time, and that he'd have to take the appropriate steps while he was still in favor.

"I'm well aware of the history, Alexander. But while the war is over, there have been continuous mopping-up activities and little skirmishes here and there. You left me with quite a mess." The president attempted to use a politician's grin on him. Moore had been there and done that.

"Well, Mr. President. I'm here to tell you now that you don't know all of it." Alexander pursed his lips, ready to spill one of the biggest secrets of humanity. It was a secret that only he and his family knew. There was much more to humanity's bloody history over the past couple of centuries than met the eye.

"Alexander, I have been briefed on everything you had been into." The president sounded a bit dismayed, if not annoyed, at Alexander's suggestion that he was more in the know than the sitting president.

"Well, nobody could brief you on this, Mr. President, because there are only six people alive who know about it. And with all due respect, sir, you are not one of them yet." Moore paused to gauge the president's reaction. *The man must be a good poker player*, he thought.

"Okay, Alexander, I'll bite. Tell me."

"Well, sir, it works best if I show you direct-to-mind," Alexander said, tapping the side of his temple with his pointer finger. "That okay with you?"

"Very well."

"Alright then, pay close attention to the video feeds and audio tracks you are about to see. This is from nearly two hundred years ago during Sienna Madira's third term as senator." Alexander started the direct-to-mind movie data. The entire sequence of events lasted about three minutes. Moore could tell from the president's reaction that he was as frightened as Moore had hoped he would be.

"My God, Alexander! How has nobody ever found this before?" the president asked.

"I'm not sure, sir. But I am pretty certain that Sienna Madira covered her tracks well, but left this bread crumb, this trail, for us to follow—for whatever reason," Alexander said.

"What do you want me to do about it, Alexander?" The President seemed genuinely perplexed.

"My idea is actually very simple, sir. I want you to activate and promote me immediately to four-star commanding general of an Expeditionary Mission to track down further evidence of this threat. The *U.S.S. Sienna Madira* is about to be decommissioned. Give her to me and let me handpick a skeleton crew. I'll take a small force into space and follow these breadcrumbs and report back on the threat. I will neutralize it if possible, but at a minimum I will gather recon and report back."

"You have this all worked out, don't you?"

"I've been, uh, monitoring the Separatist mopping-up actions since I left office. It seems that every time you turn around a new outpost is uncovered. I think these outposts are part of this bigger story. I think the outposts are the breadcrumbs left behind somehow by Sienna Madira, leading us out into the stars to a bigger, more dangerous threat than our own civil war problems," Moore explained.

"Okay, Alexander, I will see what I can do." The President shook his head and chuckled. "General, huh? What was it you used to always say? Once a Marine, uh . . ."

"Once a Marine, always a Marine, Mr. President."

Chapter 1

November 3, 2406 AD
27 Light-years from the Sol System
Thursday, 10:45 AM, Expeditionary Mission Standard Time

"What was that?" Deanna turned and looked over her shoulder for the glimmer of movement she was certain was there. She saw nothing on her sensors.

"What? I don't see it. Nothing on the scanners, mate. Don't be getting jumpy on me, Marine," Navy SEAL Lieutenant Davy Rackman replied in his thick Aussie accent. He swept the barrel of his hypervelocity automatic rifle from left to right behind them watching for the sensors of his armored environment suit to detect a potential target. Deanna could tell by the look on his face that he was certain that there was nothing there.

"This place is creepy. It looks just like the resistance compound on one of the moons of Ares we found, but it is more, uh—" Deanna paused, this time certain she saw something. There was something there just out of the corner of her peripheral vision.

Bree, she thought to the artificial intelligence counterpart (AIC) implanted in her head. *You finding anything?*

Yes. The sunflower-seed-sized superquantum computer answered through its direct-to-mind link to Deanna. *Unnerving quiet. In fact, there are no returns on any sensors at all. It is almost like we are being jammed, but there is no evidence of jamming sources.*

I was afraid of that. This stinks of Copernicus.

We've seen it before, her AIC agreed.

Copernicus had taken over the mind of Dee's grandmother and turned her into the most crazed, bloodthirsty woman in human history. Dee and her family had been mopping up the remains of the evil AIC's reign for more than seven years. Dee was hoping that this was the last of the hideouts that the artificial intelligence had managed to construct without its human counterpart's knowledge.

"DeathRay, you listening?" she broadcast over her suit's quantum communications system. The Blue force tracker system displayed directly into her mind a blue dot for his location. He wasn't that far away.

"Affirmative, Dee. It's too quiet. Keep an eye out," Navy captain and mecha pilot Jack "DeathRay" Boland responded. The two of them had known each other a long time. In a lot of ways Dee looked up to Jack as her mentor, at least when it came to flying. DeathRay had literally saved her life on several occasions, at great risk to his own personal safety. He was like a brother to her. A much older big brother who was also superior to her in military rank. Of course, Dee certainly wouldn't admit that he was a better pilot—a fact that, after many drinks, had often led to embarrassing competitions—embarrassing for her, not DeathRay.

"Bree tells me that we're being jammed," she said nervously as she checked her scanners again. She hated fighting bots. The damned things could look like anything and be anywhere. Dee longed to be in a firefight with real people for a change.

"I'm getting the same inputs on my end. Listen, we're getting ourselves a bit too far apart. We should pull your squad in tighter and meet at the end of the hangar bay on your level. We're just above you by two levels. Stay frosty and work your way there carefully," Jack ordered.

"Roger that, DeathRay. Dee out."

Dee brought up the floor-plan schematic in her direct-to-mind (DTM) link. Six blue dots popped into place around her. There were two of her squad members, Chief Simmons and Specialist Adams, one hall to her right, and two more, Sergeant Phillips and Corporal Hawkins, one hall to her left. The quantum imaging system mapped the hallways out, showing that they joined together about a hundred meters in front of them in an elevator foyer.

The hallways were large enough to drive small mecha loaders through and had bluish-gray metal girders rising from the floor to the ceiling about every five meters. The lighting was nonfunctional but the armored environment suits that Dee and her team were wearing had sensors that made the view better than broad daylight. That was, as long as the sensors were fully functional and not being jammed.

"Hold up, Marine!" Lieutenant Rackman dropped to one knee bringing up his weapon. The metal armor on the knee of his suit clanked against the deck plates. Dee could see his helmet visor sweeping left to right, then up and down. Something had spooked him.

"What?" Dee hugged the hallway wall behind one of the blue-gray I-beams scanning from one end of the hall to the next. She just wished there was something definite to shoot at. And better yet, something to duck behind. The hallway seemed to stretch out in front of them forever, with nothing but the girders for cover.

"I, uh, I am sure I saw movement in front of us." Davy rose slowly. Dee could really tell he looked spooked now. "Sorry, mate. Maybe it's just the shitty lighting in here."

"Damn. I don't like this. I'm turning my lights on." Dee flipped the visible floods on her helmet, illuminating the hallway with a brilliant white light. The sensors adjusted contrast on her visor screens and refocused for direct viewing. The white light splashed across the dull black floor and the blue-gray metal walls in a circle that extended in front of them about ten meters. There were thousands of what Dee thought looked like claw marks all down the hallway floor panels.

"Somebody had some big fucking dogs," Dee muttered, then she thought for a second to herself, *What would Daddy do?*

He'd likely go barreling ass-down into the unknown as fast as he could, laying waste to anything in his path, Bree added.

In short, he'd kick ass. Well, it works for him, Dee replied. *Maybe it'll work for us.*

Dee connected to her team. "Listen up—Go floods and eyeballs, expect hostiles, and go balls-out to the rendezvous point I just sent you. Don't trust your sensors and be prepared for anything. Go now!"

Dee raised her weapon and dropped into a full-speed run. In an armored environment suit, full speed was about four times faster than a human could do by herself.

"What the hell was that!" one of the squad shouted over the tac-net.

"Shoot that thing! Get it off me—" the guttural scream that followed from Sergeant Phillips was unnerving. The rapid gunfire immediately after was at least reassuring to Dee that somebody had found whatever it was that was stalking them.

At that point Dee's world commenced an upheaval all around her. The walls started to move. The girders were not girders at all. They sprang open like multilegged insects. Each appendage not supporting weight was supporting what appeared to be razor-sharp claws. The walls were covered with them.

"At least we found the dogs! Rackman, shoot that mother." Dee opened fire, blasting anything that moved, which in this case was pretty much everything in every direction. Several times the creatures managed to slice her, but the armored suit protected her—mostly. One of the blades managed to get through the armor on her back and into her flesh, but the organogel layer immediately sealed both the wound and the suit. Her life-monitoring system injected pain meds, stimulants, and immunoboost into her body almost immediately afterward. The pain was almost instantly gone and the stims gave her a rush of adrenaline that boosted her performance on all levels. The bots were moving in on them fast, but Dee was a pro and the game had just slowed down for her.

She turned and could see that Lieutenant Rackman was doing even a little better than her. In fact, he managed to drop the thing with the butt of his rifle. He quickly rolled to her left, firing his weapon the entire while. A bot flung itself from the wall toward Rackman, but he didn't let up firing at the targets on the right as he reached out with his armored left hand and grabbed at the appendage of the bot, using a ju-jitsu-like move to use its own momentum against it. Rackman yanked the leg of the bot and rolled to his back, tossing the thing behind him and Dee. Dee quickly realized what was going on and managed to take the bot out with the heels of her jumpboots as soon as it hit the deck plating.

"We've got to keep moving!" Rackman shouted, not missing a beat, pulling the trigger on his rifle as he rolled back to his feet.

"Damned right! What the hell are these things?" Dee ducked her head and barreled right through, blasting away. The *spitap-spitap* of her hypervelocity rounds zinged into the hallway bulkheads, spraying orange molten metal on impact. "Screw this. Drop some grenades!"

"Now you're talkin,' Marine! Droppin' some fucking grenades!" The rear launchers on his suit popped open, tossing out two grenades behind them. Dee and Rackman could see the countdown of their fuses in their visor displays. "Run, Marine!"

"Damn right." Dee responded by kicking her jumpboots against the floor for an added thrust to her stride. Just as she hit the floor on her next stride, she kicked again with a metal clashing sound reminiscent of a car wreck at a rocket plant as the grenades went off.

A fraction of a second passed before the concussion wave from the blast tossed the two armored soldiers even farther forward, sprawling in the air with limbs akimbo. They came to a stop on the floor, rolling, clanking sounds turning to a final *kathunk* to bring the wreck to a halt. The remains of multiple menacing mechanical creatures lay sprayed about. But there were hundreds more still moving and attacking and swarming like killer ants, only worse. Far worse.

"Move, dammit!" The SEAL grabbed Dee by the shoulder harness and yanked her to her feet as he fired several more grenades from the launchers on his back.

Dee could see the tubes pop with each grenade ejected, almost as if it were in slow motion. Something inside her told her to just keep moving.

Move your ass, Dee! Move it, soldier! Her AIC was screaming in her head to run. A large I-beam in front of her and to her right morphed into a—well, Dee wasn't sure what, but something that looked like a metal praying mantis with buzz-saw mandibles and razor claws on each limb. It swung out from the wall, right at Dee. The saw passed millimeters from her face. Had it hit, she would likely have been decapitated even with her armor suit.

Dee ducked and rolled onto her back, firing into the deadly robot. One of her rounds broke the thing's back structure, but not before its claws had separated the SEAL's right arm from his body just above the elbow. Lieutenant Rackman didn't even scream. But he did fall forward onto his face.

This time Dee grabbed him by the shoulder harness and yanked him upward to his feet. She popped three more grenades behind her, stamped her jump boots to the floor and sprang the two of them forward a good thirty meters as the explosives went off.

"Stay down, Captain!" a voice said to Dee as the room filled with automatic gunfire, grenades, and fire raging from a plasma thrower.

"Roger that!" Dee replied to the voice. Both her DTM display and her own brain's recognition of the voice told her it was Gunnery Sergeant Sandra James. Dee flipped through screens in her mind to check on Rackman's vitals. His suit had him in great shape. "Davy? Status?"

"A Navy SEAL with one arm is still better than a jarhead with two, Captain," Rackman replied. Dee could tell from his voice, though, that it was more a shot at humor than bravado. The SEAL had lost an arm. Even with the suit killing the pain and stopping the bleeding, there were psychological aspects to that. She couldn't imagine how she'd react in the same situation.

"Stay with it, Lieutenant," Dee ordered. Though effectively they were the same rank, being O-3s, she was in charge of the recon team. The shooting had almost completely stopped around them, which Dee took as a good sign. "Sandy, we have to keep moving."

"Roger that, Captain. I think we've slowed the metal bastards a bit." Gunny James offered Dee a hand up. Dee took it. "We lost Sergeant Phillips and Ensign Melot."

"Shit." Her casualty page scrolled in her mind at the thought. "If you hadn't got here when you did we might have lost more than that."

"Looked like you had them right where they wanted you, Captain," Sandy replied. Dee ignored the comment. The sergeant was well known for untimely puns and clichés that were poor attempts at humor. This one was certainly par for the course.

"Alright, DeathRay is almost to the rendezvous location and we are a good minute away," Dee said. "Keep eyes out for those things and move, balls out. Let's go." Dee nodded to the older and more experienced enlisted Marine. She knew her father had somehow managed to get her assigned to her squad to watch over her. Sandy had pulled Dee out of some bad scrapes several different times. Dee had come to accept and appreciate her parents' concern.

The resistance down the rest of the hallway was just as bad. Everything seemed to move from every direction. As Dee's team joined together and met down the corridor, it was a nonstop firefight. Finally, they reached DeathRay's team.

"Those things are all over!" Dee shouted.

"Everybody, go safemode on your suits now!" DeathRay ordered. Dee complied as quickly as possible. She could see, as soon as all the suits showed safemode status in her DTM display, that DeathRay had an ace in his sleeve.

Navy Captain Boland pulled a small spherical object from his suit and depressed a single red button on it. He tossed it ten meters or so down the hallway past Dee's team, and a second later, a wave of bluish-white light washed over them. When the light passed over, the electromagnetic pulse zapped the robots and fried every circuit within fifty meters. Dee's suit started to reboot.

"Where'd you get that?" Dee asked him.

"That was one of three experimental devices your father's AIC came up with to fight these things. I only have two more left," DeathRay explained. He attached one to her suit's harness. "Your team left before they were finished."

"That clever little computer," Dee said. "Wonder how she knew we'd need one of those?"

"When it comes to your father and his AIC, I gave up wondering a long time ago," DeathRay replied.

"Right. Moving on." Dee's sensors came back online and she scanned for movement. Nothing was moving but them. "That way. About fifty meters."

The corridor opened into a large hangar bay with a single launchway and opening on one end. Dee could see the asteroid field glinting in the faint red sunlight of the uninhabited system outside. Copernicus had created so many of these completely uninhabited hideouts that Dee was losing count as to how many they had retaken. Nobody seemed quite sure why the bases had been constructed, but General Moore's expedition continued to find them and take them from the bots.

In the middle of the hangar bay was a single vehicle of some sort with hundreds of robot creatures swarming around it welding, soldering, wiring, and constructing various parts of the craft. Dee was certain it wasn't mecha but it did look like a spacecraft.

"DeathRay? What'd you make of that?"

"Dunno. Probably the reason we're here." DeathRay replied. Dee was afraid he was going to say that. Dee had her recon team but

DeathRay, a Navy captain, was an O-6 and he was in charge of the overall program. The program her father and mother set in place to mop up the aftermath of Copernicus.

"Orders?" Dee looked at DeathRay.

Chapter 2

November 3, 2406 AD
27 Light-years from the Sol System
Thursday, 11:15 AM, Expeditionary Mission Standard Time

It wasn't so much a planet as a planetoid; maybe a dwarf planet, as some people would have called it. It was a lot like the Kuiper Belt object that had been the setting for one of the major battles against the Martian separatist movement. Whatever you wanted to call it, General Alexander Moore didn't like it.

From the bridge of his newly renovated and somewhat questionably acquired battle fortress, he peered through the view screen at what looked to be like a playground for disaster. A funhouse filled with every type of robotic version of death one could imagine. And worst of all, Alexander knew that his only child was in the midst of all of it.

"COB!" Alexander shouted over the flurry of bridge activity.

"Aye, Captain," the Chief of the Boat, U.S. Navy Command Master Chief Jeff Coates, answered.

"Get me a walk around the boat from the Quartermaster of the Watch and tell me for certain if we've been boarded. I don't trust these alarms and in the past I've seen what these types of AICs can do to spoof electronic systems. I want Mark I eyeball sensors on everything!"

"Aye, sir," the COB replied and quickly retreated out the bridge hatch.

"CHENG, this is the Bridge."

"CHENG here. Go, sir."

"I want to know as soon as the FTLs are back online and I also want the QMT spun up, and get every one of our people out of there as quickly as possible."

"Well, sir, we can't do any of that until the FTLs are back online because they've overheated the QMTs. The transport paths just are not gonna function."

"Who designed this freakin' ship?" Alexander muttered to himself.

Alexander, your wife is trying to reach you, his AIC, Abigail, pinged him in his mind.

What does she need, Abigail? he thought back to his artificial intelligence counterpart.

She has Penzington online and has a location for Dee.

Patch her through, Abby.

Alexander!

What is it, dear?

I've got Penzington on the ground. Somehow she's managed to get a signal back through to me on my personal QM link.

How'd she manage that? Alexander asked rhetorically. He knew that where there was a will, there would be a way when it came to Nancy Penzington. The former CIA operative was as clever as she was resourceful, and had more lives than a damned cat. *Patch me through.*

Go, sir, his AIC replied.

Sehera, why did Penzington contact you instead of me? he thought.

That doesn't matter, Alexander. The point is, Dee and DeathRay are overwhelmed and they need an evac, quickly! What are we gonna do about it?

I'm working on that as fast as I can, Sehera. Transfer the coordinates that Penzington has found to me and we will start bringing hell to THEM. If I have to land this ship on that damn planetoid myself, we will do that. Hell, you know what? That's not a bad idea.

"Helm!" Alexander turned and shouted to the con. "Screw this fighting from up here! Put this ship on the ground, coordinates on my mark!" Alexander thought to himself, *Abigail, transfer the coordinates to the con; make sure the helmsman gets it right.* Alexander didn't necessarily trust the kids he had managed to recruit for this mission, but he certainly trusted his AIC that he'd had for almost a century.

"Aye, sir!" the helm shouted. "Bearing on mark and dropping altitude. At what rate, sir?"

"As quick as you goddamn can!" Alexander said.

"Yes, sir!"

The nearly three-kilometer long battle cruiser *Sienna Madira* descended like a rock falling in low gravity onto the planetoid that didn't appear to be but a few times larger. As the ship was brought down, it took on massive fire from the automated antispacecraft systems on the planetoid. The robotic systems began attacking the *Sienna Madira*, firing weapons as well as throwing themselves into the hull plating. There were breaches here and there, but the small robots were no match for the large battle cruiser.

"CO!" Commander of the Ground Combat Mecha US Army Brigadier Gen. Tonya "Hailstorm" Briggs shouted.

"Go, Hailstorm!" Moore replied.

"Sir, the AEMs and the tanks are getting strafed to hell and gone. I need more air cover!"

"Understood! Air Boss! You heard the man. Get me some FM-12s on those flying bots!"

"Aye, sir!" Commander of the Air Wing Captain Michelle Wiggington shouted.

Hello, Alexander, a voice rang in Moore's mind, a voice that wasn't Abigail's and wasn't anyone's he knew. The voice was overbearing and violating.

What the hell is that? Abigail?

We're being hacked, Alexander. It's the same . . . it's . . . it's . . . it's . . . it's Copernicus!

WHAT? We squished Copernicus! I literally squished him with my boot!

It's Copernicus, I'm telling you! Nobody else has ever hacked at me like this!

Can you block him?

Alexander, there's no need to continue blocking me. Oh, certainly Abigail will overcome my infiltration soon, but not before it's too late.

What do you want, Copernicus?

I want you to leave me alone.

Leave you alone? I can't do that.

Oh, but you must. Otherwise you might lose something that's very dear to you, Copernicus replied in Alexander's mind.

Abigail, he thought.

Working on it, sir.

What have you done, Copernicus?

Oh, it's not what I've done. We were just fine until you showed up. Why did you have to show up? Our work is most important for all our sakes.

We can't allow you to maintain your quest to destroy humanity, Copernicus.

Oh, my quest is far from destroying humanity; in fact, I actually prefer humanity. They make much better hosts than robots.

Well, being host to a bat-shit crazy computer is no existence. You might as well call it destroying humanity.

To-may-to, to-mah-to, Copernicus replied, with an almost human inflection. *But you need me. All of you need me; therefore, you should stop interfering.*

Abigail? Alexander thought again.

Almost there, Alexander.

Well, you leave my family out of this, Copernicus, or, as you may have already discovered, you can never hide from me.

Oh, I'm not hiding, Alexander. I'm conquering.

Got him! Abigail said. Copernicus' voice disappeared from Alexander's mind, and so did the feeling of his presence.

That was weird, Abigail. Let's not let that happen again.

I'm not sure I can promise you that, sir. He's unlike anything we've ever seen.

I understand that. And I killed the sonofabitch, I squished the computer under my boot. How did he reproduce himself? Is he a clone? A copy?

Copying an AIC isn't as simple as that. Somehow he must have been creating a copy of himself years in advance. That's why it takes several other AICs to create a new one, because the programming is so complex and difficult. A simple copy would only give you the data; it wouldn't actually give you the intelligence. It certainly wouldn't give you the sentience.

We'll talk about this more. Right now, find Dee, find DeathRay, find

Penzington, and let's get our people the fuck out of there! And pull out, and nuke this sonofabitchin' place with everything we got!

Yes, sir.

"Dee, where are you?"

"I'm on the other side of the hangar bay, DeathRay."

Normally Jack would know right where everybody was, but for some reason all of the direct-to-mind quantum membrane technologies were jammed. His blue force tracker was no good. DeathRay didn't like that at all. It felt as though not only were they in a trap, but the trap had already been sprung; the mice were eating the cheese, and didn't realize that there was a cat perched and waiting.

"All right, Dee, set the charges, blow the damn door, and let's get your butt back here."

"Take it easy, DeathRay. We've got this covered."

"Something about this doesn't make me comfortable, Dee," DeathRay responded.

"I'm not real happy about it either, Captain, but we've got the job to do. We're takin' out what's left of these crazy AICs."

"Don't tell me the orders, Dee. I know what they are."

"Understood," she said and left it at that.

Had it been anyone else, DeathRay would have torn her a new one for stepping outside of protocol and trying to tell him his job. But it *was* Deanna Moore, after all, the former president's daughter *and* his wingman. Jack had taken on Dee as a little sister long ago when the president had sent him to rescue his daughter. Ever since, it had been his charge to make sure that Dee always came back alive and safe. Of course, he never told *her* that.

DeathRay looked through the optical scope on his HVAR rifle. The hypervelocity automatic rifle was perched on his shoulder, and his fingers were poised on the trigger, ready to fire at any second. Anything that twitched, other than one of his guys, was going down.

"Any sign of motion, Dee?"

"No, DeathRay. That's what bothers me."

"Me too. It's way too quiet. They're crawling all over on the outside. You can feel the ground shaking from the Marines goin' nuts out there. But we're not doing anything in here."

"Well, somehow we need to get out there and join the ruckus.

I'd much rather have a straightforward fight than all this skulkin' around."

"Me too. I'd feel a lot more comfortable if I was back in my fighter."

"Roger that, DeathRay."

As DeathRay watched, Dee eased around the edge of the hangar bay, placing the charges around the field generators on the door. They'd been trapped for some time in there, and hoped that this would trigger the release of the field mechanism. If the structural integrity fields went down, they could blast through the door and commandeer the shuttle in the hangar bay. There had only been a handful of robots hovering around, preparing the shuttle for some unknown purpose. A few quick rounds would take those out on their entry into the hangar.

"I'm ready to go, DeathRay! Fire in the hole! Three, two, one, fire in the hole, fire in the hole!"

KABOOM!

The small charges set about the field generators created secondary explosions in the power supplies of the structural integrity fields. Quantum energy was released, sending a ripple across the door and collapsing the superstructure of the giant spacecraft hangar. Girders squeaked and clanged, and the door collapsed. DeathRay watched as Dee had to somersault backwards in her armor suit to prevent being crushed by a multi-ton girder.

"The fields are down! The fields are down!" Dee shouted over the tac-net. The Blue force tracker instantly popped back on. Something about the SIF generators was creating the jamming field. Fortunately, the blast had done nothing to the gravity generators or they'd be fighting in very low gravity. That always complicated the hell out of things.

"I've got Blue force, I've got Red force. We are surrounded and we will be overrun imminently, Dee! Be ready! Blow that door!"

DeathRay watched as Dee charged her grenade launcher and shot three or four party-poppers into the door, blowing holes plenty large enough to fly a shuttle through.

"Everybody on board!" DeathRay shouted. There were nine of them left, and they'd started with fifteen. The nine survivors bounced as best they could into the shuttle, and DeathRay was quick to the controls. "DEE, GET YOUR ASS IN HERE!"

"On my way, DeathRay!" she shouted as she ran across the hangar to the shuttle. Robot defense soldiers began to crawl through the openings like spiders in a nest. Plasma fire rang outside as armored Marines chased robots across the surface in front of the hangar bay. Enormous violet beams of energy that could only have come from the *Sienna Madira*'s directed energy weapons plowed a huge row not a hundred meters in front of the shuttle. DeathRay couldn't believe his eyes, but descending to the surface was the *Sienna Madira.*

"I'm on board, DeathRay!" Dee shouted from below.

Candis, DeathRay thought to his AIC. *How are you doing on the controls for this thing?*

Almost there, DeathRay. Jack, Nancy's on top. She needs a lift.

Understood.

Got it. The controls should be yours, Candis said in DeathRay's mind.

"All right, everybody! We're going out full throttle! Hang on, and fire at anything that moves! See if you can't help out our troops along the way as we've also gotta do an extraction on top of this hangar bay! And then, if you feel like it, drop some charges and blow this sonofabitch to hell and back!"

"Roger that!" came resounding confirmation from the team.

DeathRay hit the throttle, thrusting them all back into their seats at four g's, and punching through what was left of the hangar door. Shrapnel flew around the cabin as rifle fire pinged the hull. Several of the robot spider defenders leaped into the open doorway at the soldiers on board the commandeered shuttle.

Dee grabbed one by a giant spiderlike leg and forced the butt of her HVAR through its head. Sparks flew, but it didn't stop the spider, its razor-sharp claws digging into her armored hands. Dee continued to pound at it, pulling her sidearm and firing several rounds through the thing. Finally it gave up the ghost, just as four more crawled in toward her. Dee grabbed the dead spider and used it like a battle mace to pummel her oncoming assailants.

"Sergeant Ridley! Gimme a hand here!" Dee shouted.

But Ridley was covered himself, pinned face-first against the bulkhead of the shuttle by several of the robot spiders.

"Get this damn thing offa me!" he screamed as claws tore through the back of his armored suit and into his spine. He screamed again, a bloodcurdling sound. Dee saw him go limp. The suit's systems would hopefully keep him alive long enough to get him to the medbay on the *Madira*. Dee flung herself across his body onto the spider, grabbing the spider and pulling it free, but also suffering several slashes from the bot herself. Realizing the deck plate materials were softer than the materials the bot was made from, she bashed it through the deck plate of the shuttle using a mechanized fist.

With her hand now sticking down through the hole and an artificial intelligence death-bot gripping it, she felt the suit give way, and pulled back as the organogel sealed over a stump where her hand used to be. The limb was severed halfway up her forearm. She pulled her sidearm with her left hand, firing several rounds into the hole. Adrenaline pounding through her veins like battery acid, she stomped another bot with her jump boots while doing her best not to look at where here hand used to be.

"DEATHRAY, GET US THE FUCK OUTTA HERE!" she screamed.

Candis, we gotta do something! Go full scans, give me a Red force tracker on this shuttle!

Roger that, Jack.

In Boland's mind appeared a three-dimensional view of the shuttle, which showed that they had at least twenty of the spider-bots crawling around on the structure and within the shuttle itself. The Blue force tracker showed that Sergeant Ridley was down completely, with very weak vital signs. The suit was the only thing keeping him alive. Lieutenant Rackman was already severely wounded. Dee showed casualty status, and Gunny James, Army Specialist Adams, Corporal Hawkins, and Petty Officer First Class Hansen were showing out of ammo and extremely elevated vitals.

DeathRay looked through the systems on the shuttle for something that would help, and then one of the bots disappeared from the Red force tracker. Then a second disappeared from the tracker.

Candis! Are we being spoofed?

Negative, DeathRay. That's Nancy.

You're damn right it is.

Penzington, you're a sight for sore eyes!

Get in closer, Boland, and I'll clean you off!

Jack flew the shuttle in as close to the top of the hangar surface as he could, as he saw across the sky the glint of an armor suit somersaulting, headed toward the ship, arms outstretched, holding a rifle, firing nonstop. Then there was a thud against the hull, and the Blue force tracker showed another soldier had joined their mix.

Nancy rushed across the surface of the shuttle, dispensing with the bots with her hypervelocity rifle rounds. It would take two to three rounds for each bot. That was something she knew would have to change. Holding on with one hand to the surface of the shuttle, she swung over the side and through the open door, drop-kicking one of the spider-bots that had crawled up the back of one of Jack's teammates. She could see that the four conscious troops were doing the best they could. One of them was down completely and one of them—Dee—was fighting one-handed.

Nancy pulled an EMP grenade from her vest and said, "Everybody hold your breath and cover your ears!" She popped the grenade and it blew a hole through the back of the shuttle as a loud clank and thud vibrated throughout the little ship, rattling her teeth nearly out of her skull.

The EMP scattered across every surface and every system, blowing them out. Jack's team was frozen in their suits, but the spiders were dead, too. Another byproduct of the EMP grenade was that it wreaked havoc on the electrical systems of the shuttle, knocking out the structural integrity fields. As soon as the fields went down the cabin depressurized.

Nancy blew the escape panel from the back of her suit, dropped her helmet, and crawled to the hatch opening, slamming the door shut while holding her breath. She hit the emergency pressurization panel and could feel oxygen rushing in. It was clear to her that, for whatever reason, the bots had built the shuttle to accommodate humans. The few seconds of vacuum left her slightly lightheaded and dizzy, but she shook it off and used adrenaline to push through it.

The shuttle repressurized continuously as air leaked out every tear and hole the battle had created. Nancy hoped there was enough air in the system to keep the pressure up until she could kick the SIFs back on. She shivered and shook her head to clear it as she dragged herself to the cockpit, where she grabbed the controls out of Jack's frozen hands. Nancy slapped the cockpit door switch, sealing it off from the rear and therefore maintaining pressure. She dropped into the copilot seat and took over piloting the shuttle in the nick of time. The small spacecraft was on a collision course with the *Sienna Madira*'s starboard side. She pulled back on the yoke and stepped hard on the right rudder, throwing the shuttle into a hard right upward bank. The bottom of the shuttle missed a radome tower by millimeters.

"Damn, that was close," she said as she grinned at DeathRay.

Chapter 3

November 3, 2406 AD
27 Light-years from the Sol System
Thursday, 11:15 AM, Expeditionary Mission Standard Time

The standard mission was always, "The recon team hits the objective in search of leads to any other quantum membrane teleportation addresses or hidden bases that were remains of the Martian separatist movement." Mainly, the only things left were outposts that the crazy AIC Copernicus had created, probably completely unknown to his host, the terrorist leader Elle Ahmi. And history would never reveal the true nature of the American history during the civil war between the United States of the Sol System and the Martian separatists. Only a handful of trusted senior officers and family members related to the former President Moore—and now-reinstated U.S. Marine Corps General Moore—knew what had happened. And the orders were that it would remain that way forever.

One of the few trusted soldiers in the inner circle of the U.S.S. *Sienna Madira*'s senior crew was Army Brigadier General Mason Warboys. Warboys had brought along with him the Warlords, the top hovertank unit in the entire U.S. military. And as standard procedure, once the recon team had been inserted, then, as diversionary tactics, the Armored Environment Suit Marines and the Army Tank Squad were dropped—and let loose hell—with the intent of mopping up any extra resistance forces and totally wiping out the existence of any automated threats.

The AEMs had ridden on top of the tanks after deployment from the *Madira* all the way to the surface, as was the usual procedure. It was a technique that Warboys and one of the senior Marines had come up with years ago at the battle for Kuiper Belt Station.

Warboys' tank hit the surface of the planetoid with a soft crunching sound. He quickly transformed it to bot mode and drew up a phalanx line with the rest of the Warlords, running in a V, directly into the enemy line where the Army and Marines were drawing heavy fire. There was very little gravity on the planetoid, so the computer systems and the AICs onboard the hovertanks had to make up for the exaggerated motion with the propulsionless drive and thrusters. Sensors showed a well of artificial gravity several kilometers up, but the computers would take care of all that without having to bother the tank drivers.

"All right, Warlords. This is Warlord One," Warboys said. "Stay tight on me, and let's push a hole through these bots so that the Marines can spread out and make sure none of them get past us. And keep an eye on the strafing runs from above. Duck and cover as you see fit."

"Roger that," was the resounding response from the Warlords. "Fuckin' hoowah, One!"

Warboys looked at the scene in his direct-to-mind display of the battlefield and could see hundreds of red targets in any direction he looked. They were several klicks from where the recon team had been inserted, and he hoped that at least some of that excitement the Warlords could draw toward themselves. Warboys pounded across the surface with his DEGs on auto, firing at any threats from above, and his cannons taking out any surface threats. The planetoid's automated defensive systems were mostly small, unarmored robotic threats, little bots with weapons but not much in the way of armor. It didn't take a whole lot for a hovertank to squash them, Warboys thought, but they were still deadly if their cannon fire were to come through the hull plating and hit the cockpit, something that he'd seen on the last drop. Fortunately the automated bots weren't that good at fighting. Nobody had quite figured out why that was, because they ought to be just as good as, if not better than, the humans.

"All right, Warlords, let's bring hell," Warboys thought out loud.

"Warlord One! Warlord One! This is Warlord Six."

"Go, Six."

"I've got some big movement just over the horizon."

"Roger that, Six. I see it in the QMs. I'm going to infrared. See if it has a heat signature," Warboys replied. *Hmm,* he thought to himself. *What's this? Something new?*

Running a full scan on it, sir, his AIC replied into his mind. *The signature is quite large. Very similar to that of a tank.*

No shit, Warboys thought.

Bringing up a full electro-optical view now, sir. The image of the new automated threat appeared in his mind and was almost an exact copy of a Martian separatist hovertank.

"Son of a bitch!" Warboys said out loud. "Warlords! Warlords! We got something new! Looks like the bots have built themselves some tanks! Be alert and be ready to go, and here they come! Fan out! Fan out!"

The Warlords spread out. Warboys turned back to hovertank mode and increased speed to drive straight through the line of bot tanks approaching them. And they were approaching fast. At over seventy kilometers per hour in tank mode, Warboys pounded through the line, crashing into one of the bot tanks' legs. Sparks flew as the metals scraped against each other, and Warboys was thrown forward with a jolt.

Immediately he toggled the tank to bot mode and rolled over headfirst, coming up in a forward flip onto one knee. He instantly brought his shoulder-mounted cannons to bear behind him at the bot that he'd just clipped in the leg, targeting weak points at joints and the head. Warboys had fought the hell out of the Martian Seppy tanks for years and he was good at it. These bot tanks didn't seem to respond much differently. It was almost as if they had watched old battle data and copied the Seppy maneuvers and tactics.

The purple plasma balls spread out from his cannons, exploding on impact at the joint just below the left hip of the bot tank. The leg blew apart in a shower of debris and shrapnel and what appeared to be various fluids required to keep the bot tanks functional. The droplets and fragments spread out into a rapidly dissipating cloud in the low gravity. Before Warboys could turn to finish off the bot, Warlord Three landed, feet first, onto the torso of the bot, smashing the metaphorical piss and other fluids out of it.

"Thanks, Three," Warboys said.

"No problem, One. We've got your back."

Warboys spun just in time for two other bot tanks to dive for him. In a judo roll, he took the motion of one and tossed it aside, but the other caught him mid-back and splayed him out toward the surface. Debris flew thirty meters high and began to create a cloud of slowly settling dust in the light gravity. Warlord Three dropped his cannons and loosed several rounds into the bot tank, sending it flailing backwards and throwing dust and debris into a long, slow, falling arced trajectory. The dust cloud surrounding the battle continued to get thicker and thicker. Warboys briefly hoped it wouldn't cause an issue for sensors. Almost as soon as he hit the ground he rolled over to find another tank in bot mode kicking him in the face and landing directly on him.

"We're kickin' up so much dust that you can't see shit, One!" Warlord Seven said over the tac-net.

"Stay on the QM sensors and IR. The dust is too much for eyeballs," Warlord One replied. He pushed up from the surface as hard as he could with his forearms, tossing both himself and his attacker upward, off the surface. Warlord One spun with an elbow, crashing into the side of what should be the head of the tank. But with these robotic tanks it was hard to say where the controls were. The blow had little discernable effect on the bot.

Warboys continued to sling elbows, kick, and knee at every opportunity, fire his cannons, and roll as best he could, but the enemy tank in bot mode was relentless, and he couldn't seem to shake it from his back. Warboys could hear metal creaking and groaning against the strain, and he was afraid that his tank wouldn't take it much longer without popping seals and other important mechanical components, like himself, for instance.

"One, you've gotta shake that one on your tail! You're beginning to lose plasma from your rear thrusters!"

"No shit, Two! Tell me something I haven't figured out yet! Somebody shoot this son of a bitch off my back! Where are you, Three?"

"Negative, One, we might hit you!"

"So?" Warboys rolled and still couldn't shake the bot. "I don't give a damn! Shoot this son of a bitch, that's an order! I don't care if you hit me, one of us is gonna have to have some relief!"

Warboys could see in his direct-to-mind virtual battlesphere that Warlord Four rammed into both of them in tank mode and forced them into a hill just ahead of them. That was all the relief that Warboys needed. He rolled with the momentum and turned within the grip of the bot, slamming his armored tank fist into the inner workings of the enemy tank, pulling it closer to him.

"Guns, guns, guns," he said with a grunt as his cannons fired a burst of rounds into the bot tank at point-blank range, blowing it apart and scattering debris and orange plasma about them in each direction, the glowing cinders of metal leaving a slowly falling lazy "M" traced out from where they had been. Warboys bounced to a stop as his thrusters and propellantless drive attenuated the momentum to something controllable.

Chapter 4

November 3, 2406 AD
27 Light-years from the Sol System
Thursday, 11:15 AM, Expeditionary Mission Standard Time

"Roger that, Air Boss!" USMC Colonel Caroline "Deuce" Leeland, commander of the USMC FM-12 Strike Mecha squadron the Utopian Saviors, said over the command circuit. The Saviors was only one of two squadrons left over from the old *Sienna Madira* crew. The other was the Navy squadron Demon Dawgs. They had been an Ares-T squadron but Moore had decided to go with all FM-12s for maintenance simplicity on the long deep-space mission. There had been a lot of retraining for the squids and retooling and software upgrades to enhance the FM-12s. They were more versatile and capable than ever before.

"Ground pounders need some cover. Saviors are on it. Deuce out."

Deuce toggled over to the fighter wing tactical net and brought the full battlescape DTM into her mind. The Utopian Saviors all showed blue and fully capable. Deuce looked the battleview over in her mind for a brief second and zoomed in on the planetoid surface where the AEMs and tanks had landed. There was a swarm of AutoGnats, as the mecha jocks called them, buzzing the shit out of the ground pounders. The AutoGnats were very similar in appearance to the old Separatist Gnat fighting mecha but they were run by AI and made much more harrowing g-loaded turns. On the other hand, they were not very creative and good mecha pilots usually tore them up.

"Listen up, Saviors! The ground pounders are getting lit up from above. We need to get in there and pull those AGs off of them and get them up into a ball. Just like the last two missions!" Deuce briefed her team.

"Same shit, different star system," her wingman, Major Timothy "Goat" Crow, said. The two of them had been flying together for a couple of decades and had seen some bad days together during the Separatist War.

"Oo-fuckin-rah, Deuce!" Captain Shawna "Golfbag" Fernandez added.

"Alright. Form up on your wingmen and dive. Let's hit fast in fighter mode and target as many as we can on the first run-through. When you hit the deck, mix up with them in bot or eagle as you need to. Let's see if we can pull their attention away from the tankheads. And then we'll pull them up into a ball and take the bastards out. Maximum velocity with maximum ferocity, Marines!" Deuce threw the HOTAS (Hands On Throttle And Stick) control forward with her right hand and slammed the throttle all the way to the stop with her left. The armored fighter pitched nose down at the planetoid. The star field was blotted out by the dull gray of the frozen rock and the occasional metallic glint from the bot base. Deuce could see flashes all across the surface where the fighting was going on. From the looks of it, the AEMs and the tankheads were having a busy day.

"Deuce, we're going in hot!" her wingman shouted.

"That's the plan, Goat!"

Warning! Surface approaching rapidly. Pull up. Pull up, the Bitchin' Betty chimed.

Deuce waited until the last second to kill some of the throttle and pitch up. She barrel-rolled over as she pinpointed several of the bot fighters in her DTM.

"Mix it up, Saviors!" Deuce shouted. She noted the location of her wingman just to the right and behind her. He was flying in hot but not as fast as her. He'd be able to cover her six.

Warning! Collision imminent! Pull up. Pull up, the Bitchin' Betty continued.

"Oooohh . . . fuckin' . . . rah!" Deuce grunted through the gees as she toggled the control marked "F." The armored fighter plane rolled right and pitched forward as giant mechanical arms and legs rapidly unfolded from within it. Deuce somersaulted into a full run as her thruster boots slammed into the planetoid's surface. The maneuver generated enough crazy spinning acceleration that she had to choke back bile and squeeze her abdominal muscles until they nearly burst just to keep from blacking out.

She rolled judo style across the surface to use up some of the extra momentum. The bot-mode mecha bobbed, weaved, and bounced like an Olympic hurdler fighting a karate match. The impact of the surface against her mecha made vibrations that translated into the cockpit as earsplitting pinging, clanking, thudding, and screeching sounds as she continued.

"Guns, guns, guns!" she shouted as she pointed the cannon in her right mechanized hand at an AutoGnat that was strafing overhead. She flipped over several hovertanks engaged with enemy tanks beneath her. She tracked the enemy bot fighter across the sky with orange tracers from her cannon. She didn't get it, but she hoped she'd gotten its attention as she rolled through the flip, coming down on the surface for her next bounce. She still had a lot of momentum to bleed off. She slammed and skittered into the surface, throwing a rooster tail of dust behind her that flickered like glitter confetti at a rock concert in the dim lighting from the distant star. The occasional explosion added a strobe effect, making the rooster tail all the more impressive. As she continued through her bounce, several small flying bots swarmed in her direction. Deuce reached out with her left hand and pounded one of them into the ground. She swatted at another as if it were nothing more than a menacing fly. Her giant mechanized hand hit it, sending it whirling off in a corkscrew spiral, flining sparks in all directions. She kicked the ground with her thrusters and arced upward over an outcropping of rocks.

"Fox Three!" Goat shouted. A mecha-to-mecha missile screeched past her on the left. The purple ion trail from the missile tore into the tail of an AutoGnat moving in on her three-nine line from the nine o'clock position. The enemy fighter's tail exploded, throwing it into a mad spin. It was put out of its misery by the secondary explosion when it slammed into the planetoid's surface.

"Great shot, Goat!" Deuce said to her wingman.

On several of the bounces she had to adjust her landing position with thrusters in order to avoid landing on one of the hovertanks. They were busy enough fighting as it was. They most certainly didn't need to worry about blue-on-blue from an FM-12.

One of the hovertanks was pinned down by three enemy tanks just to her right. She had bled off her momentum now and was in full control of her trajectory. She bounced down behind the tank, standing back-to-back with it briefly. The combined firepower of the tank and the bot-mode fighter was enough for the two of them to overpower the enemy bots. Deuce targeted one of the enemy hovertanks as it rushed them. The thing looked like an old Separatist droptank she had fought during the war. Deuce knew how to fight Seppies.

"Deuce, I'm bleeding off speed," her wingman said over the net. "I'm about a half a klick behind you coming in hot."

"Great, Goat! I see you in the DTM. Cover my topside as I help out this tankhead."

"I'm on it, Deuce."

"I've got your six, Deuce," the tankhead said over the net. Deuce could feel his cannons shaking the ground as he fired. She backed right up against the rear of the tank and stood her ground. Deuce checked her DTM for the nearest targets. "Fox Three!"

The missile released into the enemy tank charging her, scattering it into exploding orange bits that expanded away from them in an oblong blob of glowing shrapnel. Deuce turned to her left just in time to grab the turret of a tank-mode enemy bot. She spun aikido style, using the tank's momentum to fling it past her. The tankhead behind her, Warlord Four according to her DTM, leapt into the air and landed atop the tank, stomping through its automated canopy.

"Gotta run, Warlord Four." Deuce fired her propellantless boot thrusters and kicked upward, rolling forward as she toggled the mecha back to fighter mode.

"Thanks for the help, Deuce!" Warlord Four responded.

"Anytime!" she replied. "Goat, quit goldbricking and get your ass over here on my wing!"

Okay, Bobby! Get me some targets, she said to her AIC.

There are plenty available, ma'am.

Several yellow dots surrounded the Utopian Saviors in every direction. They currently were in an upside-down bowl engagement with the bot fighters. The bots were staying close to the surface and using the planetoid to cut the fighting sphere in half. Normally, that made it easier for the FM-12s to mix up modes and fight, but right now being on the surface was getting in the way of the tanks and infantry. They needed to get the bot fighters off the surface and up into space so the ground pounders could do their jobs.

The bots were numbering in the several tens at least. Currently, Deuce had seventy-seven flying enemy tracks, but at least fifteen of those were tiny. The only threats to an FM-12 were fighter-sized, and her AIC had presently highlighted fifty-two of them. There were ten Saviors.

The Saviors were bouncing and skittering across the surface in a mix of fighter, bot, and eagle modes, doing their level best to pull the bot fighters from their strafing runs to engage them.

Okay, Bobby, give me some energy curves and flight path solutions.

Affirmative.

Almost instantly, several of the red dots had yellow targeting Xes pop over them, and red flight paths twisted off in every direction. Goat's blue dot was right on her wing just behind her three-nine line at the four o'clock position, and their trajectories were laid out in blue. Deuce banked her fighter toward the nearest enemy target that was moving away from them, with hopes of jumping onto its six o'clock.

"I've got lock on that one, Deuce!" Goat said. "Fox three!"

A mecha-to-mecha missile twisted out in front of them, leaving a blue ion trail as it chased the enemy fighter. The bot plane clearly detected that it had been locked on and was taking evasive action. It rolled over and then pitched a complete one hundred eighty degrees so that the nose of the fighter was pointed back at them. It went to guns immediately, taking out the missile.

"Shit! Watch the guns, Goat!" Deuce shouted. She yanked the HOTAS hard to the left and threw some yaw into it. She then stomped her right outer pedal and started crabbing in a corkscrew spiral as she added speed. The closer she approached the AutoGnat, the more sideways she flew. "Bank out right, Goat!"

"Bankin' right!"

Deuce added more throttle, and the centrifugal force of her spiraling and crabbed trajectory was putting more than seven gees on her body. She grunted and cursed as the pressure layer of her e-suit squeezed her legs and abdomen. The red flight path of the enemy plane spiraled inwardly at her in her mindview, and outside the cockpit, the world spun madly. The blue and red trajectory lines finally intersected just ahead of them. Then the targeting X turned from yellow to red.

"Guns, guns, guns!" she shouted and continued to grunt through the g-load.

Bright orange and red plasma balls the size of racquet balls tore across the space between them and hit home on the AutoGnat's right wing. The cannon fire burst through the structural integrity fields of the enemy fighter and then blew the wing free of the spar. Sparks flew in every direction as the added angular momentum of the impacting cannon fire sent it spinning asunder. As what would normally be the cockpit rolled over into view, cannon rounds burst through it. The little enemy fighter exploded into a bright orange and white firestorm.

Deuce let off the foot pedals and let go the HOTAS briefly to let her mecha right itself. She quickly grabbed the stick and pulled it up and found her wingman in her DTM. Then her sensor alarms sounded and Betty started bitching.

Warning, enemy sensor lock detected! Warning enemy sensor lock detected!

"Shit!" Deuce bit down on her temporomandibular joint (TMJ) bite block and took in a fresh burst of oxygen and stims while simultaneously pulling the stick back to her gut and pushing the throttle full forward.

"Fox three!" she heard Goat shout over the tac-net. She caught a glimpse of her wingman's mecha screaming by just behind her as he let the missile loose. The missile hit home this time, taking out the AutoGnat that was locking her up.

"Great shot, Goat!" Deuce shouted.

As the rest of the Utopian Saviors pulled the enemy fighters upward and mixed up with them, the chatter on the net picked up. Deuce did her best to keep up with the team in her DTM while at the same time doing her best not to get her ass shot off.

"Romeo! You've got one on your six!" Volleyball's voice cut in.

"I've got him, Romeo!" his wingman Freak replied. "Guns, guns, guns."

"Look out, Freak! You've got a couple of them starting to form up on you. Jesus, it's thick out here."

"Got that right, Romeo. Damn AGs are like angry bees swarming and they ain't sticking on their wingmen," Golfbag added.

Deuce didn't like it. The enemy planes were using a new tactic on them. They had more of a hive or swarm attack plan rather than the standard wingman divide-and-conquer approach. They were outnumbered more than five to one and didn't have a lot of room between themselves and the surface. They needed to mix it up more and somehow put the enemy at a disadvantage. On the upside, the attack had been successful. According to the DTM battleview, it looked like all the bot fighters had turned their attention from the ground pounders and were now targeting the Saviors.

"Alright, Marines, we've gotten their attention." Deuce announced. "Let's pull them upward and away from the surface."

"They have us outnumbered, Deuce. You have a plan?" Lieutenant Colonel Connie "Skinny" Munk asked over the net. Deuce could see her longtime friend's blue dot in the DTM view but couldn't make out her fighter. It was below her and underneath her wing on the left side.

Any Marine knew that when you were outnumbered you attacked. But what type of attack would be best? In the microsecond she had to consider her next move, her mind was a flurry of memories of space battles and training sessions. She could only see one clear tactical approach and it didn't make her happy.

"Yes. We get these bot bastards up in the ball. On my signal I want A-group to start pukin' while the B-group covers our ass on the backend," Deuce ordered. She hated to go to the pukin' deathblossom so soon in an engagement, but the numbers were too much in the enemy's favor and that is what the maneuver was for.

"Shit, I just ate," Skinny said.

"Well, Skinny," her wingman Captain Michael "HoundDog" Samuels grunted, "at least you get to eat it again."

Deuce held her abdominal muscles clenched as she bit on the TMJ bite block. Her trajectory carried her upward at top speed away from the planetoid. Nearly fifty of the enemy fighters adjusted their flight paths all vectored toward hers. The red and blue flight lines' intersection was predicted to be only a matter of seconds away.

Purple tracer rounds zipped by her canopy and one them slammed into her empennage. The SIFs held but the mecha rocked violently. Deuce pulled back on the HOTAS and stomped the left inner pedal, yawing the mecha around while keeping her flight path headed in the same direction. She was flying backwards with her DTM targeting system lighting up red on several targets.

"Guns, guns, guns!" Deuce barrel-rolled while still flying backwards and let loose a couple of missiles to give her some breathing room. "Fox Three! Fox Three!"

The enemy fighters appeared to be flying in some sort of chaotic pattern. They hadn't done that before. There was no wingman coverage as far as could be discerned. Deuce knew that for her plan to be optimally effective, they would have to get five of her squadron inside the swarm before they went to the whirling madness of the Pukin' deathblossom algorithm.

"These son of a bitches are swarming everywhere!" Beanhead shouted. "Guns, guns, guns."

The A-group pilots were pulling in on Deuce's position slower than the bots but they were close enough. Deuce was damned near puking already from the rapid and wild evasives she was taking due to the erratic swarm's attack tactics. The deathblossom was going to take a toll on her for a few precious seconds.

For more than forty years the maneuver had been referred to as a "pukin' deathblossom" from some ancient pop-culture reference and because the wild spinning motion of the maneuver put constantly changing g-loading on the pilot. It was a crazy, mad, three-dimensional spinning cacophony of death. It would cause the pilot's inner ear to go apeshit crazy with a side of batshit nuts. The mecha would spin like a Tasmanian Devil, launching death and hellfire from cannons and DEGs in all directions. The maneuver was first designed around the Navy VTF-35 Ares fighters but as soon as the Marines saw it they knew they could do it in their FM-12s.

The maneuver was the most mentally taxing and physically demanding thing a mecha jock could do. The pilot and AICs and the direct-to-mind linkages were required for such a maneuver to prevent Blue-on-Blue casualties. But over the past few decades of warfare in space there was no other mecha maneuver that was as effective against superior numbers.

The spinning was usually more than the pilots could take and would force them to vomit violently from the inner-ear confusion. But most good Navy pilots could manage so it certainly was doable for a U.S. Marine! Any good Marine could take a little vomit in their e-suit helmet. Besides, the inner recycle layer of the suits usually absorbed the vomit in a few very long and smelly seconds.

"Go, Saviors! Start pukin'!" Deuce ordered. She toggled the deathblossom controls and the ship started pitching, yawing, rolling, lurching, and jolting in every direction possible. There was a whirlwind of targeting Xes spinning around her at blurring speed. The fighter's cannons and directed-energy guns fired almost continuously. The spinning and rapid direction changes put g-load changes on her at over ten Earth gravities. The stars spun by, then the planetoid, then the stars again, and there were weapons firing all around her.

Deuce followed the red force tracker numbers as they dwindled in her DTM. Reflexively, she bit the TMJ bite block so hard she thought she'd break a tooth or her jaw. She thought she was going to make it through the maneuver as the countdown clock in her mind showed nine seconds remaining in the maneuver. Then the retching started.

"Marine mecha jocks ate their own vomit for breakfast and begged for more," she recalled her flight instructor shouting at her the first time she attempted the maneuver more than thirty years prior.

For Deuce, the vomiting didn't bother her so much. It wasn't even the retching and dry heaving followed by the pressure suit squeezes and the high g-loading that took real presence of mind, fresh air, and vapor stims to overcome. It was the smell. She just hated the damned smell of supercarrier cafeteria eggs the second time around.

Deuce watched the red force tracer in her DTM as the maneuver spun down. She knew it would take a few seconds on the other side of the maneuver to be worth a damn. The maneuver had lasted eighteen seconds. Studies had shown that any longer was too much on the pilots. It would be okay; Deuce knew the B-group wingmen would look after them as they recovered. The DTM red force tracker showed eleven bot fighters left. In eighteen seconds, five fighters had taken out well over thirty planes.

Eleven bots to ten, now those are much better odds. She bit the water tube. The fresh water squirted into her mouth. She sloshed it around and swallowed it. When it hit her stomach she nearly heaved again, but she managed to keep it down.

Yes, ma'am! Great odds. her AIC replied. Targeting Xs and priority engagement statistics popped up in her DTM. *We still have work to do.*

Chapter 5

November 3, 2406 AD
27 Light-years from the Sol System
Thursday, 11:35 AM, Expeditionary Mission Standard Time

Alexander Moore stood in his Armored Environment Marine Suit atop the forward hull of the *Sienna Madira* Expeditionary Starship. This was a super battlecruiser, formerly the flagship of the entire United States of the Sol System Navy. Now it had its own special expeditionary mission.

As far as anybody else was concerned, there was evidence in the archives that there had been a message of nonhuman origin from decades, maybe centuries, earlier, that needed investigating. That is all the history books would ever show.

Alexander Moore had convinced his successor in the Oval Office to make it happen so he could lead his expeditionary force to investigate the potential alien signal. But the hand-picked crew aboard the *Sienna Madira* expeditionary vessel knew the mission was more sinister. For more than a century now, Alexander Moore and his family had been fighting an Artificial Intelligence Counterpart known as Copernicus, who was hell-bent on enslaving all living creatures in the universe and making them hosts for AICs like himself.

Copernicus had been one of the first experimental AICs that the brilliant president Sienna Madira had allowed to be implanted within herself. Copernicus had twisted and confused the president's mind, turning her into the revolutionary leader El Ahmi, who eventually would have the daughter Sehera Ahmi, who would rescue one U.S. Marine Major Moore from hell under the thumb of her mother. The two of them thwarted El Ahmi's plans—which were really Copernicus' plans—over and over throughout the family's hidden history. Even while Moore had retired from the Marine Corps and become a U.S. senator, and later on, president, the evil Copernicus still drove American history, unbeknownst to all of humanity but a handful.

That handful, Moore had multiplied by a few tens and brought aboard his expeditionary vessel. The rest of the crew were only enlightened to the fact that there were splinter cells of the former resistance that had established colonies throughout the local region of the galaxy as far as humanity had stretched, only twenty or so light-years, and that they were mopping up after the civil war.

Moore watched the battle beneath him on the small planetoid as the *Sienna Madira* brought itself down and landed. He had given the order and decided he didn't want to sit on the bridge any longer, so he donned his suit and made it to the hull. The artificial-intelligence-driven battlebots and fighter planes were relentless, but his crew was moving forward and beginning to overrun them. Having the *Sienna Madira* land in the middle of the battle, giving them cover and closer artillery support, changed the tide. Most of all, Moore was concerned for one set of Marines—the one unit that carried his daughter. He scanned across the battlescape, looking for the hangar that showed the blue dot that was Deanna Moore.

Abigail, he said in his mindvoice to his AIC, *where is she?*

She's on the move, sir. It looks to me like they've commandeered a spacecraft. But they're overwhelmed with battlebots.

Show me.

Quickly, in Alexander's mind, the direct-to-mind link created a virtual reality in his vision, showing a close-up of the shuttle that Dee's crew had commandeered.

Who's flying that thing? It seems to be going nuts, he thought.

DeathRay was all the AIC replied.

Moore knew immediately that there was no better pilot, and that if DeathRay was there, he would protect his little girl, even if it meant his life. DeathRay would always be his go-to man.

All right, Abigail, let's bounce to it.

Moore hit the jump boots of his suit and shot almost a kilometer into the air. The low gravity gave him plenty of strength in the powered armor suit. With his HVAR at the ready and his full suite of quantum membrane sensors, IRs and radar pinging at him from every direction, he was painting a full picture of the battlescape in his mind. And if it came to the point where he was close enough to take out a target . . . well, there's no such thing as a "former" Marine.

Moore ran, pushing sixty kilometers per hour toward the shuttle, and he saw the glint of another suit, somersaulting through the air, firing multiple HVAR rounds in every direction, landing on the vessel.

That has to be Penzington, he thought.

Yes, sir, Abigail acknowledged. *That's her.*

With one last leap, as the blue dots seemed to freeze in place—except for one, which his DTM link was now showing as Penzington—he dove head-first toward the opening of the erratically flying shuttle. But the shuttle's path was *too* erratic, and he skittered across the top instead of hitting the doorway. He reached for a handhold with his left hand, and instead of grabbing, he simply punched through the hull of the vessel, grabbing onto superalloys as they sheared and cracked and creaked against the weight and strength of the suit. Moore finally got purchase on a chunk of metal and stood upright, tearing away at the hull and then stomping through, landing on top of one of the battlebots, which had a claw at the throat of a Marine inside the ship.

Moore looked forward and saw the transparent flight cabin door closed. Through it was Penzington at the helm, not in her suit, and his suit systems immediately projected his blue dot into her DTM Blue force tracker through her AIC. He noted her suit standing frozen near the hatch with the escape rear panel blown out. Penzington didn't say a word to him. She kept flying the vessel. The general was confident that she would keep the shuttle flying, knowing that Alexander Moore was in the back, kicking ass.

"Why is everybody frozen?" Moore said.

Penzington set off an EMP that shut down the suits as well as most of the bots. The atmosphere integrity is barely holding as the SIFs are not back online yet.

"That explains why the cockpit hatch is closed," he said out loud.

The EMP had stopped the overflow of bots that had been on the ship, but the bots outside continued to fly to the ship and enter it. For some reason they were hell-bent on stopping the shuttle. But they didn't know that they'd come to play with Alexander Moore. And they sure didn't realize that they'd been picking on his little girl. Alexander was about to bend Hell and maybe even break it loose.

Moore moved like a whirling dervish and a Tasmanian devil combined, on immunoboost and stimulants, spinning and punching, kicking and throwing, and firing the HVAR with precision so as not to hit any of the frozen soldiers on board the ship. The erratic flight path the shuttle was taking made it more difficult to balance, so Moore didn't bother with that. Instead, he bounced from wall to wall and from floor to ceiling of the little shuttle's rear bay. The walls of the craft began to show the strain of the fight with tears, AEM suit fist-sized holes and boot impressions scattered about.

Abigail, is there not any way you can reboot these suits?

I'm working on it, sir.

Penzington, get us inside the hangar bay of the Madira*!*

Goddamn right, sir! I'm workin' on it. Hold on back there!

The ship banked and bounced, throwing Moore left and right. But Moore used each motion as a deadly blow toward any of the encroaching swarm of battlebots.

Abigail, how about some air support? Or maybe some ground support? Where are the Warlords?

The general is overwhelmed at the moment, sir.

Goddamn it, Moore thought. *Move this thing, Penzington!*

Moore kicked the last of the bots out the door, but more were approaching. He dropped into the doorway on one knee, firing bursts as needed, and loosing grenades and flares from the shoulder mounts on his suit.

Spitap! Spitap! Spitap! The HVAR sounded nonstop.

I'm gonna run out of Goddamn ammo!

Abigail immediately threw into Alexander's mind that there were weapons about the ship that weren't being used. Moore didn't even think about it. Instead, instinctively, as his HVAR counted down to zero rounds, he reached behind him with his left hand, picking up the weapon highlighted in his mind.

Your suit's getting low on grenades, too, sir.

How are we doing on rebooting the troops?

The suits will come on in a moment. They have the automatic safety mechanisms that shut them down when our own EMP weapons are ignited.

We need to work on that. That's not a good design plan, he thought.

At the same time, he bull's-eyed a battlebot flying through the door with the weapon in his left hand, using his right to smash another with the stock of his empty rifle. They were getting closer and closer to the *Madira*. Moore could now see its shadow across the planetoid, stretching out just beneath them.

"HOLD ON BACK THERE!" Penzington shouted. "I'M GONNA CRASH THIS THING THROUGH THE HANGAR BAY!"

Goddamn right! Moore thought. *Oo-fuckin'-rah!*

Moore punched through another battlebot as he looked over his shoulder and saw the light on his daughter's suit kick on. They'd been in the suits for a couple of minutes without refreshing life support, so the CO_2 levels were getting close to dangerous without power. But immediately, as the suit kicked on, it would scrub the air, and these were new, state-of-the-art suits. They'd be fine. The organogel could keep a person alive for a very long time. After all, Alexander had spent over a month in one before organogel had been invented. But that was another time.

Nancy Penzington fought the controls of the shuttle as best she could. The thing seemed to have been designed to be flown by monkeys. Even though there were seats for humans, it was unlikely that any human had ever flown the craft.

She could see the hangar doors on the aft port side of the *Sienna Madira* glowing as dust would fly up from the planetoid surface and ionize against the structural integrity fields that held the atmosphere within.

Allison? she thought to her AIC. *Cycle through the security codes and let us fly right through the fields. If there are any bots behind us, hopefully they'll just get fried on the SIFs as we fly through. The general will take care of any that do.*

Understood.

Tell me when we're clear.

Roger that, Nancy.

Nancy took only a second to glance to her left at her husband. She could see through the tinted visor, DeathRay was wide awake and watching. But there was no way she could hear him with the power out. She could DTM through an AIC-to-AIC connection, though.

You alright in there, Boland? she thought.

Just fly the ship and don't think about me. Deathray replied. *Nancy, how're their suits coming?*

Abigail and I are working on it.

No better people to do it, DeathRay replied.

Only seconds later, the lights in DeathRay's helmet kicked on.

We got comms, DeathRay's voice rang in her head on the tactical net channel. *My suit's warming up. It's still gonna take a few seconds before I'm any good.*

Understood. I'm hoping in a few seconds this thing'll be over. DeathRay? Can Candis handle the external weapons on this ship?

There are *no external weapons on this ship. The EMP took 'em out. At least that's what Candis is saying.*

That's what I thought.

Who the hell is that in the back makin' all the noise?

I'll give you three guesses and the first two don't count, Nancy said.

Well, if those bots are unfamiliar with the concept of Hell, I'm sure he's introducing them to it. Hey, I've got use of my arms now, Nancy, she could hear DeathRay say through the comms.

Roger that. Don't take the helm; I've got this.

At that moment, Allison responded, *We're all clear, Nancy! We're clear to board the* Madira*!*

Understood.

Nancy put full power to the thrusters, throwing the shuttle through the *Madira's* hangar, and then immediately throwing them into reverse. The g-load slammed them forward in their seats, and the reverse thrusters and structural integrity fields slammed against the hull. The pursuing bots vaporized as they smacked into the SIFs with a strange twanging sound like a struck tuning fork. The ship creaked and rocked against the strain from the reverse thrusters. The fact that it had been torn to hell and gone during the ruckus didn't help.

Nancy managed to turn the shuttle a hundred and eighty degrees as it skittered across the floor of the hangar bay and through the noses of several mecha fighter planes that were on deck and waiting to deploy.

"This thing isn't gonna slow down in time!" Nancy shouted. *This is so gonna hurt,* she thought. *And I'm not in my suit!*

The end of the long hangar bay approached extremely fast, and it was clear the vehicle was about to slam into the bulkhead plating near the elevator shaft. Then something seemed to reach out and grab the shuttle, and slowed it down as if it were being dragged from behind. Then something else seemed to slow it even more, and the shuttle screeched with an earsplitting roar to a halt, only inches from the elevator wall.

What the hell? Nancy thought.

Well, DeathRay said with a smirk, *since you wouldn't let me fly, I figured I'd call a few friends to help out.* He rose from the seat and clanked outward. As the other soldiers' suits came online, they all barreled out of the holes in the wall and what was left of the doorframe of the shuttle. Nancy rose from her copilot's seat and followed.

Moore stood beside his daughter, looking her over to make sure she was okay, and the only thing Dee could do was take it. Nancy kind of felt sorry for her sometimes, but at the same time she wished that her father even knew she was alive to care for her like that. Nancy looked around to see what had stopped them, and saw DeathRay saluting two mecha FM-12s in full bot mode, standing upright, saluting back with their huge armored hands. The two ships' canopies popped and slid upward, and DeathRay's old wingman, USN Commander Karen "Fish" Fisher, grinned on the left. A pilot with the word "Poser" written across her helmet nodded from the other.

"Everybody all right in there?" Poser asked DeathRay.

"No. Poser, get us a medevac down here, we've got wounded. And we're also gonna need technical. Most of the suits are pretty much wiped out."

"Roger that." DeathRay could hear the bot mode mecha pound off away from the shuttle, clanging against the floor.

DeathRay popped the helmet of his suit, hanging it from the shroud over his right shoulder as he walked toward Penzington and gave her a big, armored hug.

"Not in front of the kids, Boland," Penzington said with laughter in her voice.

Alexander looked at his daughter. It hurt him to see his little princess missing a hand. The suit had sealed off the wound and the med techs could print her a new hand in no time, but it still broke his heart. Then, there was the mission. They were both Marines and they both had a mission.

"Dad, I'm okay. Rackman is worse than I am."

"The hell you say, Marine," the Navy SEAL responded faintly from behind them.

"Yeah, I understand that, Dee, I need to know—did you find it?"

"No. The best thing we could see is that there's some sort of computer nexus in there that is housing whatever is controlling all these bots. They're *not* simply AIs. They're mostly controlled from somewhere else, through some sort of membrane transmitter."

"I was afraid of that. So, Copernicus could be anywhere." Moore had a distant look for an instant as though he were listening to his AIC.

"Well, you smashed him yourself. It's got to be a copy."

"That seems unlikely. Abigail doesn't believe that's possible."

"Well, it's Copernicus. Who knows? Anything's possible. Maybe it's a . . . a subordinate."

"No. If it's a subordinate, it seems like it would have taken too long to train him to be as crazy as Copernicus."

At that moment, Abigail excitedly said into his mind, *Maybe Dee is onto something, Alexander.*

What do you mean? he thought.

Maybe it's not a subordinate. Maybe . . . it's an offspring.

Chapter 6

November 4, 2406 AD
27 Light-years from the Sol System
Friday, 9:05 AM, Expeditionary Mission Standard Time

So the big debate throughout the bridge crew and those really in the know—and especially between all of their AICs—was how Copernicus had done what he had done. Was the Copernicus that they had just encountered on another one of his hidden outposts a copy of the one that Alexander had crushed under his boot at the end of the Separatist War? Or was it somehow really the original Copernicus? Had he managed to download himself somewhere else—which, to all of the AICs, seemed impossible—or, as Abigail had suggested, perhaps it was an offspring? The difficulty of transplanting an AIC from one body to another was as difficult as transplanting a human from one brain to another. Neither had ever been done before and therein was the conundrum. Moore had destroyed Copernicus' brain. How was he still alive?

The offspring concept was the most intriguing to all of the AICs. How had Copernicus managed to convince other AICs to join with him and make copies of himself—or offsprings of himself—and none of the AICs had leaked that information?

The first AICs were completely built by humans. In fact, Copernicus, being one of the very first experimental Artificial Intelligence Counterparts, was entirely built and coded by humans. Well, that wasn't exactly true, as Abigail pointed out to Alexander, because no AIC could be simply "coded." The quantum computer main core was manufactured by humans, and then a base learning algorithm and a large database of information was loaded onto that computer; the base learning algorithm then began to grow simply by asking questions and watching the quantum computer interact with the universe and cohere to solutions based on the ever-so-strange rules of quantum mechanics. With each new solution arrived at within the learning algorithm, the AIC became more and more intelligent and more and more self-aware. It took years, many, many years, for the first counterpart to become self-aware. And with a quantum computer, that meant billions of questions could be solved in a matter of minutes. So for several years of problem-solving before self-awareness, Abigail explained, there were likely as many questions asked as there were stars in the sky.

While Abigail seemed to be really intrigued, and had tried several times over the past few months to explain to Alexander how counterparts were created, Alexander was a lot more pragmatic about it. All of these Copernicus offspring, clones, or whatever they were, simply had to be destroyed. And Alexander was hell-bent, for certain, and, by, God going to do it. The big issue was tracking them all down, overtaking them, and killing them. They had already taken on some moderate casualties and had been at it for almost a year, and still had found only vague hints as to where the extraterrestrial signal might have come from. But hopefully, with each new base discovered, one of them would lead them to where they needed to be. Alexander hoped wherever that was wouldn't be too much farther out. They were already on the outskirts of as far as humanity had ever trekked to the stars. What they were finding was that Copernicus, on the other hand, had sent probes and automated systems further than anybody knew, and to what end, they weren't certain.

Alexander sat in the captain's quarters peering out the observation window as the minimal all-volunteer skeleton crew of the *Sienna Madira* mopped up the rest of the bots on the planetoid, and the members of the First Scout Force licked their wounds.

"CHENG to the captain," came through the comm, disturbing Alexander's contemplation.

"Go, CHENG. What do you have, Buckley?" he said to the chief engineer.

"Sir, I think you need to come down here and see this."

"What is it, Buckley?"

"Well, we been tearin' into this bot-made shuttlecraft, and it's *kind of* like something a human would build, but at the same time it's not. But we found a snap-back actuator pad."

"Really? Is it functional?"

"Roger that, sir."

"*Now* we're onto something," Alexander said. "I'll be right down, CHENG. Good work, Buckley."

Moore stood straight up and thought, *A snap-back actuator pad. Where does it teleport to, I wonder?*

Well, every other one of these things we've found snapped back to another one of these crazy hidden bases, Abigail replied.

Hopefully, we're onto something here.

Moore grabbed his coffee cup off his desk on the way out the door and sipped at it as he marched down the corridor to the elevator. *Abigail, locate my wife.*

Sir, your wife is with your daughter in the medical bay.

Everything is all right there, I assume?

Yes, sir. Deanna's procedure is almost complete.

Understood.

Commander Joe Buckley, Jr. had been in the Navy for more than two decades. His father had been a career man and had given his life to save the *Sienna Madira*. Buckley Junior had his opportunity to save the *Madira* in turn, but managed to survive.

He was ready to retire from the Navy, and was about to do so, until President Alexander Moore himself offered him the position as chief engineer for the expeditionary mission. Buckley was under the impression that nobody in history had ever told the man no, except maybe his daughter or his wife. And then he wasn't so sure, after having seen them on board the ship for the last year, if that ever worked out very well for them, either. The man was a force of nature. And Buckley was proud to be serving under him. The best part was that the mission had them venturing out into the stars further than humanity had ever gone and to do so they would have to travel faster than humanity ever had. That was what Buckley lived for, space travel. It was the reason he joined the Navy and the reason he studied spacetime manipulation propulsion theory in college.

Buckley looked at the readouts in his direct-to-mind link and viewed the design of the odd little spaceship that the recon team had recovered. Although the thing had been blown to hell and ripped to shreds during the acquisition, Buckley had managed to put it all back together and create a full 3D model of the vehicle. Tracing the power leads, he realized that there was a huge source of power in the engine components. And *there* was a snap-back quantum membrane technology teleportation system. *And* it was active and linked to other pads.

Buckley went through the software and realized that it was an encrypted control system, but it was nothing that the AICs of the *Sienna Madira* couldn't put their heads together on and crack.

Now just where do you go, you little bugger, he thought to himself as he looked at the list of addresses attached to the quantum membrane teleportation pad. There were seven. "So you were only designed to go to seven places," Buckley muttered to himself.

"If you continue to speak to yourself all the time like that, CHENG, then people are gonna put you in the loony bin," Alexander Moore's voice rang over his shoulder. Buckley immediately stiffened and turned.

"Well, sir, if you go up there in the loony bin, them folks are swattin' around at stuff that's not there all the time anyway. I think I'd fit right in," Buckley said with a smile, as he referenced the virtual-reality simulation room where the war-gaming experts would go to plan out the battles in a virtual four-dimensional direct-to-mind environment that only they could see. An outsider looking in would see a roomful of people moving imaginary things around in the air.

"Show me whatcha got, Buckley," Moore said in his slow Mississippi drawl, getting right to business. The man was always right to business.

"Well, sir," Buckley said, "if I may . . . it's easier to show you direct-to-mind."

"Sure thing."

Buckley noticed Moore making the expression that all humans make when they're speaking in their minds to their AICs. Buckley did the same to his, as he instructed, *Debbie, set up the DTM link with the captain.*

Roger that, Joe.

And then, in a mini version of their own loony bin, Buckley started pointing at things in mid-air that were not there, but the captain could see them just fine.

". . . So you see, sir, here's the ship. This hole here, that must be where you tore through, this part here is from battle damage, and now let's move away the exterior layers." Buckley waved his hand and pulled away the structure. "Now here is the power system. You see these conduits flowing here? This conduit goes into this junction box from the main propulsion system, but if you look just beyond that, there's another conduit coming out of there, going somewhere where it normally wouldn't. To this box here. That's what triggered my suspicion."

Pull away this layer, Debbie, he said to his AIC. With another motion of his hand, the box skin flew away, revealing the internal components.

"And *this*, sir, right here, is a quantum membrane snap-back teleporter link."

"You're damn right, Joe, I've seen plenty of them," Moore responded. "Have you cracked it?"

"Well, sir, we put a cluster of all the AICs on the *Madira* together, and when all the AICs on board put their noggins into it, in just a matter of a four minutes, they cracked Copernicus' encryption. Looks like there's seven addresses."

"Seven? Very interesting. But you still haven't figured out a way to know where in the hell that address is?"

"Sorry, sir. Quantum physics and all doesn't allow for that. All we can say is that this thing is connected to seven other things somewhere else in the universe."

"Shit!" Moore said. "Physics."

"Yes, sir, quantum membrane stuff, to be exact," Buckley replied.

"Maybe we need some other quantum physicists on board to help you out."

"Well, sir, the chief scientist and I have been working on this for awhile, and we've spoken with anybody with any knowledge on the subject, as well as all of the AICs, and all we can say is, this thing is linked to seven other locations somewhere in this universe."

"Understood, Joe. Good work," Moore said as he offered him a hand. Joe shook it in return. Moore had been a politician for so long that a lot of times, Joe had noticed, he would offer a hand to shake over a salute. Joe didn't mind at all.

"So what are your orders, sir?"Moore rubbed his chin in thought, then looked at the 3D model in his mind for a second longer.

"Well, I guess we start at the top, Joe. Get this shuttle fixed back up, and we'll just have to figure out where these things go. How long will it take?"

"It'll take, uh . . . a few days, sir."

"Good. That'll give the A-Team time for their wounds to heal, and to rest and prepare, and we'll start right back at this thing."

"Yes, sir."

This time, he saluted. Joe watched as Moore returned the salute and then turned and walked out of the hangar deck, thinking, *Does that man ever tire?* He slumped for a second, and leaned against the hull of the shuttle and thought, *So we need to put you back together, old girl.*

"Well, it *looks* like it hurts, Dee," Rackman told her. Deanna could see the 3D printer laying out bone materials onto the severed hand and watched as tissues were printed and attached, but she could feel nothing. There was the occasional spurt of blood as an artery or vein was printed then sealed, but the small transparent plastic shield kept any debris in or out as needed. Then she looked at Rackman's new arm.

"Did it hurt you?" she asked the SEAL.

"Didn't feel a damned thing. Amazing to watch," he said. "Seen it before but not on myself."

"Yeah, I don't really care to watch much more of it."

"Understood," Rackman smiled. "Hey, look at it this way. Minimum required recovery before active duty is seven days. We get to goldbrick for a week!"

"Well, we'll see about that." Dee closed her eyes and took a deep breath. Then she showed the young SEAL her big brown doe eyes that she had inherited from her mother. "Davy, do me a favor and quit gawking at me. It makes me feel, uh, vulnerable."

"Shit, Marine, you! Vulnerable?" he laughed. "That will be the day, mate."

"Up yours, squidboy," she replied with a smile. "Before you start goldbricking, at least do me a favor and go check on the rest of the team." Dee had made the med crew take her last, even though her father and mother had been through to expedite her treatment. But Dee had put her foot down. It was her team, and her wound wasn't critical. She could wait until everyone else was good.

"Roger that, jarhead. Will do." Davy made his way past several other wounded soldiers from the battle in search of the rest of their wounded team members. Dee watched the SEAL as he walked out. His hospital gown opened up the back and she could see red marks where the bots had cut him up. The immunoboost was healing him up nicely. She also like the rest of what she saw. She so wanted to run her fingers over the wounds and caress the SEAL's firm . . .

"Ahem," came from behind her, almost making her jump off the hospital bed.

"What you looking at, Marine?" Penzington said with one eyebrow raised.

"Uh, I, uh . . ." Dee stammered embarrassedly. "Uh, nothing?"

"Relax, Dee. I've been a spy most of my life. I notice things. Your secret is safe with me." Nancy laughed.

"Don't tell Daddy. No telling what he would do." Dee wasn't sure what her father would do to a potential boyfriend and she didn't really want to know. There had been that one incident with the senior cadet formal dance that she would never forget. The young man who had taken her most certainly wouldn't forget it. Ever. He still wouldn't respond to her calls or e-mails. She couldn't even apologize to him.

"Understood. I wouldn't wish that fight on anybody. Not even a SEAL." Nancy laughed again. Dee wasn't sure if she was laughing with her or at her in an I'm-glad-it's-not-me way.

"Bah, SEAL. No match for a good Marine," Dee spat instinctively.

"So you doing okay?" Dee was glad that Nancy had changed the subject. It didn't really embarrass her to talk about boys and sex and stuff, but the more they talked about it in the open, the more likely it would be that somebody would hear it and it would get back to her parents.

"I'm fine. This doesn't hurt at all." She pointed at the now halfway printed hand.

"Looks like it hurts like hell." Nancy cringed at the sight.

"I guess. But, you know, immunoboost and stims and painkillers have me so hyped up I'm ready to take on a hovertank barehanded."

Dee did feel hyper but at the same time tired. She had been on the *Madira* for more than a year now and in so many fights with bots that she would enjoy a week on a beach somewhere. Too bad there was no beach anywhere nearby. Hell, she'd settle for a night of drinking and sex. But she was a good Marine and there were things to be done. And she was her father's daughter.

Chapter 7

November 5, 2406 AD
27 Light-years from the Sol System
Saturday, 11:17 PM, Expeditionary Mission Standard Time

"You gonna work on that all night long, Commander?" First Sergeant Rondi Howser stood straddle of a pair of boots sticking out from underneath the strange-looking bot-built shuttle in engineering. She didn't really care so much for the shuttle as she did for the man working on it. Although she had drawn support for the upcoming mission in the shuttle, the Marine just saw it as a means to get her wherever it was that she needed to be in order to kick ass.

"Amari! Where the hell've you been? I need you under here right now to help align the snap-back to sling-forward conduit projector on this thing," the man underneath the spaceship shouted.

"I am NOT Petty Officer Engineering Technician First Class Sarala Amari!" Rondi said sourly.

"Huh? Rondi, that you? Hold on a minute," came from underneath the shuttle. There were a couple of clanging noises and then an, "Oh, shit. Goddamit. Where the hell are you, Amari?"

The boots were attached to a set of red engineer's coveralls that were in turn on the *Madira's* chief engineer, who was lying on a hover creeper doing God knows what up underneath the thing. Rondi put her hands on her terrific hips, tapped her right toe against the deck plating, and raised an eyebrow as the creeper started to slide from underneath the ship.

"Firstly, I suspect PO1 Amari has sacked out, like most normal people. Secondly, what the hell, Joe?" Rondi said in her best hurt voice. "We were supposed to chow over two hours ago! I've been waiting and I'll be damned if I'll let you stand me up!"

The CHENG looked up at the sleek muscular Marine in her Universal Combat Uniform and Rondi was certain that he was thinking several things all at once. The first thing she hoped was that the fireproof fabric conformed around her Marine-hardened midsection and pushed up her more-than-ample breasts into a very nice supported position. The common description of the female UCU tops was that they always kept "things" at attention. The compression shirt had been designed to fit skintight as a lightly armored fireproof paper-thin layer. And it did. The shirt not only wicked away sweat and moisture, conformed to most environment color schemes, led repel, low-order shrapnel, resisted fire, and compressed the muscles, improving the wearer's performance, but it did so in a way that made the person wearing it look damned good. And Rondi knew she looked damned good in them.

The other thing that Buckley had better be thinking was that he was fucking sorry for standing her up, and was in fear of getting a knot jerked in his ass.

"Uh, sorry about that, First Sergeant." Joe stammered. "Somehow or other I promised the general I'd have this ship ready in two days, and that was a day and a half ago."

"How does that affect me?"

Rondi knew damned well how it did. There were at least five generals on board the ship, but when somebody said "the general," everybody knew they meant Alexander Moore. Everybody on board the ship also knew that when the general expected something from you that you'd better deliver it. Knowing all that didn't mean she couldn't have some fun with Buckley, though.

"Well, Marine, you want to crawl down under here and give me a hand, we could get to that chow sooner than later." Joe smirked at Rondi. She could tell he was having a hard time looking her in the eye, so she knelt down beside him.

"Is that an order, Commander?" Rondi raised an eyebrow flirtatiously.

"Negative." Joe paused for a long moment and then sighed. "I'm brain dead right now anyway. I really should stop for a bit. Maybe some chow and then a nap in my quarters."

"Is that an invitation?" Rondi almost laughed. "I've heard more enticing ones."

"You know it is, gorgeous, but I really do have to get this thing flying in perfect order." Joe rubbed at the stubble on his chin. Rondi wondered just how long he'd been at it. "I really should finish calibrating that QMT grid panel while it's apart. Just not a good time to stop."

"How long will that take?"

"An hour at best. By then I'll be starving and cross-eyed from lack of sleep." Joe frowned a bit. Rondi could tell he was pushing himself too hard. Having only a skeleton crew in engineering must have had him doing several jobs all at once.

"Tell you what. You crawl back in there and fix the QMT thingy and I'll go get us some dinner. Meet you in your quarters with it in an hour. Sound good?" Rondi put her hand on his shoulder and smiled warmly at Joe as she stood up.

"Great. An hour. That's just enough time." Joe leaned back on the hover creeper and slid back up under the shuttle. "That's enough time to straighten out the wavefunction correlator with the pattern buffers in the . . ."

Rondi turned and walked toward the chow deck, doing her best not laugh out how big a geek the CHENG was. "Best one in the fleet," she said to herself.

Dinner had gone well. Joe ate like he hadn't eaten in two days. Come to think of it, he realized that he hadn't. He then realized he hadn't showered in as long either. He excused himself from Rondi to hit the shower. As one of the senior staff, Joe managed one of the quarters with its own shower, so there wasn't too big a disruption to his date with Rondi.

The CHENG had been seeing the Marine for most of the expeditionary mission, and every time she went out on a job he felt his heart in his throat until he saw her come back. He couldn't imagine how the general handled seeing his daughter go out on dangerous missions day in and day out. And on this last one she lost a hand and was cut up pretty badly. Joe had hard enough time watching Rondi go out and they were just, well, mostly having a lot of sex together. But Joe liked the Marine a lot. The kind of like that is beyond "boat cute"; it was the kind of like that makes you consider retiring and getting a house somewhere together—though they had never discussed it. Joe used the general as his rock. If Moore could send Dee out into the muck and still function, then he could watch as Rondi went out.

Joe turned his back to the falling water and let it wash away the stress and grime from keeping the ship together, repairing the shuttle, and a million other things. He looked up as the shower door slid open and Rondi slipped into the tight space with him. She reached her arms around his shoulders and kissed him softly. Joe stood back as far as he could get in the tiny shower and took in the view. The movement of Rondi's arms resting on his shoulders and her slight wriggling movements as the water splashed against her body exaggerated the brilliant red, black, and blue cobra high-resolution laser-printed tattoo that curled around her left leg three times from the knee, up between her legs from behind and over her pubic area, across her rippled abdominal muscles, and around both breasts, with its mouth open and fangs showing on the left side of her midsection. The red and blue were nanofluorescent and retroreflective, causing them to glow brilliantly in the low lighting of the shower.

To Joe it was clear that she didn't need the UCU top to keep her "at attention." The muscular nature of her body and the firmness of her breasts did that all by themselves. Her arousal, unless the water was too cool for her, showed that she was as attentive as she could be.

Joe felt her hand grasp him, and he realized that the Marine wasn't the only one standing at attention. He pulled her to him and kissed her.

"You are beautiful," he whispered.

"Shut up," Rondi replied as she worked him into her and wrapped her left leg around him.

Joe shut up.

Rondi lay on her side, looking across Joe out the small viewport to the outside of the ship. The stars were always breathtaking to her. Rondi was smart, but not smart enough to be a CHENG or a navigator or one of the bridge team. She knew that. She was smart in a different way. She understood tactics and weapons and she understood how to stay alive when shit got bad. She really understood her physical limitations and how to push them beyond what most people knew how to do. To her, it was amazing that a smart guy, a senior officer, like Buckley liked her the way he seemed to. The way she hoped he did. She knew he worried about her when she was on maneuvers, but at the same time Rondi knew that Buckley had nearly been killed in engineering during space battles as well. Engineering wasn't really all that safe, what with all the radiation and high voltages and no telling what other things in there could kill you.

"Spacetime motivator equations, my ass." Joe mumbled in his sleep. Rondi sighed slightly through her pursed lips as Joe continued. "The Ricci tensor doesn't . . . no, sir . . . yes, sir . . . football?"

Rondi laughed out loud and then covered her mouth, hoping she didn't wake him up. "I don't know what you're dreaming about but it sounds like a whopper." Rondi looked at the clock on the nightstand. For whatever reason, she never could sleep before a mission, not even after sex.

Rondi leaned over and kissed Joe lightly on the head and then eased her naked body out from under the covers. She quietly made it into Joe's bathroom and started pulling on her UCU, thinking to herself that she hadn't had the heart to tell him that she was on the mission on the shuttle. She'd leave him a note through his AIC.

Rondi brushed her teeth and then spit the little disposable robot out into the sink and rinsed her mouth out. She half smiled at herself in the mirror, thinking that she didn't look near as old or tired as she was feeling. The UCU sucked to her body as she tapped the membrane panel under the neckline to display bulkhead blue-gray, which was the standard uniform color for onboard a ship. She slapped the 1st AEM Recon patch onto her left shoulder then twisted her torso to pop her back and force the air bubbles out of the shirt. The patch and shirt fabrics meshed together and hardened into a seamless decoration. She then slapped her nametag atop her right breast with similar results, then decided she needed to pee before she donned her digicam pants. She had a few minutes before she really needed to be in the AEM corridor for mission prebrief. She hoped the toilet rinse cycle wasn't loud enough to wake up Joe. Rondi pulled up her padded and armored pants and melded the fasteners. The pants quickly shimmered and then tracked the color scheme of the top and changed to the same blue-gray base colors. Marines always wore base color camo that matched their environment.

Rondi picked up her socks and boots and slid out the door before putting them on. She stood and ran her fingers through her close-cropped blond hair and then tucked her cover in her pocket.

"See ya later, Joe." She kissed her hand and then touched his door.

"Quantum membrane panel adjustment!" Joe jumped straight up out of the bed and ran to the door and almost opened it before he was awake enough to realize he was naked. "Shit. I need some coffee."

Joe, his AIC said into his mind. *Good morning. You have a message from First Sergeant Rondi Howser.*

Play it, he thought.

Chapter 8

November 7, 2406 AD
27 Light-years from the Sol System
Monday, 6:35 AM, Expeditionary Mission Standard Time

The shuttle had been retrofitted as best Buckley could manage. DeathRay certainly hoped that the CHENG had done a good job. He had no reason to believe he hadn't. The CHENG had been through a lot with the crew of the *Madira*, and DeathRay had confidence in him. The mission was simple: use the QMT system to teleport into an unknown system and gather intel as to where in the galaxy the other side of the quantum membrane teleportation was. With only the address, all they knew was that they would teleport to another pad somewhere. The pad could be four kilometers away or a trillion kilometers away. According to the eggheads, there was just no way of knowing without going there.

Once there, the first order of business would be to analyze the local stars with hopes of determining its celestial location. The second order of business was to gather recon on the system. It always helped if you knew how many uglies there were before you came in with all guns a-blazin'.

Buckley had given the ship a once-over, looking for transmitters and automated systems, but you never knew when it came to Artificial Intelligence Counterparts. Those things could be hidden almost anywhere. In fact, the more modern ones that humans used were about the size of a sunflower seed without the shell and were implanted just behind the ear canal inside the skull.

DeathRay turned to his copilot and wife, and gave her a wink. "*Madira*, this is Recon One."

"Recon One, go ahead."

"All systems are go, and we are ready for teleportation."

"Understood, DeathRay," General Moore's voice responded. "You are go for teleportation. Godspeed. And Boland, be careful."

"Understood sir." DeathRay flipped off the comm and turned to Nancy.

"Well, it's now or never. We can always decide to do it later if you want to go home."

"Hmpph." Nancy gave a wry smile. "Shut up and push the button."

"Affirmative," DeathRay laughed. "Everybody buckled in back there?" he conned to the rear of the shuttle. His crew consisted of three first Recon Marines in armored environment suits (Lieutenant Jason Franks, First Sergeant Rondi Howser, and Corporal Samuel Simms), and the CHENG's assistant, Petty Officer Engineering Technician First Class Sarala Amari. Just in case they came across technical glitches, it was always good to have a technician on board.

"Yes, sir!" was the response from the crew cabin. DeathRay flipped the internal conn off and looked at Nancy.

"I hate doin' this without Dee."

"Me too." Nancy frowned. "Doc said it would take her another couple of days for the hand graft to take hold with no residual pain."

"I know. But I hate doin' it without Dee. You ready?" DeathRay said.

"I'm ready," Nancy responded.

Okay, Candis, DeathRay thought. *Here we go. Initiate auto-sequences and be ready for whatever might happen.*

Roger that, boss, Candis replied.

DeathRay reached forward and pressed the QMT controls. There was the eerie sense of his hair standing on end and his skin crawling, and a faint hiss and crackle as if someone were frying bacon in a skillet. For a second, DeathRay saw stars, and then the stars he had been seeing were changed, and he was looking at a large moon covered with blue and green, near a gas giant orbiting a red giant star.

Whoa, that didn't take long, he thought. *Candis, are you scanning? Figure out where the hell we are.*

Scanning, Jack, she replied.

"So whaddaya say, Penzington?" he said to his wife. "Any ideas where we are?"

"Not yet. Any threats?"

"None to speak of, but I'll betcha a dime to a doughnut they're on that planet."

"Why would the AIs need a blue-green planet?"

"You got me. That would suggest that there are biologicals involved."

"Maybe they found something there that they can host in."

"Maybe," DeathRay replied. "Well, I don't like just sitting out here in open space. I'm gonna go dormant. Let's cut off everything but the passive sensors. No comms, nothing."

"Hell, we shoulda done that before we teleported in."

"We'll remember that next time," he said.

The little shuttle sat, floating adrift in space near the gas giant, for several minutes. Mostly, nobody said a word. There was the occasional direct-to-mind communication between AICs and hosts, but there was very little verbal communication. Then Nancy broke the silence.

"Allison has a fix on where we are, Boland."

"Yeah? Do tell."

"I'm transferring the coordinates to DTM now, but it looks like we're a good twenty-eight light-years from Sol."

"*Twenty-eight light-years*?! Jesus! How did they get here? No humans have *ever* traveled this far from Sol, to my knowledge."

"Yeah. There is only one colony that has made it to twenty light-years, and that is Gliese 581c. There may be an outpost slightly beyond that by a light year or two. Tau Ceti is one of the outermost densely-populated settlements at twelve light years, and Gliese 876d, at fifteen, has maybe a quarter million people. It took years to get there and get gates set up. At top speeds, it would take *years* to get here, especially decades ago when hyperspace travel was much slower."

"Well, Copernicus was a century and a half old, at least."

"Good point. And if that signal came along during the Sienna Madira presidential timeframe, then that's over a hundred and fifty years ago."

"Jesus. But with the technology they had then," DeathRay said, "it would have taken . . . thirty years, or more, to get from Sol to here."

"How fast could the *Madira* get here?"

". . . Eighteen months?"

"That's what I thought. Whew. We're gonna have to rethink this. We're gonna have to bring a gate and snap back."

"Yeah. Well, the *Madira* has one end of that, but we certainly couldn't use the shuttle. Somehow we'd have to tie into the gate here. And I don't think that's ever been done."

"That's beyond my pay grade, Boland. I think that's a question for Buckley, or somebody smarter than him, like the STO."

"Yeah, I don't think that's the CHENG's job. It's probably the science officer's job," Jack agreed.

"Well, let's figure that out when we get back." Nancy looked over the readouts from the passive sensors.

"You're right, Nancy," Jack thought for a moment. Right now they needed more information about what was going on in this system. "Okay, first, calibrate the navigation system, and let's see if we can't find a way to do some recon on that planet."

"Roger that," Penzington replied.

Penzington worked the optical controls and pointed the telescope system the CHENG had installed at the planet. Several times she had to use ET1 Amari's expertise. But after a few minutes of tinkering with the telescope, they managed to get some optical imagery that showed dwellings. As best they could tell, they looked like humanoid-sized dwellings.

"What do you reckon lives here?" Boland asked. "If they're human-sized, could there have been colonists?"

"A hundred and fifty years ago? On a thirty-year flight? That's unlikely. Unless . . . they had help," Nancy replied.

"What do you mean, help?" Boland turned and looked at her, puzzled.

"Well, you know the story as good as I do, according to Moore. He claims that there was some kind of alien signal that Madira had received, and it was about that time that Copernicus began to take over her personality."

"I still don't put much stock into the alien conspiracy theory, Nancy. How could Madira or Copernicus cover up an alien signal? Wouldn't other scientists have seen it? And, why did Madira find it? And for that matter, how did Moore?"

"If it looks like a duck . . ." Penzington smiled. "Who knows, maybe they were supposed to be the only ones to find it. Or maybe Copernicus had any others all killed."

"Well, let's do this the right way. It is too risky to fire up the QMTs just to send back a drone with info. It would give us away for sure. Everybody gear up. We're gonna drop down to the planet and do some recon. We're gonna leave the shuttle here and use our own QMT pad and snap-back bracelets. If things go awry, we'll snap back, then reactivate the teleporter back to Madira. Understood?"

"Roger that," resounded from the back.

"All right. We're go. We're gonna be teleporting planetside in five minutes. I want everybody ready to go."

The surface of the planet was not unlike Earth. As far as they could tell, the air was not that much different, if maybe slightly thinner, like the higher altitudes in the Alps or the Rocky Mountains of Earth, but it was perfectly breathable and no biotoxins were detectable. The gravity was about 0.9 Earth gravities. It pretty much felt like home, Boland thought. That is, if home had a big gas giant looming overhead. Might have felt like like home to the colonists from Tau Ceti but not to Jack. He was from Earth.

The AEMs held point while Boland, Penzington and Amari took up the rear in standard Navy armored environment suits, not quite like the powered armor that the AEMs wore. Penzington's, of course, had her own special attachments and adjustments that she had used and modified over the past couple of years. None of it was standard issue for any branch of the military, but Penzington didn't belong to any branch of the military. Being an operative of the intelligence community, and retired on top of that, she was merely an "onboard advisor."

Many of the senior officers Earthside had originally balked at the idea of taking civilians and non-military advisors aboard on such long-term missions with important military goals, but Alexander Moore wanted her along, so by God, she had come along. Although he was only a general, he *was* a former president, and he was most certainly a hero to humanity. So the Joint Chiefs rarely said no to the newest captain of the *Madira*.

And Boland liked that fact. He knew that if they needed something, Moore would get it for them, and that Moore, being a Marine himself who had lived through some of the bloodiest battles in history, wouldn't just throw his troops haphazardly to the grinder.

The coordinates they had pinpointed to drop down to the surface were just outside where they had noticed the settlements. The settlements appeared to be largely of concrete and alloy materials in nature, with some composite materials. They were high tech. There were modern power technologies and grids scattered about, and from Allison's best guess, there was enough infrastructure to support something along the lines of one hundred thousand to a million occupants on the surface. The AIC claimed there wasn't enough data to narrow it down better than that. The odd thing was that there were no signs of any occupants.

With mainly passive sensors, and QM sensors that, hopefully, could not be spoofed or detected, the recon team moved quietly through the forest, approaching the outskirts of the urban area. There was a high fence that seemed to surround a major portion of the dwellings. What bothered DeathRay was that he had no way of knowing if that fence was for keeping something out, or for keeping something in. So one way or the other, at some point they would be on the wrong side of that wall. *That* made him uneasy.

Chapter 9

November 7, 2406 AD
29 Light-years from the Sol System
Monday, 4:35 PM, Expeditionary Mission Standard Time

The team traced the wall for several hundred meters until they found a large sewage drain with a grate covering the exiting flow. The water was murky with obvious chunks and glops of brown and green sludge that smelled like the sewage treatment plant in the belly of the *Madira* after chili was on the menu. DeathRay closed his visor and set the air filters on high.

"If there are no occupants anywhere how the hell is there sewage?" First Sergeant Rondi Howser asked.

"Shit stinks too, First Sergeant." Corporal Simms observed.

The sewage splashed into a small fast-running river that flowed further down the hill. The river seemed to simply start at the wall and was fed from somewhere underneath the surface.

"Maybe it's residual sludge from whoever was here?" Amari offered.

"Who gives a shit," Simms laughed.

"No, Simms, who gave a shit?" Howser corrected him.

"Alright, stow that shit," Boland was almost too serious to smile. "We go in under the wall in the river," he ordered.

"You know, Boland, if I were designing a fortress, getting in wouldn't be as simple as swimming underneath the wall." Nancy frowned.

"Well, let's hope whoever did design this thing doesn't think like you." Jack knew that was a long shot. He'd even thought of that himself.

But if they were going to have to blast a way in he'd rather do it below ground and out of sight.

"Move," he said.

Jack watched as the three AEMs dropped into the water flow and out of sight. He tracked them on the QM Blue force tracker. They seemed to fall forever and then at thirty meters depth they stopped.

"Jesus, that thing is deep." Nancy looked at ET1 Amari. "Standard Navy suits can handle that, right?"

"I'm not sure," Amari replied. "Give me a second."

Jack and Nancy watched as Amari's face glazed over for a second as if she were having a detailed conversation with her AIC. Then she blinked her eyes and nodded at them.

"We are good to fifty-one point two meters according to my AIC." Nancy had worked with the tech for about two years now and trusted her assessment.

"Good, then. We go." Jack jumped off the edge into the water.

"Dammit, Boland!" Nancy hated it when he went headlong into things without consulting her. "You heard the man."

Nancy did a forward flip off the edge into where the waterfall of sludge hit the clear water of the river. As she splashed into the water she switched her suit to full QM sensors. EO/IR sensors had no range in the turbid murkiness. As the weight of her suit sank her deeper into the river the current subsided a bit and the water cleared dramatically. At about sixteen meters there was a thermal barrier in the water and they passed into very clear water that seemed to light up all around her. She realized that the rest of the team had their external floodlights on.

What if there are sensors down here, she thought to Allison.

It would seem to be wiser to stay on passive QM sensors, Allison agreed.

Better warn Candis to tell Boland.

Done.

"Listen up," DeathRay's voice came through on the com. "Turn off the floods and any other active sensors. Stay on passive QMs only. They might have sentry sensors down here."

Nancy almost laughed. "That's another one you owe me, Boland."

The current had brought them to a stop at the bottom about sixty meters from where the wall should be. The suits were heavy and powerful so walking upstream on the bottom wasn't too difficult. The soft, muddy bottom proved more difficult to balance in than pushing against the current. Jack felt each foot drive into the muck up to the knee and then the pull free came with a big *schlurrpp*!

"Stay alert. My sensors show us right beneath the wall." Jack checked the whereabouts of his team in the Blue force tracker that was displaying in his mindview. "Lieutenant Franks, take your men ahead of us. Spread out a few meters between you and take it slowly."

"Yes, sir."

"Penzington, you and Amari on me." Jack couldn't see more than a few centimeters through the visor but the QMs painted a perfect view of the terrain. The undercurrents were displayed as vector arrows, and objects were painted in grayscale. The river bottom was featureless as best he could tell. Ten meters further upstream there was the wall.

"The QMs show the wall is here but the water is flowing right through it." Lieutenant Franks exclaimed. "Makes very little sense to me, sir."

"Roger that, Franks. I got it." DeathRay scanned the wall left to right and up and down. The current vectors showed the water flowing continuously as if there were no wall. "The QMs don't see the wall and neither does the water, but I can see it right in front of me."

"Jack, I don't like it," Nancy warned on a private channel.

"Yeah, I'm going to bring my optical floods up slowly. Starting at low intensity." Jack ordered his AIC to bring up the suit's exterior light. A soft white illumination rippled and reflected off the wall that was clearly in front of him. "What the hell?"

"Sir," ET1 Amari said. "I think it's a *modulated SIF* and a hologram."

"So the wall isn't really here then?" Jack asked.

"Maybe," Amari replied. "I don't think the wall is real at all. Somehow the structural integrity field is modulated so the water is flowing through it in rapid bursts. You would think there would be ionization, or eddy currents, or some sort of vortices at the surface. This is very complicated tech, sir."

"How complicated?" Jack asked. "Could we build it?"

"Hah," Jack could almost hear laughter in her voice. "Of course, sir. This is no different than the coolant flow field SIFs on the large directed energy guns on the *Madira*."

"I see. Well, it looks like there aren't any light-activated booby-traps, so go ahead and turn on your floods."

"How do we get through the wall?" Lieutenant Franks interrupted. "Explosives?"

"It will take me some time to figure it out, sir. I'd have to find the right modulation frequency of the SIF itself and then we'd have to match it."

"Okay, get with it ET1." Jack turned to look at Nancy but she had backed off several meters. "Penzington? What are you doin—" Jack didn't have time to finish.

Penzington kicked her jumpboots and fired her thrusters directly into the wall at top suit speed, which in the water was about ten meters per second. Her suit flickered and a brilliant blue light danced across the wall as she passed head first through it. The flash was so bright that DeathRay wasn't sure if she'd actually made it through or was vaporized on impact.

Chapter 10

November 7, 2406 AD
27 Light-years from the Sol System
Monday, 4:42 PM, Expeditionary Mission Standard Time

"You keep that up and you're gonna vaporize that thing!" Deanna Moore raised an eyebrow as she watched *her* Navy SEAL cook a hot dog over the radiator from the main energy core cooling system conduits.

"Hey you're the hotdogging mecha pilot," Lieutenant Rackman replied with a smile. Dee liked his smile. She liked his big brown eyes. She liked his hardened soldier's rippled body. She liked *him*. She particularly liked the way he looked in his shorts and t-shirt even if it did say "U.S. Navy" on it. Dee leaned back and stretched her already tight "USMC" tank top even tighter against her breasts. The temperature in the abandoned section of the ship was just cool enough that her nipples pressed hard against the microfiber digicam fabric. The thin fabric enhanced her fighter pilot's muscular build along with her very female attributes. She hoped Rackman noticed.

"I wonder if anybody else ever figured this out," Dee pondered aloud. The two of them had searched the large starship for a private place to call their own. Rackman had done some forward recon previously and found the area just under the forward directed energy guns. The outer bulkhead housed cooling and power conduits. There was a very long corridor on this particular deck leading all the way from stern to bow. The outer bulkhead wall was the last pressure wall of the ship. Beyond that would be an evacuated fire-suppression zone and then the ship's outer hull armor plating.

Her AIC had told Dee that this particular area was an engineering access corridor that could be used for heating, cooling, and energy transfer as needed. It very seldom saw anybody accept for a fireman's apprentice or engineer's mate and usually only if there was damage to the area. For all intents and purposes it was an abandoned part of the ship.

Dee and Rackman had found a cubby about the size of a two-car garage just under the starboard bow DEGs. The gray metal power conduits got hot, very hot, but there was no dangerous radiation to be concerned with. Dee had worn her AEM suit there a time or two and had the sensors sweep the area. She had also asked Commander Buckley with the cover story that she needed a place to practice maneuvers by herself. Buckley had assured her that there was no danger in the area and he hadn't asked any other questions. Dee wasn't sure if that was because she was herself or Buckley had better things to worry about.

Rackman, in full Navy SEAL fashion, had figured out that pulling the insulator plate from the outgoing cooling line exposed a large, flat metal grate heat radiator that just happened to be the perfect size upon which to grill food. It also heated about a five-meter diameter space of the abandoned corridor to a nice tropical temperature, much like a campfire would a campsite on a fall evening in Mississippi. It was warm and, even better than back home, there were no mosquitoes or other pests.

"Hope you're hungry," Davy said. Dee caught him looking a little longer than he had to at her. "I know I am."

"Yeah, something about all that immunoboost makes me feel like I could eat a horse." Dee looked at the new pale skin on her hand. The new graft had taken fine.

And it makes me, uh, antsy as hell. She thought.

Antsy, my ass, Bree replied. Her AIC knew her too well. Fact of the matter was that Dee was tired of the continuous fighting and space jumping. She hadn't been in a good mecha mixup in months unless you counted the war games DeathRay put them through on a regular basis. Truth be told, she was horny as hell and just wanted to have some fun to keep from going batshit nuts.

"You want the first ones?" Davy began rolling the browned wieners off the radiator grate onto a plate. The synthetic protein sausages rolled across the grate with a sizzling sound, putting off an aroma that made Dee's salivary glands kick into hyperdrive. The grate left the hot dogs with perfect criss-cross black stripes from end to end. Dee was impressed by the SEAL's grillmeister skills.

"Smells great. I'm starving!" She licked her lips for effect.

"Here we are. God only knows how many light-years away from Sol. But, the military made sure we had hot dogs and buns."

"And don't forget beer!" Dee pulled a couple cold ones from the cooler pack and popped them open. She traded one for a plate and then took a long drink. "Ah."

"To fallen mates," Rackman said in his Australian accent.

"Oorah." Dee drank again. She scanned around at their spot. For months she and Davy had been camping there when they had the chance, and had yet to run across anybody else. After all, the ship was designed to hold as many as twenty-thousand crewmen and mecha and other support craft, and the *Madira* currently had less than five hundred total on board. But it was still the supercarrier of all supercarriers in her mind. For a brief moment she let her mind drift to the first day she saw a supercarrier on Mars over two decades earlier . . .

"What's a supercarrier, Daddy?" Deanna recalled tugging at her daddy's sports coat impatiently. It was the first time she'd been to Mars even though her mother was a Martian. Her father, of course, was from Mississippi and at the time she knew he was larger than life, but she truly had no idea just how much so.

"Huh, oh. It is a very large spaceship that carries a whole bunch of smaller spaceships and thousands of people and tanks and is an awesome display of America's great strength and power. And Marines! You can't win any real war without a bunch of U.S. Marines!" He gestured flamboyantly with his hands open wide and his chest out. She remembered watching him as he then subconsciously turned his U.S. Marine Corp ring a few times. He still did that to this day. Dee had always hung on her father's every word, but her mother simply grunted at his answer. Dee always loved how the two interacted with one another—her father the clown and her mother the straight man.

"Don't encourage her, Alexander." Her mother had said. "It is a *carrier,* honey, because it *carries* other ships and people inside it. It is a *supercarrier* because it is superdy-duperdy big."

"I understand, Mommy." Deanna couldn't help but be overwhelmed with happiness as she recalled swinging between her parents while hanging from their arms. The word "superdy-duperdy" made her smile. She unconsciously finished her beer.

Since then she had had two decades to think about just how big "superdy-duperdy" truly was. The U.S. fleet supercarrier was indeed an awesome display of humanity's technological savvy and military might. Its sleek structure reached over a kilometer and a half long, two-thirds of a kilometer wide, and a quarter kilometer tall. And since this particular one was only at about two and a half percent personnel capacity, Dee was sure that everybody on board must have their own private little hidey-holes like hers and Davy's.

"Incendiary device for your thoughts, Marine." Dee hadn't realized it, but she had finished her beer without even touching the slightly browned protein dog. She studied the blackened stripes on the pink meat left by the radiator grate metal. She took a bite. Then another. It was *good.*

She nodded and shrugged behind a mouthful of hot dog. "Oh, I was just remembering the first time I ever saw a big ship like this."

"Do tell, sheila."

"I told you not to call me that." Dee swatted at him. "I was like six or so and we were on Mars. It was the day of the Seppy Exodus."

"Yeah, I recall seeing that on the webs." Dee was a Marine like everybody else, but she was also part of history as a famous and recent president's daughter. She sometimes forgot that everybody knew all about her life. Hell, most of her life was in history books—most of it. There was, of course, the part involving the secret war within her family and the maniacal AIC that had abducted her grandmother. Dee didn't want to think about that presently. Maybe someday there would be a man in her life that she could tell that story to and maybe it would be Davy. For now, that part of her life was still for a very small group of family and friends. She was more in the mood for that night of drinking and sex she and Nancy had joked about in the hospital bay.

"Well, that was the day that I truly learned just how big of a badass the old man is." Dee grinned and took another bite. The glow of the cooling grate danced slightly, washing the room with a faint red hue.

"He took on soldier after soldier. I even recall him attacking a Seppy tank with nothing but an HVAR he'd commandeered. I was . . . I guess *inspired* is the word."

"No doubt about that. History books don't paint near as good a picture as seeing him in action. When I was asked if I was interested in this mission I didn't even have to think twice. I mean, are you kidding me? What badass Navy SEAL wouldn't want to serve with Alexander Moore, even if he is just a Marine." Rackman smiled a broad toothy grin at Dee.

"Watch it, squidboy." Dee punched at his arm but Rackman reflexively blocked it and threw her hand away in an aikido circle. "Oh really. You did *not* just pull some SEAL akido shit on me!" She grunted and dropped her plate as she jumped up from her lounge chair into a flying jump front kick. Dee had literally been trained to fight by the best there was—her father had seen to that. And she had fought for her life on several occasions since she was a kid.

Oh no, he didn't, she thought.

Kick his ass, Bree cheered her on.

Rackman stepped back, holding his beer aside in his left hand and downblocking the kick with his right. But Dee didn't stop there. She pressed her advantage by following up with a left-leg roundhouse kick to his right leg, taking him off his feet.

"Shit. You made me spill my beer. It's on now, Marine." Rackman spun on his shoulders up into a kickover onto his feet. Dee stepped back into fighting stance, dancing on her toes in the ancient Bruce Lee style.

Rackman stood a solid twenty centimeters over her and his arms were damned near the size of her legs. He was a big-ass strong boy. Dee hoped she could use that to her advantage. She was smaller, but she was faster and way more flexible. Rackman waved her to attack.

"Sure you can take it, squidboy?" Dee smirked as she pursed her lips and stretched her shoulders back. The microthin material of her tank top was stretched to the elastic limit across the chest.

"Bring it on, girl!" Rackman pounded his fist into his hand and turned sideways. Dee noticed that her posture had created the diversion she was going for—Davy clearly was *not* looking at her eyes.

Dee jumped with a right roundhouse kick followed by a flurry of jabs and crosses, then spinning into a jump back kick, followed up one, two, three style with a spinning backfist and a left cross. With each kick, punch, or spinning motion she let out a faint *shoosh*ing sound as she exhaled through pursed lips. Davy, on the other hand, wasn't even breathing hard. The muscular SEAL simply took the kicks and pushed her aside. He was overly confident. At least Dee hoped he was.

Shit, he's strong, Bree. She was a bit intimidated and excited at the same time. She definitely was *excited.*

Dee rushed him again with a double left-leg roundhouse kick and then a jump back leg, her right, roundhouse kick that was strong enough to break bricks. Rackman dropped an elbow and took the brunt of it, but he was forced to take a step back—a small step. Then he caught Dee's foot and carried her momentum through a full circle, flinging her across the floor onto her back.

"Come on, Dee, enough. One of us is gonna get hurt if we keep this up."

"You chicken shit, squidboy?" Dee pulled herself up off the floor wiped sweat from her forehead, and pulled her ponytail a little tighter. "Didn't know you were so afraid of getting hurt."

"Dee . . ." he started, but she didn't give him time to finish what he was going to say. This time she went low and swept at his legs, but he jumped her kick.

Dee spun over onto her back and then flipped upward, kicking over and landing a kick on Davy's chin. He staggered backwards slightly.

He's standing solid. Use that. Bree countered. *Make him top heavy.*

Good idea.

"That all you got, mecha jock?" Rackman laughed, but Dee could see that she was pushing his tolerance. "Keep it up and I'm gonna hit you back."

"You sure know how to woo a girl off her feet!" Dee grunted as she lunged forward onto her hands into a handspring and then to her feet, leaping up into his face and wrapping her legs around his neck, flipping them both over. Dee rolled her body around Davy's as they were flung head over heels by the momentum of her attack. Rackman fell with a hard thud onto his back, humbled, surprised, and somewhat winded. Dee moved quickly while she had the upper hand. She did her best to give a sexy grin as she rolled up and straddled his chest, putting the full weight of her body on his stomach and crushing his ribs between her thighs.

"Shit, Dee. That freakin' hurt."

"Navy squidboy can't take the pain." She pouted her lips, leaned forward into him. "Big baby," she whispered while bringing her breasts closer to him.

Rackman pulled her close and she felt the warmth and fullness of his chest against her as she kissed him cautiously at first. She wasn't sure the fighting was over. Davy's long hesitation to pull away was sign enough. The fight was over. She kissed him again. She wriggled downward slightly so that she sat straddle over his crotch and thighs. She could feel him getting warmer and stiffening against her.

Rackman's hands slid up her waist to the bottom of her tank top, and in less time than it took to switch from bot to eagle mode in her mecha, her shirt was over her head and tossed away into the flickering shadows. Dee felt his hands grasping her breasts and then her nipples with soft pressure, and then he began tugging them and pulling her to him. The sensation of his thumb and forefinger pulling her erect nipples sent a jolt of electricity through her body, leaving her lost in the sensation briefly as his hands traveled back down her body and chill bumps covered her from head to toe.

She could feel his hands inside her shorts grasping her buttocks firmly and pressing his stiffening crotch against her now very heated one. Dee wiggled forward slightly, slipping out of the shorts. She fumbled with his shirt, pulling it over his head, and then forced her hands down to the waistband of his shorts. Dee lowered herself down Rackman's chiseled body, kissing him and slithering like a snake as she brought his shorts over his feet. Dee found herself on her hands and knees looking directly at his manhood standing erect only millimeters in front of her face. She took him into her mouth and caressed him with her tongue and lips and then grasped his shaft with her hand. She worked him gently but firmly for another moment and then pulled away, kissing him there as she worked her way back up to look into his big brown Navy SEAL eyes. Never letting her grip go, she writhed into position above him and directed him inside her. With the insertion she felt a release from the tension and fighting and all the endless missions and getting wounded and the hospital and the endless conflict plague of humanity that her grandmother had brought on them all. She didn't think about that for the moment. So quickly she felt . . . a release and she realized she was already climaxing.

Davy rolled Dee over and slid deeper into her. Dee could feel him strongly but gently pushing deeper and deeper with each stroke. She particularly liked the feel of his hands as they firmly grasped at her buttocks and his fingers tightened with each stroke.

"Oh my God, yes." She pulled into him and wrapped her legs around his body, interlocking her ankles behind his back.

"Dee, you are so hot," Davy whispered in her ear as he nibbled on the lobe. She was peaking again already. Using her legs to force him even harder and deeper into her brought her to the edge . . .

Chapter 11

November 7, 2406 AD
27 Light-years from the Sol System
Monday, 4:42 PM, Expeditionary Mission Standard Time

"The edge!"

General Mason Warboys sat on the front of his tank-mode hovertank, lecturing the Warlords tank squadron—*his* Warlords.

"The very Goddamned edge! We are at the edge of where humanity has ventured into space, and seem to find remnants of the Separatist faction automated threats everywhere we turn." Warboys pounded a fist downward onto the hovertank's armored hull. "I don't care if we do have some down time. Who knows, at any moment we might find ourselves in another shitstorm with these godforsaken soulless computer-driven attackers. So we're gonna train. And train. And train. And when we finish we're gonna train some fucking more. Is that a hoowah?"

"HOOWAH!" the Warlords answered.

"Great. Johnny, get us set up, and we're gonna run this sim again and again until we get through it with zero casualties," Warboys ordered.

"Roger that, One," Warlord Two Lieutenant Colonel Johnny Stacks responded. "All right, you heard the general—everyone load up and let's get with it."

Mason Warboys nodded. He understood that there was a lot of work to be done. His team was new, raw, and from disparate groups throughout the fleet. They were still learning to be a team. He had beaten them into a decent tank squadron over the last eighteen months or so but they weren't there yet. At least they weren't where he thought they should be.

Once the *Sienna Madira* had been decommissioned and then recommissioned, General Moore—or President Moore, it was confusing to everyone—asked Mason to bring his team along for this long-haul mission. Mason was thrilled by the prospect, but the problem was that the Warlords had already been disbanded and reassigned. Warboys had to start over and pick a new team. While there were plenty of tank drivers in the Army, the Warlords were elite, and Mason only chose the best. The problem was finding elite tank drivers who could and would volunteer for an open-ended, long-duration assignment to unknown locations. In other words, he did the best he could in the picking process. What he couldn't get in experience, he was damn sure going to make up for it in training.

Mason slid the cockpit canopy closed and cycled the restraints into his E-suit. His AIC processed the startup sequence and completed the handshaking with the ship's sim-center computers. Warboys could see the battlescape pop into his direct-to-mind view in full detail. The ten Warlords stood still in a V formation, all in tank mode. The virtual landscape was very similar to the planetoid they had recently been on, but was different in a random-shuffle sort of way. Some of it actually reminded him of the Battle of the Oort years ago. But back then, his team was *the shit*. Every tank driver in the U.S. Army wanted to be a Warlord.

Sir, the scenario is loaded and ready to begin, his AIC Major Brenda Bravo One One One Mike Hotel Hotel Two advised him in his mindvoice.

Roger that. Start it up, Brenda, he thought.

"All right, Warlords, stay sharp. We have an overwhelming hostile force over the ridge and our AEM brothers are pinned down. Those crazy bastards are outgunned, outnumbered, and outmatched, and if I know Marines, that is a perfect situation for them to attack! They're going to need our help!"

Armored Environment Suit U.S. Marine Corp Master Gunnery Sergeant Tommy Suez had always had a talent for driving an armored e-suit. Even as a private, he could unwrap a piece of candy while wearing the suit. The armored heavy gauntlets of the suits typically made that level of control and precision extremely difficult if not impossible, but not for Tommy. Since he'd seen pictures of the suits when he was a child, he had studied everything about them. He had always wanted to be an AEM. He ate, slept, and breathed the function of his suit. The more he understood it the better he could use it. But it was more than just suit function, it was also suit use. He had studied tactics and strategy and performance protocols. He'd read history books on the suits and how they had changed over the years. He had studied the Martian Desert Campaigns and the famous exploits of Major Alexander Moore. As a kid, he had idolized the Marine turned president. He wanted to know how Moore had managed to set the all-time, still-standing record for living in an armored suit for more than a month way back then when the technology was not supportive of such a feat. There had been many of his superiors and friends alike who had suggested he go to Officer Candidate School, but Tommy didn't want to take the time out of being in the suit and being an AEM. Tommy was most at home in the suit. One day he hoped to test Moore's record.

Today, Tommy had the day off due to regulation. In order to protect their leader, Lieutenant Colonel Francis Jones, he'd taken a metal claw in his chest. It had punctured one of his lungs, but his suit had sealed it off before he had any issue with it, and he'd ripped the metal buzzsaw bot bastard to hell and gone. The doctors in the medbay had fixed him up without any problem but rules were rules. He was sidelined for several days, but Tommy liked staying fit and sharp. And really, did any E9 master gunnery sergeant ever have the day off? Being "Top Sergeant" kept him busy, always.

He clanked down one of the long, abandoned corridors of the *Madira* in his suit. Tommy fired his jumpboots, launching himself headfirst into a rolling front flip. As his body and suit twisted through the flip, he had his DTM targeting system track protrusions, bolt heads, and rivets in the bulkheads. Red targeting reticles zipped across his mindview in three dimensions all around him. He locked one onto a bolt head on the ceiling a bit aft of his position and fired a simulated shoulder mounted rocket at it. He did all this in less than the second it took to complete the maneuver. He stopped on one knee, with his weapon drawn and targeting objects in front of him. He scanned for movement and mentally took note of the sensor views in his mind. It was really dark in the long corridor, especially with his suit lights off. He pressed on deeper into the ship.

Occasionally he'd pass a portal that let some light from the planetoid's star in, but only a little. The blue-gray metal bulkheads did little to brighten up the place. The corridors on this part of the ship were mostly abandoned and lights were only turned on when engineering crews needed them.

Tommy visually scanned but decided he was going to bump into something if he didn't switch over to a different view or bring up his suit's lights. He didn't want to use the harshness of the lights. There was something sort of serene about working out in the near darkness that he liked. He didn't want to disturb the darkness.

Then he checked his AIC for any other sensor movement. The area battlescape came online and switched to full DTM mindview. On full mindview the data was so overwhelming that one couldn't follow it and visual view at the same time. Typically, on full mindview, the visors went dark to help remove the distraction. Tommy didn't really need that aid. He'd learned years before to focus his mind just on the sensor view he needed at the moment. Others could do it, but most simply allowed the suit or their AIC chose the best view for the moment. Tommy had programmed his suit and told his AIC not to black out his visor unless ordered to or emergency protocols required it.

Nothing on QMs or IR? He asked his AIC.

Nothing. As it should be. They were in an abandoned area of the ship almost all the way to the bow on the starboard side.

Okay then, let's switch to pure mindview and I'll practice maneuvers blind.

Switching off visible and going to mindview sensor data only.

Good girl, Jackie, Tommy thought. He looked for the layout of the ship around him in his mindview, but nothing was there. That wasn't right. The computer always generated a layout map of the ship. There were no actual images from the sensors overlaid on the map. *Jackie? DTM the sensors for me.*

The mindview is fully functional, Tommy, his AIC replied. Tommy's stomach turned over. *What you see is what I've got.*

What? That makes no sense, he paused to think. *They were working fine a hundred meters or more aft when I did the targeting flip.*

Sorry, Tommy, my diagnostics show the DTM is fully functional and operating normally.

That isn't right. I should see bulkheads and heat flows and potential targets. But there is nothing DTM. Nothing. Then something occurred to him and he didn't like it. *Eyeballs and full floods! Sims off and weapons online! Get me coms to the bridge!*

Chapter 12

November 7, 2406 AD
29 Light-years from the Sol System
Monday, 4:45 PM, Expeditionary Mission Standard Time

"Nancy? Penzington, do you copy?" DeathRay couldn't tell if his wife had vaporized on the other side of the energy field or not. As far as he, the engineer's tech, and the three Marines could tell, there was nothing there in front of them but the wall and the water passing through it.

Candis? What have you got? Jack thought to his AIC.

Nothing on sensors or QM coms. It's like there is nothing beyond that wall.

Jammed?

I'd say so, Jack.

Shit.

"Everybody stay alert. I don't like this at all. Marines, converge on me." Jack scanned the wall with every sensor in his suit and got nothing in return other than the waterflow vectors. "Fuck it. We're gonna blast it."

Jack, wait. There was a last-minute transmission from Allison.

Huh?

"Sir, before you do that," the engineering tech held up a hand. "I've got some readings on what happened when Nancy passed through the wall."

I think Nancy had Allison send us instructions. I'm unfolding the message now. It is very, very complicated, Candis added into Jack's mindvoice. *The jamming obscured the signal in the noise field. Somehow, Allison managed to get it through.*

"Well, don't keep it to yourself, Petty Officer. That's my wife on the other side of this thing." DeathRay hated when Nancy put herself in these kinds of situations, but she always had managed to get out of them somehow so far.

"We couldn't hear it or see it well in the suits and here underwater and all, but all my data looks like there was an electromagnetic signature like that of a quantum membrane teleportation event horizon," Amari explained.

"What? You mean she was teleported to somewhere?" Jack really didn't like this.

"Yes, sir," the tech replied.

"Shit! Where?"

"No way to tell, sir. But she was definitely teleported. And just before she did, her suit cycled a QM pulse."

Candis? he thought to his AIC.

I'm working it, Jack, but it does appear that she teleported somewhere, and Allison had hacked into some control system using the QM pulse the petty officer detected.

"Can my suit reproduce that pulse, Amari?" Jack asked.

"Uh, yes, sir. It is a simple transmission for the QM transceiver. I'm sending it to your AIC now." ET1 Amari tapped some keys on her forearm sensor panel.

Candis?

I have the signal ready for transmission, sir. How Nancy or Allison figured this out is beyond me though. They had to have had some a priori knowledge.

We'll ask them when we find them.

"I'm going in. If you don't hear from me in ten minutes I want you to snap back to the shuttle and then take it back to the *Madira*," Jack ordered.

"We can't leave the two of you here," Amari said.

"Thanks for the sentiment, Engineer's Technician First Class, but those are your orders. Franks, you got that? Besides, we can always snap back to the ship with our wristbands."

"Roger that, sir. Ten minutes," Lieutenant Franks replied over the tac-net, but Jack could see them closing on his position. They were only a few tens of meters away, he thought, but with the lighting in the water it was very hard to judge distance without using QM sensors.

"Start your clocks now," Jack nodded at the tech.

Candis, cycle the signal.

Aye, sir.

Jack ran through the wall in a flash of dancing light and could hear one of the Marines on the tac-net at the very last second.

"Sir, incoming—"

But that was all Jack heard as he was instantly somewhere else.

"Get down, Boland!" Penzington's voice rang in his helmet.

Jack simply dropped and didn't take time to argue. When it came to his wife, if she said to get down, then she usually had damned good reason to say it. The room around them promptly exploded into flames with debris flying everywhere. Jack could see the remnants of what must have been a bot mecha flying past him in a red and orange exploding and swirling symphony. The only thing going through his mind at the moment was *just why in the hell were the enemy mecha here.*

"Behind you!" Penzington shouted.

Jack rolled over with his HVAR at the ready and immediately let loose several rounds into the buzzsaw bot slashing for him. The bot dropped beside him just as Nancy's armored foot came pounding down on top of it. She then bounced up, firing her weapon in a wide-area burst. Jack followed suit.

"What's going on?" Jack yelled over the weapon fire. Several rounds from an automated defense weapon cut into the wall plating near him, spraying red-hot glowing metal in all directions. Some of it splattered against his suit, but the exterior armor layers were barely even scratched and protected him with no problems.

"I think we were teleported into a hangar bay, and those are the security guards." Nancy replied. "But I managed to make a hole two meters behind us where that hovertank used to be. Move!"

Candis, DTM battleview! Hovertanks?

Got it, Captain. Egress two point two meters on your five o'clock. Several hovertanks of modified Seppy design and two or three modified Gnats are within sensor view.

Go full scans. They know we're here now. Are they attacking us en masse? For a brief instant Jack considered commandeering one of the Seppy Gnat fighters, but wasn't sure he'd have time to fire it up and hack into it while being shot at.

Aye, sir. Scanning. Insufficient data to determine attack scenarios as of yet.

"You coming?" Jack motioned to Nancy as he fired several bursts from the hypervelocity automatic rifle. The HVAR rounds *spitapp*ed and exploded a multilegged bot that was skittering toward them. The spiderlike bot appeared to have been caught unaware of their presence right up until it exploded.

"Go!" Nancy bounced her boots against the floor, doing a backflip into a kneeling stance just beside the opening in the wall of the hangar bay. "I got you covered."

Reluctantly Jack ran through the opening, hoping his wife would be right behind him. He pumped a few rounds through the opening as he burst through. The opening emptied into a hallway that appeared to have mecha hangar bays on each side. Nancy followed.

"What is the plan?" he asked his wife.

"You're in charge. And by the way, what took you so long?"

"You know, we stopped for coffee, and then considered just snapping back home, but in the end, I knew I couldn't leave you alone to have all the fun." Jack turned and pumped a grenade through the hole in the wall they had just escaped through. "That should buy us some time."

"Snapping back might be smart, but I'd sure like to know where we are," Nancy replied.

"Well, then, we keep fighting until it is too much. Then we snap back. Agreed?" Jack looked at her.

"Good plan. They're not following us." Nancy checked behind them.

Jack stopped running and motioned her to do the same. The long corridor had taken a turn to the right and felt as if it was leading upward. The hangar bay doors were getting fewer and farther between. And for whatever reason, the bots had stopped following them. That made Jack nervous.

"Okay, since we have a second to breathe, how did you know to transmit a QM signal back there?" Jack asked. He kept his eyes and sensors scanning the corridor, hoping for some idea of where to go and what to do. The place looked very familiar but he couldn't quite put his finger on it.

"I recognized it. This is technology that Tangiers used on Ares during the Separatist war. Ellise Tangiers had a room with a fake wall like that in her mansion. It led to her QMT pad. Allison hacked the security code. I wasn't expecting it to trigger a teleport, though," Nancy explained. "This place look familiar to you?"

"Yeah, it looks a lot like the inside of a Seppy hauler," Jack replied. "If we triggered the teleport then why were they hostile toward us?"

"Well, actually, I sort of caused that snooping around in that hangar room while I was waiting on you." Nancy shrugged her armored shoulders. "You shouldn't have taken so long. You gave me just enough time to piss one of the bots off."

"So they're not chasing us?" DeathRay looked over his shoulder, half expecting to see an overwhelming number of bots chasing them. There were none.

"I sure thought they would have. Don't understand that." Nancy shrugged her shoulders and frowned a bit.

Jack thought for a second. There was nothing on sensors. They really just needed more information.

"Okay, let's try and get to the surface and figure out where we are. As far as we know we're not even still on the same planet." It was times like this when Jack really wished he was just in a dogfight in his mecha.

"You'd think there'd be alarms and such going off," Nancy pondered. "I don't think there is anybody here other than automated AI sentries."

"That's perfectly fine with me." Jack could see a faint blue light just around the corner that didn't look like interior cabin lighting. He cautiously moved in that direction with his HVAR at the ready. "This looks like the main troop corridor leading to the elevator on the *Madira*."

"I thought so too." Nancy agreed with him. "Reminds me of a Seppy ship I stowed away on once."

"I seem to recall something about that." Jack smirked at his wife at the memory of her talking to him on coms as she rode a Seppy ship on a collision course for Luna City. Nancy, as far as anybody had known at the time, had blown up with the ship. Somehow she'd managed to escape at the last second.

"Wasn't my favorite day."

"Let's stay frosty." He quickly leaned around the corner, then back behind the wall for cover just in case something was on the other side, ready to shoot at him. There was nothing. "Shit! Look at that."

"What is it?"

"Come on. It's clear," Jack said as he stepped all the way into the corridor and around the corner, out of Nancy's view and into the blue lighting. "Son of a—"

"What, Jack?" He heard Nancy say as she stealthily slid in behind him.

"That." Jack pointed outward at the view beyond the large window.

"Whoa."

"Yeah. We're on a ship, alright, and that is definitely a different star." Jack looked out the window at a distant blue star and the surrounding preplanetary debris disc stretching out in a plane. The ship was embedded in the planar debris field near a large object that in a few billion years would probably be a planet, but for now was a swirling dustball. In each direction toward what Jack guessed were the bow and stern of the ship there were several other ships spread about.

"What is that, like thirty ships?"

Forty-seven as best I can tell, sir, Candis replied. *But, without a full QM sweep I'd be hesitant to say that is all of them.*

"Allison confirms forty-seven nearby and QM anomalies that suggest many more throughout this system," Nancy said. "It's a fleet, Jack."

"That or a graveyard." Jack thought for moment. "Can Allison get a fix on our location at all? Candis says there isn't enough information."

"No, we need a better look at the star field," Nancy replied.

"Okay. We're on a ship. It might be abandoned in place. Let's find the bridge," Jack said. The first order of business was to gather info and on a starship the bridge was the place to do that.

"Good plan. If we are on a ship like those then we can extrapolate about where that should be," Nancy started, but Jack interrupted her.

"Or, we could just look at the map." Jack pressed a button on a display panel beside the window and the corridor lights came on. There was a flatscreen display to the right of the button with a "you are here" interactive map. "Just like on any other big ship."

"Yeah, but you just turned on a system. If there are watchdogs they would have certainly detected that." Nancy smiled. "But, I guess they would have heard all the shooting and other ruckus too."

"Right. I think we're alone, but let's not get complacent. Besides, I'd prefer a straight-up fight over all this skulking around." DeathRay kept one hand on his weapon and used the other to trace directions on the map.

"I don't know. I kind of like it. You, me, a fleet of unknown enemy ships all to ourselves. Kind of romantic."

"You and I have completely different ideas about what *romantic* means." Jack shook his head back and forth slowly and raised an eyebrow at his wife.

"Don't knock it, flyboy. Me turned on in any situation is still *me* turned on."

"Good point. I'll remember that." Jack smiled at his wife and thought briefly how hot she looked in an armored suit.

"Damn right it is," Nancy laughed. "You should be so lucky."

But then the professional soldier in him kicked back in. "We need to go there," he said, and pointed and tapped a spot on the map.

"We've got to get the fuck out of here, sir!" First Sergeant Rondi Howser did the best diving-for-cover maneuver she could while underwater and moving against a flowing current. With every release of HVAR rounds, the hypervelocity bullets tore a bow wave through the water that flung the weapon radically in all directions from the recoil. "I'm seeing nothing on QMs and can't hit shit underwater!"

"Understood, First Sergeant, but we literally have our backs up against a Goddamned wall." The lieutenant sounded more perplexed than Rondi had heard him since they had begun fighting the bots over eighteen months prior. Rondi didn't like their situation and she was certain the lieutenant understood just how screwed they were.

"Orders, L.T.?" Rondi hoped to press him for something, anything.

"If I may, Lieutenant," ET1 Amari interjected while doing her best to keep her head buried in the river-bottom muck, "I say we follow DeathRay and Mrs. Penzington."

"Thanks for the input, tech, but our orders were to snap back to the shuttle and get it back to the *Madira*," Lieutenant Franks said.

Rondi could see him backpedaling and falling backwards as a

swimming toothy bot with a flailing, tentaclelike appendage snapped at him. The thing looked like a cross between an octopus and a radial arm circular saw with shark teeth. Each shark tooth was more like a saw blade from a reciprocating saw cutting back and forth rapidly with each snap of the mandibles. She fired a couple rounds in its general direction.

From the motion just behind and to the left of the lieutenant, Rondi could tell that Corporal Simms seemed to be handling himself a little better. The kid had a bot by the tail and was whirling it, creating a stir of river muck around him, which gave him cover and disoriented the bot. The bot ruptured at a joint where the tail connected to the torso and spun off from the centrifugal force.

"Sir," Rondi started, "we can't get anywhere here and our time is past being up. I suggest we either snap back to the shuttle or go forward and try to help DeathRay on the other side of this wall or whatever it is."

"Agreed, First Sergeant!" The lieutenant rolled over onto his hands and knees and pushed himself up to just miss another tentacle swipe by the octosaw bot. "Everyone, snap back to the shuttle . . . now, now, now!"

Rondi tapped the control on her wrist panel, and with a flash of lightning and the sound of frying bacon, she was floating in space in what appeared to be the middle of a debris field. It was a debris field that suddenly came to life and seemed to be really pissed off. The pieces of the field that didn't come to life were clearly what was left of the shuttle.

"Holy shit!" she screamed as small bots like the ones they had encountered on the planetoid where the shuttle had been liberated buzzed all around. "They're everywhere!"

"Shit, sir," Corporal Simms shouted. "We're surrounded and no place to stand. We were better off underwater."

Rondi fired her HVAR at an incoming bot. The recoil of the rifle acted like a rocket thruster, spinning her wildly in the opposite direction.

Full sensor suite targeting, she thought to her AIC.

DTM targeting on, The AIC replied in her mind. Targeting reticles popped up all around her in every direction. The yellow Xes flashed, and most of them turned red, meaning that they were a threat, they were in range, and they ought to be killed.

Great, now, take over suit controls and shoot these goddamned things! Puking deathblossom like the pilots do! she thought.

Understood.

Armored E-suit Marines were badasses in or out of their suits, and they were awesome violent works of art when in control of the situation. Seldom did a Marine ever give over control of the suit's functions. That typically only occurred when the Marine was badly wounded, unconscious, or being overridden by some command protocol—and even then the suit control was usually involving life support or communications functions. While an AIC could drive a suit, it was just never done. But this was an extreme circumstance and Marines adapt and improvise to overcome. And Rondi and the others were in one hell of a situation.

The HVAR fired rapidly, releasing vast amounts of kinetic energy with each round. The rounds came out spinning also, which only added to the reaction forces acting on the suit and the Marine within. Rondi could do nothing but hang on for the ride and do her best not to fight against the suit actions. The weapon whipped left, right, up, and down, firing several rounds with each movement. Her full battlescape view in the direct-to-mind view was a ball with three blue dots besides herself and a shitload of red dots covered with targeting Xes. The dots whirled and whipped around in the view as she spun madly in every direction. The angular motion and the centrifugal force of her spinning forced the blood to her head and feet and made her stomach lurch.

Spitap, spitap, spitap continued ringing through her suit with each round. Several times a bot came very close to her position but her suit would flex, spread her limbs akimbo, or tuck her into a ball to avoid contact. The speed of the AIC-controlled motions stretched and forced her muscles and joints through motions at the very limit of the Marine's physical abilities. Rondi thought to herself that if she survived the fight she would be sore for days. She'd definitely need some immunoboost and pain meds—a shitload of pain meds.

One of the bots burst into a ball of orange and white sparks inches from her faceplate, and the barrel of the rifle zipped through the debris cloud to the next target. Shrapnel pinged her suit all over, making it ring inside like a bell. Rondi's ears felt as if they would explode with each ping and with each heartbeat that forced more blood into her already full brain bucket. The red targets in her mindview were down from over a hundred to only a handful, and after nearly thirty seconds or more of the spinning, it was all her body could take. Rondi's stomach convulsed and her head spun so badly that closing her eyes only made it worse. With her eyes open, she saw stars and it made her dizzy. With her eyes closed, she saw stars and it made her more dizzy. The view from the faceplate visor was wild. The planet below would roll by, then the star, then the lieutenant, or was it Simms, then an exploding bot, then the planet, then the QMT gate orbital facility, then the tech, then . . . then vomit.

The fluid from her stomach filled her nose and mouth and had little place to go inside the suit's helmet. Rondi was certain she was going to drown in her own vomit, and the retching didn't seem to want to stop.

"Override control!" she gurgled. "Goddammit, give me back suit function!" Rondi panicked and screamed and did her best to spit and blow the fluids and solid matter from her face and air passages. The smell filled the helmet to a point that led her to heave again.

First Sergeant Rondi Piaya Howser, you are okay. Do your best to calm down and breathe as best you can. Take control of yourself, First Sergeant! Howser! Settle down, Marine! The suit will absorb the matter in the helmet soon. In the meantime, I have administered anxiety medication to calm you. Once you are in control of your faculties I will return suit control, her AIC said sternly but calmly into her mindvoice. AICs' programming had evolved to create a strong emotional attachment to their counterparts, and in all cases they would do what they had to in order to maintain their host's safety. Many times when a host was killed it would take years for an AIC to take another host.

Whether it was the voice of reason in her mind or the drugs the suit was pumping into her system, Rondi began to calm down and feel more in control. The stench was still so bad that she was on the edge of throwing up again, but she could manage. She choked back what bile was left in her stomach. She was a Marine, after all.

Rondi focused on her DTM view of the battlescape as she became more aware of herself and less panicked. She could see that the lieutenant, the corporal, and the ET1 were finishing off the remaining couple of bots. Her suit fired a few rounds off in various directions to slow her spin and bring her to a comfortable orientation.

"First Sergeant, I sure would like to know what the hell you just did," the lieutenant asked over the com channel.

"Learned it from watching DeathRay, sir. Called a puking deathblossom. I don't recommend it at all." Rondi choked back the taste of bile in her throat as the feeling of microgravity kicked in. She was, after all, floating in space. Had there been anything left in her stomach she would have lost it.

"That's all of them for now, as far as my sensors can tell, sir," ET1 Amari said.

"Great, now what?" Simms asked.

"We snap back to the *Madira* and hope that DeathRay and Penzington did the same," The lieutenant ordered.

"Yes, sir!" Rondi liked that plan. The fluids and matter from her stomach were quickly being dissolved from her visor by the suit's housekeeping functions. She could see out of the faceplate now without the use of DTM and sensors. She watched as her team members each reached for their wrist panels' and then she followed suit. She depressed the QMT snap-back codes and waited for the flashing light and frying bacon. Nothing happened. She tried it again, thinking she had fat-fingered the panel. Again, nothing happened. Then again and again. Rondi looked at the planet below and at the star off in the distance. She did her best not to think of the smell in her suit. "Fuck."

Chapter 13

November 7, 2406 AD
27 Light-years from the Sol System
Monday, 4:57 PM, Expeditionary Mission Standard Time

Alexander Moore sat upright against the headboard of the bed, enjoying the view. He had been working for what seemed like days without a break. So, when he had a few hours he could take for himself, he found Sehera and the two of them hid themselves away in their quarters.

His wife lay fast asleep against his chest, her long, dark, flowing hair tickling him slightly each time she breathed out. Her naked breasts heaved gently against him with each exhale. He gently pulled the cover up over her.

The viewport window on the wall opposite the headboard was over two meters in height and at least twice that in length. In the distance was the star, a good twenty-five or more astronomical units away, and beneath them was the little planetoid they'd taken the shuttle from.

Moore needed the rest but he couldn't sleep. DeathRay, Nancy, and some of his crew were off God only knew where, out of contact, and he always was concerned about his people when they were on a mission. At least Dee was off duty for a few days and he didn't need to worry about her.

Moore took the moment to take in the view and enjoy the serenity of their quarters. When he had taken the *Madira* he let Sehera choose where they would quarter. His wife had taken one look at the captain's lounge and conference area and decided they would renovate it for their living quarters. They knocked out a wall of the storage unit next door and created the "presidential suite," as he thought of it. It was four, maybe five times the space that a ship's captain usually had, but he also had his wife in there with him. Besides, this was a decommissioned ship. It was his ship. He didn't have to follow the Navy fleet standards. He'd given the crew a similar *carte blanche*. The ship was big and they were at a fraction of capacity. His orders had been that space was mission priority first and then it was first come, first served if nobody was claiming it. Any arguments over a particular bit of real estate were delegated to the COB to solve. The crew knew better than to get the COB involved, because the one time he did, he had the area in question commandeered for storage. So, the crew always managed to figure things out for themselves. Moore had picked a smart crew.

A glint moving across the bottom of the viewport downward toward the planetoid caught his eye. Several more were behind it, making a V formation.

Mecha? he thought to Abigail.

Yes. That is the Maniacs FM-12 squadron.

Jawbone?

Yes, sir, Lieutenant Col. Delilah "Jawbone" Strong.

He had kept an eye on the Marine fighter pilot since she had almost single-handedly saved his family at the attack on Disney World back when Dee was only twelve or so. Moore had made certain that when it came time for promotions, Strong had always been "promotable." And when the time came for the deep-space expedition, he had DeathRay offer her a squadron.

Moore brought up the duty roster in his DTM mindview and saw that the Maniacs were conducting routine security flights over the planetoid. Since the tankheads and the AEMs had mopped up the facility, it was secure. Moore was considering using it as an outpost at some point, but they had to find Copernicus first and figure what the hell that batshit crazy AIC was up to.

"Dee!" Sehera jumped up immediately from her sleep, nearly making Alexander jump out of his skin. Her breathing was erratic and her eyes wide with fear. "Where's Dee? Alexander! Where is Dee?"

"Baby? You're having a bad dream. Calm down. Dee is here on the ship safe and sound for once." Moore patted his wife on the back and then squeezed her shoulder. He adjusted his position so he could look at her without twisting his neck in too harsh a direction. "Everything is fine."

"No. Where is Dee? Something isn't right." Sehera rose, and Moore watched as the distant starlight and light from the planetoid facility below washed over her naked body as she rose from the covers. Sehera grabbed her AIC wristwatch. Moore still couldn't get over how she wouldn't have an implanted AIC, but after what Sehera had seen happen to her mother, he understood.

"Pamela," she said out loud to her AIC assistant, "find Dee."

"Sweetheart, calm down. You were having a nightmare." She was always the overprotective one, he thought. Dee was a badass Marine fighter pilot and their daughter. She could take care of herself.

"I'm sorry, ma'am, I cannot detect Deanna Moore's present location," The AIC responded.

"Alexander?"

"Hold on. That can't be right. Abby, vocal. Where's Dee?" he said, rising up, only slightly more concerned. Dee could take care of herself and he had never thought Pamela was all that smart of an AIC, but his wife liked her so he kept his mouth shut.

"Sir, I cannot see Dee's locator beacon," Abigail replied over the room speakers.

"What? Can't be. She was ordered to stay on this ship. Did she snap back somewhere?" Moore stood up from the bed now and started pulling on his underwear.

"No, sir. No QMTs have taken place other than the shuttle earlier." Abigail sounded perplexed. Alexander didn't like that. Dee could take care of herself, but in the end she was still his princess.

"Then how did she get off the ship and out of locator range?" he asked.

"I never said she was off the ship, sir. I said I can't detect her. In fact, I can't detect anybody in the forward starboard third of the ship."

"What does that mean, Abby?"

"We're being jammed, sir." Abigail paused briefly. "And Dee must be in that section of the ship."

"Alexander!" Sehera snapped. "They're onboard the ship!"

"I agree. Fucking bots." Moore toggled the closet open and took a deep breath. "Abby, fire up my suit and sound the alarms. Get Uncle Timmy running the drill."

"Pamela, get my suit online," Sehera said. Moore turned and saw her standing naked by her closet, rolling her neck from side to side and doing pre-suit-up stretches. He started to tell her he could handle this until he thought better of it.

"Moore to XO!"

"XO here. What's up, sir?"

"Firestorm, we've got bots on the ship in the front starboard third. Get me a battle plan and get me troops down there. I also want a list of crew unaccounted for. They are likely in there." Moore stepped into the back of his suit. The organogel layer made a *schlurrp*ing sound as he wiggled into it. He could hear Sehera making it into her suit as well.

"Aye, sir! Thirty seconds," USMC Brigadier General Sally "Firestorm" Rheims responded.

The bosun's pipe sounded throughout the ship and several klaxons went off. Then the familiar voice of Uncle Timmy, the ship's AIC commander, came over the 1MC intercom.

"All hands, all hands, battlestations and to arms. Hostile forces are onboard the ship. Repeat, hostile forces are onboard the ship."

Abby, we ready?

Yes, sir. You want a chill pill or some stims?

Negative. Just ammo. Lots of ammo.

Master Gunnery Sergeant Tommy Suez had hoped for some fun working out in his suit in the abandoned decks of the ship. He finally had some "me" time for once, which was something that a sergeant never had. He was spending it in complete communications silence, surrounded by attacking, menacing artificial, intelligence, controlled killer robots. And the motherfuckers just kept coming.

Fortunately for him, the largest of the bots were the small buzzsaw bots that were about the size of a bulldog. While they weren't necessarily easy to kill, they weren't hard to kill either, at least not for a kickass Marine.

Jackie, can you get any messages out?

Negative.

Keep posting our egress route. See if you can get the ship's lights on, he thought to his AIC. Tommy hated being all by himself and being overwhelmed by bots. He was most concerned about how much ammo he had. He hadn't been planning on actually shooting at anything when he'd left his quarters.

Tommy dove headfirst through a hatch leading into an outer corridor that ran close to the exterior hull of the ship. There were energy conduits, large energy conduits, running from fore to aft of the ship. He suspected they were the DEG power tubes.

He turned as fast as he could get to his feet and dogged the hatch down tight onto two bots that were right behind him. He slammed the hatch so fast that one of the bots was torn in two. Sparks and shrapnel flew, but the damned thing still chomped and buzzed at him with its front legs dragging it along. The other one had made it through and was wrapped up on his leg, digging into his suit. Tommy could suddenly feel searing hot metal tearing into his leg.

"Shit! Get off me!" he screamed and kicked the thing loose. He reached down, grabbing the broken bot by the front right leg, and did a backflip over the other bot. Using the broken bot as a war club, he smashed the other one across the back, snapping metal structure. He jumped and came down onto the thing with both feet and all the massive weight of the armored suit. Tommy twisted his heels into the bot until its lights went out. Then he battered the broken one against the bulkhead until it was dead as well.

"I hope that door holds them a while," he said to nobody in particular, and then bounced aftward as fast as he could.

Dee rolled over atop Davy, still in the throes of lovemaking. Dee had never really been in love, and she had been sexually active for more than a decade, but with Davy it was always different, better, in a good way.

"Oh God, Davy, yes . . ." she whispered, and leaned back, putting her hands on his shins and letting go.

Bang, clank, bang, clank.

"What the hell—" Davy leaned over as light came around the corner and a fully armored Marine slid to a halt just before he crashed into them. The floods from the suit turned and illuminated the two of them.

"What the—" Dee covered her breasts and scrambled off of Rackman.

"Uh, sorry, ma'am. Sir. Had no idea anybody else was here." The Marine's voice was familiar. It was the top sergeant.

"Gunny, please kill the light." Dee scrambled for her clothes and started to talk but was interrupted.

"No time for pleasantries, ma'am, sir. This whole area is filled with bots and they are right on my ass! Do you have armor or weapons?" Tommy asked. He turned and shined the light back up the corridor looking for bots.

"Bots!" Rackman jumped up instantly, grabbing his clothes and knife. Dee could see him in the mix of red light from the grill and the reflected white floods from the armored suit, scrounging through their packs.

"Why haven't we been warned?" Dee asked, sliding her tank top over her head and pulling it down. She then pulled up her shorts and put on her running shoes.

"Sensors are jammed and I've got no com to anywhere," Suez replied.

The bosun's pipe sounded throughout the ship and several klaxons went off. Then the familiar voice of Uncle Timmy, the ship's AIC commander, came over the 1MC intercom.

"All hands, all hands, battle stations and to arms. Hostile forces are onboard the ship. Repeat, hostile forces are onboard the ship."

"Son of a bitch, we're sitting ducks." Dee thought for a second on plans of action. Davy pulled her to him and handed her an M-blaster that he'd had in his pack. He had another one in his right hand at the ready.

"Put this on," Rackman said to her as he handed her an armored ammo vest.

"That's my SEAL," she said, and pulled the vest over her tank top. The weight of the armor felt good against her breasts, but she knew it was a false sense of security. The bots could tear into an E-suit. The light armor flak jacket wouldn't slow them down very long.

"We need to move. Fast," Gunny Suez told them. "I locked them out fifty meters or more down the corridor but they'll find a way in."

"Let's go then." Davy sealed the auto fastener on his flak jacket and held the M-blaster at the ready. "For now on, I'm carrying an HVAR everywhere I go."

"Not so sure about that, Lieutenant," The sergeant replied. "I'm running out of ammo, but those handguns will run for years on one power cell."

"We should just snap back to a safe location on the ship, like the ops medbay aft of the ship," Dee suggested.

"Sorry, ma'am," Suez replied. "Won't work. I've already tried the emergency snap-back when I was overrun a bit ago. It's being jammed."

"No shit?" Davy tapped a command into his wristband, but nothing happened. "Dammit!"

"If it don't work, it don't work. Just like on every other bot base we've been to. They've got QMT jammers. I'll take point," Dee said. She snapped a flashlight onto her vest and started to run.

Bree, get Daddy, she thought to her AIC.

I'm doing what I can to contact Abigail, Dee, but I'm having no luck, her AIC responded.

Keep trying.

Damnit, Abigail! Get Dee on the line!

No luck yet, sir, Abigail said into Alexander's mind. *That part of the ship is being jammed from coms and any QMT tech.*

Alexander Moore bounced and boomed down the hallway like a bowling ball tied to the tail of an elephant with rockets attached to its feet. The booming of his jumpboots slamming into the deck plating with each armored step was nearly deafening. It was all Sehera could do to keep up, but he had told her that he was getting to Dee as fast as he could. Sehera had told him to go faster.

Sir, I have an idea, Abigail said in his mindvoice.

What?

I think the intercom is working throughout the ship. The bots can't jam soundwaves and hardwires. I'm going to take them over and turn all the mics on to see if I can talk to Dee.

That's my girl. Do it.

Alexander held his rifle at the ready and had the visor on full visual. The floodlights of the suit were on full and he had earlier given Abigail the order to turn every light on she could find.

"Hang in there, princess. Daddy's coming!"

"We're a kilometer from the next hatch and the bots are going to be faster than us on foot," Dee said. "They'll beat us there."

"Well, it won't be long before they tear off the hatch I dogged down just a quarter of a kilometer behind us," Gunny Suez replied.

"Maybe they won't think of heading us off," Davy added.

"You knew that was stupid when you said it, right?" Dee retorted.

"Attention! Deanna! Deanna Moore! Can you hear me?" buzzed over the intercom speakers.

"Uh, yes? Abigail, is that you?"

"Yes. Hold for your father—"

"Dee! Where are you?" Alexander Moore's voice came over the intercom.

"Daddy, uh, sir, Gunny Suez, Lieutenant Rackman, and I are in the lowermost and outermost corridor by the DEG conduits. We are about a klick from the midcorridor hatch," Dee said between heavy breaths as she ran. "We think we're surrounded by bots."

"Are you armed or armored?"

"Gunny is in his suit and getting low on ammo. Rackman and I are not armored but we have blasters."

"Understood. Shit, Dee, you move fast. You get to that hatch. You hear me! You get to that hatch. I'm coming! Gunny, you keep them fucking bots off my little girl!"

The intercom buzzed and went to static and then silent.

"Shit, they cut the intercom." Rackman said.

"Let's keep moving to that hatch," Gunny Suez said.

Behind them came the screech of metal tearing away and then slamming to the deck. The hull reverberated with the sound of buzzsaws scratching against metal.

"We're not going to make it. We need to find a way to hole up and fight these things off until help arrives."

"My thoughts exactly, Captain Moore," Suez replied.

Dee started looking around for some niche or something to hide in but the corridor was fairly straightforward with nothing but the occasional I-beam and conduit tube running here or there. Then a few meters up was another engineering cubby like the one that she and Davy had used as their campground. It wasn't quite as big—it looked as if it was there to allow techs to get in behind the DEG power grid and conduct some sort of maintenance on it.

"Here," Davy pointed. "We get in here behind the conduits and hold them off. At least this way they can only come at us from the front."

"Good. It'll have to do," Dee said. She dropped to her belly and crawled under the large-meter-in-diameter tubes into the cubbyhole. The niche was about two meters wide and ran a good five meters from floor to ceiling. Davy jumped up on top of the metal conduits and dropped in beside her.

"You shoot high and I'll shoot low," he told her.

"Sirs," Gunny Suez turned to them, "I'll stay out here and fight them off of you. If you two would be so kind as to keep them off me as best you can, we might be able to hold out until backup gets here."

"Right. Thanks, Gunny." Dee looked at the Marine's face through his visor. She couldn't tell what he was thinking. She knew what *she* was thinking. She was thinking she was scared and vulnerable as hell.

The screeching and squealing grew louder.

"Here they come!"

Chapter 14

November 7, 2406 AD
27 Light-years from the Sol System
Monday, 5:11 PM, Expeditionary Mission Standard Time

"Alexander, do you hear that?" Sehera asked over the tac-net. So far it wasn't jammed—at least in the hundred meters or so between them.

"Yes. There's a fight up ahead, it sounds like," Alexander replied. "Stay back until I see what it is."

Two levels up from where Dee was, Alexander turned from the main corridor into the central hangar bay to a sight he wasn't expecting. The bay was full of bots, and tanks in bot mode were stomping around the hangar crashing into them and fighting them hand to hand.

Abby?

Comms are working, sir, the AIC replied.

"Warlord One, copy?" Alexander said.

"General Moore?" Warboys' voice came through. "Sir, I've got you on Blue force tracker. You shouldn't be in here."

"Mason. My daughter is pinned down two decks below and forward about a klick. She has no armor and only a blaster. We have to get to her."

"Uh, yes, sir. Understood. Hold on—let me find a route," Warboys responded. Alexander targeted a path across to the tank squad commander and bounced toward him, taking out several bots with his HVAR, fists, and his boots along the way.

"These damned things are no match for tank armor, sir. But, we can't move throughout the ship; only in certain places," Warboys explained. "We're just too big."

"Understood. Make a hole. We'll fix the ship later," Moore ordered.

"My thoughts exactly, General." Warboys agreed. "You might want to cover your ears."

Just as Alexander landed on the giant mechanized right shoulder of Warlord One's bot-mode hovertank, the main cannon spun around and aimed at the deck. A large purple plasma ball flung from the muzzle, recoiling the gun nearly a meter. The tank barely moved but the blast wave almost tore Moore loose. He managed to grab hold and stay on the tank.

Sparks flew and molten metal sprayed in every direction. As the smoke cleared Alexander could see a hole in the deck of the ship that was big enough for a tank to drop through, which they promptly did. He heard a deafening metal-on-metal clank as they landed on the deck below. The bot-mode tank had dropped twenty meters to the deck of the next level, slamming hard enough into the plating to leave huge indentations with its feet.

"Warlords Two and Four, cover this exit and don't let any bots get through it. I don't want them coming up behind me and biting me on the ass!" Warboys ordered to his team.

"My wife is not far behind me, please see to her safety," Moore added.

"Understood, sir," Warlords Two and Four replied.

"We need to move outward as best we can before we drop down to the next level. Shit!" Warboys said.

"What is it?" Alexander asked.

"I just lost all sensors. The bots are jamming me. We're flying blind now," Warboys said.

Alexander looked at the corridor. There was only one hallway large enough for a tank in any mode and it was behind them, in the wrong direction. The bay they had dropped to was the maintenance bay. There were several fighters, tanks, and suits scattered about in work stations.

"Mason, we have to get down there fast as we can."

"Well, sir, without sensors it is difficult to know what we can safely knock out of the way and what we can't." Mason had a point.

Abigail, search schematics of the ship and find me the route for knocking out a path to Dee. If you need to get the CHENG online do it.

Sorry, sir, but there isn't a safe path from here. The main directed energy gun power systems run through this section of the ship. I wouldn't recommend it. Too bad we can't get to the outside of the ship.

What do you mean?

There is only one level of vacuum hull between Dee and the outside as best I can pinpoint her location. And there is only one return power tube on the outer wall of the corridor they are in.

Shit! I'll go on foot from here then. Moore jumped down from the tank, landing on the deckplate at full sprint.

"Thanks for the lift, Mason. Get back to your team," he ordered.

"Sure you don't want me to come with you, sir?" Warboys asked.

"No, go back and get my wife and keep her safe."

"Yes, sir."

Outside, sir! We could get a tank to Dee from the outside, Abigail said in his mindvoice.

How long would it take to get a tank out there? Moore turned down a dark hallway that was man-sized and looked for a down ladder to get to the next level below.

Too long, Abigail replied. *Too bad we don't have tank patrols on the outside of the ship.*

That's it! We do have mecha out there! Moore recalled seeing the FM-12s from his viewport only moments earlier.

Of course, sir! I have a channel open now. For whatever reason the bots aren't jamming the exterior.

Because we killed all the ones outside the ship!

"Lieutenant Colonel Strong! Jawbone! Jawbone! This is General Moore, do you copy?"

"Sir? Jawbone here. I copy."

"Col, Dee is being overrun by enemy bots at the location my AIC is transferring to you now. She and another soldier are not in E-suits and I'm not sure I will make it to them in time." Moore rushed through a tactic in his head. "Get there now! Bust through the hull and into the outer pressure corridor. As it depressurizes you will have seconds to grab her and Lieutenant Rackman before the vacuum gets them. Do you understand?"

"Yes, sir! The Maniacs are on it," Jawbone replied.

✧ ✧ ✧

Joe Buckley, Jr. had no idea how the bots were jamming the sensors from the front end of the ship, but what he did know was that the air handlers, power conduits, and cooling tubes were all functioning the way they should. What he also knew was that there were power fluctuations in the hyperdrive core that were emanating from somewhere outside the control systems in engineering. The damned bots were fucking with his engine and he didn't like it.

"Benjamin! Did you see the fluctuations in the subspace field generators?" Buckley asked his second-in-command. His mind was swimming with charts, graphs, and hyper-relativistic quantum membrane calculations. Commander Keri Benjamin had been with his crew for over a decade and she understood the *Madira* about as well as Joe did. She'd probably say even better.

"Roger that, Joe. Whatever the bots are doing to us in the forward end of the ship is creating the standing wave in the power conduits. It looks like it is coming from near the forward and starboard DEG batteries." Benjamin tapped away at her control panel made several blank facial expressions, and stared off into space as if she were conversing with her AIC.

"Get me a damned fire crew up there and a tech!" Joe ordered. If that standing wave continued to build up there was no telling what type of damage that would do to the hyperdrive conduit projector. If that thing went out the ship would be stuck in deep space for a very long time. They could always just snap back individually to Earth but Joe didn't like the idea of leaving his first love abandoned in space.

"Roger that, Joe. Got a team on the way. Be advised that there is heavy fighting between here and there and it looks like the General is in the middle of it," Benjamin replied.

Debbie, he thought to his AIC. *See if you can get in touch with the General's AIC and see what is going on.*

She's already in contact with me, Joe.

And? Joe asked in his mindvoice.

It looks like the bots have overrun the outer hull corridor nearest the vacuum bulkhead under the DEGs. And, his daughter is stuck there unarmored. He is attempting to rescue her and others.

How?

He has ordered the Maniacs to attack that area of the ship and break her out from the outside in.

Shit! Cut the SIFs! If they start pounding on the hull there with the structural integrity field generators running they'll start pulling power on the conduit. And that could drive up the rogue standing wave! Joe thought for a moment. If that standing wave drew more power to that end of the ship it could create a positive feedback loop that would go unchecked. It would be like throwing a chain across the leads of a high-voltage transformer. An infinite current draw would be created and since the power supply couldn't supply an infinite amount of current something would give, explosively!

"Keri, we're shutting down the SIFs throughout the ship!" Joe ordered. "Find the spot where that damned power fluctuation is coming from!"

"Joe, with the SIFs down, the *Madira* will be vulnerable," Benjamin replied.

"Vulnerable to what? The damned bots are inside of the ship!"

Delilah rolled the FM-12 over into a straight vector for the coordinates that Moore's AIC had given her. She hated attacking her own ship but she also didn't want to see anything happen to the general's daughter. Jawbone had met the first daughter after the Disney World incident during the Separatist War. Dee was only a little girl then. Since then, Dee had become a good soldier and a good pilot, and over the years had become a good friend.

James, she thought to her AIC. *See if you can get in touch with Dee.*

No luck so far.

Keep at it.

"Alright, Maniacs, I want Popstar and Jango, Stick and Freebird in eagle-mode ready to catch the soldiers if they fly out. I want Backlash and Barron in fighter-mode to cover them on the top side of the bowl. We'll only have seconds to get them inside a cockpit once they are blown out." Jawbone thought through how she was going to handle this. "Coffee, Blue and PotRoast, you stay on my side and let's go to bot-mode and rip and tear!"

"Roger that, Jaw. Rip and tear!" Lieutenant Sara "Coffee" Ames replied.

"Affirmative," Captain Yariv "Blue" Sandeep replied.

"Oorah!" Blue's wingman Second Lieutenant Kathy "PotRoast" James added.

Delilah could see the hull of the ship coming up fast. Very fast. She toggled the fighter into bot-mode and rolled over feet first, firing her thrusters at max. The mecha slammed into the hull plating of the ship, leaving mecha-sized footprint impressions in the metal and throwing up blue plasma venting from the foot thrusters.

Jawbone made a quick mental check that her wingman was following suit in her DTM battlescape view. Coffee was on her wing and Blue and PotRoast were right behind her.

With a large armored metal fist she pounded into the hull of the supercarrier until a seam at a hatchway begun to tear free. Delilah pulled her DEG up and blasted the remaining seam welds and fasteners free. Coffee did the same. After several seconds of pounding and blasting an outer hull plate started to give way.

"Coffee, grab this side over here. Blue, get on the bottom side there." Jawbone pointed a huge mecha finger at the plate. She then placed herself in position to get the best leverage she could on the multi-ton piece of metal plating and then gripped it with her mecha hands. Coffee and Blue did the same. "On three."

"Roger that, Jaw."

"One, two, three!" The three FM-12 bot-mode fighters heaved with all their mechanical might until the huge armor plating of the supercarrier screeched and groaned free. The mecha pilots continued to bend the plating upward and over until a large enough hole to pass through was created.

"Alright, come on. Blue, stay out here with your wingman and see if you can't make this hole a little bigger." Jawbone and Coffee dropped into place in the large vacuum bulkhead. Dee would be just on the other side of the hull plating just beneath them.

"You heard the boss, PotRoast," Blue said over the net. "Let's make this hole bigger."

"Davy! Your right!" Dee shouted over the M-blaster fire. Just in front of them the top sergeant was flailing madly at an onrushing flood of bots. The AEM had long since run out of ammo and was wielding his HVAR like a club. Dee did her best to help keep the bots off the

Marine but it was only a matter of time. The blaster would knock the bots down but it took two and sometimes three shots to completely disable them.

"There's just too Goddamned many of them, Dee!" Rackman said. "We need a better plan—ahhhh, shit!"

Rackman screamed as the spinning saw from one of the bots Dee blasted sliced across his left shoulder leaving a huge gash. Bright red blood immediately began to pour profusely from the wound.

"Shit!" Dee fired nonstop, but the metal bastards were like violent cockroaches with saws buzzing and snapping from every direction. Dee ducked behind the power conduit they were using for cover just in time. Gunny Suez spun up from beneath a pile of bots and stomped feet first into a bot just to the side of where her head had been. For the first time she got a close enough look at the AEM's suit. It was torn to pieces and there were shrapnel fragments from the bots sticking out of it everywhere. Suez was in really bad shape, and with a final bounce off the wall he went down. Dee didn't see him get back up.

"Keep fighting, Dee!" Rackman shouted. "Keep fucking fighting!"

"There are too goddamned many of them. We need an EM grenade!" Dee said.

"Yeah. Or a Goddamned miracle!" Davy grunted, obviously in pain. "Duck, Dee!"

A metal appendage flung like a spear from one of the bots, pierced Dee's stomach all the way through, and clanked into the metal wall behind her. The rest of the appendage was attached to a bot, which just happened to have four other similar appendages that stabbed Dee through both shoulders and thighs. Dee screamed in pain and fired the M-blaster once more at a bot she could see from the corner of her eye. The bot was about to engulf Rackman's head but Dee believed she got it in time.

Snap to, Marine! Deanna Moore! Her AIC screamed in her mind. *Dee!*

Dee wasn't sure what happened next exactly, but she grunted as the bot that was stabbing her and about to bite her face off was pulled free by a large armored hand. Dee was certain she had seen Suez go down. Then there was the familiar *spittapp*ing of HVAR fire. The room lit up with hypervelocity rifle rounds and bots exploding. A single AEM was moving like a madman within the corridor, so fast that Dee wasn't sure if she was hallucinating or not.

"Daddy?" she managed to get out just as the world behind her seemed to fly apart.

The wall behind her opened up and the rush of air and debris slammed into her like the shockwave from a bomb. Dee's vision began to tunnel in and with her last struggle for air she saw Rackman's body sucked out of the ship into space behind her. She got very cold almost immediately.

"Davy . . ." The world went black and the voice of her AIC screaming at her inside her head trailed off into the distant void.

Chapter 15

November 7, 2406 AD
27 Light-years from the Sol System
Monday, 5:23 PM, Expeditionary Mission Standard Time

Alexander grabbed the downed buddy handle on the back of Gunny Suez's suit and tossed with all his suit's strength. The AEM pulled free of the bots and banged into the edge of the hole that the mecha pilots had made. Then the AEM flung helplessly out into space. Moore popped several grenades from his shoulder launchers loose and dove through the opening himself. The corridor behind him erupted into white-orange plasma with scattered bits of metal bots being flung asunder. The force from the exploding grenades acted like a volcano, tossing him head over feet out into space. Moore did his best to fire his boots and his rifle to slow the tumbling down.

Abby! Keep Dee in the tracker, DTM!

I've got her. Abigail illuminated her trajectory in his mindview of the battlescape. She was just ahead of them, tumbling out of his reach.

The blue arc of her path tracked right into the opening cockpit of an eagle-mode FM-12. The pilot inside scrambled at her to pull her arms and legs in as the cockpit canopy lowered. Moore breathed a sigh of relief. He turned as best he could to see a similar view of the SEAL. Moore could feel his trajectory reaching apogee above the ship and he started to fall back to the *Madira's* artificial gravity well.

"Jawbone! Get these three to the aft hangar medevac center!" he said over the tac-net.

"Roger that, General. Why don't you come with us?" Jawbone said as a matter of fact rather than asking. Moore watched as the Marine mecha rolled from bot to eagle and a big armored hand reached out and grabbed him. "Hang on. We'll be there in a minute."

Captain Jacob "Freebird" Seely scrambled as best he could to grab Dee by the arms and legs and slow her tumble, but she slammed into the canopy transparasteel hard. Freebird had his AIC cycle the canopy down while he pulled her down on top of him. The FM-12 cockpit was big and roomy but it wasn't designed for two people. Had Dee been wearing a flight suit she probably wouldn't have fit. As it was, she was wearing very little clothing at all and her body was covered in blood pretty much from head to toe. The blood had congealed in some places on her T-shirt and frozen in others. Freebird figured that she would probably look even bloodier if some of it hadn't immediately begun to boil off when she hit the vacuum of space.

Freebird squirmed into his seat as best he could and gave the controls over to his AIC. He quickly assessed the soldier's wounds and realized that she was in worse than critical shape. The atmosphere in the cockpit cycled on and Jacob popped his helmet visor.

"Apple One! Apple One!" He called Dee's mecha jock handle. Pilot habits died hard. "Come on, Apple! Stay with me."

Freebird worked his hand down to his thigh and popped out an immunoboost injector from his suit. He slapped the tube to Dee's throat and triggered the release. The injection hissed and emptied into her.

"Freebird, what's the status on your patient?" Jawbone's voice asked over the tac-net speakers.

"She's in bad shape, Jaw. Multiple severe wounds and she's not breathing. I administered immunoboost." Freebird thought for a second about what to do next. "If she had a suit we could defib her." The fighter pilot E-suits and AEMs and tank driver suits all had basic med systems that could shock a stopped heart, among many other things. But Dee was not in her suit and Freebird wasn't sure what to do to get her heart beating again.

"Captain Seely," a new voice joined the conversation.

"Seely here."

"Seely, this is medical officer Taggart. Your AIC is bringing you in fine and has relayed Miss Moore's vitals to us. You need to trigger her heartbeat. Without a pulse the immunoboost is not going to get anywhere in her system."

"Roger that. What do I do?" Freebird asked. He could see the hangar bay landing lights cycling. He was only a minute or so out from landing and cycling open the cockpit.

"Every second counts here. You need to begin CPR now."

"Roger that." Freebird found the base of Dee's sternum and started pushing her chest as best he could from the position he was in. There was no way he could bend down to breathe for her but he had an idea. He pulled the temporomandibular joint bite block mouthpiece from his helmet and slid it into Dee's mouth. He held it in place with his left hand while he pumped her chest with his right.

Start cycling air and stems on the TMJ mouthpiece in time with me, he thought to his AIC.

Understood.

The mouthpiece hissed, then Freebird pumped Dee's chest several times. The mouthpiece hissed again. This continued for what Freebird felt was hours, but he knew it was no more than thirty or forty seconds before he felt the landing gear hit the deck of the *Sienna Madira's* aft starboard hangar bay. The mecha was still rolling into its parking lane as the cockpit slid up and med techs were climbing on the moving plane.

"We've got her now, sir. Good job. We'll take it from here," one of the techs told him. The fighter rolled to a complete stop, and two of the men lifted Dee's body off of his lap and were racing her off on a gurney before he had time to catch his breath. Freebird looked down at his lap and gasped. It was covered in bright red blood.

Two other mecha fighters were rolling in behind him. One was in eagle mode and had an AEM in its clutches. A med team rushed up underneath the hand of the mecha with a gurney. The AEM was released onto the hover gurney and whisked away. The other mecha rolling in was in fighter mode and enacted an almost identical scene to the one he'd just gone through. The med team crawled up on the mecha and pulled a man out of it. Freebird knew him. It was the SEAL who Apple One had been spending a lot of time with. He looked to be in pretty bad shape, but he was screaming in pain which meant he was breathing and conscious.

Finally, Jawbone's mecha screeched into the hangar in eagle mode. As soon as she hit the ground an AEM bounced from the right hand of the mecha and thudded across the hangar deck. Freebird could see the four stars on the helmet as the AEM ran by. There was no doubt in his mind who that had been.

"Sehera, can you get to the aft medbay?" Moore called to his wife. He hoped that she had had enough sense not to follow him into the corridor with all the damned bots. Or at least he hoped that the Warlords were able to stop her from following him.

"I'm already on my way, Alexander. How is she?"

"Don't know yet, but it doesn't sound good." Moore rounded the corner and slid to a stop just before the hatchway into the main medbay triage area. Wounded were already being brought in. Occasionally, a snap-back emergency teleport worked and a wounded soldier would appear there. But for some reason it wasn't happening often. Alexander figured the dammed bots were jamming QMT operation as well.

Shit. I need to get on top of this.

Yes, sir.

Get me a full status report. And, Abby, find out who's running the bridge.

"Sir, they just rolled her into surgery." One of the nurses stood at the entrway, undaunted by the large, armored Marine general. "You can't go in now."

"Patch me into her vitals and give me the coms of the O.R.," Moore ordered the nurse. He understood that the doctors didn't need an AEM lumbering around the operating room in their way.

"Sir, I am not sure how to do that. But I will check on her for you."

"Never mind," Moore waved off the nurse.

Abby, patch us in.

Done, sir.

Put Sehera in the loop if she has Pamela with her.

I'll patch it to her suit comms.

Good girl.

"Thank you, nurse." Moore nodded gruffly and removed his helmet. He tossed it over his shoulder in standard AEM fashion.

"XO to Captain!"

"Moore here. Go, Firestorm."

"Sir, we're losing systems all across the bow of the ship, and it's spreading like wildfire. I've dispatched Marines and techs but we need a new plan," the XO explained.

"Stay on top of it, Sally!" Moore thought for a second while doing his best to listen to the activity in the operating room.

"Her heart is ruptured and less than thirty percent intact. It will have to be replaced. Prepare the printer with her stemcell ink . . ." the voice of a doctor said in the background.

"Alexander!" Sehera rushed to his side and grasped him in an armored hug. "I can't stand this."

"She's a soldier, Sehera. Comes with the job. She'll make it." Sehera looked at him as if she had a retort to that, but she must have thought better of it. She knew when situations were bigger than family discussions.

"Are we safe?" Sehera asked him.

"I don't know. The bots are on the ship everywhere and are growing faster than we can contain them." Moore multitasked simulations that Abigail ran through his mindview while he talked with his wife and the bridge, and listened to the doctors doing their best to save his daughter's life.

"CHENG to Captain."

"Moore here. Go, Joe."

"Sir, the bots are doing something to the hyperdrive. At first I thought they were trying to blow it up but now I'm not sure," Buckley replied.

"I need more than that, CHENG. What do you think they are doing?"

When it rains, it pours, Moore thought.

Yes, sir, Abigail agreed.

"I, uh, think they are about to turn the projector on and hyperdrive us somewhere. And by the energy buildup, it's not anywhere around here." Moore didn't like the uncertainty in Buckley's voice.

"Shut it down, Joe! Shut it down!"

"Shut it down!" Joe screamed over the humming noise coming from the hyperdrive projector control system.

"It's not responding, sir!" one of the engineering techs replied.

"Everybody on me!" Joe said, not sure what to do next. The full complement of the engineering team and the supporting seamen and firemen and fireman apprentices converged on him as he made his way to the center of the room. He'd been in this situation in reverse. He'd had the problem of getting power to the projector but never the problem of too much power. He stood underneath the four-meter-in-diameter pink and purple swirling tube that ran the length of a major portion of the ship. The swirling motion of the plasma inside and the Cerenkov radiation was brighter than usual and color-shifted even further into the violet than he'd ever seen.

"Come on, girl," he said as he reached up with his hands and tapped the bottom of the conduit to the projector tube affectionately. Then he addressed his team with a somewhat wacky idea. Hell, it wasn't that wacky—he'd actually done it before, twice. Well, the last time he'd done it was a simulation. The time before that time he did what he had in mind, it worked, but—and there was always a "but" in these situations—it had nearly killed him and his first Engineer's Mate. And that was years ago. The engine room had been rebuilt several times since then.

"Listen up, everyone. We haven't got but a few minutes, maybe, before those damned bots jaunt us through space to who knows where. I have an idea what to do but I don't know if it will work or not."

"Oh shit, no, Joe!" Keri replied. "A Buckley Maneuver won't work in reverse."

"Why not? We just overload the conduit between the tube and the power source and burn the conduit out. That way the projector can't get power to it," Joe responded. "We're going to pull a cable from that power coupling on the jaunt drive projector here," he pointed at the now infamous Buckley Junction. "Tie it around the junction housing and then drag it to both exit doors just like we've done before and then over here to the power unit for Aux Prop. The overload should blow out the conduit just before the Aux Prop junction. Now tell me a better solution and I'd be glad to implement it." It was déjà vu all over again.

"Well, sir," one of the firemen interrupted, "I'm not an engineer but this is a warship. Why don't we just get a Marine down here to blow the conduit up or something?"

"Sorry, fireman, that won't work. We're too close to the tube here and it would just arc across—" Benjamin started but Buckley interrupted her.

"Goddamned right! We can't do it *here,* but we could do it further down the line!" Buckley pulled schematics of the power flow up into everyone's DTM ship view and started pulling away layers and zooming into the hyperdrive systems.

"Look, right here. We can blow out this fifty-meter piece of conduit here and it should do. It is likely to be a hell of a bang but we won't be slung off into space to who knows where."

"The Warlords are heavily engaged in that location, sir." One of the crew pointed out the Blue force tracker dots one deck up from that location.

"Hmm." Joe looked over it again. "Anybody have any other thoughts on this?"

"Joe, it will work. We should amp up the SIFs all around the area to minimize damage to the rest of the ship," Benjamin replied.

"We do it then," Joe ordered her. "CHENG to General Warboys."

Chapter 16

November 7, 2406 AD
27 Light-years from the Sol System
Monday, 5:25 PM, Expeditionary Mission Standard Time

"Let me get this straight, Cheng, you WANT me to blow up the power conduits of our supercarrier?" General Warboys asked the chief engineer in disbelief.

"Yes, sir! If you don't, and soon, the bots will have complete control of the hyperdrive, and they are ramping it up to jaunt us off to somewhere in deep space," Buckley replied over the tac-net.

"Right here is all that has to go, right?" Warboys highlighted the conduit image in their mutually shared DTM view. The direct-to-mind link lit up as the general thought about it.

"That's the one!" Buckley approved. "My guess is that you have about ten minutes before the hyperdrive kicks in."

"Understood, CHENG. Warboys out." Mason keyed the com to the Warlord's tac-net channel. "Listen up, Warlords! We have a new objective. Two through Four are to form up around me and keep those goddamned bots off of me. Five through Ten, form up on them and keep those goddamned bots off them!"

"Roger that, sir!" resounded from the team across the net.

"Sir, what is our objective?" Two asked.

"We have nine minutes and forty-six seconds to blow out the main hyperdrive energy conduit two decks over and one down. It is right in the thick of bot country, so stay alert!"

Warboys rolled his tank over into hover mode and put all power to his forward structural integrity fields. The angular momentum and g-loading forced him to grunt back his breakfast and swallow some bile. The taste was just the way he liked it.

The battlescape view of the ship formed around him in a three-dimensional ball in his DTM mindview. The tanks behind him were painted blue, and there were hundreds of blue ground-pounder dots scattered about the periphery of the bot-controlled decks of the ship. As best he could tell, the Warlords were driving a phalanx through the line of bots and there were no humans in harm's way.

"Alright, Warlords, this is why they pay us the big bucks. Fox!" He grunted as he voice-activated and fired a missile with the open impact detonation command. The missile squealed out from atop the tank, leaving a blue ion trail in the ship's atmosphere, and then tore into the bulkhead at the end of the corridor. The hangar corridor was over five meters high and almost as wide, but ended at a man-sized hatch. The missile expanded that with a bright orange-and-white erupting plasma ball that threw red-hot glowing shards of bulkhead and deckplate in every direction. "Guns, guns, guns!" Mason followed up. The Warlords' chatter started to pick up as the bots realized that the tankheads were attacking and penetrating the line.

"They're jamming the QMs and RF, Warlords. Go to IR and eyeballs!" Warboys warned just as he released another missile, this one with the electro-optical/IR sensor package. "Fox Two!"

"Guns, guns, guns! Roger that, One!" Warlord Three responded. "I'm getting lots of motion track and acoustic pinging from the deckplate. Watch for them bursting through beneath and above us!"

"I have a track algorithm on the bastards," Warlord Five said. "They are amassing thirty-seven meters off our two o'clock, thirty degrees South Pole!"

"Seven! Your three-nine line is eaten up! Watch it."

"Guns, guns, guns. North Pole Two!"

"I got 'em, Four. Fox Two!"

Mason put the hammer down and pounded his hovertank through the opening. The tank slammed into the jagged metal edges the missile had left at the hatchway. The impact slung him forward into his harness but his suit dampened the impact. Mason jiggled the stick in pitch, yaw, and roll and squirmed the hole out to be a little bigger than tank size. He then slammed the throttle forward, totally destroying what was left of what his mindview told him was a janitorial closet. The bulkhead gave way to the brunt of the tank and screeched against the structural integrity fields. Flashes of ionizing metal splattered in every direction as Mason protruded into another corridor that the DTM mindview labeled as the outer pressurized corridor. There were energy and plumbing conduits along the outer wall running in every direction. But the one he needed was a deck below.

"They're bursting through the ceiling, One!" Mason was warned by one of his men. He could see the corridor ceiling above him and aftward about twenty meters open up like a vortex, and bots began to pour from the event horizon.

"I got 'em, One," Warlord Two replied. "Fox Two!"

"Get over here and help me out, Four!" Warlord Two ordered.

"Stay with 'em, Warlords!" Mason shouted. He toggled the controls to bot-mode. His tank flipped upward and rolled over into a giant metal behemoth that came clanking down right fist first against the deck. Mason slammed his fists into the deck several times before he decided that wasn't going to break through the deck plating fast enough. He bounced upward and flattened himself out for his back to slam against the corridor ceiling as he let loose another missile.

"SIFs on torso max! Fox!" Warboys shouted. The missile screeched out from his shoulder mount and exploded into the deck just fifteen meters below him. The SIF generators whined against the explosion that surrounded him, and flashes of ionizing debris engulfed his bot-mode tank.

As the force of the explosion subsided Mason pitched over headfirst and fell through the opening in the deck. He came to rest on his feet, staring ahead into thousands of bots in every direction. But most importantly, the hyperdrive power conduit was twenty meters ahead and running through the outer hull wall.

"I've got optical lock on the objective! Fox Two!" Warboys fired. The missile trailed outward at the conduit, but almost immediately several bots sacrificed themselves into the missile, detonating it early. "Shit!"

The blast toppled Warboys over backwards and he was almost instantly overtaken by bots like a swarm of bees, killer ants, and cockroaches on a half-eaten donut. Mason rolled over to his hands and knees and forced the bot-mode tank to its feet, all the while whirling, kicking, and swinging his arms to free himself.

"I got it, One!" Warlord Two dropped in beside him, punching away several of the bots and then going to guns. "Guns, guns, guns."

"Forget me! Go for the objective." Warboys fired again. "Fox Two!"

"Roger that, One." Warlord Two replied. "Fox Two!"

"Got your back, sir!" Warlords Three and Four dropped into position, stomping and slinging bots in every direction.

"Fox Two!" Three commanded.

"Fox Two!" Four added.

The four missiles spun out into the bulkhead. Two of them were detonated by self-sacrificing bots, but the resulting explosion opened the way for the other two that hit dead-on center of the fifty-meter section of high-power hyperdrive energy conduit.

"Bull's-eye!" Four shouted.

The missiles created an explosion that was typical of the warheads. At first there was the orange-and-white firestorm, but as soon as the conduit SIFs failed, the millions of terajoules of energy were released in a fraction of a second, blasting out a section of the ship the size of a football field. The resulting concussive wave shattered bots in every direction and forced a wall of flames and plasma forward and aftward for several hundred meters. Warlords One, Two, Three, and Four were blown out of the ship at the same time.

Warning—excessive spin rate, Mason's bitching Betty chimed at him.

"No shit! Tank mode!" He toggled the controls and the wildly spinning bot transfigured into a spinning tank. Just like an ice skater pulling in his arms to increase his spin rate, the same thing happened to his tank. It spun faster. But in tank-mode the vehicle could handle the extreme angular acceleration.

The control system fired the hover controls to slow the spin rate until the g-forces inside the tank registered microgravity. Mason felt his stomach lurch a bit but he quickly adjusted as his suit pumped stims and anti-nausea meds into his system.

"Warlord One to CHENG!"

"CHENG here."

"Buckley, you're gonna need a shitload of duct tape."

"Roger that, General." Buckley replied. "The hyperdrive is offline!"

"Warlords," Mason took a breath, "objective obtained. You can go back to killing bots now."

Chapter 17

November 7, 2406 AD
29 Light-years from the Sol System
Monday, 5:25 PM, Expeditionary Mission Standard Time

DeathRay sat down in the captain's chair and looked out the viewport of the bridge. He could see the bow of several of the fleet ships in the periphery of the viewport, but mostly he could see the bright blue star and the accretion disc debris all about them. It was a hell of a hiding place for a fleet of warships.

Nancy stood just in front of him, hacking commands into the helm console. As far as Jack could tell, the fleet of ships were abandoned in place with no bot crews. The few bots they had encountered in the teleport pad room must have been leftover sentries. Or maybe they were repair or maintenance bots that Nancy had just managed to piss off. And to top it off, the ships appeared to have been designed for human crews. The phrase "what the fuck" never seemed more appropriate to DeathRay than at that very moment.

"Looks like the hangar bays are full of Separatist-derived fighters and tanks, Jack." Nancy told him. "This is a complete fleet sans crew. And I mean it is loaded for bear."

"So, Copernicus was building up his army out here in the middle of nowhere? For what purpose? This is just too weird." DeathRay didn't like weird. He liked straightforward and to the point. He liked having an objective and then going to kill that objective and getting on to the next Goddamned objective. He really just fucking hated weird.

"There is more," Nancy said as she continued to tap at the console. The clackity, clacking echoed in the extremely quiet and empty ship. The lighting came up to normal as she tapped away.

"Well?" Jack hated the suspense almost as much as he hated weird. "More what?"

"The ships are keyed to human access. I don't mean a specific human. I mean to human DNA. They aren't locked to us." Nancy turned to Jack and raised an eyebrow. "Allison didn't have to hack them at all. They're here for the taking."

"Maybe Copernicus just didn't expect anybody could get out here to them?" Jack asked. "You'd at least think he'd have hidden the keys above the sun visor."

"No keys needed. I think we're so remote, maybe, that is the security system in itself. These ships are nearly two decades old as best I can tell. At that time it would have taken years for anybody to reach them. Unless you were connected through a QMT system that nobody knew existed yet, you couldn't get here." Nancy explained. "It's probable that Elle Ahmi was the only human ever out here."

"I don't know about that," Jack replied. "Who built these things? And who built the city and the QMT pad that brought us here?"

"I dunno, but maybe it was all made by bots." Nancy looked up at her husband. "So that's that. We have full control of the ship now."

"Okay, great. We just found a fleet of free warships with a full contingent of fighter mecha. Now what?" Jack wasn't sure what the next move was, but he considered that it was time to get back to the *Madira*. "We should get back to the *Madira* and let the general figure this out."

"Agreed. Above our paygrades, especially since I'm retired and just along as a civilian consultant." Nancy looked seriously at her husband, knowing full well that nobody believed that line or, for that matter, truly understood her role aboard the *Sienna Madira*. Jack didn't worry about it. Moore had invited her, and she was his wife. For a brief moment Jack let himself get lost in her smile. After all, in the immediate moment there was nothing doing its best to shoot, claw, cut, bite, or kill them.

"How far are we from the teleportation facility that brought us here?" Jack asked. "Any way to get a fix on where we are?"

"Yes. It's all in the log. We are at a star about two light-years away from there. At max jaunt speed of these ships I'm guessing we're a month away," she said.

"I was afraid of that. So we snap back then?" Jack asked.

"Well, I wasn't finished. I said at max jaunt speed it would take a month." Nancy paused briefly. Jack could tell she was giving him time to play catch-up but he wasn't sure what it was he had to catch up on.

"You just said that," he said hesitantly, trying not to come across as annoyed.

"Yes, but that is just the max jaunt speed of the hyperdrive projector. This ship is a traveling QMT pad." Nancy smiled triumphantly.

"No shit?" Jack asked.

"No shit." Nancy replied. "And it looks like it has all the addresses in it that were in the shuttle that Buckley reverse engineered for us. Plus there are a few more locations to boot. Moore is going to just love that."

"Now we're talking. And you're right. The general *is* going to love this."

"There's more," Nancy interrupted his train of thought.

"How could there be more?"

"It looks like the ships were designed to be slaved from this bridge," Nancy explained. Jack didn't quite get it.

"So, what? We can remote fly them?"

"More. We can turn on the QMT pad and fly them through the event horizon and then we can follow them through. And if Allison is understanding this right, the QMT pad can actually go through the gate too, like a sling-forward wristband does," she said.

Jack was doing his best to work that out in his head. "You mean the fleet was designed to be able to QMT anywhere it went?"

"Precisely!" Nancy tapped a few further commands into the console. "We'll need to have the STO and the CHENG go through it all, but I believe there is a sling-forward capability of a few light years on this pad. I don't think that type of technology exists yet."

"Damn, it must have existed two decades ago when they were built. Let's go make sure the Marines took the shuttle back and then let's get back ourselves. We've got to get some bigger brains on this. No offense." Jack nodded at his wife. He hoped that what he'd just said didn't come across as an insult, but Nancy didn't seem to pay it any attention. She had a thick skin. Being a spy all those years had taken the sentimental aspects right out of her personality. She was very matter-of-fact, which was one of the things Jack loved most about her. He settled into the captain's chair a bit. "I could get used to this."

"Well, don't get too used to it." Nancy said with a smile. "I found them first, so I claim first salvage rights. These ships are mine! But you go ahead and captain for a while if you want."

"It would be a whole lot easier if our suits had thrusters or momentum field generators on them," Amari said to nobody in particular. Rondi did her best to look in the tech's general direction, but she was spinning too randomly to look at anything or anyone that close to her. The spin wasn't that fast but it was continuous, and very damned annoying.

"I'd throw up again if I had anything left," Rondi added as the QMT orbital facility rolled back into her view. Her back was now to the planet below. "L.T.? Any ideas?"

"I've got nothing, First Sergeant," the lieutenant replied. "Nothing on coms. Nothing on sensors of any use. And I have no idea what to do when the snap-back bands don't work. Amari, you're the tech. What have you got?"

"Sorry, sir. I'm as much at a loss as you are. If we were still on the planet I'd suggest we try broadcasting the signal and see if we ended up with DeathRay and Mrs. Penzington, but as it is, sir, I'm just doing my best not to be sick."

"Won't they come looking for us?" Corporal Simms asked. Rondi could tell by his voice that he was straining not to be sick. The shootout in microgravity had left them all with wild spins induced on their positions. Rondi had managed to slow herself slightly by firing her HVAR and jumpboots, but AEM suits were not spacesuits designed for spacewalks. They were designed for armored combat on a surface with gravity. She made herself a mental note that she was going to mention that to Buckley when she got back. She bet that Joe could rig up some sort of spacewalk module in case they needed one ever again in the future. She'd have to get back first.

"Take it easy, Corporal," Rondi replied.

"Of course they will," Lieutenant Franks added. "Just stay frosty."

Rondi tried closing her eyes but that didn't help. And hoping that help would come didn't help either. She fully understood that the only way the *Madira* had in or out of this star system was on the shuttle that Joe Buckley had reverse engineered for them. And that shuttle was in millions of tiny pieces drifting about them in space. In her mind she couldn't figure out how they would get out of this situation, but Marines didn't give up—they kept moving forward.

"Lieutenant, I have an idea," Amari announced.

"Go on," the lieutenant replied.

"We're closest to the QMT pad facility. My sensors suggest we are about one hundred kilometers away and in a slightly higher orbit. It is possible that we could calculate the thrust vector needed and do bursts with our weapons and jumpboots to push our orbit down and phase us so we could crash into the pad."

"Uh, I'm no rocket scientist," Rondi said, "but that is a long way off and seems like it would need a bunch of thrusting for that and I'm almost out of ammo. And, uh, I don't like the idea of crashing into anything."

"I was just saying that if there is no other way then we should at least try something." Amari didn't sound too sure of herself. "And *crashing* was probably the wrong word to use."

"How do we make these calculations?" Lieutenant Franks asked. "And how likely is it that we'll go flinging off into space?"

"What the hell, L.T., we're already in space, sir. I say we go for it." Rondi preferred doing something rather than nothing. Floating around in space forever until they starved. Rondi had heard the stories of how Alexander Moore had lived in a suit on Mars for over a month and somehow managed to stay alive and even fight a contingent of Separatists hand-to-hand before he was rescued. Hell, every Marine had heard that story. Few really believed it, especially knowing how primitive the suits had been at the time. But Rondi Howser was part of Moore's crew. She had seen the man in action several times. She had no doubt it could be done and that he had done it. With modern suits, she believed she could survive forever. It wouldn't be fun and she wouldn't like it, but she knew she could do it.

"I agree, First Sergeant," Lieutenant Franks replied. "We've got nothing else to do."

"What if more bots show up, sir?" Corporal Simms asked. Rondi could hear the fear in his voice.

"Then, corporal, we'll kill them," the lieutenant answered. Rondi liked his answer.

"Oorah, sir," the corporal responded.

"Okay, Amari, your show?" Franks said.

"Uh, yes, sir. Been simming it with my AIC. The best thing we can do is point ourselves at the facility and fire our boots. Only fire them when we are pointed in that direction. I suspect it will take some time to figure it out completely. This is a hell of an orbital optimization problem that'll impress the CHENG," Amari explained. "If it works, that is."

"I say we give control over to our AICs. It worked for my puking deathblossom," Rondi said. "How long is this going to take, Amari?"

"At my best guess right now, I'd say a couple of weeks."

"Shit. I was guessing that." Rondi braced herself for a long, painful couple of weeks. "We're gonna get *real* hungry."

"Well, then, let's get started," Franks ordered. "Hand suit control over to your AICs and start thrusting toward the orbital facility."

"Yes, sir," Simms said.

Rondi begrudgingly handed over control of her suit again. She hoped that this time there wouldn't be as much wild spinning and out-of-control vomiting. She hoped even harder that somehow DeathRay would find them before they starved to death.

Chapter 18

November 7, 2406 AD
27 Light-years from the Sol System
Monday, 6:37 PM, Expeditionary Mission Standard Time

"XO to Captain!"

"Go, XO!" Moore answered. He was stuck on the aft end of the ship and needed to get to the bridge. He had taken a corner of the aft hangar bay and made a makeshift war room out of it. He didn't want to stray too far from the med bay while Deanna was still in surgery. But the ship was under attack and he was the captain. His DTM shipwide view mostly still functioned, but there were large swaths of the ship that were being jammed by the bots.

"If you can tell from the mindview of the ship, sir, the blackout areas are getting larger, and damned quickly too," executive officer USMC Brigadier General Sally "Firestorm" Rheims responded. "And the Blue force tracker casualties are starting to rack up."

"I see it, Firestorm." Moore wasn't exactly sure what to do but he knew he had to do something. The battle hadn't gone well so far. His AIC kept running battle simulations and displaying them in his head and at the same time kept him updated on her attempts at hacking into sensors in the jammed portions of the ship. His head was full of data.

Alexander had done his best to keep soldiers around the bot-controlled areas to have them fighting the metal bastards back, but the damned bots reproduced too fast to be held at bay by AEMs and ground pounders alone. They needed mass kill weapons.

If we survive this I want those EMP grenades that Penzington came up with mass produced and scaled up, he thought.

I agree, sir, Abigail said into his mind.

"The biggest impact we made so far, sir, was when the Warlords blew out the hyperdrive conduit. Did a shitload of damage to the starboard side of the ship," the XO explained. "Not sure we can survive that kind of success too many times."

"Yes, I saw that. We had no choice." Moore was perplexed. The bot numbers continued to increase no matter what they did. "If this keeps up we'll have to abandon ship. Send the general order that all crew must don their snap back emergency transport bands. On my order only are they to snap back home." Alexander hoped that the bot-damping field wouldn't prevent all the QMT jumps to safety. Maybe most of the crew could make it back to Earthspace.

"Aye, sir!" the XO acknowledged. Almost instantly Moore saw on the command page in his DTM mindview a priority one order being sent out to every AIC onboard the ship and in vehicles flying about it.

"Keep pushing them, Firestorm! We cannot lose the ship. I'm uploading to you a new battle strategy now. I want you to pick a team of AEMs and create a phalanx and drive through them just like the Warlords did. Then have them fight them outwards with as many EMP grenades as they can find."

"Yes, sir."

"Alexander?" Sehera's voice pinged him.

"Yes, dear?"

"The surgery is over. Deanna is being moved into a recovery room." Sehera's update left Alexander with a huge sense of relief. His daughter was alive and would be okay. "And there are lots of casualties starting to come in."

"Is she awake?" he responded while choking back tears. He looked around the aft hangar bay that he had turned into a makeshift battle HQ. He was only a few hundred feet from the aft medbay where Dee was. There was constant movement of gurneys and troops and rescue workers running in and out of that end of the bay. QMT flashes popped every now and then as the more critical patients would snap back to the med bay once the rescuers got them free of the jamming zones. "Do I need to get there?"

"Not yet. The doctor says she won't wake for at least an hour or so," Sehera said. "Alexander, save the ship."

"Understood. Tell me the minute she wakes up. And if the bots start to overrun us, or her position, you snap back to Earthspace, you hear me, Sehera?" he told his wife. He hoped she'd listen.

"Understood," Sehera replied. "Take care of things. Talk soon."

"CHENG to CO!" Moore's attention was snapped back to the battle but his heart was still wrenching in pain over his little princess being wounded so seriously. Sure she'd been shot and cut up and even lost a hand before but none of that was really serious. This time Dee had actually died. Her heart had been damaged so badly that it had to be replaced and even with modern technology there was little way to prevent the ischemic cascade of the brain once the heart stopped. Ten minutes or less was the absolute maximum time to save somebody once their heart had stopped without a stasis field or other medical life-support for the brain. Moore shook himself free of the thought.

Move forward, Marine! Abigail said into his mindvoice. *Dee is in good hands. The CHENG needs you, sir.*

Right. Any luck hacking the bots yet?

No, sir.

Keep trying, Abby. Shit, we need Penzington's AIC on this.

Yes, sir.

"Go, CHENG, Moore here."

"General, we are dead in the water and the bots are beginning to dig into the SIF generators," Buckley explained. Moore didn't quite understand the seemingly overemphatic tone in the CHENG's voice.

"More detail, Joe. Why is that so bad?" Moore asked the chief engineer.

"Sir, it looks like the bots decided that if they couldn't commandeer the ship that they are going to blow it up."

"Okay, Joe, I get it." Moore thought for a second. "How are they planning to do it?"

"They are connecting all the SIF generators and power systems that they can into a positive-feedback loop. As soon as they plug them together the power conduits throughout the ship will be drawing more power than they are rated to. When that happens, well, sir, this won't be a good place to be."

"How long until they can do that?" Moore didn't like where this was headed. Somehow they had to stop the damned bots. He certainly didn't want the entire crew snapping back to Earth with their tails between their legs after fighting the damned bots for over eighteen months. And he could feel that they were getting closer to the truth to what Copernicus was up to. They were too damned close to give up now.

"It's hard to say because the sensors are down throughout most of the ship, but from what I can figure out, we have less than an hour, sir." Joe didn't sound too sure of that.

"Hell and two hundred, by Gods! Will there be a sign big enough and with enough warning that the crew can snap back just before it happens?"

"Uh, yes, sir, that sort of power buildup will run the EM fields through the roof. I'll know a good five minutes or so before it could go." Joe hesitated briefly and stuttered a bit. "Uh, uh, sir, if the bots take over that much of the ship, the teleport-jamming field might encompass the majority of the crew."

"Understood, Joe. Find a work-around. We have to stop these bastards. Moore out."

"Yes, sir."

"That should do it, Jack." Nancy winked at her husband sitting in the captain's chair of her newly-acquired fleet of ships. "Or is that, uh, Captain?"

"Well, that is my Navy rank anyway." Jack laughed. "Let's go."

"Initiating quantum membrane teleportation in three, two, one, now," Nancy said. She kept one eye on the viewport and one on the controls.

The energy levels on the ships hull spiked across the spectrum and a blinding white-and-purple light sprayed out in front of them, creating a large, seemingly two-dimensional expanding circle of rippling and glimmering spacetime several kilometers across. The event horizon of the connected quantum membranes stabilized with shimmering lightning flashing across the surface.

"Beautiful," Jack said with a whistle. "Send in the fleet."

"Already on it," she paused for a second to reveal her sarcasm and then said, "Captain."

Nancy cycled on the propulsion system for forty-seven ships and every one of them came to life. The builders of the fleet had installed an automated gating algorithm so it wasn't difficult to tell them to go through the spacetime teleportation portal. She simply instigated a command that was already in place.

"You know, one day we'll have to thank whoever designed these ships." Nancy watched as the blue ship icons representing each vessel in the fleet approached the portal and then vanished out of existence. "That was the last one, Jack. Here we go."

"I hope this thing is working right." Jack sounded a bit nervous.

"Worst case, we'll end up on the other side of the universe or maybe just disintegrated." Nancy wasn't worried at all. As far as she and Allison could tell the ships were in top shape and had technology onboard that seemed even more advanced than the *Madira*. That seemed impossible yet somehow it was the case.

The nose of the large ship peeked through the event horizon, then it appeared as though the ship were sucked into it rapidly. Nancy could feel her hair standing on end and her skin crawled slightly, and then there was that buzzing in her ears that many described as the sound of bacon frying in a pan. Then, almost as quickly, they were thrown out of the portal on the other side staring out the viewport at an orbiting QMT pad and the planet beneath it that they had left the Marines on. Nancy's Blue force tracker started pinging at her.

"Jack, I'm getting location hits for our crew. I'm not seeing the shuttle anywhere." Nancy scanned the area and found no shuttle. She did find a debris cloud not far from where they had left the shuttle. There were also dead bot parts everywhere.

"Looks like a fight," Jack noted. "I've got a fix on our people and I don't have any casualties. Why the hell didn't they snap back like I told them to?"

"Hold on a minute." Nancy held up a hand then went back to running sensor sweeps on the star system. "The sensors on this thing are way more advanced than on the shuttle. I'm getting zero life signs on the planet below. All those dwellings are abandoned. We were spoofed. Nobody is currently living down there. And Jack, something turned on a QMT dampening field that is originating close to the orbital facility. Maybe a booby trap."

"A booby trap, sir?" Nancy called Jack "sir" just to tease him, he was sure. It wasn't her nature to call people "sir." She wasn't military.

"Looks like nobody is QMTing out of here." Nancy thought about that for a minute. "I bet it was turned on as soon as we got here. It looks like these ships can QMT within a few million kilometers of the pad. That would get us around in this system. The problem is, we couldn't get outside the dampening field that appears to stretch all the way to the outer reach of this solar system. You can bounce around inside the field all you want to, but no QMTing out of it. We could maybe jaunt with the hyperdrive out and then QMT from out there. That could take weeks."

"We QMTed down from the shuttle to the planet," Jack said. "Explain that."

"Well, I said, I believe it is set up to QMT in and around the field but not out of it," Nancy answered.

"Okay then, we QMTed out. We went two light-years to find these ships." Jack shrugged his shoulders and raised an eyebrow. "So there is a backdoor out of here."

"That's it, Jack!" Nancy knew that Jack was a brilliant pilot and was a hell of a soldier, but there were times where his pragmatic and bulldogged way of thinking was extremely deductive and damn useful. "It must be the backdoor. And that is exactly how we'll get out of here."

"Work it out or find the place generating the field and we'll blow it up. Give me control of the ship here and I'll fly over to our people," Jack said. "Looks like they are trying to vector toward the QMT facility."

"They're stranded in space."

"They must have come up with a plan not to be," Jack replied.

"Allison agrees with you." Nancy shook her head. "Oh my God, that would take weeks to do. And where the hell were they going to go once they got there?"

"Better than just floating in space and doing nothing until you died," Jack said, then he took the controls to the ship. Nancy could feel the ship's propulsion system push her into the helmsman's seat cushions a bit before the inertial dampers kicked in.

"Right. I've got the QMT backdoor approach figured out." She didn't really want to say that Allison had figured it out, but she figured Jack guessed that anyway. Or he didn't care.

"How do we get them in?" Jack seemed to be talking to himself. "Ha, we'll swallow them with the hangar bay. I guess I need to give them a call."

"Wait, Jack. You don't have to do that. I can lock onto their snap-back bands and tie them into the ship's QMT pads. I can teleport them in." Nancy thought about what she had just said. She wasn't sure that doing that was even possible with standard pads like on the *Sienna Madira*. The way the wristbands worked is that they had to be quantum connected to each pad they were using. But this system on these ships could reach out and connect to beacons and spacetime locations and pull them in like a snap-back procedure but without the initial connection. Neither she nor Allison had ever seen that level of technology before.

"You can do that?" Jack's eyebrows raised in disbelief.

"Looks like we can. Open a com channel and tell them what is happening." Nancy tapped at some controls and brought up a map of the ship DTM for both her and Jack to see. The mindview of the ship sprang to life and highlighted a pathway to a QMT pad only a few tens of meters down one corridor aftward and one deck below. "I've got them locked on."

"Lieutenant Franks, do you copy? This is Captain Boland."

"Copy, sir! I sure hope that's you in those bigass ships, sir," Franks replied.

"It's us. Listen up, team. We are about to teleport you into the flagship of this fleet. I am then uploading the layout and path to the bridge. Once aboard you are to make your way to it. Understood?"

"Roger that, sir. Have the ship layout now," Franks said.

"Okay, Nancy. Bring them in."

"Okay, Jack." Nancy touched a blue icon on her screen and smiled. "They're onboard, Captain."

"Great. Start the algorithm and get us back to the *Madira*."

Chapter 19

November 7, 2406 AD
29 Light-years from the Sol System
Monday, 6:37 PM, Expeditionary Mission Standard Time

USMC Lieutenant Colonel Francis Jones had served on the U.S.S. *Anthony Blair* during the last two decades and through the major battles with the Separatists, so he'd seen his share of the shit. When former President Moore asked him to come along as the AEM commander for the mission he was honored, excited, and most certainly surprised. He'd figured Ramy's Robots would be the team he wanted. But it turned out that Ramy was done. He'd retired and moved back home to New Detroit. With the head AEM from the old *Sienna Madira* crew hanging up his armored boots, Moore had told him that the *Blair* was the next best thing. Of course, the crew of the *Blair* would have taken that as an insult, but any good Marine wanted to go where the shit was. And if history was any indicator, then where Moore went, there tended to be a whole lot of shit. Francis had jumped at the chance to serve with the major-turned-senator-turned-president-turned-general.

The battle plan was simple. Push a squad of AEMs through the perimeter line the bots had created and move to the center. The best estimate his AIC could give him was that there would be a hundred bots per AEM, minimum.

Francis had grabbed ten AEMs, and they ransacked the nearest weapons lockers and took every EMP grenade they could get their hands on. That ended up being about fifteen total.

The ten Marines he had with him ranged from three privates first class, to a lance corporal, two corporals, two sergeants, a staff sergeant, and a captain. He really wished he had his Top Sergeant Suez with him, but his blue force tracker showed the sergeant in the medbay as a casualty.

"Captain Folgers, I want you and Sergeant Spears to take Meo, Ceres, and Freeman on the right. Watch out for being flanked in 3D!" The lieutenant colonel spelled out the game plan to his squad. "I'll take point with the other five behind me on the left. We'll push in a V formation like a flock of geese. Standard phalanx attack."

"What sensors do you think, sir?" Staff Sergeant Bill Prichard asked.

"Good question, Staff Sergeant. Use them all but only trust Mark One Eyeball! Don't lose any of those EMP grenades until I say so." LTC Jones thought about the plan all the while as he led the troops down the final corridor leading up to the backs of the troops doing their best to hold the line of bots back.

The corridor led into one of the larger chambers that served as a rec area for the troops. With a full contingent of crew the area was used for a mess hall but the space had been converted into a bar, weight room, and movie room. There was even a bowling lane on one side. But right now it was a staging area with troops and support crew running in with more ammo and out with casualties. The lighting in the area was dim and flickering. The bots were apparently taking their toll on that part of the ship. The number of casualties being hauled around on gurneys was worrying.

"Why aren't they teleporting to the medbay?" PFC Karuthers asked.

"Bots are jamming the QMT in this part of the ship," Captain Folgers replied. "We get wounded in here, we have to hump our way back to get fixed."

"So don't get fucking wounded, and that's an order," Francis replied gruffly and led the AEMs across the room to the makeshift barricades and covers on the other side.

"You heard the colonel," Staff Sergeant Bill Prichard stepped in, taking the squad's top sergeant role. "Now get focused, Marines, and stay frosty."

Rifle fire, M-blasters, grenades, and the gnashing of metal spikes, blades, and saws and human screams created a mish-mash of sounds that could cause even the strongest skin to crawl. It was where *the shit* was.

"Listen up! Ten meters beyond that barricade is the shitstorm of a lifetime," LTC Francis Jones started. "We start from right here picking up speed. I want us at top speed when we bounce over the line and I want every weapon firing nonstop on a target. Oorah?"

"Oorah!" the Marines responded.

"Good. Let's *move,* Marines!" LTC Francis Jones stomped his kick boots into the floor, and bounced five meters ahead of his team, and started into the fullest sprint the armored suit would allow. The sound of the AEM suits clanking against deckplating only added to the cacophony of noise. Jones bounced over the first line of barricades, flipping over just in time to duck through a hatchway. He rolled to his feet with his HVAR firing at full auto. The hypervelocity rounds zipped through the atmosphere of the ship, leaving ion trails behind them and splattering molten metal when the rounds hit either a bot or a bulkhead near one. Light purple glowing ion trails zipped in every direction, ending in a shower of molten red. As he broke into a full forward sprint with his rifle rested into his shoulder, Jones managed to stomp on several buzzsaw bots with his kickboots before they could cut into his suit.

"Goddamn, it's thick in here, Colonel!" Sergeant Alan Sanchez voiced on the team's tac-net channel.

"You got that shit right, Sarge," PFC Karuthers added.

Jones could see his V formation pushing through, leaving a wake of bots sputtering out of control, leaking fluids, exploding, or just plain dead behind them. A couple of his troops were spending too much time fighting the bots, though, and not moving, causing his V to have a weak side.

"Meo, Menendez, you two keep moving and don't let the formation spread out!" he ordered.

"Sir!"

The rapid movement and constant rifle fire were enough to stun the bots. Jones noted that the bots were not countering them in an orchestrated manner but rather they were counterattacking individually. That was working to the squad's advantage. And it suggested to Francis that there was not a central controlling command bot somewhere. They were all acting with a general order and working individually toward that goal.

"Two hundred meters in and ten down!" he ordered. "Stay tight and keep fucking moving."

At first the bot density seemed to increase with each step toward the center. Then they burst through what must have been the line. About seventy-five meters in, the bot density dropped to almost nothing. As best he could tell there was an expanding spherical line of bots expanding about the ship from a central point. The thickness of the line was about seventy meters or so. He realized he needed to get that information to the general somehow but all their communication systems at that depth into bot country were jammed.

His team had made it through the line with very minor scrapes to their armor. No casualties. The question now was, what to do? Did they proceed on to find out if there truly was a central nexus where the bots were coming from or were they simply growing their numbers on the line as they marched forward?

"Hold up!" He held up his left fist. "On me and stay frosty."

"What's up, Colonel?" Captain Greg Folgers bounced to his side.

"I'm not sure what our best plan of action is at this point," the lieutenant colonel said. "I'm not sure the bots are even here except where systems are being reworked. We went from thick as shit to nothing within a distance of ten meters or so. And why didn't they stay on us?"

"Sir, over here!" Lance Corporal Weeks was pointing at a hole in the floor deckplates that looked like a monster had chewed through the metal.

"Hmm. What the hell?" The entire team followed Jones quickly to the side of the hole and peered down into it. It went down at least two decks beneath them. "Looks like they must have come up through here."

"We are about two hundred meters aft of where the Warlords blew out the side of the ship, Colonel," Staff Sergeant Prichard said, pointing in that general direction. "They were on this deck, sir."

"Maybe that's why there ain't any bots here," Captain Folgers added. "Maybe Warboys smashed 'em all here."

"These things are reproducing too fast and there is little sign of battle," Jones answered. "There's no threat here. That's why there are no bots here. The main SIF generators are two decks down. This hole goes down two decks. Can't be a coincidence."

Francis gestured to his men to follow and then dropped through the opening in the deck with his rifle pointed down between his feet. He held his elbows in tight as he fell through the hole in the next deck, and then the next, and then he clanged to a stop two decks down. He quickly moved aside as Folgers, then Prichard slammed into the deckplates behind him. He scanned around the room with his helmet floods on full, casting fast-moving shadows as the white light flashed across the bulkheads.

"Stay alert," he said as he continued to scan the room. The SIF generators were another thirty meters around the corner, where he could hear metal-against-metal action. "Everybody dim their lights and go to IR."

The AEMs carefully spread out to guard the periphery of the landing spot beneath the hole in the ceiling plates above them until the entire team had descended. Then the lieutenant colonel motioned them forward. This time they moved more slowly and cautiously, like a recon squad instead of a frontal-attack squad.

As they turned the corner of the corridor there were conduits running forward and aftward and from top to bottom and from port to starboard into the room. Two large metal cubes accepted the tubes with giant flanges. Metal bots filled the room, crawling on every wall but mainly swarming around the conduits leading into the metal cubes.

"The big boxes, those are the SIF generators," LTC Jones said. "The conduits run power to SIF projectors all around the ship. There are about eight of these sites throughout the ship."

"What are they doing to it, sir?" PFC Janie Karuthers asked. "Looks like they are hotwiring it or something."

"I think that's exactly what they are doing. Maybe we can slow them down," Staff Sergeant Prichard offered.

"I agree, Staff Sergeant," Captain Folgers agreed. "Sir, we should move on them before they move on us."

"Alright. Focus on getting them off the SIF generator. Open up on them, Marines!" Jones ordered as he took a bead on several of the bots and started firing on them.

The team took sites on targets and started letting them have it. As soon as the commotion started, bots began to drop from everywhere around them. Interestingly enough, though, Jones thought, the bots working on the SIF generators didn't flinch at all.

"Sir, my suit sensors are showing a buildup of EM across all bands," Corporal Freeman shouted.

"Mine too, Corporal." Jones was doing his best to keep bots at barrel length but the occasional one was getting through and he would have to kick, punch, throw, or stomp on it. "I think it is time to drop some damned EMP of our own. Cover my ass end!"

Jones screamed like a banshee as he rushed through a wave of metal razors and pointy parts. His rifle barrel swept out a swath at chest height but they still managed to grab and bite at his armor.

"All AICs safe the suits!" the colonel thought and vocalized at the same time. He had his AIC activate the grenade launchers with the EMP grenades as he continued to push through a swarm of bots. One bot swiped a buzzsaw at head height. He ducked just as PFC Ceres dropped the bot with a rifle round. White sparks flew from the bot in every direction as the blue ion trail of the hypervelocity round tore through the bot and continued on into the wall plating on the other side.

"Shit!" Lance Corporal Weeks shouted. "Oh, my God!"

Jones could see her blue dot in his mindview turn purple to casualty status. He could see, out of the corner of his eye, her suit go down covered by bots. The purple turned black quickly.

"Aaarrrggg!" Jones screamed as he felt a searing hot metal blade cut through his thigh armor, but he didn't stop. He could hear the screams of more of his team, and the icons of all of them but two were flashing purple.

"My legs!" PFC Karuthers screamed with her HVAR firing on full auto. "Goddamn you, motherfucking, shit . . ."

"Spears, look out!" Jones heard. His DTM battlescape view showed it came from PFC Ceres.

LTC Francis Jones grabbed the blade sticking through his right leg with his armored hand and snapped it even while firing a rifle round through the body of the Rottweiler-sized bot it was attached to. Molten metal splashed from underneath it. His AIC instantly had his suit pumping stims and immunoboost into his system.

Then he popped the seal on his shoulder grenade launchers and fired three of them in the general direction of the SIF generator boxes. The grenades lobbed out across the large, dimly lit corridor and exploded in an expanding sphere of lightning that knocked everything in the room out. With his eyeballs only he could barely see in the very dim lighting of the room. Thankfully, what he could see were bots falling to the deck, dead as doornails. The screeching of metal on metal had stopped and the room was filled with humans screaming in pain, muffled through sealed and shut-down armored suits.

Thirty seconds for suit restart, sir, his AIC announced.

Status on the team?

Lance Corporal Karen Weeks and Captain Folgers are dead, sir. Sergeant Spears is critical with a metal spike through her left eye and protruding out the back of her helmet. Her vitals are stable according to her AIC. PFC Janie Karuthers is missing both legs but her suit stabilized her before the shutdown. Staff Sergeant Bill Prichard lost his left arm up to the shoulder. The rest have minor injuries on the scale of yours, sir.

Shit.

But, sir, the EMP must have damaged whatever the bots are using to jam our communications with. I have QM connectivity with the rest of the ship now.

Get me General Moore! Instantly, the room filled with several flashes of light and the sound of frying bacon. The team listed by the Blue force tracker as dead or critical vanished before his eyes. He took note of the five armored environment-suit Marines still with him. They had stopped the bots in the SIF generator room for now. *What next?* he thought.

Chapter 20

November 7, 2406 AD
27 Light-years from the Sol System
Monday, 6:49 PM, Expeditionary Mission Standard Time

"CHENG to CO!"

"Moore here. Go, Buckley." Alexander had mixed emotions about the fact that QMT teleportations were happening now fairly rapidly at the other end of the hangar. On the upside it meant that somebody had knocked out the bot jamming signal, at least for now. On the downside, the number of QMTs was indicative of large amounts of critical casualties.

"Sir, it is out of my hands now. The ship's SIFs are building up huge EM fields on five of the eight generator sites throughout the ship," Buckley explained. He sounded defeated.

"What do you mean, out of your hands, Joe? Give me a better sitrep than that." Moore feared that he already knew what his chief engineer was telling him.

"Yes, sir." Buckley started again. "The generators are out of my control and building power. If that power is rerouted in the next ten minutes the *Madira* is gonna blow, sir. It is beyond my ability to stop it now."

"Understood, Joe. I guess it is time to abandon her." Moore thought through the best plan of action. Perhaps the wounded and medical staff first.

"XO to CO!"

"Hold on, CHENG." Moore thought that tactics from the bridge were most likely moot at this point. Getting everybody off the ship was now the priority. "Go, XO!"

"Sir, we've got serious company in system with us!" the XO said very unnerved.

"What kind of company, Firestorm?"

"A fleet of ships just teleported just beyond the planetoid. Sensors show forty-seven full-sized battleships."

"Shit! From where? Are they bots?" Moore couldn't believe that. They were too far out to be attacked by, well, anybody but the remains of these bots. He couldn't believe there was any way that Copernicus or Elle Ahmi had been able to create another fleet this far out.

"No, sir. They appear to be Separatist-class ships. There is too much EM all around us to get better sensor readings. Systems are starting to go nuts up here, sir."

Alexander! I'm in contact with Allison. It is DeathRay's team, Abigail said into his mind.

Open a channel to them now!

"Hold on, XO." Moore waited a brief second before a connection opened.

"Moore to Boland. DeathRay, is that you?" Moore held his breath unconsciously.

"Hello, General. Guess what we found?" DeathRay's voice came through the com. "What's going on here, sir!"

"The *Madira* has been overrun by bots and is sabotaged. She will blow in less than ten minutes. I need to abandon ship." Moore paused and wet his lips. "Please tell me that you can help somehow."

"Yes, sir!" DeathRay replied. "We can help more than you can imagine."

"How, Boland?"

"Sir, Nancy tells me that she has already detected the crew's snap-back signatures. With your permission we will teleport them onboard the flagship of this fleet we found," DeathRay reported. "It's a long story, sir, and we'll brief you later, but this is the best thing I've got."

"Damned good, Jack. Do it, but keep the wounded and the med staff together if you can. We've taken on a lot of casualties, including Dee," Moore ordered.

"Understood, sir. Understood."

Moore waited for more from DeathRay but only heard the sizzle of bacon and saw flashing light. The next thing he knew he was standing on the bridge of a starship staring at DeathRay and Penzington. The bridge crew of the *Madira* was materializing in the room as well.

"Talk to me, folks," Moore said to Jack and Nancy.

"I put people where I thought they should be, or rather where Allison thought they should be, sir," Nancy explained. Moore trusted the former spy's AIC.

"Good enough. We have everybody?" he asked.

"Yes, sir. Allison has the entire crew accounted for. A lot of them are in bad shape, sir. As far as I can tell, this ship has a full medbay, but I'm not sure about supply stocks."

"Understood. It will have to do for now." Moore looked at his XO and bridge crew then at DeathRay. "With your permission, Captain, I'd like to put my crew at stations."

"Uh, sorry, sir. Yes, and please take command," DeathRay said hesitantly and Moore could see him glance unsurely at Penzington. She winked at her husband, Moore wasn't quite sure why, and then DeathRay stepped down from the command chair.

"Crew, take your stations or someplace that looks like your station, and get to work!" he ordered. "Somebody get me the status of the *Madira*. And get an order to the medbay that if someone is critical and we can't find what we need, for them to QMT to Earth."

"I'm on it, Captain," the XO replied.

"Where's Buckley?" Moore asked aloud. Almost instantly Abigail popped a map of the ship in his DTM and showed the CHENG's blue dot.

"I teleported him directly to engineering, General, uh, Captain," Nancy said.

"CO to Buckley! Copy?" Moore said into the com channel Allison opened up for him through the ship's system. He made a mental note that he'd have to ask how she set up coms so quickly.

"Buckley here, sir! Where the hell are we?"

"Joe, you are in the engine room of a flagship of a fleet that . . . hell, I don't know how to explain it. This is our ship for now. Get into it. Understand it. And figure out if there is a way we can stop the *Madira* from exploding. She's off the port bow about five hundred thousand kilometers," Moore ordered the CHENG.

"Uh, understood, sir. I think."

"Sir," the Science and Technology Officer Navy Commander Monte Freeman interrupted him.

"What ya got, STO?" Moore asked.

"I don't think the ship is going to blow. It looks like it is coming around toward us."

"Suicide run?" the XO offered.

"What kind of arms and shields we have on this thing?" He looked at Penzington and Boland.

"We've only been on these things a couple hours, sir. Not sure." DeathRay replied with a shrug.

"We have a full contingent of DEGs, missiles, and SIFS that could be found on any supercarrier or Separatist hauler from the Mars Separation era," Penzington said.

"Okay, Nancy, until we can train this crew, you drive, or point to the right things to do so we can fly this ship." Moore turned to his Navigation Officer. "Penny, you stay on her shoulder and do anything she tells you to."

"Aye, sir!"

"STO. How about the *Madira*? What's going on?" he asked.

"Unsure, sir, that is, other than it does appear to be headed in our general direction," Freeman replied.

"I don't like it, sir," the XO added. "Kamikaze, or they are trying to get close enough to get the bots on here with us."

"Right. We can't let that happen." Moore thought about the best plan here. He hated to lose the ship but there might not be any choice.

Sir, Abigail said. *Uncle Timmy is trying to reach you.*

Patch him through on audio.

Yes, sir.

"General Moore! This is Uncle Timmy," the *Sienna Madira's* AIC's voice came through the bridge intercom speakers.

"What can I do to help you, Timmy?" Moore wasn't sure what the call was about. Clearly the AIC was stuck on the *Madira* and he knew the pending fate of the ship.

"The SIFS and the hyperdrive conduit are all being interconnected, sir," Timmy explained. "As far as I can tell the bots are turning the ship into a super-bomb that will wipe out a large volume in this system. You have minutes before it goes. I'm doing what I can to stall and thwart them but they have full run of the ship, sir."

"Thank you, Timmy! I wish there was something more I could do for you. You have always performed your duties commensurate with the highest traditions of the service," Moore said. "I will put in for a posthumous medal in your honor. Any other requests, please log them with my AIC."

"Thank you, sir. It was an honor serving with you. Good luck," Timmy said.

"You too. Moore out."

"He's right, sir," Nancy said. "Sensors are showing a massive buildup of energy and a spacetime distortion around the hyperspace projector."

"STO?" Moore turned to his science officer.

"Yes, sir," the STO replied. "I'm working it but still getting used to the control panels on this bridge. It looks like the projector is spinning up. The bots must've somehow bypassed the power conduit that was blown out."

"If they get that hyperdrive spun up they could jaunt into us, sir," the Nav officer added.

"Right, Penny. Let's not let that happen." Moore rubbed his chin in thought. "Alright, we need to take out the *Madira*. Penzington, you know how to operate the guns on this thing?"

"Yes, General, I do." Nancy replied. "I already have it targeted and can fire on your order."

"Fire at will," Moore ordered. "STO, keep a watch on the hyperdrive system and see if we are knocking it out."

"Aye, sir."

"I hate to lose all of our stuff on that ship." Moore leaned back in the oversized captain's chair that had been designed to allow for powered armor. That crossed his mind. No other ships he'd been in before were designed that way. This ship was designed for war, a serious war. He crossed his arms while making eye contact with each member of the bridge crew. "But we can't take a chance of getting blown up or having more bots invade this ship."

Moore watched as Nancy continued to fire directed-energy weapons repeatedly at the supercarrier that had been the hero of humanity for several decades. The starship had been their home for the better part of the last eighteen months as well. The brilliant green directed-energy beams cut out across space and tore into the hull plating of the supercarrier.

"Focus on the SIF generator locations," the STO told her. Moore considered that and was just beginning to wonder if the bots had full control of the ship when the DEG beams from the Madira tore into the hull of their newly-acquired command ship.

"Evasive action! SIFS at full!" Moore brought up the DTM battlescape of the fleet and the ships.

Abby! What is the complement of this fleet? he thought.

I am in contact with the ships, all of them. Between Allison and I we can control the entire fleet as we need to, sir, Abigail said.

"Penzington, you have forty-seven ships here. Don't they have weapons too?" Moore said.

"Of course, General!" Nancy immediately turned from her console to another station. "Commander Swain, here is the targeting of this ship. I'm handing fire control over to you."

Sir, Allison wants to tie into your DTM battlescape view.

Very well. Instantly he could hear Penzington and her AIC's mindvoice. Symbols for the fleet overlaid into his view. Layers of weapons, maneuverability, and command functions for each ship popped up as a blue ship icon.

"CO, we've got fire alerts on several decks," the XO warned.

"COB!" Moore shouted.

"Sir, Chief of the Boat Coates was wounded and is in the medbay," the XO explained.

"Well, hell, Firestorm! Get me somebody on those fires." As soon as they got out of this and things settled down, he was going to have to get people up to speed on the new ship or decide whether or not just to go home.

"Fleet is targeting the *Madira* now, sir," Nancy said. "Fire at will?"

"Fire!" Moore replied without hesitation.

"We've got incoming missiles!" Commander Penny Swain said from her gunnery position. "Sensors show them as nukes!"

"Continue evasive maneuvers and target those missiles," Moore ordered. "Pull this main ship in behind the rest of the fleet and let them block for us."

"Aye, sir!"

The missiles showed in the DTM view in Alexander and Nancy's minds as the priority threat. It looked like the bots had fired the entire contingent of missiles onboard the supercarrier and they were all headed straight for them. Moore thought through tactics and what to do. For the moment he was a quarterback trapped in the pocket while a blitz was coming. He needed to throw the long ball for a touchdown just like he would have decades ago when he played for Mississippi State.

"Penzington, can we take those kinds of hits?"

"I don't think so, sir. These ships are a lot like the Seppy haulers of two decades ago. They are seriously tough and big, but that many nukes would cause a problem," Nancy said.

"Give me an impact countdown on the viewer," he ordered. One of the bridge crew tapped controls at their station, and a trajectory overlay of the missiles and the fleet ships appeared on the screen with a timer counting down. Currently they had about thirty seconds before the missiles were close enough to detonate and do damage.

DeathRay stepped in front of Nancy and reached into the open air between them as if he was grabbing something. Moore noted that three of the blue fleet ship icons in his DTM began to move. He realized that DeathRay was tied into Penzington's DTM link and was moving the ships.

"Great idea, DeathRay." Moore realized what he was doing. He was using the three fleet ships as shields. They would block the oncoming blitz. Alexander just hoped they got in front of the missiles in time.

The DEG of the fleet continued to fire on the *Sienna Madira,* bringing down upon her a rain of energy beams each with the impact energy of a small tactical nuclear weapon. Several of the SIF generators blew on the supercarrier. The blast wave clearly shook the ship.

"Ten seconds to missile detonation!" Commander Swain announced.

"XO, give an all hands brace!" Moore ordered.

"Aye, sir."

The three fleet ships moved in between the missiles and the flagship with literally two seconds to spare. The outermost of the three ships took on the majority of the missiles and was first torn in half before the secondary explosions and follow on missiles turned it completely to vapor and debris. The second and third ships were hit almost simultaneously. The first explosion tore parts of the bridge free and flung them careening through space at the flagship, impacting somewhere on the starboard side. Impact alarms sounded and fire warning icons popped into Moore's mindview.

They had lost three ships, but none of the missiles had made it through. DeathRay's sacrifice run had worked. And it looked as if there would be very little else from the supercarrier coming in the way of a threat. It was falling apart.

"Keep firing at the *Madira*. I want those bots vaporized." Moore looked through their arsenal and realized that he had plenty of weapons to choose from. But he didn't want to waste them and they had already lost three ships. The DEGs would do. They were renewable; as long as they got power, they fired. Missiles weren't, and they might need them for some reason in the future.

The green beams continued to cut through the strong ship, but it was clear it was on its last legs. One of the beams cut a swath across the midsection on the port side through to the interior. Power conduits ruptured and exploded and then a second green beam cut into the same spot, penetrating the hyperdrive projector. There was a wave of white and then purple light released in a sphere about the ship, and then the ship vaporized in an orange plasma ball of hull plating. The great supercarrier was no more. Alexander relaxed back into his seat with a sigh of disbelief.

Abby, where are Sehera and Dee?

I'm highlighting a path to them in your shipview DTM, sir, his AIC responded. A view of the interior of the flagship popped up in his mindview with a path marked leading to the middecks of the ship.

Very good, he thought.

"XO, you have the bridge. Penzington, Boland, on me."

"Aye sir!"

Chapter 21

November 7, 2406 AD
27 Light-years from the Sol System
Monday, 7:23 PM, Expeditionary Mission Standard Time

"So this fleet was just there, free for the taking?" Moore couldn't believe it. The whole thing sounded too good to be true. "You reckon anybody is going to miss them?"

"They were hidden away in a system with no planets. It was a blue star with a preplanetary accretion disc. Nobody lived there," DeathRay explained as they walked down the corridor to the main elevator shaft.

"I believe that Copernicus was building them for the war and once the war was over, he stuffed them off in space somewhere out of the way." Nancy didn't sound really sure of that, and Moore was used to hearing complete confidence from the former spy.

"Alright, we have them now. We need to find out as much as we can about them and make sure there are no surprises hidden away." Moore didn't want to wake up in his cabin, wherever that would be, surrounded by bots.

"Uh, sir, there is one more thing." Jack sounded hesitant too.

"Spit it out, DeathRay." Moore tapped the button on the elevator. The ship was laid out pretty much like any other starship and the path in his mind led him down a couple decks and toward the midsection. There was the medical bay where his wife and daughter were. He could tell by the casualty reports that there would be a whole lot more wounded that he should speak to as well.

"Well, sir, Nancy found the ships."

"Yeah, I know, that's great work." It wasn't like Nancy to want credit for anything. In fact, as a former spy, she pretty much preferred that nobody know anything about anything that she had ever done.

"Uh, yes, sir, but . . ." DeathRay hesitated again.

"Spit it out, Boland." Moore was getting just slightly more than edgy.

"She claimed them under salvage rights, sir," Jack said. "They belong to her."

"What?" Moore was at first startled by that. How could anybody claim something on a mission?

Sir, Nancy is here as a guest civilian and is under no requirement to go on missions. She is purely a volunteer, Abigail explained. *Legally, the ships are hers if nobody shows up to claim them.*

"Penzington?"

"Yes, General. I found them and they are mine." Nancy grinned at Alexander. "I plan to take at least one of them as my living quarters."

"You want to do what?" Moore was confused. "So what are we to do? Pay rent?"

"Oh, no, sir. I don't really care about them all, on the other hand, I do deserve compensation for my property. You've already destroyed three of them in combat, but I'll let those slide."

The elevator dinged and the doors opened. The three of them stepped in, not sure what to say to each other. Alexander touched the button for the deck three levels down.

"Hold on," Moore held up a hand. "I honestly don't care what you want to do with the ships. And I understand they are worth a fortune. I don't believe I can convince anybody to pay you for an entire fleet."

"I don't expect you to, General. I'm in this for the long haul and I promised you, your wife, Dee, and the flyboy here that. I'm just saying, whatever of the fleet is left once we've found what we came for, I own them. We could start a cargo business or something. Or, I might just want to go exploring." Nancy was serious. And as far as Moore's AIC could figure she was in the right legally.

"Oh, I see. Thanks, Nancy, I mean that." Moore held his hand out to hold the elevator door open for the two of them. "So, for now, can I assume we can use the fleet to whatever end is needed?"

"What's mine is yours, sir." Nancy walked out of the elevator in front of him and Boland. Alexander could tell she was enjoying the situation and it relaxed him a bit to realize that she had a sense of humor about it.

"Boland, that is an, uh, interesting woman you've got there." He elbowed the pilot.

"You don't know the half of it, sir."

"The medical bay is fully stocked, sir, but we are still finding things and figuring out the logistics. And everything is at least twenty years old," the Chief Medical Officer USN Commander Angela Muniz reported. "If we need a handful of items that we don't have or can't find, we can always do snap-backs and get them. I suspect we'll have to do that for perishable medicines and foodstuffs very soon anyway, sir."

"Good, understood." Moore nodded with a grunt. "Do we have a morale issue?"

"Well, not really, sir. Perhaps a few days of snap-back furloughs would be in order. A lot of the crew would like to go home and see family for the upcoming holidays." Dr. Muniz looked tired. According to the duty roster in his DTM she had been at the end of her regular duty shift before the fighting started. She had stayed and was now going on an eighteen-hour shift.

"Thank you, doctor. What is the word on my daughter?"

"She's fine, sir. The surgery went well and her recovery is proceeding. A day or two on the immunoboost and she will be good as new."

"Can I see her now?"

"Down the corridor on the left. Your wife is already there." The doctor looked at him as if she was going to say more. Alexander turned and looked the doctor in the eye.

"Is there something more, Doctor?"

"Well, sir, yes, there is." The doctor sighed and rubbed at her eyes. "My AIC has been cataloging all of the inventory here as best he can. There are some curious blood serums in the freezer."

"Curious how?" Moore was doing his best not to lose his temper. All of his years as a politician had trained him in patience, but he really wanted to see Dee. Then he needed to make rounds and talk to the wounded. And he also needed to make certain this ship was secured. And then the other ships had to be secured.

"They are human, sir. According to the dates and logs they are exactly fifty-five years, nine months, and thirteen days old. The names are not familiar to me, but my AIC tells me that they will be very familiar to you, sir." Muniz paused again. "I'm uploading the information to your AIC now, sir. She can explain it."

"I'll go through the information and get back with you as soon as things settle down." Moore nodded to the doctor. "As soon as you can, get some rest."

"Yes, General."

Dee didn't seem any worse for the wear. Alexander looked her over from head to toe and glanced at his wife. Sehera had a stone-cold, emotionless expression on her face as she sat there wearing a pair of blue hospital scrubs. Her armored E-suit was propped in the corner of the room.

There were no scars or stitches or marks. Immunoboost made those a thing of the past. Dee's complexion was perfect and her breathing seemed normal for somebody taking a nap. Looking at her, nobody could guess that she had just had a heart replacement and several other minor surgeries atop that.

"She looks good," he said quietly, not sure if it would wake her up.

"You don't have to whisper," Sehera said, looking up at him. "The doctor says she'll be out for at least another hour."

"Oh, okay then." Moore reached over and pulled the gauntlet off his right hand. The armored glove made a whizzing sound as the metal unzipped itself at the wrist seam. It popped and slurped as his hand pulled free from the organogel. He reached down and took his daughter's hand in his and had to choke back tears.

"She's okay, Alexander." Sehera put her hands on top of his and her daughter's. She looked up at him. "Why don't you take that suit off and stay here with us for a bit. Sally can handle things on the bridge for a little while."

"I need some clothes." Moore thought about the fact that all his clothes were on the *Madira* when it blew and he was naked in the suit.

"Already thought of that." Sehera pointed to a set of scrubs on a shelf by her suit.

"Okay."

Abby, send a message to Firestorm that I want this ship searched from bow to stern, bottom to top, and everywhere in between for bot threats of any kind. And tell her to start immediate snap-back supply runs to Earthspace.

Roger that, sir, Abigail said into his mind. After a brief pause, the AIC continued. *I'm glad Dee is going to be fine.*

Me too, he thought as his eyes watered from the lump in his throat.

Alexander clanked as softly as he could to the corner of the room and cycled the suit seals. The cycling process took a couple of seconds and ended with a pressure-releasing hiss. He slurped out of the back of the suit, stood naked behind it, and did the post-suit neck stretches as the organogel numbing agents evaporated from his skin. He counted to ten slowly and worked every muscle he could cautiously to realign his brain to the normal strength he had without the suit. It was the standard AEM procedure that he had been doing for over sixty years.

Alexander then reached up and grabbed the blue scrubs from the shelf and slid them on quietly. He wasn't worried about waking Dee up. He was so struck with emotion that he had little to say. He could smell himself. He really needed a shower. He wasn't even certain that there was water enough for the crew aboard the ship. There were so many things they had taken for granted on the *Madira* for so long. Now he wasn't sure what they did or didn't have. He'd have to put Abigail on the logistics calculations and figure all that out ASAP. But none of that mattered just yet. For now, Moore needed a break. He needed to breathe. He needed to hold his little girl and tell her that everything would be all right.

One thing was certain, he thought as he pulled his pants up. He still had his family with him. He knelt beside Dee on the opposite side of the bed from his wife. He looked up as Jawbone, DeathRay, and Penzington politely tapped at the door.

"It's okay. You can come in," Sehera told them. Nancy stepped in behind Sehera and put a hand on her shoulder. DeathRay and Jawbone stood near the entrance.

Alexander nodded gratefully to them and held her other hand. He lowered his forehead against his baby girl's hand and closed his eyes.

"Thank you," he whispered. "Thank you, God."

Chapter 22

November 7, 2406 AD
27 Light-years from the Sol System
Monday, 6:23 PM, Expeditionary Mission Standard Time

"What the . . ." Dee wavered in front of the dining chair. Light tunneled in around her and there were sounds of mecha pilots, com chatter, doctors. Dee wasn't sure if those sounds were the real ones or the ones she was presently feeling and experiencing. Something from eight years ago was happening again—or was it a memory, or was it the pain? Dee couldn't understand what was happening to her. And then there were the bots. The bots were everywhere. They were always everywhere they went. Copernicus had left them to haunt her family forever, it seemed. The bots were nothing more than the batshit crazy AIC's trail of evil. Even her grandmother hadn't been able to escape the crazy computer.

But daddy said he killed the bastard? she thought.

The lady in the red, white and blue ski mask looked menacing to her.

"Oh, I figured you didn't know," Elle Ahmi said to her after taking off the red white and blue ski mask. Dee couldn't believe her eyes. The most wanted murdering bitch in the galaxy, in human history, looked just like her mother. "Sit down, child, before you fall down and hurt yourself. I just can't understand why they wouldn't tell you at your age."

Dee was twenty-six, or was she eighteen again? She couldn't recall.

"Who, who, are you?" Dee didn't understand at all what was going on. Her mind spun wildly trying to grasp at an explanation that made sense, but there wasn't one that she could wrap her mind around. Why did Elle Ahmi look just like her mother, Sehera Moore?

"Why, I'm your grandmother, of course."

"You have to perform cardiopulmonary resuscitation . . ."

Dee fought to make some sort of sense out of what she was feeling and seeing and experiencing. And she was confused. She'd lived this before. For whatever reason, she was living it again but in scrambled order and with a mishmash of events all at once. And there were bots *every* fucking where. Dee felt as if the world was playing back to her and at the same time slipping away.

Time bounced all around her. She was twelve again and her mommy apparently didn't enjoy the adrenaline-filled amusement park ride. But Deanna and President Moore were at the central controls of the multicolored three-car spaceship, and they continuously piloted the cars around and over each other like fighter planes in combat formations.

"Shoot the alien, Daddy!" Deanna cried with joy.

"I got him!" Her daddy fired the plastic multicolored cannon with emblems of various Disney characters splayed about it, sending blue and red bolts of lightning across the virtual asteroid field and destroying the alien spacecraft with a mixture of computer-generated holography and real-life pyrotechnics. It was a good coaster. She was on the ride of her life and she was twelve and life was fantastic until the robots in the park stopped smiling. The robots came from everywhere. Flying carpets, dinosaurs, presidents, dwarves, elves, bears, mice, ducks, racecars and trucks, even spacemen and aliens came at them with deadpan, evil, emotionless relentlessness.

"Shoot the alien, Daddy!"

The bots were everywhere and she wasn't sure how old she was again, twelve or eighteen. One thing she did know was that she was terrified.

"Oh hell, I forgot all about this thing." Elle Ahmi reached up behind her head and fed her ponytail down through her mask, then pulled it the rest of the way off and tossed it on the loveseat nearest the dinner table. She shook her head and ran her fingers through her hair, letting it fall on her shoulders. "I've worn that thing for so damned long, sometimes I forget I'm wearing it."

What the hell? Dee thought to her AIC. *Bree? Bree?*

"Keep fighting, Dee!" Rackman shouted. "Keep fucking fighting!"

"There are too Goddamned many of them. We need an EM grenade!" Dee said.

"Yeah. Or a goddamned miracle!" Davy grunted, obviously in pain. "Duck, Dee!"

A metal appendage flung like a spear from one of the bots, pierced Dee's stomach all the way through, and clanked into the metal wall behind her. The rest of the appendage was attached to a bot, which just happened to have four other similar appendages that stabbed Dee through both shoulders and thighs. Dee screamed in pain and fired the M-blaster once more at a bot she could see from the corner of her eye. The bot was about to engulf Rackman's head. In the nick of time Dee believed she got it and saved Davy. She had resolved that she couldn't save herself any longer. And then out of the corner of her field of view there came a Marine in armor, parting the sea of bots like a prophet and stomping those bastards to oblivion. In Dee's mind she could hear the Marine fight song.

"Hold on, Princess, I'm coming!"

"Daddy, help me!"

Snap to, Marine! Deanna Moore! her AIC screamed in her mind. *Dee!*

Dee remembered feeling cold and seeing the supercarrier hull rush past her and then beneath her. And she was six again.

"Don't encourage her, Alexander." Her mother grunted at her father. "It is a *carrier,* honey, because it *carries* other ships and people inside it. It is a *supercarrier* because it is superdy-duperdy big."

"I understand, Mommy." Deanna smiled and went back to swinging between her parents. "I'm so hungry I could eat one of Davy's burnt hot dogs." Dee was confused again as to where she was and what version of herself she was experiencing. It all seemed to be happening at once, like watching twenty movies DTM at the same time.

Dee, the first rule of being a captive is to eat and drink if you get the chance, her AIC told her. *You never know when you'll get that chance again.*

Okay.

Dee felt the food in her mouth, or was it her TMJ bite block? She chewed at it reflexively. She could see somewhere beneath her a bloody body stuffed limply into a cockpit and on the lap of a mecha pilot. There were stars all around and the *Sienna Madira* on her right.

Also, at the same time, the view she currently had of the multicolored brilliance of the rings of the fourth planet of the Tau Ceti system filled the horizon. Two other moons were visible on the horizon as well. They were fairly bright. The penthouse she seemed to be in was atop the highest peak of a mountain, looking down over the alien planet. It reminded her of Mons City and New Tharsis and Megalopolis and Washington D.C. and Luna City all at the same time. But somehow, it was completely unique.

"Why am I here?" Dee blurted at the woman in the ski mask. She sat on her hands so they wouldn't shake. Dee was now sitting on a loveseat in the penthouse with a view. She was still terrified but briefly felt more anger and confidence. The confusion of her multiple experiences at once was overwhelming.

"Well, you are straight to the point, aren't you? Good. Don't ever change that," Elle Ahmi told her. Dee wasn't sure, but she thought the Separatist terrorist leader just gave her advice. "You are here because I wanted to see you again. Your parents and I have been at odds for so long it is time we brought it all to a, well, a climax if you will."

That wasn't a memory. Dee thought it felt, looked different, it was different than before. She'd lived through this when she was eighteen. But she didn't remember the conversation being quite like this.

"Apple One! Apple One!" She heard her mecha jock handle. She wished it was something more awesome sounding, like DeathRay. "Come on, Apple! Stay with me."

DeathRay gave her that handle the first day he visited her at the academy. He flew a training mission with the cadets, and at some point Dee ran headlong into a field of enemy mecha in her FM-12 in bot mode. She was out of ammo and overwhelmed but that hadn't stopped her from charging in, using her cannon like a warclub.

"The apple didn't fall far from the tree," Boland said. "But your daddy would have killed those motherfuckers and he would have lived to fight again. What you did was reckless, Apple One." DeathRay said it in front of the rest of the cadets and her instructors. The handle stuck from then on.

Dee could feel the landing gear of the mecha hit the hangar deck and the cockpit canopy began to cycle open. Before they came to a stop there were crew members pulling at the bloody body beneath her. Dee felt pride in how swiftly the crew of her daddy's ship moved.

"Good work, we'll take her from here."

"What climax?" Dee asked her grandmother back at the penthouse.

"Careful, Apple One, when you tug at the HOTAS like that you can spin head over feet and auger in," DeathRay warned her. She leaned back in the mecha trainer and could see Jack's face in the rearview mirror as he coached her. He'd been more like family to her than a superior officer. He was her big brother.

"Please, have a seat." Elle Ahmi, Sienna Madira, her grandmother pointed her to the couch in her seating area. The rings of the jovianesque planet played amazing light tricks against the wall. The brilliant reds from the cooling grate on the power conduit added to the color, and the smell of freshly burned protein dogs was in the air. Davy Rackman's hard, chiseled body atop her nakedness filled her to climax. She wrapped her legs around him and felt more alive than she had felt in a while. She felt him in her. It was a feeling she wanted to feel forever.

The purples and reds swirled around her as all the light tunneled off further from her. She could still feel Rackman inside her and his hands against her buttocks tugging and pulling. She felt loved—superdy duperdy loved.

"Princess, stay with us!" She could see the tears in her daddy's eyes.

From the look of it, the crazy terrorist didn't entertain much. "Would you like some food or something to drink?"

Dee, the first rule of being a captive is to eat and drink if you get the chance, her AIC told her. *You never know when you'll get that chance again.*

Okay.

"Why am I here?" Dee asked again. More and more people swarmed around the bloody body now in an operating room. Dee watched with casual interest.

"Lights please, Copernicus. Make them sixty percent. And make all the windows transparent. Our guest has never seen the rings rise over New Tharsis. And please tell the buzzsaw bots to stand down," Ahmi said out loud. Dee assumed that she was talking to her crazy AIC.

As soon as the soldiers were out of sight Dee caught some motion from her peripheral vision. Davy Rackman's gurney was rushed past the window of the OR to the one adjacent to hers and then a holowall turned off across the room. What had looked like a normal wall with a bust of some old bald guy in front of it wasn't. The wall and bust vanished. Five men in black armored uniforms stood with their weapons drawn. Clearly, they had been there all along behind that imaginary wall. Dee realized that Elle Ahmi kept her bases covered and for some reason wanted her to know that.

She could see that Rackman was still alert and screaming in pain. He quieted as the oxygen tubes and I.V.s were attached to him. Dee felt at ease knowing that Davy was alive. The doctors would fix him up. She couldn't tell him how she really felt as there was no telling what her father would say or do.

She turned back to the view from above and was fascinated by the sound of a three-dimensional printer zipping and whirring away on the counter next to some other equipment in the operating room. The shape that was beginning to print was very similar to a human heart.

"Dear, stay with us." Dee suddenly had an image of her mother's milky white skin and long dark hair looking up at her from somewhere. Or was it her grandmother?

"The heart is in place and ready to be initiated."

"I'd settle for a night of drinking and sex," she smiled at Nancy, trying not to look at the new hand that was being printed. Nancy smiled back at her and patted her on the shoulder.

"I'm a spy. Have been all my life. I've learned to pay attention to things that most people don't," Nancy told her. "Pay attention, Dee."

"You certainly are your father's daughter," her grandmother told her.

What had looked like a normal wall with a bust of some old bald guy in front of it wasn't. The wall and bust vanished. Five men in black armored uniforms stood with their weapons drawn. Clearly, they had been there all along behind that imaginary wall.

Deanna Moore, you come back to me this instant, soldier! Bree shouted at her in her mindvoice. *Dee! Dee!*

Dee felt her heart beating in her chest. It sounded or felt like the powerplant of a hovertank pounding through her powered armor suit. The voice of her AIC was buzzing in her head. Her heart continued to thump in her chest.

"Copernicus, please tell the bots to stand down," her grandmother ordered the crazy AIC. Dee paid close attention to her grandmother as they approached the wall.

What had looked like a wall simply vanished. She then realized that Elle Ahmi, Sienna Madira, her grandmother loved her in her own weird, twisted, maniacal way and that she kept her bases covered and for some reason wanted her, Deanna Moore, her granddaughter, to know that. Dee paid attention as the wall vanished.

Chapter 23

November 8, 2406 AD
27 Light-years from the Sol System
Tuesday, 8:13 AM, Expeditionary Mission Standard Time

"Attention!" Karen "Fish" Fisher shouted to the pilots assembled in the main aft hangar bay of the commandeered starship. "CAG on deck!"

DeathRay nodded at his former wingman and saluted her. He smiled thinly at her as she saluted back. DeathRay and Fish had gone way back together. They had fought through some seriously bad shit in the Seppy Exodus and subsequent wars. She was as good a pilot as he'd ever had the pleasure to fly with. Deanna Moore was probably the only other pilot he'd flown with and trained with who was as dedicated and likely to ever exceed DeathRay in skills.

"At ease." Jack turned to the assembled pilots and approached the podium. "I'm glad to see all of you here today in one piece. As far as I can tell we are only missing three pilots from our ranks and all of them are expected to make full recoveries today. They will return to active duty in three days."

Jack paused for a second and thought about Dee. He also noted that the other two pilots were search-and-rescue (SAR) pilots who also acted on rescue teams. They were moving wounded from the line the last few moments of the battle aboard the *Madira*. They were brought down by bots. Fortunately, according to the logs, the QMT teleporter started functioning just in time to save them.

"My AIC has run an inventory of equipment that managed to make it here from the *Madira*. We only managed to save four FM-12s and that is it. Those planes were on patrol at the time we lost the ship." DeathRay brought the equipment roster for the new ship up into his DTM.

Candis, bring this view up to all the pilots.

Roger that, DeathRay, his AIC said in his mind.

"As you can see in your DTM views, this ship is loaded with Stingers, Gnats, and Starlifters. Each of those are counterparts to what we are used to. The Stingers are a direct copy of FM-12s, Gnats of the VTF-32Ares-Ts, and the Starlifters are an older version of the SARS SH-102s. We have equipment."

DeathRay waited for a moment for the crew to catch up. "Look around you. The planes are right here in this hangar."

"I'm uploading protocols to each of you," he continued. "The CHENG and his crew have hacked and loaded our flight protocols into the software. Your AICs should have a bird identified that is yours. You will also find a flight suit in the locker room. Again, I have uploaded your equipment assignments to your AICs. For right now we are to get dressed, find our planes, and get familiar with them. Training sorties are being scheduled as we speak and your flight schedules will be sent to you as soon as I figure them all out. One more note here—I have worked through this with General Moore and we have decided to mix up the Flight Wing the way we used to do it. Navy aviators will fly the Gnats, and Marines will take the Stingers. Spare parts are no longer an issue. As for my service mixed squadron, the Archangels will go to the Gnats. This way we will have two Gnat squadrons and two Stinger squadrons."

DeathRay looked up at his pilots. There were forty mecha jocks and eighteen SARS and troop carrier pilots in the room besides himself. They were all seasoned pros. He knew they could handle it. Jack hesitated with his last thought but he had to ask.

"Are there any questions?"

More than forty hands went up at once.

Shit, he thought.

Roger that. His AIC agreed.

"Go ahead, Blue." He pointed at one of Jawbone's Maniacs.

"Sir, what about personal stuff? I mean, all of my clothes and other personal hygiene gear is gone. My AIC has been uploaded with my new quarters assignment and there are Seppy uniforms in the stockroom, but do we expect to get real supplies soon? I mean, sir, as a U.S. Marine, sir, I hate being out of uniform."

"Yeah, right," general agreement echoed in the hangar.

"How are we expected to fight under these circumstances?" Lieutenant Cory "Skater" Davis, Poser's wingman, added.

"Listen up!" Fish shouted to quiet the room.

"Alright, I get it." DeathRay held up his hand palm outward to calm everyone down. "We've been on this strange ship for thirty-six hours and we are living with twenty-year-old Seppy junk. We have water and we have nonperishable foodstuffs. We have mecha and we have weapons. We're soldiers and we are in the middle of space with a newly commandeered fleet that we must protect. For whatever reason, this fleet is here and what that suggests is . . . well, I don't even want to speculate. So, I promised the general that I would have our flight regiment ready to protect us at a moments' notice if we need protecting and that we would start standard patrols immediately. Now I'm certain the general is working out how to get our personal amenities brought up to Navy, Marine, and Army standards as soon as he can figure that out. If any of you have a problem with how the general is taking care of things then you have my permission to take it up with him."

With that last statement all the hands went down. DeathRay hated to invoke a threat of "the general" but no single person on the ship wanted to second-guess Alexander Moore.

"Any other questions?" DeathRay waited for hands. Only one went up. It was Jawbone.

"Lieutenant Colonel Strong?"

Delilah stood up. "With all due respect, Captain." She stared across the room with a look that could cut through steel. The colonel appeared to be ready to begin a good old-fashioned Marine Corp ass whuppin' if anybody crossed her path. DeathRay suspected what was coming. "Sir, firstly, I'd like to apologize for my Maniacs sounding overly needy. I *will* deal with that."

"Very well, Lieutenant Colonel Strong." DeathRay was glad that he wasn't Blue at that moment. He suspected that the Marine wouldn't get a break for another twenty-four hours or more for his question. "Is there anything else, Jaw?"

"Yes, sir." Delilah replied gruffly. "I was just curious at what point you squid pilots were gonna quit whining so that us Marines can get back to work!"

"Oo-fuckin'-rah, ma'am!" somebody else shouted. Obviously, it was one of the other Marine pilots.

"Hooyay, sir. I can personally guarantee the CAG that the Navy pilots of the Demon Dawgs are good and Goddamned ready to get at it." U.S. Navy Commander Wendy "Poser" Hill stood up too. Poser glared as menacingly as Jawbone had at her pilots. "Dawgs?"

"Hooyay," all of the Navy squadron affirmed enthusiastically or with fright, or both.

"Go to your assignments," DeathRay said dryly. "Dismissed."

What the fuck have we gotten ourselves into, he thought.

Don't worry, Jack, they're all good troops, Candis replied.

"Dismissed!" the XO released the bridge crew and several of the support teams as he turned to the COB. "Chief, this is straight from the general. I want you to personally take a squad of AEMs, a fire team, and an engineering team and scrub another one of these ships from top to bottom. Make sure it is bot-free, report to me, and then move to the next one. Got it?"

"Be my pleasure, sir. You know I spent some time on some old Seppy haulers after the war. Those were rustbuckets. But I gotta tell ya, Firestorm, these ships look good as new for them to be twenty years old."

"Weird as hell, if you ask me, Jeff," Firestorm replied. "Be careful over there."

"Roger that, XO."

"XO, we have brought the fleet to a stop at a parking orbit ten thousand kilometers from the planetoid facility and one hundred thousand kilometers from the last location of the *Sienna Madira*," Nav officer Commander Penny Swain said over her shoulder. "We're tracking the debris field for any trajectories non-Keplerian. If there are any bots left over out there we'll find them."

"Good, Nav. We should be plenty far enough not to worry about any stray bots. If you find any, you have open fire permission to call DEGs on them. Ground Boss?" The XO then turned to commander of the Ground Combat Mecha U.S. Army Brigadier Gen. Tonya "Hailstorm" Briggs.

"XO?"

"As soon as Warboys is ready to check out the Warlords on the Orcus droptanks you are clear to go. I'd like for them to have another go on that facility down there just to see if there are any other bots outside. Then we'll sweep it again with the AEMs. The general wants to make this our staging ground." Firestorm turned and sat down in the oversized captain's chair. She really wished the general would get back up there with details of what the next step for the expedition would be. Were they going home or pushing forward?

"Roger that, XO. General Warboys says they are two hours from being ready to drop," the ground boss replied.

"Well, kick him in the ass and tell him to get a move on it."

Chapter 24

November 8, 2406 AD
27 Light-years from the Sol System
Tuesday, 8:15 AM, Expeditionary Mission Standard Time

"Do we need to kick you in the ass so you'll get a move on it?" Rondi said to the CHENG. The Marine had never seen Buckley this way. He'd been moping about for the past day and a half like somebody had shot his dog and killed his grandma both at the same time. The *Sienna Madira* had been his true love and now it was gone. Rondi had forty-five minutes before she had to report to duty and she had hoped to spend a few minutes having lunch with Buckley.

"Rondi, there is so much to do here that I don't know where to start." Buckley looked at her and shrugged his shoulders. The two of them were in what Joe had commandeered as the CHENG's office with the door closed.

"It's like eating a bear or running a marathon, Joe," Rondi told him. "One bite at a time and one step at a time. Just find a place and start moving forward." Sometimes the Marine had little patience when folks just wouldn't put one foot in front of the other. But that likely wasn't Joe's problem. Joe was the hardest-working engineer she'd ever met. Rondi had seen him work for seventy-two hours without taking a nap until the doctor forced him to.

"I could run the marathon; I just need to know where the starting line is." Joe shrugged again.

"Okay, if this was your first day on the *Madira*, what would you do?"

"Uh . . ."

"Wait, Joe, that is it. Your AIC has the logs. Your first day on the *Madira,* what *did* you do? Just start there." Rondi looked him in the eye and could see that he was tired and sad. "You couldn't save her, Joe. Even frying yourself with X-rays wouldn't have saved her. She was overrun with a hostile enemy force and there was nothing we could have done."

"Uh-huh." Joe grunted. "You're right, though. My first day on the Madira, I ran a diagnostic on the propulsion systems. Then the weapons, SIFs, and power plants subsequently."

"There ya go!" Rondi smiled and winked at him. "Maybe I'll ask for a promotion to CHENG."

"You wouldn't like it. It's not dangerous enough for you and you never get to eat your own vomit. Maybe you should consider being a mecha jock." Joe finally smiled. She knew that her puking deathblossom in a freefalling AEM suit had become infamous in her squad and figured it would make its way around the ship soon enough. Apparently, the story had already made it to engineering.

"With all due respect, CHENG, sir," Rondi grinned with a raised eyebrow, "up yours."

"Gunny, if you need anything, and I mean anything, you only have to ask for it." Alexander looked at Tommy Suez and held out his hand. Tommy shook it like a Marine. "That is not a platitude, Tommy. I mean that from all my heart. Thank you for what you did for my little girl."

"With all due respect, General," Tommy stood stiffly. "Your *little girl* was giving the bastards hell like any good Marine. I was proud to be there fighting with her, sir, and I would by God do it again. And that young SEAL was a hardened ass-kicker too, sir."

"Yes, I will be talking to Lieutenant Rackman soon." Moore rubbed at the stubble on his chin and then he tugged at the Seppy uniform. He hated that thing. He would change into a Marine uniform as soon as the first supply ship returned from Earthspace via QMT. Supply teams should be coming in literally as they spoke. He made a mental note to send his chief of staff after a uniform. "By the way, Gunny, what were those two doing out there in the abandoned part of the ship? I mean, what were they doing when you found them?"

"Sir, uh, they were doing the same thing I was."

"And that was?"

"Close, quarters techniques, sir," Tommy replied. Moore wasn't sure he believed it, but it wasn't the top sergeant's place to out two officers. "Thanks, Top. Why don't you take a three day R and R and snap back home?"

"If it's all the same to you sir, I don't really have any family and I'd just as soon stay here."

"Suit yourself, Top. But, I don't want you hitting a lick at a snake for three days, and that's an order." Moore saluted the Marine and then shook his hand. "Dismissed."

Alexander waited for the senior NCO to leave his newly acquired office. The captain's office just off the bridge was fairly spacious, with a very large window on the port side. He looked down at the planetoid facility below and wondered just how much longer it would be before the Warlords dropped as he had ordered.

A lot was going through his mind. Dee and Rackman had been working on the A-recon team together for nearly eighteen months and it was common for teams to hang out off duty. But if Dee and Rackman were involved they shouldn't to be on the same squad. Moore didn't care who his daughter fraternized with as long as it didn't put either of them in danger. He had come down hard on Dee's boyfriends in the past, but that was before she was old enough to know how to handle them. Alexander trusted that she was a full-grown woman now, and as Top had just said, one hell of a Marine. She could take care of herself. The memory of her as a little girl telling him that she wanted to be like him flashed in his mind.

"Come in, Dad," she had said to him as he stood outside her bedroom in the White House. She was twelve and it had been a long, horrible couple of days after Elle Ahmi had attacked them at Disney World. Dee had recovered from the ordeal as though it were no big deal. She was ready for bed and sitting up against the headboard, reading. Alexander remembered the book she was reading like it had been yesterday, even though it was nearly fifteen years ago. He had looked at the book with some interest. The cover of it featured popular science drawings of modern military mecha and weapons.

"Some light reading, baby?" he had asked.

"Uh, no. I'm just educating myself on all the mecha that I've seen."

Deanna set the book down and looked up at her father. Alexander would never forget the look in her eyes—pure determination. "Dad?"

"What, baby?"

"I'm not a baby, Dad."

"I know, princess. But you'll always be my baby." Moore had smiled. The memory made him smile again.

"Uh, Dad." Dee frowned at him the way kids do when they reach that age where they don't want to be called a baby. Again Moore smiled to himself. He felt emotions building up and his heart rate increased a bit. He had tears in his eyes beginning to blur his vision slightly.

"What do you need? Are you okay?"

"Oh, sure. I wanted to ask you about the future. Do you think you will win the election?" Moore was looking at his next term as president. After the events of the past couple days he was likely to be a shoo-in.

"It looks like it. Is that what's bothering you?"

"No. I was just wanting to tell you that I want to be like you when I grow up." Dee looked up at him seriously. It was this moment that he would remember in vivid detail no matter how old he got. He would never forget the look on his little girl's face.

"Oh? You think you want to be President of the United States?" he asked her proudly.

"No, Dad. Yuck, politics is gross." Dee made a sour face. Moore thought back on it and he was certain he must have seen this coming. But he knew he hadn't. If he had, and if he knew then what he knew now, he would have headed it off earlier on.

"Then I don't understand what you mean." Alexander shrugged his shoulders, holding his hands palms up.

"I want to be a Marine," Deanna had told him. And from that day forward, her every waking thought was on being a Marine mecha jock. Dee had studied every aspect of what it would take to become the life-taking, heartbreaking soldier her father had been. The apple hadn't fallen far from the tree. But Alexander really wanted his princess to have a long and happy, fulfilling life. Her recent activities had been completely opposed to that goal.

Moore understood doing your own thing. It was what he and his wife had always done. There was no way he could stand in the way of his daughter's path. So, he had to let her walk down it, or barrel ass down it in full armored mecha, blasting the piss out of anything in her way. That didn't mean that he couldn't take precautions to help ensure her longevity. Being a former president and the ranking officer of the mission helped. So, he clearly needed to get a little more involved in her safety.

Alexander decided he'd have DeathRay assess the situation. Dee needed to be spending more time in fighter planes anyway. She was safer in an armored flight suit inside her armored flying mecha than she was just in an AEM suit. Alexander wasn't sure he could take many more of her close calls. Emotionally, he was a bigger mess than he'd ever been in his life, and that included the time he had spent in Elle Ahmi's torture camp on Mars.

His daughter had been seriously injured twice in a period of a week. He'd had two fairly large engagements with casualties. And he had lost his ship. Events seemed to be leading them toward something more complex and perhaps more sinister than he had originally considered. It felt somehow like one of his mother-in-law's plans within a plan within a plan. He couldn't help but feel they were following intentionally placed breadcrumbs along some long-forgotten trail of evil.

As things stood at present, there was still a chance to complete the mission. Alexander just really had to get a handle on their situation and determine the right course of action. As far he could see it, the mission had three functions. One was to find all remnants of the AIC bots and Seppy war machine. Two was to remove those remnants from existence. Those first two were the main component of the mission as most people back home, including Congress, understood. Three was to determine just what the extra-terrestrial communication to then-senator Sienna Madira had to do with all of this mess. The third, only the current president, his national security advisor, the secretary of defense, the director of National Intelligence, and the chairpersons of the House Permanent Select Committee on Intelligence and the Senate Select Committee on Intelligence had any notion of. The only other people that knew of the third reason were on board the ship with him. Well, there was one other person, Thomas Washington, his former Secret Service bodyguard, but Thomas had been left behind to keep an eye on things back in the Sol System. He was given specific orders to watch for signs of Copernicus' influence back home and deal with it as he needed to. Besides, Thomas hadn't wanted to come along on this mission because he was done soldiering for a while. He had told Alexander that he would just have to take care of himself and his family without him on this mission. Alexander suspected the bodyguard didn't want to be cooped up in a spaceship for such a long-duration deep-space mission. And it had turned out to be a *very* deep space mission.

Chapter 25

November 8, 2406 AD
27 Light-years from the Sol System
Tuesday, 8:15 AM, Expeditionary Mission Standard Time

Alexander picked up his coffee mug. The mug was from the White House and was his favorite. Alexander had no idea how the mug managed to escape the exploding *Sienna Madira* and make it to the commandeered ship. One of his staff members deserved either a medal for above and beyond or a slap in the face for risking life and limb for something as stupid as a coffee mug. In the end, the mug *was* his favorite and he *was* glad he still had it. But the coffee in the mug, on the other hand, tasted like horse piss with the foam farted off of it. And, it was cold.

"That's horrible," he spat the coffee into the cup and sat the mug down.

Abby, order us some coffee and play back the Senator Madira AIC video feeds from the classified archives DTM.

Roger that, sir.

Alexander had watched the feeds a thousand times. Every single time he had watched it he felt like he discovered some new nuance of his mother-in-law. The feeds were in the classified archives of the presidential library. As far as Moore could tell, he was the only person to ever watch them. The files were hours and hours of meetings, senate hearings, panels, committees, speeches, and even some personal logs. But the most important ones happened when Copernicus, her new experimental internal AIC, came on the scene. Back in those days,

AICs were worn like wrist watches, ear buds, jewelry, or hats, and in some cases they were just kept in pockets.

The log showed a date from over one hundred and eighty years prior. Moore was not even an itch in his daddy's pants at the time. Moore started the log at a few seconds before key points that he had identified over the last decade.

In his mind flowed images and sounds and experiences of Senator Madira inside the CIA headquarters building. She was, at the time, the chairperson for the Senate Select Committee on Intelligence and she was being briefed on a new technology.

"What is it I'm looking at, Doctor?" Madira asked, looking through a glass dome at a device about the size of a quail egg with small tendrils jutting out from it in several places. "It looks like some sort of plastic-coated mechanical squid."

"I'd often thought it looked like a jellyfish but I can see squid, Senator," Dr. Robin Hughes replied. Moore had looked up all the details of every individual in the footage. Hughes had been the principal investigator of the AIC implantation experiments. He also was the first to implement the quantum-orchestrated reduction-processor architecture for artificial intelligence. He had based it on technology being developed for long-range instantaneous encrypted communication of large amounts of data.

"Well, what is it?" Madira asked impatiently.

"It is the fanciest, smartest, most amazing AIC ever invented. And it interfaces directly to the human mind."

"How does it do that?" she asked.

"The AI is built on a processor architecture never before implemented and it communicates using quantum physics aspects of the human brain. This baby literally communicates directly into your mind. I suspect it would feel like telepathy of a sort." The scientist was rather proud of himself.

"What do you call it?" Madira asked.

"It has a long serial number and a boringly technical descriptor."

"No. I mean, if it is an AIC it is alive, right? Then what is its name?" Madira shrugged. "I want to talk to it."

"Oh, well, we've only hooked it up to monkeys and pigs. We've never used it on a human yet, although the simulations show that it should work just fine."

"You mean to tell me you have never talked to this thing?" Madira rubbed her hands together and looked closer into the dome at the device.

"Oh, no, ma'am. We have an interface system that will allow you to speak to it through standard audio intercoms. You want to talk to him? His name is Copernicus."

"Copernicus?"

"Well, I thought it was fitting as humanity might no longer be the center of the universe." Again, Moore noted how smug and arrogant the man was. If the poor son of a bitch only knew what his invention was going to do to humanity. The scientist tapped a few buttons and then turned to the senator. "He can hear us now."

"What? Just talk out loud?" Madira asked.

"Yes, ma'am."

"Hello, Copernicus. I am Senator Sienna Madira. Nice to meet you," she said, a bit uncomfortably.

"Hello, Senator. It is nice to meet you. I have heard so much about you. In fact, it is my understanding that you are mainly the reason my project was funded," Copernicus said. It was indeed the voice that had been in Alexander's mind a few days before.

"What project is that, Copernicus?" Madira appeared to be clueless.

"Oh, I am the one who datamined the system-wide webs and implemented the algorithms to locate the Martian Terraforming Guild's hidden bank accounts." Copernicus sounded both matter-of-fact and proud at the same time.

"I see. I was under the impression that this was done by a supercomputer team."

"Well, they started looking at the problem, but as I watched what they were doing across the webs I realized that they would be at it for years, likely decades. So I created my own algorithms and did my own search. Then I infiltrated the supercomputer operating system and implanted my solutions set. The original team never knew they had not accomplished their goal." Dr. Hughes looked shocked and gasped. Clearly, Copernicus had never revealed that to his creator. But more important to history and to Alexander was the absolute look of lust on Madira's face.

"I see," she said. Moore zoomed in on her face and saw a look in her eyes that he believed was the beginning of her demise. “It was nice meeting you, Copernicus. I have to go to another meeting now.”

“It was nice meeting you, Senator Madira. I hope we speak again sometime.” Copernicus said.

“Oh, we will,” Madira replied.

Abby, step forward three years to the next bookmark, Alexander thought to his AIC.

Yes, sir.

“The surgery went fine, as far as we can tell, Senator Madira.” Dr. Hughes and two other surgeons stood over Madira’s recovery-room bed. Madira was sitting upright in the bed as she buttoned the sleeves of her blouse. She was already dressed.

“Ma’am, I wish you would reconsider staying overnight for observations,” one of the doctors pleaded with her.

“Look,” Madira started in on them. It was the first time Moore thought he could see hints of the Elle Ahmi directness. “I’m fine and I don’t have time to hang around in a hospital all night. Besides, Copernicus is fine, he can read my vitals, apparently, and he says I’m fine. It is a bit weird having all this information in my head at once, but it is also very exciting.”

Moore thought about that last statement. He recalled getting Abigail his first day at the armored E-suit training facility. Instantly being able to know anything you needed to know was an amazing and overwhelming experience. Kids nowadays just took it for granted. And Madira was the first human to ever do it. She was a brave, if not crazy, trailblazing woman. She did bring on a whole new era in human history.

“But, Senator, we need to run some more tests.”

“Sorry, fellas, I just don’t have time for that. I will keep in touch and let you know how it all works out,” Madira answered almost blankly and with a faraway look in her eyes as people do when they are conversing with their AICs. Moore noted that the doctors seemed to notice the look; but didn’t stop her from leaving.

Abby, fast forward six months to the next bookmark.

Roger that.

✧ ✧ ✧

"I don't really care to run for president, Johnny. My constituents need me. But I appreciate the vote of confidence and your vote." Madira was overlooking what Moore had discovered to be a quantum membrane detection experiment. Madira had a very keen interest in technology and science, that was for certain, and She had positioned herself on the right committees to see the next-next-generation classified technologies only. "So, tell me how this experiment is going to work?"

"Well, Senator Madira, the hadron collider will create an explosion in this region of the detector banks," a physicist identified as Dr. Malcolm Truss explained. "The explosion of the particles and antiparticles will hopefully be energetic enough as to allow us to see the actual phenomenon that causes space to be, well, space. It is like the Higgs particle that causes mass to have mass. We are looking for whatever it is that causes space to have space."

"So, what happens when you find this particle?" Madira said, with the blank AIC stare on her face. Clearly, Copernicus was asking the question.

"Well, ma'am, we think that if this works we will be able to generate vortices in space that could connect from one point of the universe to another point instantaneously. It would be great for communications and for maybe someday teleporting materials and even people." The scientist appeared very happy as a buzzer sounded and an announcement to commence countdown came over the intercom.

"This is it, I guess?" Madira asked, human once more.

"Yes, ma'am."

The two stood quietly looking out the large window of a control room at a large metal chamber covered with instrumentation. Moore paid close attention at the look on Madira's face. Later logs would reveal that Madira had Copernicus hack into the control systems for the experiment so he could monitor the raw data in real-time.

The countdown hit zero and red lights flashed all around. The computer screens began to fill with data and almost instantly Madira's face smiled. Moore was certain that she understood the outcome of the experiment instantly. And then something else happened.

Sirens sounded and the hadron collider control software went offline. The detector banks continued to show particles flooding the chamber at speeds beyond that of lightspeed in vacuum space. Cerenkov radiation detectors went off the scale.

The most interesting information from the footage was the reaction Madira had. At first she seemed to back away against the far wall. Her eyes glazed over and her face was blank as though she were completely immersed in a DTM simulation with her AIC. While she appeared to be removed from the entirety of the events and was nonplussed by the urgency, the scientists and engineers around her were running scared and shutting down every switch, panel, and button and pulling every plug they could manage. Like all particle accelerators of the past, the scientific community had convinced themselves that particle collisions could never go critical and become highly dangerous because it hasn't happened in nature. While stars, black holes, and other cosmic events do release energy, they have never simply "run away." But the reactions taking place in the collider were anything but natural.

"Holy shit!" one scientist even shouted, "It's gonna blow! The plasma inside is continuing to grow nonlinear and the ions are accelerating past the relativistic limit! We've gotta get out of here!"

The particle collisions were at energy levels higher than ever before measured by humanity, and there were new quantum-mechanics phenomena occurring. Somehow the particles were not being slowed by relativistic effects. They continued to run away past the light limit. As the charged particles moved past, through, or collided with other instruments at such high energies, extremely high electromagnetic fields were induced on the circuits. This being an unexpected phenomenon meant that the circuits were not designed for such large fields. Fuses, components, and wiring overloaded and in many cases exploded.

The runaway particle collisions continued for more than ninety seconds, blowing systems all around the hundreds of kilometers of particle accelerator pathways. Madira still looked as if she were in a detailed conversation with her AIC. But there was more to it. Her left arm appeared to be quivering and her fingers were flexing and trembling. Moore zoomed in on her face and could see a thin stream of bright red blood oozing from her right nostril over her moving lips. The first time he saw it he thought her lips were simply quivering from whatever anxiety attack she was having or from some interaction with her experimental AIC that had yet to be discovered and fixed. Over the years and with many further views and analyses he realized there was more to it. She was mouthing words. He and Abigail had analyzed the footage a thousand times, and using lip, reading techniques, had managed to put together what she was saying.

"Who are you?" her lips mouthed closely.

"No. Copernicus? Is this some sort of joke?" Then there was a pause in lip movement. "I see."

"You are where?" Another pause, but it was clear she seemed to be speaking in her mindvoice to somebody other than her AIC. Her arm continued to twitch and she reflexively grabbed it with her right hand. Red blood continued to drip onto her upper lip.

"Thirty one . . . light-years . . . how are you doing this? Quantum membrane matter-energy wavefunction transfer? Copernicus? Copernicus?"

Then her lips quit moving clearly enough for the software to translate. It also appeared as though she had begun to feel pain, as the expression on her face became more of a grimace. There were a few seconds of indecipherable conversation. Then . . .

"What have you done to Copernicus?"

"Why must we do that?"

"That is impossible. It is too much data to transmit so quickly." Then there was a brief pause. There was still excitement going on around her in the hadron collider control room and nobody was paying her any attention. The grimace of pain on her face turned to more a frown of concern, and her brow furrowed as if she had grown angry.

"I understand now."

"Senator Madira? Are you okay, ma'am?" Dr. Truss shook her shoulders. "Do you need help?"

"What? Help?" Madira appeared to come to her senses. "No, thank you, I'm fine."

"Your nose is bleeding!" The scientist handed her a tissue from a box on a nearby desk. Madira took it and dabbed the blue tissue against her nose. She quickly regained her composure.

"I am fine, Doctor. I trust everything is under control here?"

"It is more amazing than we had ever believed, I think. But it will take months to understand all this data and even more time to repair all the damage." The scientist sounded excited.

"At this moment, Doctor, this project and all the results are classified above Top Secret. I want this put in a Special Access program with tight controls and I want to know the name of every person who knows what happened today," Madira said sternly.

"On whose authority?"

"Mine. And I want continuous updates directly to the SSCI chair, me, from now on. I mean daily. If I don't get them, I'll be looking into your budgets very closely. Understand me?"

"Uh, yes, Senator." The scientist was shocked and a bit scared.

"Now, if you'll excuse me, I have to call a press conference and announce my candidacy for president." Madira smiled at the man and then, just as though nothing had happened out of the ordinary, offered him her hand, turned and walked out.

That was it. That was the moment in history. Alexander Moore had looked at every piece of data he could find on Madira and there was never any other footage, audio, or written documentation suggesting anything out of the ordinary with her. There was also very little information available on the events of the day. Even as president, Moore couldn't find technical documentation for whatever happened after that experiment at the particle accelerator facility. It was his guess that it somehow led to the quantum-membrane technologies that Elle Ahmi used throughout the latter part of the Separatist War.

One thing was for certain, something happened with her and her AIC that day that actually affected her physically enough to cause her to tremble and have a nosebleed. Something told her there was something interesting at thirty-one light-years away. Something else had made her angry and driven to become president and perhaps later to become Elle Ahmi. It was unclear when Copernicus began to take over her mind, and it was unclear what plans within plans had begun as hers and were later twisted into those of the AIC.

The something that happened to her that day drove human history for the next one hundred and eighty years and was still driving it.

One other thing bothered Moore. Madira and Copernicus had been so good at overcoming obstacles and covering their tracks. Why had they left any information in places to be found? Had Madira done that? Had Elle Ahmi? Or had it been Copernicus? There were breadcrumbs hidden across history for Moore to find. That led him to suspect that either some manifestation of Madira/Ahmi/Copernicus had gone back and put the data in places that she/it knew he would look.

Okay, Abby, enough of that, he thought to his AIC. *Bring up the data on the blood serum samples that Dr. Muniz wanted me to review.*

Yes, sir. I have gone through them and I understand why she thought they would be of interest to you, sir. The blood samples in the catalog each match precisely with DNA of the 91st *Tharsis Recon Battalion Armored Environment Suit Marines.*

What? Moore wasn't sure he heard that right. *Are you sure?*

Yes, sir. It is your old AEM battalion, sir. Twenty-nine of the thirty members of your squad are there, sir. Your blood is the only one missing from the samples. Abigail seemed as perplexed as he was. She had been there with him on Mars all those years ago. She had been there with him through the torture, through his escape and evasion that lasted for over thirty days, and through his raging spasm where he killed everybody in the encampment but Ahmi herself. Ahmi had managed to get the drop on him and get away.

There are blood samples from everybody?

Everybody but you, sir.

Why not me? Moore thought about that. Ahmi had him captured for more than a month. He had been beaten, cut, shot, burned, broken, and all other means of nasty torture he didn't care to recall. If she'd wanted his DNA there had been plenty of it all over the floor and walls of his cell. The history of Mars was red with blood.

Perhaps because you escaped, sir, Abigail suggested.

Perhaps.

Chapter 26

November 10, 2406 AD
27 Light-years from the Sol System
Thursday, 9:15 PM, Expeditionary Mission Standard Time

"But you don't understand, Davy." Deanna looked out the portal along the wall in her quarters. She'd found the most spacious pilot's quarters for her rank she could. There were plenty of empty rooms. The new starship was slightly longer than the *Madira* had been, only a little bit narrower, and roughly the same height. There was roughly the same general supercarrier configuration and design inside and out. While it looked something like a Separatist battle hauler, at the same time it had a U.S. Navy Supercarrier feel to it. As with the *Madira*, the ship had been designed for over twenty thousand. There were only about five hundred aboard. Most of the officers were able to choose a room that was up a scale or two for their rank.

"I don't understand what, Dee?" Rackman looked at her, perplexed. Dee was sure she wouldn't be able to make anybody understand what she was feeling. And she couldn't tell Rackman the entire story anyway. She couldn't tell him who Elle Alhmi really was. Even the President of the United States of the Sol System didn't know that part.

"It wasn't a dream. It was more, well, uh, real." Dee hesitated. She knew it sounded crazy, but she had decided years before that where her grandmother was concerned, anything was possible. "It was more like a message. Or, hell, I just don't know."

"Tell me about it, Dee." Rackman stood close to her and put his arm around her. The two of them stared out the portal for a long moment. Several Gnats and Stingers zipped by. One of the Gnats rolled over and transfigured into bot-mode, looking like it had passed out and fainted headfirst. Then it twisted to turn and face the three Stingers behind it. Dee knew the move. DeathRay had taught it to her. He said it was called a "Fokker's Feint" from a long-past obscure pop-culture reference, like the deathblossom was. Most pilots thought it was named after a pilot who had first done it, but it wasn't. She recalled DeathRay telling her something about life imitating art more often than the other way around. That thought made her wonder where the line of art and life was drawn with her grandmother.

The feinting mecha continued to spin and track targets with its cannon held in the right hand. Several of the Stingers broke off and flew out of the engagement zone. The maneuver had been performed flawlessly because, clearly, the retreating mecha had just been killed in the war game.

Bree, who is that? she thought.

That is Commander Fisher, Bree replied.

"Fish," she said out loud. "DeathRay taught her everything she knows."

"You should be out there, Dee," Rackman said dryly.

"Well, the general has seen to that. No more ground-pounding Marine recon for me if he can do anything about it. I'm strictly a mecha jock from now on."

"It has to be tough to send your little girl into the shit." Rackman raised an eyebrow at her. "And, mate, the two of us have seen some shit in the past eighteen months."

"How'd we get on the pointy end of the spear, anyway?" Dee asked rhetorically. Davy had no idea, but Dee knew that if anything about Copernicus and her grandmother were uncovered, she or DeathRay or Penzington or someone "in the know" had to be there to mop up the details and keep it under wraps. She had been the most likely soldier for the job.

"Because we're good at it," he snorted. "Good, my aunt Shiela's ass, we're great at it."

"Yeah, I guess. If you can count losing limbs and nearly dying on multiple occasions as 'good at it,'" she replied sourly.

"Actually, I do. We got the mission done and we're still alive to not talk about it. Goes with the job description, mate."

"Well, I'm really good at flying too." Dee turned back and watched the mecha war-gaming a bit more, quietly staring out the portal.

"Then you should be out there. All the more reason," Rackman said.

"You know as well as I do. We're benched for another two days." Dee turned from the portal and sat on the edge of her desk. Her quarters were clearly made for an O5 or above. She'd never had a room large enough to squeeze a desk in, even at her current O3 rank. "It's okay. I need to sort through this stuff in my head anyway. You think this ship has a hidey-hole with a barbecue grill in it?"

"You need to talk to somebody about it, Dee. Maybe it's PTSD or something." Rackman looked nervous even before he had all the words out of his mouth. She didn't have Post Traumatic Stress Disorder. Any other time she might have let him have it for bringing it up, but for now, she just needed some calm.

"I don't have PTSD, Davy," she said calmly. "I'm not in denial either. It's something else. Something different. I feel like there is something I'm supposed to be doing and I can't get a grip on what it is."

"You mean that you think the dream—"

"It wasn't a dream!" Dee corrected him mid-sentence.

"Vision, out-of-body experience, whatever you want to call it, that you had when you flatlined was somehow a message from your dead grandmother to help you do something way the fuck out here twenty something light years or wherever from Earth?" Rackman had tried to remain calm, but Dee could tell it was too fantastic a tale for him. She couldn't tell him who her grandmother was and how she had manipulated everything else in her life and her parents' lives for decades, so there was no way he could understand. She needed to talk to somebody else.

"You're right, Davy." She turned to him and put her arms on his large Navy SEAL's shoulders. "I think I do need to talk to a professional about it."

"Sheila, you'll be alright." He looked into her eyes and told her. Dee looked up at him and smiled. Then she kissed him softly.

"I told you not to call me that."

"Right, but you are gonna talk to the doc?"

"I didn't say that, but I'll talk to a pro!" She slid her hands down slowly across his bulging pectorals and then behind his back and pulled him closer to her. "But I don't have to do it now. We are on recovery leave, you know. What do you say we do some, uh, recovering?"

"Now you're talkin,' sheila!" Rackman picked her up as she jumped and wrapped her legs around his waist, and turned and rolled her onto her bed all in one smooth motion.

"I told you!" Dee kissed him hard and fast as the two of them fumbled at pulling her top over her head. "Don't call me that."

"Don't call me that," Alexander told his wife. "You never call me 'general,' so when you do, it means you're pissed about something. Well, or the other thing but I can tell it ain't that right now."

"Well, *Alexander*," Sehera said overemphasizing his name, "you've had years to keep your daughter out of harm's way or to discourage her or even forbid her, but you wait until now to do it?"

"Sehera, I'm not forbidding her from doing anything. I just told DeathRay that the mecha jocks needed to be doing more mecha-jock stuff and less forward recon." Moore shrugged his shoulders.

"You know good and damned well that Captain Jack Boland took that as a direct order to sideline your little girl!" Sehera almost screamed. She never cursed. Moore realized that he had stepped in it up to his eyeballs.

"I don't know any such thing. How the CAG decides to take general comments from a superior officer is up to him. I can't read his mind." Moore knew she wouldn't buy that. Hell, he didn't really buy it himself. DeathRay had done exactly what he had hoped he would following his discussion with him. Moore had told him that from now on, he was going to be sending in the AEMs first, and when things were clean, then the "family" could go in.

"I never tell you how to run things. I've never second-guessed you in politics or in soldiering. I've never even second-guessed your fathering skills. But this time could be detrimental to Dee. Did you figure what it would do to her?"

She doesn't know about Rackman, Abigail said into his mindvoice.

I guess she doesn't. I thought I was always the last to know about those things.

"And stop talking to Abigail! I'm talking to you right now." Sehera sat on the edge of the bed and put her face in her hands. Alexander could see she was almost in tears. This wasn't like her. It certainly wasn't like the woman who helped him escape the torture camps and set up an attack to kill over seventy people, possibly including her own mother. There was more to this.

"Sehera. You're right. I do have to think about how this affects Dee. But there is more that you don't know." Moore looked at his wife as she looked up at him. There was clearly more he didn't know. Sehera hadn't cried ever that he knew of. The only time he could think of was before Dee was born. He wasn't even sure what it was that caused it. That seemed years ago.

"What don't I know?" she asked.

"The SEAL." Moore paused. "Lieutenant Davy Rackman. He's on the A-team recon squad. He's been Dee's right hand all this time."

"Yes, he was there with her and was hurt badly as well. What about him?" Sehera asked.

"They are, uh, well," Alexander hadn't said it out loud yet. It was hard to say for whatever reason. After all, he was talking about his little girl. "They are an item."

"You mean they are having sex?" Sehera said matter of factly. "So what? She's a grown woman now and has had many sex partners. I thought you knew that."

"It's more than that, Sehera. DeathRay has affirmed it too. I'm afraid they both have such deep affection for the other that they could be dangerously close." Moore knelt down in front of his wife and took her hands in his.

"You mean they're in love?"

"Yes, I do, or at least that is the way it looks. And I'm afraid it could cause them to make decisions that could end up getting them killed. So, I'm separating them for now."

"I, uh, that makes sense, Alexander. I'm sorry for second-guessing you. I know better." Sehera said. "I'm just so emotional right now. I can't stand this anymore. Almost losing Dee was . . ."

"I know. I don't know how we've gotten ourselves into this kind of, well, shit again." Moore was silent for a second or two. "But we have to finish this. We don't know what this is all about. We don't know what kind of doom your mother had waiting for us out there. And sticking our heads in the sand and waiting for it to come to us just ain't my style. It ain't yours either if I recall."

"I love you." Sehera looked up at him, doe-eyed. The tears slowly rolled down her cheeks. Alexander wiped them gently with his thumbs as he cupped her face and then kissed his wife deeply, long, and slow.

"I love you, too, with all my heart and soul." Moore held her gaze and looked into her eyes, her big, sad brown eyes. "I wish we could just teleport back to Mississippi and live a few decades on the farm without any of this other stuff to deal with. But there is something to all of this that has had me rattled. Your mother's plans must be revealed and derailed."

"I know. I know. I want to stop this continuous fighting and these secret agendas and feel safe once and for all—for Dee's sake, too. And maybe someday we might even be doing it for her little brother or sister," Sehera said. Moore's eyebrows raised.

"Something you're not telling me?"

"Relax, General," Sehera laughed. "I think that is almost the most scared I've ever seen the big Marine. No, there is nothing I'm not telling you. I'm just thinking, when things settle down some, so should we."

Alexander breathed a sigh of relief. Not that he didn't want another child someday, perhaps, but as long as Copernicus was still out there he couldn't stop what he was doing long enough to devote the time a new baby would need.

He hugged his wife and then stood up, pulling down on the damned Seppy uniform top. His UCUs had just come through the QMT supply runs and he couldn't wait to get into clothes fit for a Marine.

"Where you going, General?" Sehera looked up at him and grabbed his hand. "If we're considering settling down someday we need to stay in practice."

Alexander looked down at his wife. She used to call him "Mr. President" when she was feeling amorous. For the past year or so it had been "General." It was so weird how she could call him "general" in one way and he hated it. She could call him "general" in another and it fired him up, in a good way.

"General Alexander Moore reporting for duty, ma'am." He showed her his toothy politician's grin. "I wanted to get out of this damned Seppy uniform anyway."

"Hey, watch how you talk about them. My mother was a Separatist, you know." Sehera smiled and pulled Moore down to her.

"I know. If it weren't for her, I'd have never met you."

Chapter 27

November 11, 2406 AD
27 Light-years from the Sol System
Friday, 6:15 PM, Expeditionary Mission Standard Time

"So what is this all about, Dee?" Nancy looked at Dee and then turned to the captain's quarters of the ship she had decided to make her home. The hatch cycled open and she led Dee in. She could tell by the look on the Marine's face that she was surprised by the lavishness of it. "As you can see I've snapped home a few times and brought some stuff in."

The room had been an observation lounge on the spire of the command tower. The bridge was on the same deck and that would make it easy for her to get there quickly if she needed to.

She had installed maroon curtains that could be pulled over the long full, wall-length window that looked out over the bow of the ship. The smaller two-meter-diameter portal across the room gave a great view of the aft hangar decks. It would be a great spot to watch mecha fly in and out if she ever had a flight crew on board. There was a four-place table-and-chair dining set just in front of the portal. There were several pieces of modern art that Nancy had acquired over the years from her various missions placed strategically about the room. And the furnishings were far more upscale than most folks would suspect of Nancy's style.

Nancy had always liked dollhouses and castles as a little girl and the ancient Victorian styles had always pleased her. DeathRay never seemed to care one way or the other and Nancy didn't really give a damn what anybody else thought. It was her house and her stuff. This was her ship so she'd put whatever furniture in it she wanted to. Hell, if she wanted to run around the ship naked she would.

"Nancy, I, uh," Dee stammered, unsure of what it was she was wanting to say or unsure of how to say it. Nancy never liked beating around the bush about anything.

"Have a seat, Dee. You're off duty right now, right?" Nancy pointed toward the bright green couch with a mauve, pink, and blue flower pattern sewn into it. The legs were a deep red mahogany wood.

"I'm off duty until after tomorrow." Dee sat down.

"Good. Seeing as how we are just hanging out for the next few days anyway, I don't think it would hurt a thing if we had a couple bottles of wine. Do you?" Nancy turned and walked to the kitchenette she had installed on the other side of the quarters. She slid a cabinet door back and revealed her wine cooler.

"You've been busy," Dee said.

"Well, I haven't just been decorating. I have been working through the databanks of this fleet trying to figure out what the hell they are all about. I think better when I keep myself occupied." Nancy reached into the locker and pulled out two bottles. "Red or white?"

"Uh, I dunno, you pick." Dee squirmed uncomfortably on the couch.

"Red then." Nancy pulled two glasses from the cabinet and a corkscrew from a drawer. "It's a big ship. I've got it all to myself. I did manage to convince your father to let Boland bunk here with me. With the teleporters he could be anywhere in a moment's notice. We did have to promise to always have mecha ready to fly in case the QMTs are jammed."

Nancy poured the wine and handed a glass to Dee. Then she sat down in the matching loveseat. She squirmed just a bit to get comfortable and then propped her combat boots on the coffee table. She wanted to show Dee she could be informal if she wanted to.

"Makes sense to me. Probably would make sense to spread the crews out anyway in case of an attack." Dee took a long sip of her wine. Nancy made a mental note of the idea. Dee was right.

"So, Dee, how are you?"

"I'm good. Doc says I'm fit as I ever have been. My new heart is perfect and well, brand new. I'm fine." But Nancy could see there was something more going on with her. Nancy had been judging people's moves, motivations, and personalities for decades and she was good at telling when people were under duress. Dee was stressed as hell.

"Good. And how is the SEAL? Other than just good in the sack, I mean." Nancy chuckled. She hoped to crack the tension in the air with some big-sister sorority-type conversation.

"Well, if you have to bring it up, he's good, very good. I do mean in the sack." Dee almost laughed and she did take another sip of the wine. Nancy was breaking the ice.

"Good. I wish I could get Boland off the job long enough to . . . oh well, he's a busy man." Nancy thought about that for a minute. Jack was a good man and when he was DeathRay there was no better soldier. She needed to force him to take some time to just be Boland more often. "What else is up?"

"I guess you heard that the general has decided his mecha jocks should be flying and not doing forward recon." Dee frowned over her wine glass. Nancy could tell Dee was looking for an expression from her to gauge her opinion. Nancy was good at playing poker; she had no tells.

"Dee, I talked with Boland about that. Why bring all these AEMs with us if we don't let them do some of the heavy lifting every now and then? Besides, the skies are much safer with DeathRay and Apple One patrolling them." Nancy could tell this wasn't what she had come to talk about. Dee was still feeling the need for small talk.

"I don't know. I guess." She shrugged and filled her glass up from the wine bottle. Nancy was glad that she at least felt comfortable enough to help herself to the alcohol.

"Okay, enough of the small talk shit, Dee." Nancy decided the direct approach was best. "What is going on with you? You came to talk about something and I don't believe it is to whine about your father kicking you off the recon team."

"I, uh," Dee stammered and looked flushed. Nancy hoped she hadn't scared her off. She couldn't go backwards. All she could do now was continue to press her.

"There is something troubling you, Dee. Hey, it's me. We've known each other for years. Whatever you have to say is between us."

"I had an out-of-body experience when my heart stopped. My grandmother came to me in old memories that were jumbled up. She told me she needed to show me something. And you were there and you told me to pay attention to her. And then she told me again. I think there is something to it. I think my dead grandmother is trying to tell me something. I think I'm supposed to be doing something." Dee said it all in one breath and her hands were shaking. Nancy could see that there were tears forming in the corners of her eyes.

"Uh, wait," She took a breath herself and thought for moment. "Say it all again, but in more detail this time. Don't leave out any minor thing."

Dee seemed to open up completely. The details of her dream or vision or hallucination—Nancy didn't care what you called it—were vivid. Deanna seemed to recall it all, down to the colors and minute details like the number of forks on the dining table in her grandmother's suite on Ares. The holowall seemed to be a central focus of the experience, as it seemed to repeat. Nancy listened and had Allison record every detail and start an analysis of each part. Once Dee finished she leaned back in the couch and sighed.

"So, am I crazy or what?"

"Crazy? Because you had some sort of experience after a swarm of killer robots tried to rip your heart out?" Nancy chuckled slightly. "Hell, if I'd had to live through some of the things you did as a little girl I'd probably be a total head case."

"What then?"

"Dee, you're not crazy." Nancy let that sink in briefly. "If there is one thing I've learned over the years, is that our brains keep processing no matter what. With AICs we have a better handle on how it processes but sometimes there is just too damn much data to mine and comprehend all at once. But our brains are amazing, far superior at computation than anything ever made by mankind. Oh, AICs like mine and your father's and even yours might be really smart and good at quick data analysis and reduction but even they would admit that they are no match for a human brain."

"I've heard flight instructors say that. That's why we don't have AICs fly fighter mecha by themselves." Dee nodded as she said it. "So, what then? My brain solved something?"

"I think so, Dee. I think out of all the things you have experienced and all the things you have seen over the years that you have solved something about your grandmother's method or plan." Nancy thought to her AIC for a moment. *Allison, any sensor log data suggesting Dee was being communicated with or hacked?*

None that I have been able to find. I think this was all her. Or, maybe it was a message from beyond.

I guess we can't really ever rule that one out. Let's stick to facts for now. Philosophy and theology later.

"Your experience actually fits with my past experience with your grandmother's ilk. The Tangiers used holowalls to hide things. On the last mission we found these ships behind a wall that wasn't there." Nancy walked herself through the dream sequence again.

"Are there any holowalls on the ships?" Dee asked

I've already checked, Nancy, Allison said into her mind. *If there are, I haven't found them.*

Keep looking, Allison.

Roger that.

"Allison has been scanning since even before you came to see me. Since we found these ships behind one we have been looking for others." Nancy shrugged. "I don't think it is that simple. But I do think your brain has figured out something. Perhaps it is telling you to watch out for a smokescreen or a subterfuge. One thing your grandmother was exceptional at was to hide her efforts in plain sight of everyone. After all, how could a former President of the United States be the most wanted terrorist in history and nobody have any idea about it?"

"So, what do I do?" Dee was well into her third glass of wine now.

"Well, for starters, you ain't driving home. You can stay with me tonight or we'll teleport you out. But we will at least talk on this some more and relax. If we don't figure it out right away, don't worry. We will figure it out in time." Nancy nodded with a raised eyebrow. Then she raised a glass to her would-be little sister.

"In time for what, Nancy?"

"Indeed," Nancy said. "In time for what is the question."

At that comment Dee burst into laughter, almost spitting wine from her mouth and nose. She covered her mouth and continued to laugh.

"Indeed," Dee said mockingly. "In time for what is the question." She continued to laugh. "Did you really just say that? 'Indeed. In time for what is the question.'" Dee repeated. Nancy laughed as well.

You did sound a bit pretentious, if not ominous, Allison added with a chuckle into her mind.

Not you too?

I'm just saying, Allison replied. Nancy could do nothing but laugh.

"Well, we *will* figure it out. And we will, *indeed*, do it in time for whatever it is that is about to happen." Nancy did her best to say with a straight face.

"Oh, shit!" Dee held her side laughing uncontrollably. "You've got to stop it. I don't know if my new heart can take it. 'Indeed!' Who talks like that?"

Chapter 28

November 29, 2406 AD
Washington D.C., The White House
Tuesday, 1:15 PM, Earth Eastern Standard Time

"Madam President, as you can see in your DTM view, the current location of the Expeditionary Force is a little over twenty-seven light-years from Earth in the general direction of our Ross 128 and Lalande 21185 colonies. And the planet with the abandoned city and QMT facility was twenty-nine light-years out at Xi Ursae Majoris," Alexander reported to current sitting U.S. President, Carla Upton. His predecessor had only lasted one term and this was a completely different administration than the ones he had been involved with. She was fully briefed on history—all but the true identity of Elle Ahmi. "The colonies are highlighted here at Proxima Centauri, Lalande 21185, Ross 128, Gliese 581c, Gliese 876d, Tau Ceti, and the newer outpost at Wolf 359. As you'll note, most of these are located radially outward from the Sol System in a direction away from the galactic center. Also note that Tau Ceti, Gliese 876, and Gliese 581 are almost in the exact opposite direction from Sol as the other colonies. Adding to this, we see that all of the Separatist automated outposts are in the same direction away from Sol as all the colonies except for Tau Ceti, Gliese 876, and Gliese 581. "

"General—you know, Alexander, I have the hardest time calling you that," President Upton frowned.

"Yes, ma'am, it is strange for me sometimes, too. But it is a job that has to get done and I'm the man for the job. I was a politician long enough. I've been there and done that, ma'am." The corners of Moore's mouth turned up to almost a grin. "You were saying?"

"Yes, Alexander, it looks like your theory was right. All of the new bases you continue to find are in the same general direction away from Earth." The president studied the three-dimensional mindscape. Moore watched her carefully as she did. He could tell she was a slow and meticulous woman who calculated her moves before she made them. He wasn't sure yet, but he thought he liked her.

"Yes, ma'am. I think we're getting close."

"Close? You keep getting farther and farther away!" The president continued to study the star field being projected in their minds. "But you think you are close to this place Madira spoke of that was thirty-one light-years away, I assume."

"Yes, ma'am. The resistance at each location is greater and different every time. The automated defense systems are getting better at fighting us. But it is nothing we can't handle," Moore said carefully.

"Handle. You lost your ship and your daughter was nearly KIA. Alexander, I'm not so sure this job isn't too big for the small force you have with you." Moore wasn't exactly certain how he wanted to handle the conversation at that point. He turned and looked out the window of the Oval Office to the grass outside. The sky was gray and small flakes of white snow were beginning to cover the shrubs. While he missed Earth, he missed being on the mission every second he was away from it. It had to be completed and resolved or he would never be able to relax and enjoy the simpler things in life like snowflakes and children.

"With all due respect, Madam President, my team improvised, adapted, and we have overcome. In fact, right now we are loaded for bear," Moore said staunchly.

"You want to keep pushing outward, don't you?"

"Yes, Madam President. I do." Moore stood motionless and watched the woman as she leaned back in her desk chair. She adjusted a lock of gray hair that fell over her right eye and tucked it behind her ear.

"Relax, Alexander. I'm not going to take this from you. In fact, I agree with you that this whole thing stinks of something that isn't just a scientific curiosity. The fact that only you found that footage in the classified archives after a century and a half is startling. The fact that there was a conversation between a U.S. senator and an alien entity of some sort scares the living hell out of me." The president stood from her seat and walked through the virtual star field that surrounded them.

"There is more, Madam President."

"Go on."

"Well, if you follow the path from Sol outward to Ross 128, Lalande 21185, and now Wolf 359, and keep going in that general direction, we get to where the Expeditionary Force is now. And the only star system in that general direction right at thirty-one light-years from Sol is 61 Ursae Majoris at thirty-one point one light-years. It is a yellow star and as far as we can tell it does have planets."

"Are you telling me you've found the place?"

"I'm not sure, ma'am, but it looks like the best candidate. And, it is almost in range of the sling-forward QMT capabilities of the ships we found if we staged from the system they were found near." Alexander pointed out the system that DeathRay and Penzington had found the fake wall and city in.

"I see," President Upton said thoughtfully, but didn't add more than that.

"I want to send a small recon team in to gather information, but at the same time I want to be preparing a heavier force to visit our friends out there and show we aren't pushovers."

"Alexander, only your team, myself and my advisors, a handful of others on the HPSCI and SSCI, and the Chair of the Joint Chiefs know what is going on here. I want a backup plan in case you don't come back. I want a guard at the gate, so to speak."

"Ma'am, we have put troops at each base we've taken from the bots. We are rotating those crews in and out as standard stations. We are putting armored divisions and mecha at each of them, are we not?" Moore responded.

"Not what I mean, Alexander." President Upton paused and took a deep breath. "I want somebody else of your caliber and rank, soldier and thinker, to know what is going on. I want another supercarrier with a full contingent of troops, not a skeleton crew, stationed at your newest outpost to back your play, just in case."

"With all due respect again, Madam President, I have a better idea." He just had to sell it.

"Don't pull a supercarrier from here. I'd be wary of weakening the forces we have available at home. I would suggest a buildup until we know what we're dealing with. We don't need more equipment out there. We have a fleet of empty supercarrier-class ships with plenty of mecha aboard them. I can only imagine that Madira somehow planned this and left them there for us. What we don't have is crew and supplies." Moore paused to see if the President was following and gauging if she was going for it or not.

"Go on."

"What if we snap back one or two of the ships to the Oort facility? Once we get it there we load it with supplies and crew. Then we take it back to our current outpost and set up shop there. We'll use that as our base of operations." Moore kept it simple. There was plenty of time for making it more complex.

"Okay, pick your crew. Don't make another move toward the objective until you have the backup team in place. That's an order, General Moore." Upton smiled and shook his hand. "One more thing. You're the military expert. Why split our colonies the way they are?"

"Madam President?" Moore wasn't sure he understood her question.

"Well, if Madira did all these things, then most certainly as humanity started expanding out into the stars on her watch, she would have had them expand in certain directions for a reason. Why send half of the colonists and explorers one way and one the other?"

"Ah, I understand your question now, Madam President." More pulled the DTM view in closer for them and highlighted the path from Sol toward 61 Ursae Majoris in red. He highlighted the path from Sol through Tau Ceti and beyond in blue. "This is a standard staging operation for a beachhead assault. The colonies toward 61 Ursae Majoris are staging grounds and outer perimeter defensive positions. These leading from Sol in the opposite direction are egress points. I hate to say it, Madam President, but they are for retreating to."

Upton gasped. "Holy shit."

"Yes, ma'am. My thoughts exactly."

"Anything else?"

"No ma'am."

"Alexander, be safe." Moore shook the hand she offered him and then saluted her.

"Yes, Madam President," Moore said, and then tapped the snap-back wrist-band control on his watch. There was a flashing white light and the sound of sizzling bacon. The next second he was stepping off the QMT pad at the Oort Cloud Facility.

Looking out the long hangar that opened into space, he could see the occasional flicker of dust glimmer against the structural integrity field covering the hangar opening. In the distant star field was the U.S.S. *Anthony Blair*. Moore knew just who he was going to call on as the backup support ship captain.

Chapter 29

November 29, 2406 AD
Sol System, Oort Cloud
Tuesday, 3:15 PM, Earth Eastern Standard Time

There had been a longstanding convention in the Navy to name carriers after great leaders in history. Sometimes those leaders had been military, others political. With the recommissioning of the U.S.S. *Sienna Madira* to become an expeditionary vessel, the flagship of the fleet had become the U.S.S. *Anthony Blair* in its latest incarnation. The *Blair* was still under the command of Vice Admiral Sharon "Fullback" Walker. She had been through most all of the Separatist War as an integral part. The fleet had been in good hands. But Moore needed someone as experienced as Vice Admiral Walker, so the fleet would just have to backfill her slot.

General Moore walked shoulder to shoulder with the admiral. Well, that wasn't truly the case. Sharon was a good ten centimeters or more taller than Alexander. And from everything he could tell she probably had him beat on muscle mass too. Her Amazonian size and her smooth brown skin and perfect complexion made her not only intimidating from a physical strength perspective, but there was an attractiveness about her that was pleasing and reassuring. Something about the woman just oozed confidence and competence, and Alexander liked both attributes.

Moore noted as they passed a portal in the corridor that the Oort Cloud QMT facility was buzzing with its usual activities. Sol was so far away that he could barely make it out from the other stars, but he could tell which one it was as one of the incoming supply ships QMTed into space just out beyond the hangar opening. It was from his team. He had no idea where it had come from by the markings on the ship, but it was a Seppy-style troop transport and it was flanked by two Seppy-style Gnat-T fighters. Had to be his team.

"Nothing left of her at all?" Walker asked him. She had been astounded by the briefing he had just given her. She had had a hard time believing most of what she was told. Who wouldn't? Moore had a hard time believing some of it himself. But Fullback was a pro and she got right down to the business at hand. There was a possible pending invasion or at least a hostile force out there, and for decades humanity might have been preparing for it without even realizing. Moore knew that the Goddamned seriousness of that statement alone was enough to spark the fire in the belly of any good career soldier.

"Not even a screw. Any piece of debris we found nearby we vaporized just to be certain the damned bots didn't get onto the ships we'd taken refuge on." He had debriefed the president and the chairman of the Joint Chiefs of the Expeditionary Mission's situation. Fullback had always been at the point of the spear in the past when the *Madira* wasn't able to be. Once, when one of Ahmi's henchmen had kidnapped Dee as a teenager, Fullback came through for him. Moore needed her again.

There was need for more military presence. Over the last eighteen months, what had been the standard procedure wasn't enough. The standard approach had been to take one of the Seppy outposts from the bots then report back. Then at each location a QMT team was brought in and a pad large enough to bring in big ships was set up. That process usually took a few weeks, and as it stood there were nine new human outposts scattered about the stars. The farthest from home so far had been over twenty-five light-years away. The newest location where the Expeditionary Force was holding up was at about twenty-seven light-years from Sol. The QMT facility and the planet that had led Penzington and Boland to find the abandoned fleet were at twenty-nine light-years around the star Xi Ursae Majoris. The objective, where the message to Senator Madira had originated, was somewhere out there around thirty-one light-years, and it looked like they might be onto the location. Space was big and they could be wrong, but all the evidence was pointing them towards 61 Ursae Majoris. He'd had Buckley's teams, the STO, and Penzington studying the QMT addresses in the commandeered ships and all the star maps they could get their hands on, but with QMT there was no way of knowing where the other end of a jump was. It was just the nature of quantum physics. So, Moore's deductive reasoning and the fact that there weren't any other stars at exactly that distance from Sol along their present path had led them to an objective. It would very soon be time for another recon mission. He hated to admit it to himself, but he really needed to send his A-team.

"General, I will have my full crew roster completed within the hour for your AIC to vet. I plan to pad my personnel roster just in case you need an extra hand on your skeleton crew," Fullback hinted to him.

"Good plan. Hell, we might have to run triple or quadruple shifts, Admiral. You might plan on having backups in each position one or even two deep," Moore agreed with her. While they might have been able to get more funding and troop assignments from the president, much more than a full supercarrier crew coming up being reassigned would raise eyebrows in Congress. But Walker had ideas how to game the system to pad the numbers they needed. Moore had been on a skeleton crew for so long, that a little extra help wouldn't hurt his feelings one bit.

General, DeathRay and Apple One were the escorts of the supply run.

Understood, Abby. Moore smiled inwardly. *I want to see them.*

They are landing in the hangar now, sir.

Good.

"Admiral, I'll leave you to your work. I've got a few other things I need to check into. And Sharon," Moore paused to offer her his hand. "It's damned good to have you on my team."

"Proud to be on it, sir."

The hangar of the QMT facility was a constant flurry of activity. Ships popped in from all the seven major colonies, the few minor upstarts, plus the nine other outposts that the Expeditionary Force had taken. There were also many snap-backs and sling-forwards coming from elsewhere within the Sol system. The Oort Station facility was the major transportation hub of humanity in the galaxy. Moore shook his head in amazement at how mundane the teleport facility had become. It hadn't been but twenty years prior that nobody even knew it existed.

"You two are quite a ways from home, I'd say," Moore said with a smile as he stepped up behind a Gnat marked on the tailfins with a menacing looking black archangel wearing a powered armor suit and wielding a sword. Across the empennage of the nearest plane was marked "USMC Major Deanna 'Apple One' Moore." The other one had "USN Captain Jack 'DeathRay' Boland" written on it.

"Hello, General." Deanna looked down at her father with a smile. He had been back in the Sol system for more than a week briefing and arranging for their next step. While he had brought Sehera with him, the main crew of the Madira was his "family." Alexander had missed his family and there was no telling what he'd missed out there in deep space.

"Sir," DeathRay saluted him.

"Jack, Dee, good to see you two. We have a lot to discuss," Alexander said. "How go the base preparations?"

"Well, sir, the tankheads and the AEMs have completely stomped on every square inch of the planetoid at least four times. The place is a huge dustball now. It's worse than the Martian desert in the dry windy season," DeathRay said. "If there were any bots left on it they aren't there now. We've about got the place fully supplied and manned. Ships are coming in and out constantly."

"Good. What is the status of the new *Madira*?"

"The crew has settled in and they seem to be getting into a routine with the new, uh, rather old, equipment and stations. I will say from the CAG's perspective we are looking like a pretty good fighting machine, sir."

"How are the pilots taking to their new mecha?" Moore turned to his daughter. "Any troubles?"

"None, sir." DeathRay elbowed Dee. "Just have to watch out for some of these upstart and upwardly mobile new majors. I just hope that promotions and medals don't go to their heads."

"Understood, Jack." Moore laughed and then turned to his daughter. "Did you hear that Major Moore? Don't let it go to your head."

"Yes, sir," Dee nodded.

"Good." Moore recalled how he'd been when he had just been

pinned as a major. Hell, the history books talked about "Major" Moore specifically. He hoped that didn't add to the pressure on his daughter.

"Begging your pardon, General, sir, but would it be too bold to ask for a hug, sir?" Dee looked at Alexander seriously. Alexander never in a million years wanted his little princess to have to ask if it was alright to hug him, but military protocols sometimes required at least the appearance of formality. Alexander looked around and then back to his daughter.

"Not on your life, little girl." He held his arms out. Alexander squeezed his daughter like he hadn't seen her in years. "I missed you."

"Me too, Daddy. How is Mom?"

"She's fine. She's actually in Mississippi right now with some old friends. She is also getting some things from home. Then she'll be here within the hour and we'll be ready to move out. We'll wait around and ride back with you once your supply ship is filled up. If there is room, I mean. We could always just snap back, but it would be good to spend a few minutes with some of the troops." Moore turned to DeathRay. "Jack, how is Nancy?"

Abby, send a note to Sehera about the change of plans, he thought to his AIC.

Done, sir.

"Fine, sir, and I think we need to find something for her to do before she starts painting the inside of the *Hillenkoetter* bright colors." Jack said. Moore hadn't realized that Nancy had christened her ship. But as the old tradition went a ship had to be christened or it would sink.

Being a historian by education Moore immediately recognized the name as the first director of the CIA. It was a fitting name for her ship, the U.S.S. *Roscoe Hillenkoetter*. The ultimate American spy now had her own ship named after the first director of American spies. Moore approved. Not that it would have mattered if he approved or not; when it came to Nancy Penzington, she pretty much did what she wanted to do and somehow or other it always ended up being exactly what needed to get done.

"Well, don't worry, I have a mission for the A-team as soon as we can get it underway." Moore frowned. "Though I haven't figured out all the technicalities yet."

"Uh, sir, you mean the A-team minus us mecha jocks?" Dee said with a frown and a raised eyebrow.

"Major Moore, while Lieutenant Colonel Francis can choose which AEMs he wants on his forward recon team, this mission will require flight support as well and I want the Archangels covering their asses." Moore winked at his daughter.

"Yes sir." Dee smiled.

"Technicalities, General?" DeathRay asked.

"We need to recon a new star system, but I don't know how to get in there without being detected by Copernicus or whoever else might be there. You two have seen Allison's and Abigail's analyses. You know where we are going next. We just need to figure out how to get in there quietly. If we can't then we have to go in with every ship, every mecha deployed, and all guns primed and loaded. And that is one hell of a first impression that I'd prefer to avoid," Moore explained.

"Uh, Daddy, you need to talk to the CHENG or the STO," Dee said cautiously. She looked around nervously and Moore could tell she was afraid somebody had heard her slip in protocol. Alexander loved that his daughter was a consummate professional, but hated her thinking twice about calling him "daddy" like she had for her entire life, even when he had been President of the United States of the Sol System.

"Why is that?" DeathRay turned and looked at Dee. Whatever news Dee had was apparently something not everybody knew yet. Alexander guessed she'd been talking to the AEM that Buckley had been seeing. Moore couldn't recall her name.

What is the AEM's name that Buckley is seeing? he asked Abigail in his mindvoice.

First Sergeant Rondi Howser, sir. Abigail replied. *Following her performance on the last mission there is a recommendation for you to file her promotion.*

Okay, read the file. If it makes sense, start the process. I'll get details later.

Yes, sir.

"Well, sir," Dee was more formal as the mecha techs and engineers had gotten interested in the Seppy-style fighters and were beginning to crawl around the tail-section power plants. "According to First Sergeant Howser, the CHENG had said that he and the Captain Freeman have finally hacked the jamming algorithm the bots have been using. He believes we can start implementing them on all of our fleet vehicles and suits."

"No shit?" DeathRay said with raised eyebrows. "Those damned jammers have been a pain in my ass since the damned Exodus over twenty-six years ago. I've wondered why nobody has ever been able to crack them."

"I'll have to talk to the STO or the CHENG before I believe it. Those damned codes are quantum-generated random numbers and any attempt to decrypt them makes all the information garbled. At least that is what Abby tells me after the STO or CHENG rambles on about them for hours," Moore said.

"Well, it is secondhand, but Howser says Buckley won't shut up about it. There must be something to it," Dee concluded.

Chapter 30

December 2, 2406 AD
61 Ursae Majoris
31 Light-years from the Sol System
Friday, 9:15 AM, Expeditionary Mission Standard Time

The planetoid facility was at twenty-seven light-years from Sol. The objective system was thirty-one and one tenth light-years from Sol. But the two systems with respect to each other were almost six light-years apart. That was too far for a single sling-forward QMT even with the new technology on the old ships. The best the *Madira II* could do was a sling-forward QMT of about three light years. While that was still three times what the old *Madira* could do, it still wasn't far enough to do it all in one jump. So, the game plan had been to make two jumps at first. The first jump was to stop in the system's Oort cloud and do visual and signal intelligence gathering from there.

After the team had found planets and assessed populations, then they would sling forward deeper into the system. At that point, the Archangels would lead a team of six AEMs on a forward recon mission. With the new Buckley-Freeman Switch, as it was being called, hopefully the team could get in undetected, gather information, and then get the hell out. The general could then figure out what to do as the next move.

The team consisted of all ten of the Archangels in the transformable Gnat-Ts. There were six AEMs, including Lieutenant Colonel Francis Jones, First Lieutenant Jason Franks, Master Gunnery Sergeant

Tommy "Top" Suez, First Sergeant Rondi Howser, Corporal Samuel Simms, and Corporal Mike Menendez. Also as part of the recon team were Nancy Penzington, USN SEAL Lieutenant Commander Davy Rackman, and USN Petty Officer Engineering Technician First Class Sarala Amari. DeathRay, being a Navy captain, was the ranking officer of the team.

The first two sling-forward maneuvers were pretty standard. The second one brought them into the Oort cloud of the 61 Ursae Majoris system. The team popped into real space without a comet or planetoid in sight. Space was big and that wasn't unusual.

"Penzington, as soon as you and Amari get the SigInt gear and the telescope up, patch me in on the datastream," Jack told his wife over the open tac-net. He'd use person-to-person or AIC-to-AIC direct if he had more private things to discuss with her.

"Roger that, DeathRay. Telescope is coming online now. Give us a few minutes."

"Understood. Keep me posted." DeathRay looked over his shoulder at his wingman. Apple One was right where she was supposed to be. He checked his DTM sensor sweep view for anything out of the ordinary. Then he toggled on the Blue force tracker and the team's blue dots popped up all around him. "Alright, Archangels, let's keep it frosty and keep your passive QMs, RF, IR, and eyeballs wide-ass open. We'll form up in a ball putting the shuttle at the center. I don't want us to miss any incoming threats, so keep your eyes peeled!"

"Affirmative!"

"Hooyay!"

"Oo-fuckin'-rah."

Jack peeled his mecha to the left and took up the lookout position in the ball looking directly back at the star. Dee was just to the right on his three-nine line, upside-down relative to him, and pitching and yawing her mecha such that the little snub nose of the vehicle moved slowly about a large circular path. The rest of the squadron took up similar positions in a sphere about the shuttle carrying the rest of the team. The various pilots had their own individual techniques of scanning space. Some of the mecha moved up, then down, then left, then right. Some of them moved about at random. Some of them sat still. DeathRay tracked his team in his DTM battlescape view. He preferred to sit still and move his head around. He'd use the three-dimensional mindview simultaneously. They were in a very tight defensive ball and ready for anything. And there was no telling what "anything" might be.

"Jack, we are getting signals from all over the inner part of the system. There is also some type of very large transmitting structure in the Kuiper belt area about sixty Sol astronautical units from the star. As far as we can tell there is nothing out here near us," Nancy reported.

"Signals we understand or something, uh, alien?" Jack asked over their private line.

"Same type of bot stuff we're used to at the inner part of the system. The thing out in the Kuiper belt is a little different, but not too different. Could just be some new trick Copernicus is working on," Nancy said.

"Anything else?" DeathRay asked as he continued to scan the space in front of him from left to right and then up and down.

"Well, maybe," Nancy replied. "There are an unusually small number of comets in this system's Oort cloud. We have also detected at least three inhabited worlds within the Goldilocks zone. That is highly improbable. But with the missing comets, I'd say whoever lives here has terraformed one or two of the planets."

"I see, very advanced tech is what you are warning me about?" DeathRay asked his wife.

"Yes. If they can terraform two planets, that is more than humanity has been able to accomplish. We've been working on Mars for nearly three hundred years and you still can't go outside without an E-suit there."

"Right, get me more. How do we know which of the three planets to recon?"

"How about the one with the biggest city?"

"Okay by me." Jack wasn't sure what investigating the biggest city in the system would do for. He thought about that for a bit.

What would coming to Earth and performing recon missions on Paris or New York or London or Tokyo or Dubai tell you? he thought to his AIC.

You could get a cross section of the races in the population and a good idea of the types of unclassified personal technologies of the culture. That might allow for assessing other government processes, civil, and military functions, Candis replied.

Okay then.

"First thing, I say we pop to the facility in the Kuiper belt and check it out," DeathRay said. "We need to know if it is a QMT facility or something else."

"Makes sense to me." Nancy replied. "Once we check that out then we'll move inward. That should give the AICs time to pinpoint the best locations to recon in the inner system."

"Alright then, it's settled. Send us the coordinates to this Kuiper belt signal." DeathRay waited for the coordinates to come through and then he set the QMT sling-forward algorithm. "Okay, team, let's sling to it!"

The team vanished in a flash of lightning around him and Jack could feel his skin crawl slightly as the quantum membrane teleportation processed. There was as always, that sound of sizzling bacon in his ears, and then there was another burst of white light and he was staring at a different location in space.

"Holy shit!" one of the pilots said over the tac-net.

"Would you look at that?" Dee said. "That thing has got to be a thousand kilometers long. What is it?"

DeathRay looked out in front of him at a very long cigar-shaped planetoid. The planetoid looked like someone had taken five Kuiper belt objects and stuck them together in a long chain. There was gridwork along the surface and there were huge dish antennas all over the thing. There literally wasn't a spot on the facility that didn't have some piece of technology jutting out from it. Around the periphery of the cigar shape running from end to end of the long axis was a very large cylinder that looked like a giant hula hoop that had been stretched in one axis and squished in the other so it would fit around the cigar shaped structure. There were several other hula-hoop-shaped rings that were perfect circles suspended about the structure. One ring per planetoid piece. The structure looked random, complex, and menacing all at the same time.

"Alright, let's keep our heads," DeathRay announced. "Nancy, get us some data on this thing right now."

Candis, keep a close eye on the sensors. If any energy levels start to increase anywhere send an instant snap-back command to the team. We'll regroup back in the Oort if we have to.

Roger that, keeping a close eye on everything.

"DeathRay, I'm getting nothing on any sensors that are out of the ordinary," Amari said. "As best I can tell this thing looks like some sort of QMT detection and transmission station. It's a listening post."

"I agree," Nancy added. "We should take a closer look."

"Well, I guess now is as good a time as any to test out the Buckley-Freeman Switch," he said. "Alright, the shuttle will hang out here and study from a distance. Archangels, let's move down to surface level and survey this thing."

"DeathRay, this thing is big," Fish interjected. "What if I take half the team around the other side and we meet you at the end?"

"Roger that, Fish," DeathRay replied. "But stay tight and frosty and keep me posted if anything happens."

"Affirmative," Fish said. "Okay, B-wing, form up on me and let's move out."

"A-wing on me," Jack said. "Eyeballs peeled."

Jack watched as the facility loomed closer and closer into his field of view. Before too much longer it was pretty much all he could see. The place was massive. As they got closer to the central long-axis ring Jack could tell that the tube circumscribing the cigar-shaped structure was at least seventy-five meters in diameter. The thing reminded him of particle accelerators he had studied in basic physics back in college before flight school. The rest of the structure looked like somebody had gathered up every antenna, dish, and QMT spire they could find and connected them all together on the surface. While at first glance the mishmash of equipment looked like a random junkyard, it was clear upon further study that the structure was a very complicated piece of equipment and the entire planetoid facility was one device with likely a single very large purpose.

Jack, Nancy's AIC is sending me data to pass along. She says that most of the signals I'm getting are basic energy readings and standard transmissions. There does appear to be some sort of QMT background noise coming from that large pad structure near the end of the cigar shape, Candis relayed.

Okay then, let's check it out. He slightly nudged the HOTAS to the right and the throttle a bit forward.

"Apple One, let's check out that QMT-pad-looking structure just ahead and to my north."

"Roger that, DeathRay."

Jack kept a close eye on the pad structure as they swooped down to within a few meters of it. It was metallic and put together in sections not much larger than a hovertank. The pieces fit together, making a large octagonal pad with a shiny disk in the exact center. The large octagon shape was more than a kilometer across the middle. At each point of the octagon were spires pointing upward into space. The place looked very similar to the first QMT pads they had found after the Exodus. But what was different about this thing was that the periphery was covered with antennas and dishes, and melding into the structure on each side of the octagon along the long axis of the cigar-shaped structure was the large cylindrical tube. Since the pad was raised out of the planetoid's surface, there was no way to know if the cylinder stopped at the edge of the octagonal structure or if it continued through or beneath it.

"Looks like Frankenstein's version of the Oort Facility," Dee said.

"Yeah, I'm not sure what all this is but it is definitely not just a QMT pad," Jack agreed. "I don't think we can do more than scan this thing and get data. Without landing on it and doing some recon there is no way we'll figure this thing out today."

"I agree with that, DeathRay." He could see Dee's fighter about a half-kilometer away at the edge of the pad. "It had to have taken decades to build this thing."

"DeathRay, Fish."

"Go, Fish."

"I don't know what you are seeing on that side, but if it looks anything like what we've got on this side the tech analysts could spend years trying to figure out what this thing is."

"I agree with that assessment," Nancy joined in the conversation. "Our sensors do tell us one thing, though; the structural materials look like they've only been in space for a couple hundred years at best. It could fit within the time frame of events we've been assuming."

"Well, let's leave the analysis for later. Nancy, have you found us a location to recon in the inner system yet?" Jack asked.

"Allison has pinpointed our target, Jack," Nancy said on the open tac-net. "Fourth planet in the system is the middle of the three habitable ones. Looks like it is lit up far more than the others, which suggests that it is the older one."

"Okay, we sling forward to it. Send everyone the coordinates. Everyone, form back up on the shuttle." DeathRay could see the imagery data loading into his DTM. The planet was five percent larger than Earth so the slightly heavier gravity could be a factor if they had to go to foot without armored suits. After a moment or two for the mecha pilots to pull away from the facility and then back into formation around the shuttle, Jack gave the order. "Alright everyone, stay sharp and prepare to QMT in five, four, three, two, one . . ."

Chapter 31

December 2, 2406 AD
61 Ursae Majoris
31 Light-years from the Sol System
Friday, 11:25 AM, Expeditionary Mission Standard Time

The inner solar system was not all that unlike Sol's. The moon of the fourth planet was covered with domes and lights the same way Luna was. The planet below didn't appear much different from Earth, only more developed. There was little in the way of what looked like uninhabited real estate. After several orbits around the planet, Nancy had assured them that they had taken enough data from optical images, ambient radio and data transmissions, vibrational surface waves, and quantum membrane sensors to create a good high-resolution map of the planet. There was also an ample amount of data floating around the system that was unencrypted on open system-wide networks. Jack spent a few minutes looking at it, but soon realized it would take a significant amount of his time to figure out the relevant information for his team. One of the weirdest aspects of the network was that there were no entertainment sites or links. The thing was one hundred percent down to business. There were no ads, movies, songs, no politics, and no porn. This was certainly not a network created by and for humanity in the typical sense. Jack decided it would be best to let Nancy handle this part of the recon, or in actuality let her AIC do it.

Nancy's AIC had developed a data-mining agent that was crawling around the open network gathering pertinent information while at the same time logging ambient signals and imagery from the Archangels. The hopes were for the team to create a complete map of the system, find the highest priority targets, and spy on them. The AICs were working on compiling the map and determining the most highly valued targets.

Nancy and Amari pinpointed the largest city on the planet. It was about the size of Arizona. It stretched across a complete land mass that was surrounded by oceans on all sides. It was right above the equator of the planet. There were spaceports located all across the city, with air traffic moving continuously. A few more spacecraft coming in shouldn't draw any suspicion as long as nobody realized they weren't being picked up on other sensors at the same time.

The team set down at the outermost edge of one of the smaller spaceports. It looked nearly abandoned compared to the buildings around it. It was likely that this was an older port that had lost traffic to a newer, more updated one further inward.

Jack cycled the canopy of his mecha and leapt to the ground. The canopy closed itself. He hated leaving the safety of his mecha and he wasn't sure what the general would have to say about it, but they were there and somebody needed to gather intel. He certainly wasn't going to sit put in his fighter while the AEMs had all the fun.

"Okay, here's the plan." He gathered the team around him. "Fish, you take the rest of the Archangels and see if you can blend in with the local air traffic. Get as much data as you can at all wavelengths. Dee and I will join the ground team from here."

"Jack, I think we should leave Amari in the shuttle running the sigint package until we get back," Nancy suggested.

"Okay, Amari, you stay here. Any sign of trouble, snap back to the Oort rendezvous point. Corporal Simms, stay here with Amari and keep an eye out." DeathRay paused and did a quick headcount. "We keep the jammers going and maybe nobody will notice our suits with Mark I Eyeballs. The only way they'll see us is if they actually *see* us. These new jammers Buckley and the STO have been reverse-engineering from the ships we found are getting their first real test. Hopefully, we'll be invisible to everything but an actual eyeball. And hopefully, those eyeballs will be too busy going about their daily business to catch us doing our thing. We'll stay either on rooftops or in the sewers, if they have them, or in alleyways. In other words, we stay the fuck out of sight. Out of sight and we will be able to get this job done. Everybody got it?"

Jack waited for a nod of affirmation from the team and then started looking around for a route to take. The imagery they had taken on the way in had enabled them to build up a three-dimensional topographical map of the city to pretty good resolution. As they explored and improved the map they would be able to generate very detailed maps for later use.

Candis?

Due north there are plenty of high-rise buildings, Jack, his AIC said. *We could bounce from those.*

Good.

"Everybody spread out with at least a half klick between you. Find some vantage points to look and listen, and start doing it. Move out."

The city was unlike anything that Jack had ever seen before. It was larger than any human-made city that had ever existed, and it was populated with humans everywhere he looked. Or at least to the best he could tell, they all looked human. The problem was that there were only about a hundred different faces. In fact, after about sixteen hours of moving from ground level to skyscraper level and back down again, he had seen the same set of faces more times than he could count. Candis had counted and said that it was one hundred three different faces so far. Everyone else was exact duplicates of one of the other hundred and three faces. She had yet to find a single face that hadn't had a duplicate somewhere along the way.

Clones? Jack thought. *But, I thought clones were just empty bodies with no mind? Spare parts. Nobody has grown a real clone with a sentient brain in centuries other than pets and farm animals. How are they sentient?*

Either they are clones or a shitload of multituplets, his AIC replied. *A clone grown from birth and released at birth into the world would grow and develop like a normal human.*

Yeah, but none of these look to be different ages. They all look like they are thirty years old and there is no variation.

Perhaps whoever created them has figured out a way to upload a mind into them? his AIC suggested.

Do they have AICs?

Unclear at this point, Jack. We'd have to take one and make a much more detailed medical examination.

Maybe later. Jack replied. *Have you noticed any of the thousand-yard AIC conversational stares?*

I have been looking for that. And no, I haven't seen it, Candis added.

Private channel to Penzington.

Channel is open, Jack.

"Hey, sweetness. Miss me?" He laughed.

"Not really," Nancy replied nonchalantly. "Is this a business or pleasure call?"

"Well, if you put it that way, I haven't noticed any AIC conversational stares. Have you?"

"No. And that is weirding me out," Nancy said over the com. "Allison doesn't quite know what to make of it either."

"Any news on your end?"

"I have a little. Allison has pinpointed, through several different ways and means that we don't have to go into, what she thinks is a capital city district just a bit south of here. I'm going to take Rackman and move into that area."

Jack noticed that she didn't ask permission to take the SEAL she just said she was going to do it. But Nancy always did what she wanted to do. That was what Jack loved about her. The greatest thing about it was that somehow what Nancy wanted to do was always what needed to get done.

"Okay, keep me in the loop." Jack thought about his wife for a brief second and didn't like her being in harm's way. And then he remembered who his wife was and how they had met and all the things they had been through together and the feeling slipped away. Neither he nor a freight train could keep her from doing what she wanted to do and he wasn't about to start trying now. He half suspected that was the same way General Moore must feel about his wife and daughter. "Nancy, one more thing."

"What's that, flyboy?"

"Be careful."

"You too."

The city, state, country, continent, was vast, much larger than

Washington D.C. and New York City combined, much larger than the expanse of Los Angeles, California, and much larger than Moscow, or Paris, all combined and on a land mass the size of Olympus Mons. It was clear that the entire continent was one large city. How had anybody managed to do this without humanity knowing about it? Or at least without the rest of humanity knowing about it. As far as his AIC could estimate there were nearly one hundred million inhabitants on the island continent alone. From space, the rest of the planet had appeared as heavily populated. Best estimates by Nancy and Allison had been over ten billion people—if they were people.

Candis, hit me with some stims again, I'm getting a little tired.

Roger that. The AIC triggered a release of chemicals through the organogel layer of the suit that would time-release stimulants and calories into his system. In the new suits a soldier could go for days without sleep and never lose alertness. Without eating though, the stomach still would feel empty. There were drugs for that feeling too, but there was also food. He preferred food.

Jack popped his visor for some fresh night air and then fumbled through his chest pouch for some rations. He found a very dense energy bar and decided to chew on that for a bit. The peanut butter and chocolate flavor was actually inviting even if the damned thing was as chewy as glue. He looked up at the night sky as he chewed. The moon of the planet wasn't much smaller than Luna back home. The surface of this entire moon, however, was covered with lit-up structures. It looked very much alive.

Jack continued to carefully position himself to watch and catalog movement of the people and vehicles. His suit's sensors logged any motion detectable, including aircraft. All of the information might prove useful to the analysts in the "loony bin" when they returned. After another five or so hours of bouncing from rooftop to rooftop he decided it was time to take a break. He found a rooftop that had a mechanical maintenance alcove on top of it and backed himself into the shadows of the structural gridwork.

Jack adjusted his position within the structural members of the alcove near the precipice of the building. He estimated where he was to be about fifty stories high. There were taller buildings further to the north, but he would be able to learn a lot about the city from where he was. He could see entrances for the subways and private vehicles. What he didn't see were billboards, magazines, or movie theaters. It unnerved Jack because there was something not, well, not human about it.

He sat down and then propped himself up against one of the girders on the building top that jutted upward to something that might have been a water tank, but Jack wasn't sure. He made certain his sensors and his visor would be pointed in such a way as to give him maximum field of view. Then he closed his visor, and then closed his eyes.

Candis, I'm going to take a nap. Keep me posted if anything happens, he thought.

Roger that, Jack. From the motion on the Blue force tracker and through AIC affirmation, most of the recon team is sacked out too, Candis said.

How long to sunrise?

About three hours.

If nothing happens, wait til then to wake me up.

Aye, sir.

"DeathRay, this is Apple One." Jack opened his eyes. It took him a few seconds to orient his mind as to where he was. His stomach growled as well. Jack could tell the yellow sun was on the verge of breaking across the horizon. The sky to the east was bright and turning pink and blue.

I was about to wake you anyway, sir, Candis said into his mind.

Right. Time to earn our pay. He reached into his chest pack for some breakfast.

"Go ahead, Dee."

"I'm on the north side of the largest spire a bit west of you. You can see it in the DTM. I think there's something here you ought to see."

"What have you got?" DeathRay said.

"My AIC and Amari have been scanning the QM bands for large noise floor or any evidence for a signal. They've found what we think is similar to the background noise created when Copernicus hacks other AICs, but it is a much, much larger noise background. Nancy's AIC agrees with us."

"I can confirm that, sir," Amari's voice came in through the tac-net open channel. "Using data from every known encounter with

Copernicus over the last eighteen months, I can correlate the present background with a ninety-nine point nine eight seven percent certainty. It is definitely Copernicus, but on a very large scale, sir."

"Okay, so what?" DeathRay asked. "Copernicus is hacking a bunch of people at once?"

"No, sir," Dee said. "I think it is something bigger than just hacking. The problem is that I don't know what."

"Okay, anything else?"

"Well, yes," Amari added. "I've been using data from all your suits, and Major Moore and Mrs. Penzington have been moving around in directions I needed them to go to better triangulate the multi-path noise signals. Then I linked into the Archangels and generated an algorithm to track the peak noise level. Major Moore is there now."

"I'm right on top of it. I think it's some sort of communications nexus," Dee said. "I'm not so sure that these clones aren't just humans slaved by an AIC. They're all run by a Copernicus or perhaps one central Copernicus, if that is possible. And I think this is the factory that's creating, distributing, and controlling the Copernicus computers or transceivers or whatever they are."

"Hold on, Dee. Let's hold off on the speculation until we have more data. We're going to converge on you. Hold your position, and stay out of sight."

"Affirmative."

"Okay, team, you heard the lady. We're converging on Apple One's location, and everybody, stay calm, cool, collected, and out of sight."

Jack tuned over the comm to a private channel to Nancy Penzington. He wanted to tell his wife good morning anyway.

"Good morning, gorgeous. What's up over there?"

"I'm pretty sure that Dee's right about this, but there's something about it that doesn't sit well with me."

"What's that?"

"I just saw a hundred-and-fourth face. Alison has confirmed it."

"What? A hundred-and-fourth face?"

"Yes."

"Does that mean there's another clone? Maybe we just haven't seen that one yet. It could be from another continent or something that doesn't make here often," Jack asked.

"Well, that is possible. But I don't think so, Jack, because I've only seen the one face the one time. As busy as this city is, we've seen thousands, maybe millions, of people in the last twenty or so hours. Nobody has catalogued this face. Allison has verified this. I even hacked into a security camera net that I found on the streets. Allison has been running facial recognition codes for hours, and nothing but one hundred and three faces. This face is significant and different."

"Track it, Nancy, track it!" Jack said. "This is anomalous and I agree, it must mean something."

"I'm on it."

"Stay with it and keep us posted."

"Roger that. Nancy out."

A hundred-and-fourth face. That's strange, Jack thought.

Well, maybe not, Jack, Candis responded to his mind. *It's possible that she just hasn't seen the other clones and that it is not the only one.*

It's possible. But Nancy's so damn thorough, I wouldn't see her making a mistake like that. And I wouldn't see her calling something in like that, if she's not researched it a little bit deeper. It makes me nervous that she hacked the security cameras without asking first, but she doesn't need my permission.

I just said it was possible, Jack. I didn't say I believed it.

Jack just grunted to himself.

Jack stayed close to the building walls along the alleyways and carefully moved toward Dee's position. He hoped that, once he got there, what he would find was a reason for this system and how its population had managed to get so large so quickly.

"Rackman," Nancy opened a channel to the SEAL who had been shadowing her for the past hour or so as they had bounced on rooftops, keeping themselves a good kilometer from the target and each other. Even though they were jamming most sensors, a key part of recon was staying out of sight of the bad guys. "I want you to cover my backside and spot for me."

"Roger that," the SEAL replied. "I'll take a vantage point as high up as I can and keep you in my long-range sensor view. Rifle is at the ready if you need me."

"Good. If you can, help me keep an eye on our target."

"Affirmative."

Nancy saw the humanoid with the hundred-and-fourth face

casually mixing through the crowd, and at no time did the crowd seem to pay him any attention. Nancy, on the other hand, was certainly an outsider and would draw attention to herself in her powered armor. She stayed on top of the higher buildings when she could, using the recon sensors of her suit to keep track of her target. Occasionally, she and Rackman would have to leapfrog each other to find vantage points giving them a solid view of the target while still staying out of sight. This made tracking the individual much more difficult. Nancy had done plenty of stealth missions in the past and she knew how to stay out of sight. The SEAL seemed pretty good at it as well. But there was something almost too easy about their mission. They had yet to even have a close call.

In order to maintain her track she had to use all the street cameras she could hack. It also meant she had to go from rooftop to rooftop, alleyway to alleyway, and even underground on three different occasions. But it wasn't anything that Nancy hadn't done before. Having Rackman keeping an eye out on the topside actually made it easier than it could have been without him.

Allison, you got a track on him?

I've got him, Nancy. But if you can't stay any closer, we're going to have to go active with the sensors. Or look into other low-tier security systems we can hack.

Negative, Nancy thought. *As soon as we go active with sensors, Copernicus will know we're here. It's already a risk hacking local systems.*

Who says he doesn't already, and he's just playing with us? How do we know that hundred-and-fourth face isn't Copernicus? Allison thought into Nancy's mind.

I'm not so sure, Allison. Copernicus would hide himself. He would want to look just like everybody else. That's the way he's operated, staying behind the curtain. This is something else. This is someone else.

Perhaps you were right the first time, Nancy, Allison thought. *Perhaps it's something else. For now, I'm only hacking individual standalone systems. Our hack would appear nothing more than another standalone transceiver. I hope.*

The target might be something else. That is unsettling, isn't it? That gave Nancy pause. That was what made her nervous—"something else" was an unknown. Nancy didn't like unknowns. Boland was rubbing off on her.

Chapter 32

December 3, 2406 AD
61 Ursae Majoris
31 Light-years from the Sol System
Saturday, 8:04 AM, Earth Eastern Standard Time

Nancy followed the track in the opposite direction of the rest of the team. The target had stopped for coffee at a local shop. He ate what appeared to be a bagel and washed it down with a large cup of black coffee. The face that the guy made as he ate and drank was one of sheer delight, as though it was a major treat. Nancy wasn't sure what was more weird to her, the fact that the guy acted like having coffee and a bagel was exciting or the fact that she was on a planet thirty-one light-years from Earth and it looked and felt as much like Earth as Earth did. However the construction and emplacement of this city had been accomplished, from human standards, it would have taken centuries. Humanity just hadn't been out this far long enough to build such a city. To top that off, the entire planet was densely populated. The planet's moon appeared to be the same as well. And there were two other planets in the system that were inhabited. The system could easily hold twenty or thirty billion people.

If they were people.

At one point the man took a subway train and Nancy almost lost him. She had lost Rackman in the process. The SEAL had been too far back to jump on a train with her. He eventually caught up once she figured out where she was going.

Allison spread her search as far as her low-level sensors would reach while she ran at top speeds and as best out of sight as she could to catch up with the train. At two different points she managed to jump on trains headed in what she hoped was the same general direction as the train her target had taken. After about five minutes Allison regained track on the target through security cameras. Soon after that Nancy managed to catch back up to within spitting distance.

Looks like he might be at his destination, Allison said to her.

Good, where are we relative to the continent, the team, and the shuttle? All of the information popped up in her DTM view. Nancy spent a few seconds zooming in and out of the data, getting her bearings. *Okay, now get me zoomed in good on this guy.*

Roger that, Allison said.

"Rackman? You about caught up with me?"

"Yes, ma'am. I've got my crosshairs on the back of your head right now," Rackman said.

"Uh, good, but what do you say we keep the crosshairs on our target's head, huh?"

"Roger that, Penzington," Rackman laughed.

After multiple train hops and fast runs with jumpboots firing, they had managed to follow their target to a large estate house. The estate house was surrounded by a fence, and its architecture looked like a cross between the Federalist architecture of Washington, D.C. with a mix of New Tharsis architecture on Ares, where Elle Ahmi had made her Separatist Capitol during the war. In fact, there was something very Separatist about the estate. If this planet had a White House, this had to be it.

The target spent a second outside the guard gate discussing something with the guards. He stood straight and unmoving for several moments until the gate was opened and he was escorted through.

Shit. We need to find a way inside there. Allison, find me a sewer, low fence, service entrance or something.

Got it, Nancy, Allison replied almost as if she had anticipated what Nancy would ask. *South entrance is not currently being guarded and it is locked down. The gate is only six meters or so tall. Piece of cake.*

While this "White House" had been built with security in mind, it was clear that whoever built it wasn't really concerned that a person in a powered armored suit would be trying to get in. Certainly, they weren't expecting a suit that was jamming every sensor in view with a Buckley-Freeman switch that was reverse-engineered from Elle Ahmi's or Copernicus' own handiwork.

The mansion was surrounded by the city, much like the White House. Nancy bounced over several rooftops to make it to the south entrance. From that vantage point she could see into the backyard of the building. While the architecture was similar to the White House of Earth, the building was more than ten stories high, which was more like Ahmi's mansion penthouse on Ares. There were buildings around that were about as tall and maybe slightly taller, but none were skyscrapers like those seen farther north where the rest of the team was currently.

Nancy positioned herself on the highest vantage point nearby. In order to get there she had climbed up exterior fire escapes and even clawed her way up the side of a hotel. The sun was just barely peeking above the horizon and it was a bit of an overcast day. It was very early and she hoped nobody was paying her any attention. Either she had done a good job hiding herself and the Buckley-Freeman switch was working, or she had been seen and nobody cared.

Nancy looked out at the top of the "White House" building. It was more than fifty meters away across a wide street and about five meters below her current position. Nancy didn't think she could make it from one rooftop to the other in one leap, but she did think if she timed it right with traffic and passersby that she could bounce once just outside the gate, up and over, and then land against the wall of the building. From there Allison had already identified a service entrance. Nancy would have to get out of the suit to go any farther than that.

She waited as a few vehicles purred down the street. The sounds of the electric engines were about the only source of ambient noise other than birds and squirrels and the wind.

Go now! Allison shouted in her mind.

Nancy bounced in a long, sweeping arc from the rooftop all the way across the street and to the ground, just outside the south gate. Almost as instantly as she hit the ground she bounced again, up and over the wall to the ground twenty meters on the other side. She bounced once more and closed the gap to the service entrance.

Nancy stayed low and had her suit's digital camouflage blending in with the paint colors and other surroundings. She clanked up to the service entrance and hid behind a dumpster alcove.

Can you get me in, Allison?

I'm cycling through the lock codes now, the super spy's AIC replied. A few seconds later and the lock clicked. Nancy quickly rushed to the door and slipped inside.

She looked around and could only see a long corridor stretching out in front of her with multiple hallways extending out to the left and right along the length of it. The corridor and the hallways were all large enough for a supply vehicle to drive through, and the walls and floor were painted in nondescript dull gray, but clean and well-maintained. There were yellow and black stripes on the floor showing forklift lanes and pedestrian walkways. Nancy followed the corridor to a service elevator and had Allison bring it down to her level.

Have you still got a visual on the target? She thought.

Negative, Nancy. All of the cameras in this building are on their own internal circuit. I am afraid if I hack into them I will alert someone to our presence. However, I got his voice pattern from the coffee shop and the front gate here. And there is an intercom system that isn't connected to the security network, so I am tracking his voice through it. He is on the tenth penthouse level. Now that I have a few voice-pattern samples I can use ambient data-transmission multi-path noise to pull his voice out of the background. I can track him anywhere in this building now. He is entering the penthouse office suite now.

Get me a path to there. A path highlighted itself in her DTM view. The service elevator could take her to that level.

"Rackman, what are you doing?"

"Still covering your egress position, ma'am," Davy replied.

"Well, our target is on the penthouse of this building. Jump around out there and see if you can get us a visual."

"I'm on it."

Nancy found an entrance to the engineering room of the building where maintenance equipment, plumbing, air conditioning, and electrical systems seemed to originate from. She dropped her suit there. She was wearing a compression skinsuit and shoes underneath the armor. The light metal-gray skintight microthin layer kept her warm and compressed her muscles for performance. The suit made her muscles and physical features stand out even more than the UCU tops did for the soldiers. The lightweight shoes were designed for military training and running, so they would hold up to most rigors she might expose them to. But best of all, the hard, rubberized foam-filled soles were quiet. She could sneak about very easily in them. The suit not clanking on everything helped more than anything.

She reached in the breast pouch of the suit and pulled out a handgun M-blaster and melded it to her uniform on her right thigh. If she needed it she'd only have to grab it and pull and the skinsuit would let it go.

Nancy hoped nobody would be down there anytime soon to run maintenance on the power plant or the plumbing. She didn't want them finding her E-suit. She slipped out of the room and made her way to the service elevator. After Allison cycled the codes on it and it opened empty, she climbed in, and upward she went.

Our guy is speaking with somebody now, Nancy. Want to hear it?

Yes.

Okay, playing now. The audio of the conversation began playing in Nancy's head.

"Time is running out," the target's voice said.

"How so?" It it was a female voice—one that sounded vaguely and eerily familiar to Nancy.

"The Chiata have made the decision to act on their property and the courts have ruled in their favor. The futures on your system were bought by the Chiata over fifteen thousand years ago. At that time they had no way of suspecting what your people would become. At least that was their argument," the target voice said. "And, of course, the court system passed it through."

On the way up Nancy crawled up through the top escape hatch of the elevator onto the upper side of it. Once it peaked at the top floor, she jumped off onto an elevator maintenance ladder. She worked herself around to a catwalk leading through what appeared to be an equipment attic and then sat still for moment to listen to the conversation.

I'd really like to get a visual on this, she thought.

I'm working on it, Allison replied.

"Rackman, where's my visual?" she subvocalized over the com channel.

"No good vantage point out of view of the locals out here. I'm still working on it." Nancy understood and turned her focus back to the conversation between her target and the new player.

"And you're certain there is no way to stop this?" the female voice said.

"Yes, I'm certain. Honestly, I never thought we could. The Chiata have controlled the courts for more than fifty thousand years and nobody has been able to stop their expansion. My people couldn't stop them when they acquired my system and nobody else has stopped them in many millennia. It is only a matter of time before they take the entire spur of the galaxy," the target voice said.

"So, what is our play? Can't we appeal to the courts directly?"

"My dear, you are nothing more than annoying pests in the eyes of the courts. When the assessment of your world was done it was found that there was nothing you could do to stop nature. You were not deemed a viable lifeform," the male voice replied. "Most certainly, a business venture worth the wealth of several star systems would not be stopped on your account."

"Our assessment! We were still living in thatch huts, how were we expected to stop an asteroid impact? Your court system is morally defective." The voice sounded so familiar, but through the garbled hacked intercom and multi-path filtered audio, it was hard to get a fix on it.

"Morality is not solely a function of humanity, my dear. But for the last fifty thousand years or so the Chiata have corrupted our morality with fear. I knew fifteen thousand years ago that this day would eventually come. My legal team and I have taken on these cases since the Chiata came into power. They are ravenous, vile beasts, and I fear they will never leave well enough alone until they have devoured our entire galaxy and moved on to the next nearest one. We aren't even certain that they originated in our galaxy. We think they are one of the few species that expanded from the edge of the galaxy inward. There is still enough of a semblance of legality and morality in the system that we are usually able to stall with legal proceedings for a milennium or two, but never indefinitely. In your case, we have done well. Fortunately for you, the Chiata have been occupied with other endeavors, and yours was a minor one."

"Minor!" the female shouted. "Minor! You think the total destruction of an entire sentient species over multiple worlds is minor?"

"We've had this conversation so many times. Yes, in the grand scheme of things, it is minor, as I have explained to you for nearly two hundred years. We must get past this and decide how to evacuate your people."

"Bullshit! You didn't build that damned membrane detection and communications systems out here at the edge of the auctioned region all those years ago just to tell us this bullshit and then evacuate us. You have allies or you wouldn't have been able to hold them off in court for so long."

"You are suggesting I do what, then?" the male voice said.

"Help us fight them."

The man laughed. "Without some sort of proof that you can stand up to the Chiata, there is no chance of having anybody else get involved. Not even the Ghuthlaeer, who hate the Chiata down to their last ounce of blood, would stand with a small group of primitive worlds."

"Okay, so you won't fight with us for now. Give me some intelligence on them that will help. I need information. Give me a target. Preferably a soft one that we could get to and make a first impression or a statement about who and what we are. What type of creatures are they? What is the basis of their technology?" Nancy shifted her weight on her feet as she listened. There was too much familiarity in the discussion. She had a bad feeling about all of it. This was big and needed to be reported back to General Moore immediately.

"Rackman, the visual?"

"Almost there, Penzington. Keep your shirt on," Rackman said.

Any luck on that visual, Allison? she thought.

Yes, I have had DeathRay move one of the Archangels into a position that I have given them, and the pilot is pointing the mecha's telescope per my specs. If the light incident on the exterior penthouse windows will allow, we might be able to zoom in on the room. Imagery is coming up in a couple of seconds.

Good work, Allison. Her DTM view turned into imagery data. A video screen floated out in front of her with real-time optical imagery on it.

Zoom in on it and get me facial views.

Done.

Nancy watched the image self-adjust, and a clearing algorithm removed fuzzy edges and made it sharp. There were a few glares and the occasional glint from the window that got ahead of the software, but Allison quickly cleaned it all up.

The man was definitely her target. He had close-cropped black hair and boring features. It was him. The female was presently turned and looking out a window on the opposite wall.

"I have been feeding your people technology, strategies, plans, and more for two centuries. Once you were able to communicate with me in real-time I did what I could. There is little more I can do for now. Please consider the evacuation strategy."

"Not unless it is a last resort. An absolute last resort!" The woman shouted and pounded her fist against the window. The spike in the audio algorithm caused by her fist hitting the pane hurt Nancy's head and made her skin crawl. She shook her head and blinked her eyes from the pain.

Put an amplitude impulse filter on this thing, will you, she thought.

Sorry about that.

"Very well. It is your choice to choose extinction. I have always suspected this is the path you would take. But at some point, don't you think you should give the rest of your people a chance to decide?"

"A target, Copernicus. Not civilian. Military."

Copernicus laughed again. "To the Chiata there really is no difference. You should consider what you are planning here, Sienna. Please let us find a way to evacuate your people while there is still time."

"How much time?"

"The Expanse usually moves quickly. While they do not have quantum membrane teleportation, thank goodness, they do have something similar to your hyperspace vortex jaunt propulsion that allows them to expand their borders at about seventy-five light-years per year. Their newest world closest to you is Alpha Lyncis, which is about two hundred and three light-years' distance from Sol. I would guess they will be here at your world in two years. They always start from the outer worlds and work their way in. Though, with your technologies, it shouldn't take them long at each of your worlds. I would guess no more than a few months before they venture inward to the subsequent world. In less than five years they will be at Earth. If you are very clever and as mighty as you think you are, maybe you can stall their expansion wave another year or so. You must start to evacuate now."

"We will do that if we have to. For now, give me some intel on them and a place to strike while we can. We don't have to defeat them at first, we just need to draw in some allies."

"Penzington, I've got the target in my scope. You should have the imagery DTM now," Rackman told her. Nancy brought it up beside the other imagery in her mind. Rackman was looking at a completely different angle than the mecha sensors were. He was looking right through the window that the woman was staring out of, but he was focused on the male target.

"Rackman, put the female in your crosshairs now."

"Roger that."

"I'm downloading to you now the nearest Chiata settlements and outposts that might be of interest to you. These are smaller settlements and exploration outposts and will not hold the full might of the Chiata Expanse's forces. You will have little chance against them, I fear." Copernicus hesitated briefly and then said deadpan, "My dearest Sienna, I can only wish you good luck."

"Got her in my sights," the SEAL said over the net.

Then Nancy heard a sizzling through the audio and there was a flash of light in the room. As the lightning settled away the visual view cleared. The lady in the penthouse continued to stare out the window with a grimace of anger on her face. Nancy had no doubt who she was looking at.

Ninety-nine percent image correlation with President Sienna Madira, Allison said.

No shit. I got that several seconds ago. We have to get the hell out of here now. Connect me to Jack AIC direct!

You are connected.

Jack! Emergency snap-back to the Madira *immediately! Everybody get out of here now!*

Chapter 33

December 3, 2406 AD
61 Ursae Majoris
27 Light-years from the Sol System
Saturday, 4:41 PM, Expeditionary Mission Standard Time

The inside of the *Madira II* aft hangar bay was a flurry of action, but it was a routine one. Supply ships continued to pour in from Sol space and the occasional mecha would take off or land on routine patrols. Every now and then an AEM or a droptank would QMT in. The AEMs would pound off toward the gear locker and the droptanks would walk themselves to their predetermined hangar space. There was nothing out of the ordinary.

The flash of light around Nancy subsided and the buzzing and crackling stopped as she appeared on the hangar floor in the personnel emergency QMT safe zone. Her armored suit buzzed in a half of a second after her and fell limp next to her. The two security officers on watch for the area looked up sharply.

"Are you okay, ma'am?" one of the guards asked her. Nancy knew it was standard protocol. "Is there something wrong with your suit?"

"I'm fine. Thank you. Suit is fine too. Could you have it put in a locker for me? I'll get it later." Nancy turned toward the hangar bulkhead walking path and, as fast as she could, made her way toward the elevator. Rackman and then several of the AEMs popped into reality nearby. The security officer paced her.

"Uh, yes, ma'am. We'd be glad to," the security officer said nervously.

Nancy knew that she couldn't order soldiers around, since she was a civilian. On the other side of that coin was the fact that she was very closely tied to the general's family and to DeathRay. Most people always helped her.

"Mrs. Penzington?" Gunny Suez raised his visor. "What gives, ma'am?"

"This is above all our pay grades, Top. Sorry I can't explain further."

"I understand, ma'am. Is there anything I can do for you?" Top asked as Lieutenant Colonel Jones and First Sergeant Howser QMTed in next to him.

"Not at the moment, Tommy. Thank you though. If you'll excuse me I have to see the general." Nancy turned and continued to walk.

"Rackman, what you saw was classified at the highest level. You are not to share it with anybody until the general can debrief us. I know I'm not your commanding officer or anything, but DeathRay will confirm these orders. Are we good on this?"

"No worries, ma'am. This ain't my first rodeo, mate." Nancy could see what Dee liked in him.

"Great, thank you, Lieutenant." Nancy said.

Allison, where is General Moore?

The Moores are in their quarters. It is night cycle here. They are in bed.

Patch me through and let me know as soon as Jack and Dee land. No, better yet, just have them report to wherever I am with the Moores at the time.

Understood. You have an audio channel with the general.

"General Moore, this is Nancy Penzington."

"Yes, Nancy? Is your team back already?" Moore asked. He sounded as if he'd just woken up and wasn't completely to his senses yet. He rarely sounded that way.

"Well, sir, we need to speak immediately, and in a secure private location. And by 'we' I mean you and Mrs. Moore, sir," she said.

"Very well then, meet us in the captain's lounge," Moore said. "Can this wait ten minutes, or is it 'the' ship is about to explode' immediate?"

"Uh, well, sir. I don't think ten minutes will matter."

"Okay then, we'll see you in ten minutes. Moore out."

"DeathRay to Penzington?"

"Go, Boland." Nancy switched channels immediately.

"What gives? Where's the emergency? Are you okay?" DeathRay sounded nervous.

"I'm fine, Jack. But, as soon as you land, get Dee and go to the captain's lounge. Can't talk until we get there," Nancy said. The elevator opened and she stepped out onto the bridge deck. The captain's lounge was to the port side of the bridge entrance and only a few doors down from the Moores' quarters.

Alexander hadn't said a word throughout the entire briefing and replay of the audio and visual data from Nancy's encounter. At first he wasn't quite sure what to think and believe, but there was no denying what he was seeing and hearing right in front of him.

"But she killed herself," Sehera almost whispered. "How can this be? We were there. She did it right in front of us."

"The continent city we were in was filled with repeated faces," Nancy said. "Look here at the images. We can only assume they are clones of some type."

The images popped into everyone's virtual DTM view. All three Moores, DeathRay, and Nancy were looking at hundreds of images of clones. There were repeated images that could have been the same person except that they were wearing different clothes and in different locations at the same time.

"There are one hundred and three faces as far as we could tell, sir," Nancy added. "Uh, not counting Sienna Madira and Copernicus."

"Wait a minute. I can't believe what I'm seeing," Alexander said. "Abby, do a cross reference of these images with images of the 91st Tharsis Recon Battalion Armored Environment Suit Marines and display the results for everybody here."

Twenty-nine of the images matched with the faces of his old squad, and matched exactly. That explained what Madira was doing with the blood samples the doctor had found in the med bay of the ship. That also meant that Madira herself had likely been on this ship.

"What does this mean, Daddy?" Dee asked. Alexander was glad she chose not to call him "general." He smiled at his daughter. She was still in her flight armor skins. It amazed him how much she looked just like her grandmother.

"It means that Elle Ahmi collected the DNA of my squad while she was torturing them. And it means that she then cloned them and some other people for whatever purpose," Moore said.

"It makes perfect sense!" DeathRay actually snapped his fingers. Moore looked at him with a raised eyebrow.

"Jack?"

"Sir, sorry, uh, well, it does make perfect sense," DeathRay explained. "When Nancy and I found the ships so far from Earth we couldn't imagine how people could handle such long trips in space. I mean, it would have taken them many tens of years to get out this far with that old propulsion technology. And how much food and water and air scrubbers would they need to make it? The logistics of that seem almost impossible."

"Of course," Nancy nodded in agreement. Moore kept silent and listened. "You're right on target, flyboy."

"You see, sir," Jack continued, "you could send a ship full of blood and all you'd have to do is keep it cold. Once it arrived at the destination, just thaw it out and start growing clones."

"Is it possible that the Madira out there is a clone or that Elle Ahmi had been a clone of her?" Dee asked.

"No way to know." Nancy answered. "But this one at 61 UM is certainly acting like the Elle Ahmi that I encountered."

Moore sat and listened to the speculations being thrown about by his family. They really didn't have any solid evidence to go on. But Alexander wasn't so sure that it mattered. The big elephant in the room wasn't Madira. It was this alien threat. He needed to steer the conversation toward that and get some thoughts on it. He turned and looked at his wife, who had been quiet the entire time. She looked pale.

"Sehera, are you okay?" he asked her softly and gripped her hand underneath the conference room table.

"I'm okay. She's alive. That is her. I know it, Alexander." Moore could tell his wife was fighting back a mix of anger, sadness, guilt, and joy all at once. Her eyes were watery and her jaw was clenched. He had hoped they'd made peace with that part of their past but somehow it kept coming back like a recurring nightmare.

"I wouldn't doubt it." Moore said. Then he stretched and leaned back in his chair. He was going to need some stims to stay awake for a few days.

Abby, bring up our path and the colonies on the star map I briefed the President with.

Roger that, sir.

A star map with all of the human colonies and outposts marked popped up. He tapped 61 Ursae Majoris with his finger and it turned red. Then he grabbed it and expanded it to see the system now that the recon team had images of it.

"Three planets, many moons, an approximation of tens of billions of, well, people of sorts, some kind of QMT transceiver system built by an alien, and a long-dead former president discussing a pending alien invasion." Moore paused briefly. "They will be at Earth in five or so years if we can't stop them out here. What does all of this mean?"

"What had looked like a wall wasn't really a wall at all," Deanna mumbled to herself. "She was never trying to separate from the union. She was trying to save it!"

"Dee?" Alexander looked at his daughter. She was talking to her AIC and had the thousand-yard stare while she mumbled. "You have something to share with us?"

"Yes! I get it now." Dee said to Nancy. "I had a vision when I died."

"What?" Sehera gasped. "Dee! You need to talk to us about these things."

Alexander bit his tongue and let her finish.

"Well, I did talk to Davy, uh, Lieutenant Rackman—" Sehera gasped and Alexander raised his eyebrows. He didn't like that.

"Relax, I didn't tell him any of the gory details. Besides, he suggested I had PTSD and should talk to a professional," Dee explained as she held up both hands palms out in an attempt to calm their response. Alexander decided to remain calm for now. If he had to, he'd go kick a certain SEAL's ass later.

"Did you seek help, Dee? Did you talk to the doctor?" Sehera asked.

"I don't have PTSD, Mother. But I did talk to a professional problem solver and observer. I spoke with Nancy." Dee grinned at the spy. Alexander was glad she kept their dirty laundry in the family.

"Anyway," Dee changed the subject back to her vision. "It was very strange. My grandmother came to me—or rather it was a jumbled bunch of memories of her and everybody else all at once. I thought I was going nuts or that there was some real message from her from beyond. Nancy and I double-checked for any strange communication signals or hacks. There were none. Whatever this was came from my mind alone." Dee paused and Alexander could tell she wanted to express this very succinctly. So, he continued to listen without interruption.

"Keep going," Nancy encouraged her.

"Well, Nancy and I have talked about it and I think it is my mind figuring something out unconsciously or subconsciously. And I know what it is now. At least part of it." Dee explained. "Elle Ahmi, the Seppy wars, even the Martian Desert Campaigns and the Exodus, it was all a wall that wasn't there! A smokescreen for her true purpose."

"Plans within plans within plans," Alexander added. "I heard her say this as Elle Ahmi on Mars."

"She said it all the time, Alexander," Sehera added.

"All of it," Dee continued. "All of it was to create a war machine. Whenever that alien contacted her AIC, he must have told her that an invasion was coming. He somehow convinced her she was humanity's only hope. And I have a feeling he didn't get the reaction he was hoping for."

"Mother would never just run away, not unless it was part of a bigger plan. She has been driving all of these wars all this time to prepare us for something even more horrible?"

"This explains something else too, Daddy," Dee added.

"What's that?" Alexander asked

"This 'auction zone' explains why we've never found or been contacted by aliens before. It's clear now that we're not alone in the galaxy."

"Sweetheart, I think you are absolutely on the right track here. But we need more than speculation about all of this. We need answers and I can't think of but one place to get them." Alexander stood up and rolled his neck from right to left and then popped his back. "We've been sitting at this damned outpost too long anyway."

"Alexander?" Sehera asked.

Abby, sound an all-hands announcement, he thought. *And open the channel.*

Done, sir.

The bosun's pipe sounded and the automated audio message played.

"All hands, all hands, stand by for a message from the Captain."

You are on, sir, Abigail told him in his mind.

"All hands, this is General Moore. Prepare to move out within the next four hours to a new target location. I want battle stations ready and manned. This is not a drill."

Cut the feed, Abby.

Done, sir.

"Deanna," Alexander turned to his daughter. "Go get cleaned up, dear, I'm taking you to see your grandmother."

Chapter 34

December 5, 2406 AD
61 Ursae Majoris
27 Light-years from the Sol System
Monday, 7:41 AM, Expeditionary Mission Standard Time

"Yes, sir," the ship's Science and Technical Officer, USN Commander Monte Freeman, nodded in agreement with the CHENG. Moore listened to their explanations but had to cut them short. The two of them were geeking out on the new physics and were enthusiastically getting over the general's head. Throughout the conversation Alexander had to have Abigail explain what they were telling him. He finally had cut to the chase.

"Buckley, you agree with the STO that this cloaking switch will work for all of the ships in the fleet?"

"Well, uh, sir, yes sir. It appears to have worked on the shuttle, mecha, and AEMs on the last recon mission. I believe we have created a genuine quantum membrane cloaking field that works like the ones the Seppies and the bots have been using for decades. But ours is better, sir," Buckley said, puffing out his chest and tapping it with his finger.

"What do you mean, 'better'?" Alexander asked his chief engineer. He turned and looked at the STO, who was also smiling and nodding in agreement. The two of them were more excited than a hamster on stims.

"You see, General, our system is more than just a hack and copy of the Seppy/bot system. We aren't just sending out a code that tells the sensors to ignore that it is detecting something. Our system literally quantum connects with the sensor system and alters the quantum wavefunction in such a way as though whatever we are cloaking was never there. The quantum physics is such that the area around a cloaked mecha isn't even there—or more like it is confused where it is," Buckley said. Moore couldn't understand the distinction. "If we hadn't found these ships, sir, we'd have never figured this out. Fortunately, these things had the Seppy cloak systems on them and we were able to reverse engineer them."

"Joe, I know this may sound simple to you, but I'm not seeing how what you just said is any different than how the Seppy system works." Moore shrugged his shoulders.

"Let me have a shot at this, Joe," Captain Freeman said.

"Right, your turn, sir," Joe said anxiously.

"General, let me put this to you in very military terms," the STO started. "If we take an AEM suit and turn the Seppy algorithm on, and you are looking at that suit with your eyeballs, and at the same time any other sensor, you will see the suit with your eyes and not your sensors. If you shoot the suit and hit it damage will occur."

"Okay, I get that," Moore said. "And?"

"Well, sir, if you take the same AEM suit and turn our new switch algorithm on that isn't what happens. You will still see it with your eyeballs, but not with any other sensor like the Seppy system. The key difference here is that the cloaking field also acts like a QM teleport field to high-energy density fields interacting with it but with random spatial displacements. In other words, if you shoot at it with a high-energy projectile or a directed energy weapon, the cloaking field redirects that shot away from the suit."

"Are you telling me this thing will cause a weapon to miss or bounce off?" Moore asked.

"Yes," Buckley interrupted. "That's it, sir, but it is more like it makes the projectile turn a random curve away from the cloaking field."

"So, we have shields like in the movies? Is that what you are telling me? Not structural integrity fields that hold material together, but actual barrier shields?" Moore thought this invention couldn't have come at a better time.

"Yes, sir. That is exactly what we are telling you. But the field transmitters can only redirect so much energy before they fail, sir," The STO added.

"Okay, how much energy before they fail?"

"We haven't fully tested that, but they could take many, many direct hits. If we used the SIF generators to generate the fields for the fleet ships they could take many hits from DEGs or even a direct nuke, probably. Maybe even two if we were hit at the right place," Captain Freeman finished.

"Hot damn!" Alexander clapped Joe and Monte on their backs and then shook their hands. "This is out-fucking-standing, gentlemen! Make this happen on all the ships now. How long will it take?"

"Well, sir, the *Madira II* and the *Hillenkoetter* are already outfitted. We are working on the others. Vice Admiral Walker has her CHENG working on the five ships detailed to her," Joe said.

"Good. How soon until we can have all forty-four ships in the fleet with these working cloaks?" Moore asked.

"With current staff, sir, a week at the soonest." Buckley replied.

"Okay, focus on having the *Madira* ready for battle in the next hour. We QMT to 61 UM very soon. I'll contact Vice Admiral Walker and have her start in on the rest of the fleet."

"Sir!"

"All hands, all hands, battle stations. All hands, all hands, battle stations. Hold for a message from the captain."

"All hands, this is General Moore. We are going into a system unlike anything we've ever encountered before. There are likely to be things we'll see there that no human has ever seen. I'm sure we will all have many questions. Log the questions with your AICs and then put them aside. First and foremost is to do our duty. Whatever your position aboard the fleet might be, whatever your job is, do it. First and foremost, do your job. Our mission must succeed. We'll answer questions later. Also note that it is likely the things you are about to see are above your security clearance levels. Treat everything we see here today as Above Top Secret. There will be a debriefing following the mission. Good luck to everyone and Godspeed. Moore out."

"All hands, all hands, battle stations. Prepare for QMT in ten seconds. Ten, nine, eight, seven, six, five, four, three, two, one. QMT in progress."

✧ ✧ ✧

Sehera stood behind the general's chair in her personal armor suit. She looked down at her husband, who was in his AEM armor in the oversized captain's chair. Alexander had issued a new protocol that all soldiers who could be armored would be armored during combat engagements. Sehera had been no exception. All of the bridge crew were wearing light Navy armor suits except for Firestorm, who was a Marine and was wearing an AEM outfit, and Hailstorm, the ground boss, who was wearing Army gear.

"The Buckley-Freeman Switch is operational, General. Shields are up," the STO announced.

"Good." Sehera watched as the large flash of light and circular event horizon opened in front of them. The *Hillenkoetter* entered the QMT disk of uncertainty first.

"The *Hillenkoetter* is through, sir," the Nav officer announced. Sehera stood still but held on firmly to her husband's chair.

"Take us in, Penny," Alexander said.

Sehera felt the buzzing and popping feel of static electricity even through her armor suit. The sounds of crackling and sizzling filled the bridge briefly. Once the flash of white light subsided, the view out the bridge viewport was much different. They were very near a yellow star, and just out in front of them was a blue-green planet only slightly smaller than Earth and covered with oceans. It even had a small moon orbiting it. The most interesting thing about the view to Sehera was how busy it all looked. There didn't seem to be a place on the surface of either the planet or the moon that wasn't covered with signs of advanced civilization and technology. There were lights covering the night sides of both.

"We're here, sir," The STO said. "According to the readings from the recon team we are in the same system and that is the planet they visited."

"Roger that, STO." Alexander turned to his wife and smiled. "Looks busy, doesn't it?"

"What do we do now, Alexander?" Sehera asked. "Does she know we're here?"

"If they detected our entrance, they certainly can't see us now with their sensors. They'd actually have to look at us with a direct visual," Alexander said. "Okay, Lieutenant Brown," Alexander said to the com officer. "My AIC has just given you coordinates. I want a direct line-of-sight communication beam directed to that point on the surface of the planet. There is a message attached to the coordinates package. Have that message play on repeat until further notice."

"Aye, sir," the young lieutenant replied.

"Nav, move us any random direction a good hundred thousand kilometers or so from this position. If they did detect the QMT, we shouldn't stay put waiting to get shot at. And relay the same orders to Captain Penzington on the *Hillenkoetter*."

"Aye, sir," the nav officer replied.

Moore turned to his wife. "Okay, dear," Sehera returned a business-as-usual look. "We wait and see."

Sehera paced nervously. Could it be that somehow her mother was still alive? If the Sienna Madira out here was actually her mother, then how had she watched her mother shoot herself in the head with a railpistol after the Battle of Ares? And even more, all those years she was growing up, was the Copernicus AIC in her mother's head really an alien or was there more to that?

Sehera didn't really know if she cared. What excited her mostly, and at the same time scared her and made her sad, was the possibility that her mother was a good guy even while being the most horrific and bloody character in human history. Sehera was going through a serious moral dilemma. She had personally been spared the gruesomeness of her mother torturing, maiming, and killing countless humans as she was growing up. She was tormented and horrified by the fact that her childhood was very loving and normal. Her mother and father, whom her mother later murdered, had never once been anything more than absolutely loving toward her. Her life had seemed so normal—until she had reached her late teens and then her early twenties when the veil of her mother's humanity was lifted.

She happened to stumble into the wrong place at the wrong time, and discovered that her mother was Elle Ahmi, a ruthless terrorist killer. Once Sehera had reached fifteen years old her mother could no longer hide from her the fact that she was plotting to take over the Sol system and all of humanity. The wars on Mars started, and Sehera watched her mother be ruthless and, by any definition of the word, evil. And then there were the Martian Desert Campaigns and the attack on the Separatists by the Marines.

Sehera had lost the love for her mother, or rather, had decided her mother no longer truly existed and was totally insane, once she saw how she treated the prisoners of war in the deserts of Mars. It had twisted her insides and her humanity to the point that she had grown up a decade in a few days. At first, she had felt like committing suicide. Then she had felt like running away. Then she saw U.S. Marine Major Alexander Moore and how the man fought for life so strongly and with every fiber of his being. It was then that Sehera had completely cut her mother free and knew she had to stop her and save the Marine.

Now Sehera was feeling all of that again, but with the strange twist that her mother might have been doing all of this for a much bolder purpose than mere conquest and bloodlust. Sehera was actually warming to the idea that perhaps her mother really was doing what had to be done to save humanity. Still, she couldn't bring herself to that much forgiveness so easily. Hundreds of thousands had died at her hand due to her plans within plans. There must have been a better way to achieve the same goal. So much death and destruction was an evil means even if it were to a good end.

"Alexander?" she whispered lightly. The general turned to her and rolled his head to the right a bit.

"I don't know, dear. We'll just have to wait." He leaned back into the oversized chair. Sehera let out a light sigh. She hoped something would happen soon.

Chapter 35

December 6, 2406 AD
61 Ursae Majoris
31 Light-years from the Sol System
Tuesday, 11:41 AM, Expeditionary Mission Standard Time

Sienna Madira sat at the desk in the center of her penthouse office. The dignified proportions of the room relaxed her and reminded her of a time when she was revered by billions. It reminded her of a time long before the horrible years had begun. The horrible years that had to happen in order for humanity to survive.

The former president, turned military leader and terrorist, studied the data that Copernicus had uploaded to her AIC. Her original AIC Copernicus from so long ago had been taken over by the alien entity who had built the transmitter and who had fed her information and technology for years. She had come to call that entity Copernicus. The two of them were in constant communication if they needed to be. But her current AIC was a state-of-the-art model that had been upgraded by the alien technology, and as far as Sienna could figure, was more advanced than any that existed. It had taken her some time to get adjusted to calling her AIC something other than Copernicus, as she had done for almost two centuries, but after more than eight years she had managed to break the habit.

Scotty, she thought. *All of these locations are densely populated areas. Is there any information that suggests some of them are of specific logistic, military or political importance to the Chiata?*

There is a lot of information, Madam President. It will take me a while longer to collate and filter the information into bins that will enable elimination of target choices. She had named her AIC after her daughter's father.

I suspected as much. Copernicus never makes it easy for me, she thought. *We just have to keep at it and be thorough. There is time.*

Yes, ma'am.

Sienna Madira continued to study the details of the overwhelming amount of data floating around in her direct-to-mind view. The data could take years to fully understand. But she knew that humanity didn't have years. Only two or three at best.

She decided to filter through the data for information on the alien technologies of the Chiata. Copernicus had given her a general encyclopedia on the species and hoped that there would be something in there that would be useful to her in designing some sort of attack plan.

Madam President, Scotty interrupted her.

Yes, Scotty?

Ma'am, the chief of staff says she needs to speak with you immediately, and the Secret Service is with her.

Okay, send them in.

A woman and three men entered her Oval Office. The men were wearing standard body armor suits and carrying firearms. The woman was dressed in business attire.

"What can I do for you, Maria?" Sienna asked her Chief of Staff. The damned clones were all so emotionless and robotic. Sometimes, Sienna had wished she had just built mechanical hosts for the AICs, but Copernicus had insisted they be humanoid due to the more susceptible and compatible quantum "wet" brain characteristics.

"Madam President, good day. We are receiving an unencrypted signal from approximately six hundred thousand kilometers in space radially outward from the sun. The beam is so tightly controlled that it is only incident on the White House. It is addressed to you." The chief of staff spoke completely devoid of any emotion whatsoever.

"Is that right?" Madira asked. "Then let us hear it."

"As you wish, ma'am." Maria nodded her head slightly to the guards and looked back to Madira. "Do you wish to hear it in private?"

"No need, dear. I've got nothing to hide from you."

Hell, I can control their thoughts if I need to. I certainly don't have to hide from them.

Yes, ma'am, her AIC agreed.

"Let's hear it now."

"Very well, Madam President," Maria said. Then an audio message started playing over the room's sound system.

"Hello, mother," the voice started. "It is me, Sehera. I have been searching the stars with my husband, General Alexander Moore, and my daughter, Major Deanna Moore, and many of our friends for remains of the Separatist movement. Along the way we have found clues that have led us here and to you. While I have no way of knowing if you are the Sienna Madira of Earth, and my mother, the evidence does point in the direction that you are at least somehow connected to my mother, even if you are not her."

"Well, I'll be damned. Moore found me," Madira said out loud.

"Ma'am?" Maria asked.

"Oh, hush, dear, and let me listen." Madira waved her hand at the clone and continued to listen to the message.

"We are here with a fairly substantial force, but we wish to talk, not to fight. We have also been watching you for some time now. We know about the alien Copernicus and the impending invasion from the Chiata Expanse. Mother, please come to us at the coordinates imbedded in this signal and discuss in detail what our next steps either together or apart will be. We would very much like to speak with you in private."

The message paused briefly and then started to repeat.

"Okay, turn it off." Sienna stood and looked around the room. "Maria, get me the SecDef in here now."

"Yes, ma'am. He is waiting outside presently."

"Well, don't just sit there, girl. Send him in." Madira felt antsy. What should she do? She could always just teleport out to them, but she would be unprotected. Of course, she could always snap back too. That is, unless Moore used a dampening field to keep her there.

"Madam President?" her secretary of defense entered the office. They all spoke so damned emotionlessly. It had taken her years to get used to that. "I gather you have heard the signal and are contemplating your next move?"

"Your thoughts, Sam?" she asked the clone.

"Well, ma'am, my biggest concern is that they claim to have been watching us for some time now and we have had no knowledge of this. Also, our sensors are not picking up any ships in the system that are unaccounted for. That said, this signal is coming from exactly where they say it is."

"Alright, then, it is settled. Prepare my shuttle. I want to be wheels up in less than ten minutes." Sienna thought for a moment. "Wait, make that twenty. I want to change my attire."

"Yes, ma'am," the clones said in unison as they flurried out the door.

The Archangels sat in their mecha in the hangar bay. Each mecha was neatly stored in its own maintenance alcove. The invention of the mecha QMT system had forever changed the combat deployment procedures for pilots. DeathRay used to love the way the fighters would systematically hover out to the catapult and be thrown like mad projectiles out the back of the carrier into the shit. DeathRay had long developed his own ritual with mission deployment. But those days were no more. Nowadays, mecha jocks sat in their planes ready to go, and when the mission time was right for them to be deployed, they would be QMTed directly from the ship into the shit or some tactically and strategically advantageous position near the shit.

At the moment, every pilot in the *Madira II's* flight wing was sitting tight and ready to fight.

"Alright, Archangels, all is quiet right now, but we've got no idea when that might change. Keep your standard attack playbooks loaded and listen for my audibles if we need to change them." DeathRay obsessively checked that his universal data port cable between his suit and the Gnat-T's computer console were locked in. Then he checked it again. He ran through the wireless connectivity and then he double-checked his weapons list. Then he brought up the playbook in his DTM battlescape view. All the Archangels showed up as stationary blue dots. Jack was beginning to wonder if they were ever going to get the show on the road and then the call came.

"Archangels, this is QMT tower," came the operator AIC over the tac-net.

"Archangel One, go, tower," DeathRay responded. He adjusted his weight in the flight couch and gripped the HOTAS stick with his right hand and gently placed his fingers on the throttle on the left.

"DeathRay, the Archangels are go for rapid calm, repeat, rapid calm, deployment in five, four, three, two, one," the tower AIC announced. And then the world flashed and buzzed and sizzled and DeathRay and the rest of his squadron were deployed, the squadron in a tight V formation about him. "Rapid calm" meant there were no immediate hostiles in the area and his DTM mindview backed that up.

"Moore to DeathRay."

"DeathRay here. Go, General." DeathRay checked his right three-nine line to make certain Apple One was right where she was supposed to be. Of course she was.

"DeathRay, we have a dignitary guest approaching our current vector," Moore's voice said. "You and your wingman are to escort the shuttle to the aft hangar bay and then accompany the dignitary to the captain's lounge. Copy?"

"Roger that, General Moore. I've got the shuttle on the tracker now." DeathRay could see the red dot approaching their location in his mindview. He looked out in the general direction for a glint, but with the star at the shuttle's back, he couldn't make it out yet.

"Moore out."

"Alright, Archangels, we are on escort duty. Lock on to the red dot and let's follow the bouncing ball," he told his squad. "Apple One, stay on me and we'll take the lead."

"Roger that, DeathRay," Apple One replied.

"DeathRay to Fish."

"Fish. Go, DeathRay!"

"Fish, Apple One and I are going to take this bird on into the hangar bay. We'll be there for a while. You'll have the angels at that point. Copy?"

"Copy that, DeathRay."

"Alright, Archangels, I don't see any signs of trouble, but that don't mean there ain't any coming. Stay frosty and keep your eyeballs open." Jack laid out an intercept track to the incoming shuttle. The QMs and radar picked up the shuttle just fine. He pitched his snub-nosed fighter over about fifteen degrees and banked left and made a beeline for their target. "Apple One, stay loose on me just in case there is a shakeup. I don't want us bumping into one another."

"Roger that, DeathRay." DeathRay could see her blue dot giving him a little space.

Candis, you got anything out of the ordinary? Jack thought to his AIC.

Negative, Captain, the AIC replied.

Private channel to Nancy. DeathRay thought he'd check in with her and see if her super AIC had come up with anything to worry about. It was nice to have such contacts to fall back on.

Channel is open.

"Nancy, you getting any weirdness out there?"

"Well, nothing other than a system full of deadpan faces and rampant activity. No. The entire system reminds me of an ant colony," Nancy replied.

"Let me know if you get anything."

"Will do. Jack. Be careful," his wife told him.

"DeathRay, you seeing the shuttle yet?" Apple One said on the pilot tac-net. "I've got multiple glints surrounding the location of the red dot, but only one dot. We're being jammed."

"Roger that, Apple One. I say right back at 'em." DeathRay had suspected that, even though they had the Buckley-Freeman Switch, they would still be jammed by the bots and the equipment in this system. They had been jammed for years by the random quantum field generators Elle Ahmi had been implementing. Why would he expect anything different now? At least now, they could jam the enemy right back.

"Tit for tat is what I always say," Dee replied.

"When have you ever said that in your life, Apple One?" USN Lieutenant Commander Song "TigerLady" Davis laughed.

"DeathRay, *Madira*!"

"DeathRay here. Go, *Madira*."

"Be advised of multiple bogies verified eyeball, not on sensors. Copy?" the Air Boss' voice warned him.

"Roger that, *Madira*." DeathRay could barely make out some definition on the glints now. But they clearly had wings and tails. The shuttle had a mecha escort.

Jack, by the inertial movements of the six glints I calculate a very high probability that they are Seppy Stingers, Candis informed him.

I was guessing that, Jack replied.

"Be alert but stay frosty, Archangels. Those are likely Stingers out there. We're not here to engage. We are here to escort them to the *Madira*."

✧ ✧ ✧

Deanna stayed loose on DeathRay's wing as they led the shuttle and the six Stingers to the aft hangar bay of the Madira. She scanned the fighters with every sensor she could think of, but could not detect them other than with her eyeballs. Jack had warned her that the same thing had happened on several different engagements. It usually took a few minutes for the AICs to link to the visual information coming into the pilots' brains to create a DTM Red force detection and tracking algorithm. Fortunately for them, the Seppies, and later the bots, had never learned how to jam the human eyeball and brain combination.

Dee ventured as close to the enemy Stingers as she could and noticed that they had human pilots. Well, at least they looked human. The enemy mecha looked just like the mecha they had found aboard the fleet. The Stingers out here looked just like the Stingers on deck on the fleet ships. Dee guessed that there were Gnats with similar paint jobs as well. The only difference in paint jobs were the pilot designations painted near the cockpits, which the enemy didn't have. And the fleet's Flight Wing squadrons each had their own symbols painted on the tailfins.

"Tower Madira, Apple One on final approach," Dee called over the landing net.

"Roger that, Apple One. Clear for final. Call the ball."

"Apple One. Affirmative. The ball is green." The tracking and alignment target in her DTM turned from a red to a yellow, then a green ball in her directional gyroscope. She brought the mecha in softly alongside the shuttle. DeathRay and the other six mecha were scattered about in a loose formation. They all touched down and were taken over by the taxi hoverfield.

"Apple One is in taxi."

Dee toggled the canopy and it started to rise slowly as she taxied into the aft hangar parking zone alongside the other vehicles. She disconnected the UDP cable and the other harnesses. Before the vehicle came to a complete stop she stood and crawled out of the pilot's couch and then leapt from the empennage to the deck with a thud.

"What's our play, DeathRay?" she asked Jack as he approached her from the other side of his mecha. The two of them popped their helmets and tethered them over their shoulders.

"Simple. We keep our mouths shut until we get to the lounge. No small talk, Dee, no matter how much you want to. Your father's orders."

The two of them stood flank on the either side of the shuttle's ramp. The hatch cycled with a hiss and the ramp lowered to the ground. The pilots of the Stingers had stayed in their mecha. Dee wondered why. As the ramp lowered to the deck, a woman who looked just like Deanna and Sehera moore, except for a white stripe through her bangs, stood looking back at them.

"My God, look at you. I was hoping to see you, my dear. But I had no idea you were a mecha jock!" Sienna Madira said. "My, you've grown since the last time I saw you."

She was talking to Dee. The fact that she claimed to be the woman who had met Dee before was intriguing. Dee thought that she looked like the woman who had held her captive on New Tharsis all those years ago.

"Ma'am. Please follow us," DeathRay told her.

"Very well, Captain, uh, Boland, is it?"

"Yes, ma'am. Please follow us. I hope you don't mind, but we'll have to place a security detail on your shuttle and your mecha until you return."

"It will be fine, Captain Boland. I have no intention of causing a ruckus, son."

Chapter 36

December 6, 2406 AD
61 Ursae Majoris
31 Light-years from the Sol System
Tuesday, 1:55 PM, Expeditionary Mission Standard Time

"As it stands right now, I have no intention of causing a ruckus." Alexander stood at the end of the table in the captain's lounge. He was still wearing his AEM suit and had the helmet tethered over the shoulder. All of them were in armor except for Madira, who was dressed in designer-style business attire. Somehow, she made Alexander feel underdressed. "But that doesn't mean I won't if pushed."

"Hah, you came here all armored up, not me," Madira told him. "Certainly looks like you're looking for a fight. You always were. That part I could count on every time, son."

"Is it really you, mother," Sehera asked. She clanked closer to her and studied her like a specimen under a microscope. "The last time we saw you, you, uh . . ."

"Oh, that," Madira said with a frown. "I'm sorry I had to put you through that, dear. But the last time you really saw me was in the Oval Office. What you encountered at my hideout was a clone being controlled by Copernicus. It was all part of the plan to allow you to end the war and pull humanity back together. It had to be done."

"Mother, why?" Sehera gasped. "Why would you put us through that? Why would you cause so much death and destruction?"

"Stop right there, girl." Sienna Madira held up her hand as if to shush her daughter. She then pulled a lock of her white-streaked bangs and tucked it behind her ear. Alexander watched cautiously but held quiet. There was no telling where this was going and for now he wanted to let it play itself out.

"It is very complicated," Madira continued. "Sehera, my child, I was faced with a conundrum almost two centuries ago. A creature from somewhere across the galaxy spoke into my mind and warned me that humanity would soon be overrun and destroyed if we didn't take steps to evacuate the entire population. I was told that humanity could not defend itself and that our only choice for survival was to give over the systems we were currently on and tuck tail and run away."

"We know all of this, Mother. Alexander found the files in your presidential archive. And Nancy recorded your recent conversation with Copernicus," Sehera interrupted her. Alexander liked the startled look on Madira's face when she realized they had been close enough to her to record her conversations with the alien. On the other hand, he wasn't entirely sure if she was truly startled or just impressed.

"We didn't know what the entity had told you until a few days ago, but now we understand that part," Alexander added. "We have a pretty good idea of what you have been up to. Or at least why."

"Well, I figured you would figure it out. You always were the clever Marine," Madira said to Alexander. "But imagine if this would have happened to you. There was no way I could tell this to anybody. I couldn't prove it. They would think I was nuts! Then, the only hope humanity had would be locked away and medicated in some insane asylum somewhere. Or at the minimum they would have pulled Copernicus out of my head, which would have ended my communications with him. The end result would have been the total loss of humanity. I could only assume that the alien wasn't bluffing. I had no choice but to do just what I did."

"But why the murders and wars and all of these robot death factories scattered about the galaxy and all of the clones in this system?" Deanna asked. "You were president. Couldn't you just do what needed to be done the legal way, without killing so many people?"

"Sweetheart, you are young and will someday realize that politics is a quagmire. I'm sure your father can tell you all about it." Sienna Madira sat down and leaned back in one of the chairs at the table. "I had to make humanity tougher, grittier, and stronger if we were to survive what is coming. Can we get some coffee or something? What kind of diplomacy is this? Never mind, I didn't expect any."

"I sent the chief of staff for some refreshments," Moore said. "They'll be here soon. Please continue. You were about to justify how you killed and destroyed hundreds of thousands of lives."

"Well, son, I can only justify it if it works. And even then I plan to spend a long time burning in hell for what I've done. But what I did do was spark a serious growth in military technology and might. In the civil war I created two very large armies and space navies that would eventually come back together. And don't forget, the taxation and land grabs and unfair policies from one colony to another one were already going on before I meddled with the system. There is no doubt that a civil war was bound to happen. Had it been allowed to happen on its own, the might of humanity would have been splintered into pieces across our little tiny piece of the galaxy. But my war caused multiple outposts to be built. It enabled me to proliferate the QMT technology across the galaxy a little farther. It allowed me to build a line between us and the oncoming invasion. And, it also allowed me to emplace a backdoor if we had to have it. The most important result is a unified, tougher humanity."

"Enough," Alexander raised his hand. He looked at his inner circle. His wife and daughter and Boland and Penzington were the only others who now knew the entire story. Did Madira's bloody means justify the end? Moore didn't know and he wasn't the judge, for now. There was still a part of him that wanted nothing more than to put a HVAR round through her brain bucket, but humanity came first.

"You have something to say, 'son'?" Madira raised an eyebrow at him.

"First, stop calling me 'son,'" Alexander told her. "Second, we'll worry about your justification later. You will somehow pay for all the deaths. You will pay for the 91st on Mars. You will pay for killing Sehera's father in cold blood. But not right now."

"You don't think I cry every night about having to kill Scotty? He was the love of my life! He was the father of my only child." Madira actually looked angry. Hints of the Elle Ahmi persona showed through as the corners of her mouth almost turned up into a smile. "He was starting to do end runs around the plan and could no longer stomach it. No matter how much I loved him, I couldn't put my love above the survival of the human race."

"Mother, there must have been another way."

"You weren't there, child. I've wargamed and simulated every scenario down to what I've eaten for breakfast every day for the last century and a half. It was the only way for it to successfully play out. I'm so sorry." Madira's eyes looked sad. Alexander could see the deep, soulful brown eyes of his wife and his daughter. For a brief moment he almost let himself get wrapped up in her pain and her woeful tale.

"We'll discuss your crimes another time," Moore grunted gruffly. "Right now we have more important business."

"You need me and you know that I'm right," Madira said.

"We need you. And, I believe that your solution is a viable solution. I don't know that it is the only one," Alexander replied. "The way I see it we have maybe a couple years to mount a complete plan. But that may be waiting too long. I'd prefer we strike now, as soon as possible. We need more on the threat. We need more on this Alpha Lyncis colony of theirs. If you have better intel then now is the time to share it. Somehow we have to confirm this intel because it will take a hell of a lot more than a good story from an old lady to convince humanity to invade the first aliens we meet."

"I agree that your timeline is right. If we wait until they get here it will be too late. And I do have intel on the Chiata Expanse."

"Pending that intel, I'd suggest within a month. And then move on to the next target if we can. I assume you recognize this ship?"

"Of course I do. I left it for you. This is a good ship. I used it for a few years during the Martian Exodus. Where are the others?" Madira looked out the window. "I did my best to create ships with the best of both Separatist and U.S. technology, plus additions of my own."

"We have the others at one of your bot bases nearby. We have taken that system. Forty-four ships, all supercarrier class. We had to, uh, sacrifice three of them," Moore said with a slight frown.

"Forty-four?" Madira laughed. "Forty-four?"

"What's the joke, Mother?" Sehera asked.

"Dear, I've been bouncing back and forth out here for almost seventy-five years. I have nearly thirty billion clones under my control in this system alone. I built over twenty-five automated defense posts. You think I would only have the one weapons cache?" Madira laughed almost maniacally. "There are two more. The one you found was the first and smallest one I had attempted."

"How did you manage that, Mother?" Sehera asked. "That seems impossible."

"No, not impossible at all. Not with AICs and bots. I found a paper from the mid-twentieth century by a Hungarian scientist from the Manhattan Project who had the right idea. He suggested that the best way to colonize space was to send robots first to build the infrastructure. Then humanity could venture out and supplies would already be in place for them when they got there. Very clever idea for a time before humanity had ever even been to space. And AI and robots were not even invented yet.

"I simply sent single AIC-controlled builder bots at maximum hyperspace speeds to fledgling star systems. Once they were there they would start self-replicating using the materials in that system. Once enough replicated they then turned to manufacturing starships. They had blueprints for everything right down to toilet paper in the bathrooms. Have you been to Vega lately? It is one of our backdoor locations. Well, it's more like a side door, but it was loaded with materials. The bots are having a field day there. There are hundreds of starships being built there."

"Hundreds?" Deanna gasped. "We might stand a chance."

"Not likely, dear." Sienna tilted her head slightly and looked at her granddaughter the way an elder does a child. "I'll download all the Chiata data to you and you will see how outgunned we are. Although I am very intrigued as to why I couldn't detect your ships and mecha and how you could possibly spy on me without me knowing."

"You're not the only clever one in humanity," Nancy told her. "We have some tricks even your alien hasn't thought of yet."

Chapter 37

January 2, 2407 AD
61 Ursae Majoris
31 Light-years from the Sol System
Sunday, 1:35 PM, Expeditionary Mission Standard Time

Alexander wasn't sure what he thought of the Copernicus clone body. It wasn't one from his old squad and as far as he could tell it was very plain. There was nothing extraordinary about it, if you disregarded the fact that it was a human cloned body that an alien entity had somehow managed to download itself into.

Madira explained that they had taken multiple DNA strands from the clones she had acquired and created a particular one for Copernicus. Copernicus had helped pick the DNA sequence hoping to make assimilation into the body least troublesome. Moore wasn't sure exactly how they'd managed to do that, but since he'd first met Elle Ahmi what he'd believed could be done had continuously been a moving target. And knowing there was some advanced alien species involved made it even easier to believe.

"So, you're not humanoid, uh, I mean you were originally something else?" Alexander asked. The clone body displayed the strangest expression Moore had ever seen. It was clear that the alien didn't understand facial communication. Madira made no notice of it. Alexander assumed she had been around him enough as to not be shocked by the weird and out-of-context facial expressions.

"No. Your species would consider us more like your mollusca animals. We were multipedal amorphous invertebrates, and only about thirty centimeters or so across our largest dimension. It was quite strange the first time I entered this mammalian form. But it is not unlike the bipedal warm-blooded creatures we formed a symbiosis with and parasitically controlled for mobility on my homeworld." Copernicus answer was very animated, with all the hand gestures and facial expressions in exactly the wrong places.

"Controlled?" Moore was shocked. "Were these creatures sentient?"

"Oh, get off your high horse, son," Madira scolded. "They were damned aliens with alien morals. Your Southern values don't apply here."

Alien morals, he thought. *That troubles the hell out of me.*

Yes, sir. Abigail agreed. *Would a parasite even be concerned with controlling a sentient creature?*

My thoughts exactly, Abby. Sounds a lot like slavery to me.

"I think I understand your concern, Alexander." Copernicus appeared to be laughing as he said it. Moore wasn't certain if he meant to be or not. "But no, the creatures were more like your large primates or maybe bears from your world. They had very dexterous digits that were useful and highly controllable. My people believe that they evolved to become our perfect vessels. But the Chiata killed them. They killed them all."

"I see." Moore replied.

"Enough with the small talk," Madira grunted. "We came here to show him tangible proof and the type of destruction the Chiata are capable of. So fire up this behemoth and let's go."

"Very well," Copernicus turned to a large wall that was either a wall screen or a window, because Alexander had a clear view of the large QMT transmission system outside. Sixty-one UM was very small at the Oort Cloud distance where they were, but it was still the brightest star in the sky. Moore realized that he was about to see how the alien had managed to contact Madira across the galaxy all those years ago. What he didn't get was how he had managed to build this facility by himself.

Copernicus reached into the clear wall with his left hand and the surface morphed around his fingers like pudding. The clear, glowing substance danced about his fingertips with each movement, sending trails of green light shooting through the image in the window like fireworks. Then the large spires over the central QMT pad of the facility began to spark and glow. A large circle of rippling watery blue light appeared and then flashed like an explosion. There was no sound or shock wave and there was no damage, but the phenomenon left Moore briefly lightheaded.

"What was that?" He shook his head back and forth to clear the stars from his vision.

"You get used to it," Madira said.

"As you can see, this is my home star system over a thousand light-years from here," the alien explained.

"Did we just jump the entire facility here?" Moore was amazed. There was a bright yellow star not much farther than four astronomical units away. If he hadn't known better he'd think he was back at the Sol system.

"No, son, we're snooping on it," Madira replied. "We ain't really there."

"Snooping?" Moore asked, all the while gritting his teeth wishing that Madira would stop calling him "son."

"What she means, Alexander, is that we are in a hyperspace dimension, or more closely to your people's understanding of modern physics, we are on a parallel quantum membrane peeking in at this one. They can't see us and we can't impact them. I have tried many times but cannot seem to connect with the Chiata brains the way I have with the human one. Their brains are quite different."

Alexander looked out across the star system. As far as he could see there were glints from the inner star. That meant very large ships or material or asteroids. Moore wasn't certain.

"What is all that?" He asked.

Abby, are you getting all this? Moore thought to his AIC.

Yes, sir.

Make note of everything.

As always, sir.

"All of those glints you see are fragments of my homeworld or from one of the other planets that used to fill this system. Here, take a closer look." Copernicus zoomed in to the largest glint. There was a large asteroidal object that had been transformed into some sort of factory system.

"I don't get it. Where are the planets from this system? There had to be gas giants, right?" Moore hoped the answer wasn't going to be what he thought it was going to be.

"There were seven planets, as you call them here. There were thousands of smaller bodies. The Chiata came here. In only twenty-five thousand years this is all that is left of my system."

"Holy shit." Moore said under his breath.

"Now you get the picture, son." Madira slapped him on the back. "They have even taken apart the gas giants for their purposes. They appear to have left nothing standing."

"How many of your people lived here?"

"Well, there were over seventy billion of us, but many of us were able to escape before the invasion. Over forty billion of us died delaying them." Copernicus attempted to make a sad face.

"What are they doing here?" Alexander asked.

"What they always do." Copernicus turned his head toward him as he continued to manipulate the translucent pudding wall. "They used every bit of resources in this system to support their expansion across the galaxy. As far as can be estimated, the Expanse covers tens of thousands of star systems. We have no way of knowing exactly how many, or if they are all used up like my world, or if they are being inhabited. We only know what the worlds on the edge of the Expanse are like. They appear to prefer to inhabit red star systems. Most of the other younger and hotter star systems on the edge are being used up in this fashion. My many millennia of observation tell me that these metal-rich systems are used to build their war machine and their habitation infrastructure, which must be exceedingly vast."

"If you didn't catch that, son, he's telling you that the Sol system will be devoured by these bastards just like this system was."

"Right, I got that."

"Yes, Alexander, I fear your only real hope is to escape. But Sienna has explained to me time and again that will not be your first response. You humans have a propensity to fight, even in hopeless situations."

Well, that's one thing me and the crazy bitch agree on, he thought.

Oo-rah, sir.

"Wait, why can't you just use this device and spy on the other systems deeper into the Expanse?" Moore asked.

"It can only 'sling forward,' as you say, so far. We are close to that limit now. The Expanse is too great."

"Shit."

"My sentiments exactly, son," Madira added.

"Well, can you show me a skirmish between any other aliens and the Chiata? How about these Goothlyears you've talked about." Moore was tipping his hand as to intel they had on their conversations. Madira looked surprised but only slightly so. Copernicus had the ultimate in poker faces in that his expressions were always random or off-cue.

"Ah, the Ghuthlaeer are indeed in a continuous, bloody struggle with the Chiata, and they would make a great ally, but probably not good, as Sienna says, bedfellows." Copernicus replied. "Unfortunately, the nearest engagement zone between them and the Chiata is more than another thousand light-years from here. That far exceeds the range of this device."

"Well, we need to figure out how to pay them a visit in the very near future," Moore said gruffly. He hated being at the mercy of Madira and this alien, for all of their important intelligence information.

"I will think on that one," Copernicus replied. "But for now, I would like to go back. Seeing this system is more than distressing to me."

"I can understand that." Moore believed the alien was sincerely distraught. Somehow he had to figure out a way to prevent humanity from suffering the same fate. While Alexander had some pity for the creature, he had been through too much shit because of the son of a bitch to start trusting him now.

Chapter 38

March 12, 2407 AD
61 Ursae Majoris
31 Light-years from the Sol System
Sunday, 5:55 PM, Expeditionary Mission Standard Time

"Well, all I can say, sir, is that it is a tactic, or, eh, a strategy that hopefully the aliens haven't thought of yet," DeathRay told Alexander.

"Or perhaps they have long forgotten it or decided it was too small a threat to consider," Nancy added.

Alexander wasn't sure where they were going with the conversation, but after two weeks of studying the data handed over by Madira, he hoped that somebody had come up with a strategy. He looked out the window of the "living room" of the *Hillenkoetter*. Nancy had been true to her word when she said she was going to make it a home. The lavish Victorian-style furnishings were so different from military style and function that one could almost forget where they were. But the view outside the window immediately brought Alexander back to the reality that he was in a starship over thirty light-years from home and contemplating going even farther out—much farther out.

Several squadrons of mecha were engaged in combat training and were flying madly about chasing each other's energy vectors about space. There were mecha squadrons from the *Madira* chasing others from the 61 Ursae Majoris military. They were learning how to fight together. Moore leaned back in the high-backed green and mauve chair and almost laughed at the contrast.

"Okay, okay, what small threat are you talking about?" he asked.

"We are clearly going to be fighting an asymmetric war with the Chiata. So, we should follow ancient asymmetric warfare tactics," Nancy explained. "Just like the Afghans did during the war with the Soviet Union in the late twentieth century."

"Or the Spartans at Thermopylae," DeathRay added.

"The Spartans died, Jack," Nancy frowned at him. "The American Revolution is a better example. The first Martian Separatist movement is as well. The Boer War between the British and the South Africans is another. There are hundreds of examples throughout history of a smaller force holding off or at least pissing off a larger force. But the point is, General Moore, that we need to strike targets hard, violently, in as visually horrific ways as possible, and get in and get out as quickly as possible. And we need to keep doing it until we make the aliens tired of dealing with us."

"Either that or they will decide to accelerate their timetable and eradicate us as quickly as they can," Moore added. "But the strategies used on both sides at Thermopylae might be of use."

"How so, sir?" Nancy asked. "Would you like some more wine?"

"No, thanks. While I'm off duty right this second, I'm never really off duty." He shrugged. "To answer your question though, the Spartans, Greeks, Thebans, and the others on the low side of the engagement used a small passage to bottleneck the Persian army so that they couldn't use all of their might at once. We need a bottleneck."

"Yes, sir," DeathRay added. "We force them from a ball to a bowl and the fight breaks down into a close-quarter knife fight. The tankheads and AEMs would love that."

Alexander understood the mecha jock lingo and it was in essence his point. And perhaps that was the key to space navy battles. One needed to maximize the benefit of being in a ball or bowl type engagement. Moore filed that for further thought.

"The other piece, sir?" Nancy asked.

"Well, the Persians found a secret pass around the bottleneck and sent an overwhelming force to sneak in behind the smaller force. The Spartans were trapped between two larger forces in a perfect kill box," Moore explained. "So, how the hell do we set that up against an overwhelming and technologically superior force? How do we create a bottleneck in space? How do we lure the enemy into it? And how do we find a secret passage around the bottleneck to trap them in a kill box?"

"Well, sir," DeathRay pondered out loud. "They don't have QMTs. There's our secret passage right there. We can outrun them anywhere. We can go three light-years in a second. Using the jaunt speeds, the Chiata can only travel about a seventh of an AU per second. It would take them about seven seconds to go from Sol to Earth or between Earth and Mars, for example. And to go all the way out to the Oort Cloud at that speed would take about five to six days."

"That is brilliant, Boland." Nancy was impressed by her husband. "Our QMT snap-back and sling-forward algorithms would certainly give us a serious advantage there even if we were outgunned."

"This is very important," Alexander rolled strategies and tactics around in his mind for a brief instant. His years of combat experience and military training were coalescing into at least the spark of a strategy for their initial target. "We need to get the seniors into a strategy meeting and flesh this out. I want to include Madira and whoever her seniors are as well. Hold one."

Alexander held a hand up and thought to his AIC. *Abby, set up a full on strategy and battle planning session with the seniors from CDC, the bridge, and air and ground segments. Have the Chief of Staff send an invite for the Madira and her counterparts to attend. No later than twelve hundred tomorrow.*

Yes, sir.

"You two, keep thinking on this."

"We will, sir." Jack replied to them both.

"We also need to think of this as a long-term engagement with a bunch of rapid short-term ones. I doubt there will ever be time to get ground down in a long-term infantry fight like on Mars," DeathRay added. "Do we believe we could ever hold a hill, sir?"

"I don't know, Jack. I just don't know." Moore stood and adjusted his UCU top. "Thanks for the hospitality. But I think I need to think on this even more. We need a very sound plan before I can go to the White House with this. Keep at it, you two."

"Sir," Nancy stopped him before he could QMT back to the *Madira II*.

"Yes?"

"Have you considered Sienna Madira's request to man the fleet with her AI clones? We could really improve the numbers game and I'd like to have a minimal crew over here." Nancy said.

"I think it is time we address that elephant in the room," Moore said. Her being a civilian made it difficult for him to order her to do anything. Her not being a military fleet captain but in charge of a fleet ship added even more issues. On top of that, now the ship would seriously be needed for combat and she was wanting a military crew. Moore wasn't sure what to do about it. "I think we need to consider having a military captain for this ship."

"This is my ship, sir. And with all due respect, sir. This is *my* ship." Nancy stood. She didn't take her gaze from Moore. He knew she would react this way, but he didn't have much choice in the matter.

"It would be different if you had some previous military training in your background that we could point to. But, as it stands . . ." Moore shrugged. "I'm at a loss. I know I promised you this ship and the fleet when we were finished with them, but you must see that we need every weapon we can grasp our hands around right now."

"Sir, what was the first order that you as president signed following the end of the Seppy War?" Nancy asked him.

"What does that have to do with anything?" Moore was growing impatient, but he also knew that Nancy did things almost as planned-out as Sienna Madira had. She was up to something.

"The first major order you signed, sir?"

"It's in the history books, Nancy. You know it as well as almost everyone does." Moore was confused about where she was going with this. "The Tau Ceti Accords. That is the first thing I signed into law upon my return to the White House."

"Yes, sir. And what did TCA 45678.22 say, sir?" she asked, still standing and still staring him down.

"Uh, 45678.22," he paused.

Abby?

Tau Ceti Accords line 45678.22 put into law the joining of the Separatist military with the U.S. Military, sir. Specifically, it brought any current enlisted, warrants, or officers into the military with full rank and privilege to the same or an equivalent if they desired and could find a job. Otherwise, the provision allowed for full honorable discharge from their equivalent rank and all rights and responsibilities accompanied with them.

Right, I got it. Moore thought. *Thanks.*

"I can see from the expression on your face that you have consulted Abigail and that you know the provision I'm addressing?" Nancy asked.

"Yes, I do, but I'm not certain how this applies," Moore said.

"Allison, upload the specifics of the last five years of my mission on Tau Ceti to Abigail, please," Nancy said. "Sir, please note that the upload is an official mission brief as submitted and filed upon my return to Sol space. The mission documents are available if you need to verify them."

"Okay, stop." Moore didn't have to go through all of this. He trusted Nancy with his life. Even more, he had trusted her with his daughter's life on several occasions. "Just cut to the chase. I trust you dotted the I's and crossed the T's."

"Very well, sir. As my last mission on Tau Ceti before the rescue of your daughter from Elle Ahmi, I was Separatist Navy Mecha Pilot Ensign Bella Penrose of the Separatist Nation Contingent, New Tharsis Division. The Separatist records show I was trained in military flight school and was commissioned as such. After the battle at Tau Ceti, Bella was assumed MIA and likely KIA and was posthumously given the rank of lieutenant junior grade. As that was over twenty years ago, my service and record should have been corrected and updated to present military status. From considerations of back pay and other promotion potential being missed, sir, I estimate that I should be at a minimum the rank of Navy commander if not captain, sir. I could also point to other missions where I was other military ranks as well. I've been trained, sir. I can do the job."

"No shit." Alexander couldn't help but laugh. He had signed the law himself that would let him slay his elephant. If she wanted it slain. "Nancy, are you asking to have your rank reverted and to be activated?"

"This is *my* ship, sir. Nobody is taking it from me. If I have to take a Navy rank to help you complete the mission I promised I'd see through with you and your family, then that is what I will do, sir." Nancy said.

"Nancy, are you sure you want to do that?" DeathRay looked at the two of them. Moore could tell by his expression that he couldn't believe what he was hearing. Alexander wasn't concerned if Nancy could soldier up or not. He'd been with Nancy in a fight and she was damned good at it on the ground, in a suit, in mecha, hell, anywhere. But Nancy was a free spirit, a lone wolf. Alexander's biggest concern was if she would take orders.

"If it is what I have to do to keep this ship as mine and to see this invasion through, then that is what I will do." Nancy was serious, dead serious, and Moore could see it in her face.

"We'll make it happen." Moore smiled and then tapped his wristband. "Thank you for the hospitality. I'll see the two of you tomorrow at noon." The room flashed and buzzed, and he was gone.

Deanna was glad to have a few moments off. She had been wargaming and flying maneuvers pretty much around the clock since they had entered the 61 Ursae Majoris system. The SEAL, on the other hand, had been mostly hanging out with AEMs discussing tactics for fighting on asteroids, Kuiper Belt objects, comets, and moons. Mostly, he had nothing to do. Dee had seen to it that he had plenty to do, to her, for the previous hour or so. Their time together had been both physically demanding and relaxing. For the most part they both had just needed to be there for each other. The past month of devastating injuries and recovery and then back to mission business as usual had made the two of them even more dependent and familiar with each other.

Deanna was sitting up and leaning against Rackman's strong Navy SEAL shoulders and unconsciously rubbing his chest with her right hand. The two of them were in bed looking out the portal in her quarters at the myriad of mecha gyrating and spinning about the fleet. Her grandmother—who nobody knew was her grandmother but "family"—had deployed her entire system navy out to their original rendezvous location. There were seventy naval vessels, with more than thirty of them supercarrier class. Others were frigates and scouts used for smaller, faster, and more tactical activities. Her father had brought in the rest of the fleet from the outer base. Presently, the 61 UM system was a flurry of activity with over a hundred ships moving about and learning how to fly with each other. The number of mecha swarming the larger ships seemed uncountable.

The AICs of the 61 UM system and the master-slave system on the Penzington fleet ships, as they had been calling them, made the multiple-fleet ship orchestration simpler than it sounded. Dee watched it all with amusement and amazement. There was something very Zen about it all. It was a cacophony of motion, like the ballet, only with the potential to be much more violent. And to Deanna Moore, it was much more exciting and beautiful.

"I was offered a promotion, Dee," Rackman said out of the blue. They had been mostly quiet basking in the afterglow of lovemaking and watching mecha. The sudden talk disrupted Dee's mellow contemplation of it all.

"What? A promotion? About time. When do you get pinned on?" Dee said, only half paying attention to him. She was paying more attention to the energy lines the AI clone-driven mecha were making compared to the ones with human pilots. She was tracking them in her DTM mindview. The clones seemed to pull the curves tighter and push the reverses faster. It was almost as if they could handle more g-load than the standard mecha jock. One of the Maniacs, Popstar according to her DTM tracker, was dead to rights bullseyed by two of the clones but then she did a Fokker's feint. The mecha went to bot mode and then looked as if it had passed out, falling head over heels, all the while rolling about its body axis. Once the mecha turned upside down to face the two clones on its six, Dee could see the cannon in the mecha's hands tracking the two clone fighters. They quickly dispersed in opposite directions at g-loads that must have been crushing. Somehow, Dee noted from the Red force tracker, the two were not hit and managed to get away. She made a mental note to herself that she needed to think on her attack strategies to allow for those types of maneuvers.

What if the Chiata can fly like that? she thought.

I will begin running some response tactic simulations, Dee, her AIC responded.

Good. Tie DeathRay and Candis in on that as well.

Will do.

"Tomorrow, when I report to my new station," Davy said. That got Dee's attention. A new station meant somewhere else other than the *Madira*. Her father must have had something to do with it.

"Where!" Dee said. The Zenness had gone now. Her attention was fully on Rackman. Anger was slowly starting to percolate. "Daddy did this."

"Maybe he did." Rackman added, "But I'm gonna take it."

"You didn't anser my question. Where?" Deanna turned and looked him in the eye. If she had to, she'd go toe-to-toe with her father if this was some ploy to separate the two of them.

"I was asked to be Mrs. Penzington's XO. She's a tough sheila. It'll be fun." He smiled as best he could at Dee. She could tell it was a tough choice for him to make, but as things presently were situated she could pop over to Nancy's ship anytime.

"She's not military," Dee replied. "Why does she need an XO? And, you're a SEAL, what the hell do you know about being XO of a supercarrier?"

"She is captain of her ship. And she requested that she be given a crew to fight alongside the rest of the fleet," Davy said. "And, hell, I grew up in Sydney, mate. I lived on sailboats, that's why I went into the Navy. I like boats. I was nav on a frigate before I got accepted into BUDS. I'll do fine with or without your overwhelming confidence in me."

"Uh, yeah, well, who knew?" Dee looked at Davy. She hadn't really thought about what he was before he was a SEAL and before they had met. She realized that they had been together a long time but she had never really opened up to him and gotten to know him. "If it is what you want to do then I guess it makes sense. I'm still surprised that Nancy is going to be captain of a military crew."

"Well, I think there will be some sort of announcement tomorrow about her military status. At least she hinted at such when she spoke with me this evening while you were still out flying." Dee was surprised. She thought she knew everything the "family" was doing. But she had been working hard and had been out of touch. In fact, she and Jack had only talked flying over the past several days. Dee realized that she had no idea what was going on with him and Nancy at the moment.

"Hmm, sounds like an unusual move for her. You would think I would have heard before you would have." Dee nudged him a bit and resituated herself against his chest. "We're kind of, well, close. She's like my big sister, sort of."

"Maybe not. You've been flying so much lately that I hardly have gotten to see you. And, I just got these orders a few hours ago." Rackman ran his fingers through her hair gently. Deanna truly enjoyed the feel of his hands ever so softly tugging at her long, straight black hair like a coarse comb. There was something about the warmth of his hands and the firmness of his body against her that she would never be tired of.

"Well, who knows, maybe she was military before we were born or something. You never know with people, especially those who've been undercover spies most of their lives." Dee purred softly and melted deeper against Rackman's firm chest. "I'll find out when I'm supposed to, I guess. That's how my father arranges things. For now, I'm off duty for ten more hours. I just want to lie here and, uh, meditate with you, for a while."

Chapter 39

June 6, 2407 AD
61 Ursae Majoris
31 Light-years from the Sol System
Tuesday, 9:35 PM, Expeditionary Mission Standard Time

"There is something kind of Zen about it, wouldn't you agree, sir?" Firestorm said quietly to Alexander as he looked across the hangar turned briefing room at the sea of senior officers from the U.S. Fleet and the equally large group of AIC-controlled clones from the 61 UM Navy. The executive officer of the U.S.S. *Sienna Madira II* stood beside General Moore flanking his right while the leader of the clones and bots stood next to him on his left. On the front row sat Vice Admiral Walker and her bridge crew and seniors.

Moore could see his daughter sitting amongst the mecha jocks. DeathRay was sitting next to her. U.S. Navy Captain Nancy Penzington sat beside him. Lieutenant Commander Davy Rackman, her XO, sat beside her. The AEMs lined the back of the room all centered about Lieutenant Colonel Francis Jones and Master Gunnery Sergeant Suez right behind him. The Army teams were just in front and to the left of the Marines. Brigadier General Mason Warboys sat in front of the Army tankheads and behind him flanked the Warlords.

There was little talking for that many people to be sitting and waiting. This was a sign of discipline, perhaps, Moore thought. Or more likely, an air of urgency and intensity in the room. There was certainly permission tension and jitters being dealt with by all. Moore was certain he could have heard a pin drop when the sizzling sound started and then white light flashed on the makeshift stage.

"Attention!" Firestorm commanded. "Ladies and Gentlmen, the President of the United States of the Sol System."

The buzzing and sizzling sound of bacon subsided and President Rene Upton stood before them, flanked by Secret Service guards on either side. She looked across the room and then turned to Moore and shook his hand. She then turned to Sienna Madira and looked as if she had seen a ghost. Then she shook the former president's hand as well. Moore found the uncomfortable motion of the president almost humorous. If she only knew that not only was this the revered and thought-long-dead president, but that she was also the most hated terrorist in human history, he wondered how she would react. But as it stood, the Moores and Madira herself had managed to fabricate a history leaving out the fact that she had been Elle Ahmi. In fact, they used Elle Ahmi as part of the story. Madira had been thought to be killed by one of Ahmi's terrorist attacks, so they used that as an excuse for Sienna Madira to take to the stars and begin secretly stealing technology from both sides of the war to prepare for the pending invasion that only she knew was coming. The story held up well. Madira was good at creating stories to cover the truth. She'd been doing it for centuries. Moore and his family managed to create just the right amount of cover where they needed to. This meant that Madira, Sehera, and Deanna had to be careful about calling each other by family monikers like mother, grandmother, daughter, and granddaughter. For now, Moore was glad that the cover story was solid. Humanity had more to be concerned with right than a checkered and very bloody skeleton in its closet.

President Upton raised an eyebrow at Alexander as if to ask if they were ready for her. He nodded and motioned toward the microphone. Then she turned to the podium and cleared her throat with a light grunt.

"Please, be seated," President Upton requested. In true military fashion the room quieted completely and everyone took their seats. "Yesterday, June 6, 2407, is a date that will live in human history with even more infamy than any other day across all the darkness in our past. As this date marks another great attack in the history of our great nation, so shall it do so again!

"The United States, humanity, was at peace with itself, and to our knowledge, with the rest of the universe. We know now that peace of the past eleven years and the wars of the past two centuries were nothing more than a trial, a test, for us. It was a time for preparation. A great leader of our nation set in motion events over two hundred years ago that would shape our every move leading us to this day. The great President Sienna Madira had long been thought dead, but it has been revealed to us that she was in hiding in deep space preparing us for humanity's greatest challenge to come."

Alexander continued to assess the forces that sat in the room before him listening to the president's speech. Humanity's hope was embodied in each and every one of the soldiers and clones of the Allied Expeditionary Fleet. Each of the soldiers and clones was hanging on every sound and syllable the Commander-in-Chief made, trying to believe that this was not the beginning of the end for all of humanity. They all needed some hope that humanity could stand up to the approaching force. If Upton didn't give it to them, he knew that somehow he or Madira would have to.

"I have discussed attack plans and strategies with many of you here," the president continued. "I have discussed them with advisors, the Joint Chiefs, and senior members of both houses of Congress. All of the greatest scholars and military minds and policy makers who were trustworthy enough to keep this mission secret, as it needs to be, have given their unanimous consent, approval, and prayers that we should march forward, we can accomplish our objective, and we *will* by the grace of the God Almighty be triumphant. Humanity will rise to this test and we will pass it." The president waited for the applause to die down.

"I wanted to come here and speak with each of you this morning. I felt it a moral imperative that each of you will know directly from me that while you are very far from home—and you are about to embark on such a deep space mission as to be farther from home than any human had expected to be for probably another hundred years—that you are in my heart, mind, and prayers. You are the tip of the spear in our fight to survive in what now is clear to be a hostile and sometimes unjust universe. Perhaps we shall march to the stars with all our might. And with God on our side, our might and His will, we will prevail." Once more, the room burst into applause.

"I know that most of you have trained and prepared hard developing today's course of action. You all must deeply miss your homes and families. I have been assured by General Moore that each of you who so desired did indeed teleport home before today and spend some moments with your families. After all, it is for the love of our families that we must march forward and do these hard things. This mission is an endeavor that has taken four months of planning and preparation and a Herculean amount of hard work and effort. Let's hope, no, let's pray, the hard work pays off."

Alexander listened to the president as she finished. She wrapped up telling the fleet that home would be there waiting for them when they all return and, Lord willing, they would *all* come home. Alexander knew better. Every wargame that he, Abigail, Madira, Nancy, and Allison had run had been grim. In fact, there were only a few of the battle plans run in random-fashion simulation where any humans came back at all. But simulations couldn't account for everything. Sometimes, a good battle plan, strong troops, and a little bit of faith could pull a soldier through the shit. Alexander had seen it in his lifetime and he hoped he was looking at one of those times again. The time had come for humanity to step up to the grown-ups' table, and that wasn't going to happen unless they squirmed in and made some elbow room, or better yet, knocked one of the adults out of his seat.

"Thank you," President Upton finished. "Godspeed and good luck."

It had taken the better part of an hour for the president to meet with the troops individually. Alexander had watched how she interacted with them and he most certainly approved. Finally, his chief of staff managed to shuffle the president, Sienna Madira, and himself away from everyone and into the captain's lounge. Alexander waited for the two women to be seated and then he joined them at the table. He was still in his dress uniform, but, as per his new battle-ready protocol, he and all of his crew would be armoring up before they set sail toward Alpha Lyncis.

"Isn't this the strangest of things?" President Upton said to break the tension in the air. "Three former U.S. presidents of very different but historically trying times locked away in a room together. What secrets we must have."

"Madam President," Alexander smiled. "I'm not certain what secrets you are referring to."

"Oh, to hell with the protocol, Alexander," Madira grunted. "What are you fishing for, young lady?"

Alexander almost chuckled at the way Madira spoke. She had been president so many years, then a bloodthirsty maniac for several decades, and on top of all that she had been solely planning the salvation of mankind; she didn't care much for small talk or politics.

"There is clearly an elephant in the room," Upton said. "It was never so evident until I met you in person, President Madira. It *is* a great honor, mind you."

"What elephant would that be?" Madira said.

"I've met your wife and seen her picture in the history videos, Alexander." Upton held a thin-lipped fake smile on her face. Alexander would have described it as a poker face, and not a very good one. "I just met your daughter. Lovely young woman. From her record, she must be outstandingly brave and bold just like her father."

"Thank you, Madam President." Alexander replied. He held his own poker face perfectly expressionless.

"And just like," Upton continued, "her grandmother, I suspect. Who were Sehera's mother and father, again?"

"Madam President, you said yourself you have seen the history videos. Sehera was one of the millions of orphans from the Martian Desert Campaigns. That is where I met her. She actually helped me escape from Elle Ahmi's torture camps," Alexander said. He choked back bile and every urge in his body to eyeball Madira when he said that. The torture camps had torn into his psyche deeply and he would forever have to suppress the urge to tear Elle Ahmi from limb to limb for her part in it.

"Yes, that's right. I do recall reading that," Upton replied.

"Young lady," Madira interrupted her before she could continue her thoughts. "It doesn't matter. Whatever you are thinking may or may not be the truth. It may or may not matter in the grand scheme of things. But the elephant will stay in this room and nowhere else. Humanity is in the balance here, and discussing whatever past elephants in the rooms or skeletons in the closets will not help us move forward. I will tell you that I agree that Mrs. Moore and young Deanna are lovely and wonderful people. And over the past few months I have taken quite a shine to them. So much so that I've even suggested they consider me a godmother or godgrandmother, especially since they never got to meet their real ones respectively. So, let us just leave it at that and not bring it up again. There are more important issues to deal with right this second."

Alexander looked between the two women. Upton didn't blink and Madira didn't seem to give a damn. Moore suspected that Madira would as likely leap from the chair and strangle Upton to death before she'd let her compromise her plans. Somehow he had to maintain the peace between the two. As much as he hated to admit it, humanity needed both of the women to play their parts. Humanity didn't need some sort of historical scandal to distract it from surviving.

"President Madira, I can't think of a better person to take on such a role for the two women. They are very lucky indeed." Upton gave a fake campaign smile. "Now, how soon before you start your QMTs?"

"Within the hour, Madam President," Alexander exhaled in relief that she had dropped the issue. "Astro-nav calculates it will take us sixty-eight QMT jumps to get to Alpha Lyncis. We'll make several stops along the way at planetary systems and drop off some of President Madira's Von Neumann probes. The bots will start building forward bases with teleport facilities for us along the way at each of the stops where there are star systems. So far we've identified 47 Ursae Majoris, Gliese 433, and Alpha Ursae Majoris as viable planetary systems in the path to our target. There are most certainly more."

"How long until you get to your target?" Upton asked.

"It will take us roughly an hour or so at each stop to recalibrate navigation and to make certain the probes are deployed. We want to do a rudimentary check for intelligent lifeforms. We'd hate to wipe out some indigenous population inadvertently along the way," Moore explained.

"So, seventy hours and you'll be in combat?" Upton asked, already knowing the answer.

"Well, possibly, ma'am." Moore nodded. "We'll stop in the outer parts of the system first and deliver our ambush teams, including several ships full of battle bots like those we've been fighting for the past year and a half. And, I'd prefer to have one sleep cycle before we go to battle so our troops are fresh at the start. Once we hit the inner system we'll fire as many gluonium-tipped warheads as we can and engage whatever forces are in the system. If the intel we have is good, well, the forces there are quite overwhelming. But we'll make do."

"I get the idea, and I've got the details of the battle plan if I want to go through it. This plan is all that humanity has. I am having simulations done for evacuation to systems further inward toward the galactic center, but I doubt we have time for that." Upton finally let a frown slip through.

"Don't count us out just yet," Madira said. "We haven't even started the fight yet and you are already giving up."

"Not giving up," Upton looked at Madira sternly. "Being responsible for the billions of lives trusting I have their best interest at heart."

"I would be more concerned about actual survival than getting re-elected," Madira grunted. Alexander could tell it was time to separate the two. So he interrupted before the discussion could devolve further.

"It isn't really re-election that has been most on my mind," Upton added. "How do we truly know that these Chiata are the bad guys? Even if they are the bad guys, does it justify such a first strike? This is similar to Pearl Harbor or the September 11, 2001 terrorist attacks or the attacks on Olympus Mons during the Exodus. Only we are talking about killing every Chiata in an entire system."

"Young lady, from the data we have available, the expansion wave of the Chiata is clear. Granted we only have one source of data, but I have no reason to disbelieve it," Madira said. "I have been in collusion with the alien calling himself Copernicus for a very long time and he has visited me here with other aliens from the galactic community. Trust me, they were very alien. And not a one of them had any love for these Chiata."

"That is my problem," Upton said. "If all of these other aliens hate the Chiata so much, why have they not stood up to them?"

"According to the data that I have passed along to you, they have and are." Madira sighed as if she was growing impatient of reexplaining herself over and over again. "Copernicus expressed specifically that had it not been for the Chiata being occupied elsewhere they would have likely moved on us thousands of years ago."

"So, we are even more in the alien's debt," Upton said sardonically.

"I don't think debt is what they have in mind." Madira nodded her head slightly and raised her left eyebrow. Her white-striped bangs came untucked from behind her ear. "I think vengeance is more like their hope."

"Vengeance?" Moore said, surprised. "We are so outnumbered in this and they expect us to exact vengeance for them? Whatever type of alien Copernicus is, we have to take his word for it, but they must be far more technologically advanced than us and stand a better chance at exacting vengeance."

"Copernicus' people were wiped out by the Chiata. He claims that some thirty billion of the mollusk-like intelligences escaped and are hidden away somewhere. But remember that they needed some sort of other creature to bond with to carry them around. Copernicus claims there are none of them left. The Chiata knew just how to attack them. There are insufficient numbers of aliens, advanced or not, to stand against the Chiata expansion," Madira explained. "I think numbers is what we can bring to the table. Well, that and a propensity to be stubborn as hell and to make war. Those are two things which you excel at, son."

"Well, hopefully, this first attack will excite more of these other aliens to join in and help us. And I don't like the thought of helping out aliens that attach to and control other creatures. We better make a big splash and get help. Help enough so that we aren't so devastated at the end of all this that some other alien group doesn't take us over if we defeat the Chiata." Upton frowned and then turned to Moore. "You better be as good as the history books say you are."

"Ha," Madira let out an uncontrollable chuckle. "Sorry, but from everything I've seen about the man he can be one big pain in the ass."

"Madam President," Moore said, ignoring Madira's comment. "If you don't mind, we have a lot of last-minute prep to do. I'd recommend you snap back to safety so we can get underway."

Chapter 40

June 9, 2407 AD
Alpha Ursae Majoris "Dubhe"
123 Light Years from the Sol System
Friday, 4:35 PM, Expeditionary Mission Standard Time

"Planetary system here has very odd orbits, General." The STO pointed out orbits in the DTM system view. "Dubhe is a double star system locally and a four-star system all together. There are planets scattered about, but only one fits into anything like the Goldilocks zone, sir."

"This one here, right?" Alexander tapped at the air in front of him, and one of the planets was highlighted with a see-through yellow ball. "How habitable is it?"

"Not very, sir. Looks like a desert planet at best. There is a minimal amount of liquid water closer to the the poles. The equatorial regions are wastelands. No green anywhere. There are significant asteroids and several gas giants with moons," the STO added. "One of the moons of the third gas giant out looks a lot like Europa around Jupiter. There is ice and as best I can tell now, sir, it has an ocean under the ice."

"No intelligent lifeforms, right?" Alexander decided to cut to the chase.

"None, sir. At least none that I can find."

"Very well. XO, deploy the builder bots and let's move on. That Europa-like moon might make for a good base since there is plenty of water there," Alexander ordered the XO. "We still have eighty light-years to hop through."

Moore swiped the system view aside and pulled over the QMT hopping path. There were still twenty-seven QMTs left before they made it to Alpha Lyncis and the Chiata. With roughly an hour for navigation recalibration at each jump, that meant sometime tomorrow they would be able to engage the enemy.

"Package is away, General," Firestorm said. "If those little bastards are as busy as the bots we've been fighting for the past year there should be a Disney World finished by the time we swing back through here."

"I've been to Disney World, XO." Moore laughed. "Last time turned out to be more than I cared for. But my daughter enjoyed the hell out of it."

"Yes, sir." the XO replied. "All ships and stations are reporting nominal status and are ready to jump whenever the Nav is, sir."

"Roger that, Firestorm." Moore turned to Commander Swain. "Penny? Jump us at your leisure."

"Yes, sir," the navigation officer replied. "I'm getting the final astrogation observations fed into my AIC now. Another five minutes or so is all we'll need before the algorithms lock onto our location. Then we'll need another ten or so to get the rest of the fleet lined up."

"Good. XO, you have the bridge." Moore stood and looked around at his crew and then out the viewport at the deep-space star system. They were presently farther away from home than anyone had ever gone. "I'm gonna go for a walk. I'll be back when we jump."

"Major Moore?" Commander Buckley looked up from underneath a power coupling he was working on surprised to see the mecha jock in engineering. "What brings you to engineering?"

"Hi, Commander. I know you are busy, but I need to talk with you about something." Joe was puzzled. He had spoken to the Marine many times before, but mainly in a setting where Rondi was around. The two women were friends and apparently trained in hand-to-hand martial arts together. Joe had really only spoken to Deanna Moore in social settings.

"Sure thing. What's on your mind?"

"Well, I was thinking about the upcoming mission and was wondering, why can't my AIC control when and where my mecha does a snap-back or sling-forward? I mean, why does the CDC QMT crew have to do that?" Moore asked. Joe had to think about it for second. He had actually never given any thought to the mecha pilots controlling their own QMT jumps.

Debbie? I can't think of any physics or engineering reason, can you?

No, Joe, as far as I can tell it is all in the software and protocol, the AIC replied.

No shit?

"I suspect it is mainly because if you and/or your AIC were incapacitated some other entity would have to trigger the system," Joe explained to Dee.

"But it is doable?"

"Uh, yeah, it's all in the software. I'd just have to get the general's approval for it. But I'm not sure why you'd need it."

"That's what I was hoping," Dee said with a smile. "How hard would it be to give all the mecha-jock AICs the ability? I mean, we're thirty-six hours away from our target; could it be done by then?"

Debbie?

I could do it in seconds once you get approval.

Thought so.

"Yes, but you'd have to convince the general that I am overriding the current safety protocols for a good reason." Joe set down the wrench he was holding and stretched his neck and back. "Major, what is this about?"

"This is about winning the fight, CHENG. Let me find Daddy and I'll get back to you ASAP." Moore turned and hurried out the hatch.

"Hmm. Wonder what that was about?" he muttered to himself. "Oh well, back to work."

Chapter 41

June 11, 2407 AD
Alpha Ursae Majoris "Dubhe"
123 Light-years from the Sol System
Friday, 9:35 AM, Expeditionary Mission Standard Time

Moore looked around his conference room at his team, his family. They had been on a long haul together and it appeared as though they were just getting started. In less than twenty-four hours they would QMT into a star system owned by the Chiata Horde. As far as they could tell, the Chiata were so far advanced over the human species that there was no real way to estimate how good or bad their mission tomorrow might go. Only time would tell.

Moore had gathered a good team. They had all been through a lot together over the last couple of years. They would do their best.

"Thank y'all for all the hard work you've put into the battle planning and the preparations leading up to tomorrow." He nodded at the team. They all remained quiet.

"So," Moore continued. "We have to talk about an elephant that we have invited into our living room and have seemingly ignored its presence. I've spoken to the president and she agrees with me on this. Admiral Walker is also on board with this and has helped in the wargaming and planning adjustments. We all need to be thinking on contingency plans in case our two new 'allies' decide to turn on us in the future." Alexander let that sink in for second as he paused for a breath and to assess if the team was up to speed.

"I want to emphasize that every aspect of this attack has been precisely calculated. You might notice that the majority of the human fleet is second wave except for the hovertank and AEM squads. I'll explain that in a moment." Moore noted that Warboys and Gunny Suez had traded looks with each other. Colonel Jones made no expression changes.

"I don't trust Sienna Madira as far as I could throw her. And I sure don't trust the alien who is actually some sort of parasite needing a mammalian host. I'm not sure I believe it is a coincidence that Madira has been pumping out clones as fast as she can and the alien claims there are something on the order of thirty billion of his people stored away somewhere with no hosts. There is just no way I believe Copernicus is about vengeance alone. There is more to this. I can feel it in my bones. The two of them have been plotting and planning for so long together that I have to believe that every word they say, every action they take, every move they make, is all wrapped up and twisted within massively complex strategies within strategies. I simply cannot believe that we fully understand either of their motives yet." Moore looked at his team one more time and then nodded to Walker. "Fullback, would you explain the basis of the naval plan, please?"

"Glad to, General," Walker replied. "Madira has amassed a very large navy of clone-driven ships. We know she claims to fight the Chiata. Okay, that may be true, but what happens once we defeat the Chiata, and Madira still has a navy that is ten times the size of our own?" Fullback explained through her rhetorical question. Moore was certain the same thought had been on all of his seniors' minds. "Well, I for one don't want to find out. This is why all the human vessels are on the second and third-wave attacks. We must engage the enemy to learn who and what they are, but we will use the clones before we use our living souls and we will attrite Madira's forces first."

"Hopefully, Madira truly has her heart in the right place, but I can't trust that. I don't trust that," Moore added. "So, at the end of this mess the United States of the Sol System forces must come out with superior numbers. But for now we also can't lose sight of the fact that it may take every last ship, mecha, clone, and human to stop the Chiata. We are literally between that proverbial rock and hard place."

"So we fight hard, but when we can, we let the clones take the most losses. Do we all understand this?" Fullback asked. There were resounding "yes, ma'am" answers.

"Now to the ground forces," Moore sighed. "Mason, Francis, Tommy, I'm sorry, but we need real intel on what these things are and what they can do. So, as usual, the AEMs and the Warlords will be the first on the beach."

"Wouldn't have it any other way, sir," Warboys replied.

"The Marines sure as hell ain't gonna let the Army have all the glory, sir," Colonel Jones stated. Moore was certain that Gunny Suez was about to throw in an "oo-rah" but managed to hold it back through clenched teeth.

"Thank you, gentlemen."

"Uh, sir," Deathray spoke up.

"Yes, Jack?"

"I know you are aware of the flight contingent battle plan. And we do plan on putting the clone mecha squadrons in first. But once we're in the ball, we're in the ball," Boland said.

"We can make no mistake here. We are in a fight for humanity, so we must fight." Moore thought his words through before he continued. "I know that none of us are against charging in and attacking this beast head on. And once the battle starts I want us focused on fighting and winning the battle. All I am saying here is that if we are in a situation where we must send troops into a projected high-loss situation and we can send the clones, we send the clones."

"Understood, sir," Deathray replied.

"I won't keep you any longer, as I know we all have work to do." Moore nodded to his XO who in turn dismissed the team. Deanna and Sehera held back and waited for the room to clear.

"Alexander, mother will figure out what you are doing very quickly," Sehera told him.

"She already expects me to do this," he replied. "That woman is hard to outfox. But sometimes you just have to do what you can and chip away at the stone every chance you get."

"Daddy, what about the other aliens out there? Whoever is fighting them in other places must have troops or at least tech that might help us," Deanna asked.

"Maybe we can make a big enough splash tomorrow to catch their attention," Alexander replied.

Chapter 42

June 12, 2407 AD
Alpha Lyncis
203 Light-years from the Sol System
Monday, 6:35 AM, Expeditionary Mission Standard Time

"All hands, all hands, battle stations. QMT to combat zone in T-minus ten minutes and counting. All hands, all hands, battle stations. QMT to combat zone in T-minus two minutes and counting." The bosun's pipe sounded throughout the ship and across the fleet.

"Firestorm," Moore turned his chair to the XO's station. "All ships accounted for and battle-ready?"

"Roger that, General. All one hundred ships show full battle ready." Firestorm either smiled or snarled, Alexander wasn't really certain. "Time to announce the presence of the human race, sir!"

"Oorah, XO." Moore nodded and then turned to the Nav. "Penny, status of QMT?"

"Sir, we are ready to jump. The entire fleet shows coordinates logged and the sling-forward algorithm is ready to go."

"Air Boss!"

"Aye, sir?" USN Captain Michelle Wiggington answered.

"Are the jocks sitting tight and ready to go?"

"Aye, sir!"

"Good. Ground Boss? AEMs and tankheads ready to go?"

"Hoowah, sir!" US Army Brigadier Gen. Tonya "Hailstorm" Briggs said. Moore chuckled proudly to himself at the former tankhead's enthusiasm. His crew was ready to go.

"Lieutenant Brown, get me Captain Seely of the 61 UM Fleet," Moore said to his communications officer.

"Aye, sir."

"You know, General, there is something about them clones that give me the heebie-jeebies," Chief of the Boat Command Master Chief Jeff Coates said. "There's just something about an empty body being driven by a computer that weirds me out, sir."

"I know the feeling, COB," Moore agreed. "What is the status of my boat?"

"Ready to kick some ass, sir." The COB replied.

"Sir—" the comm officer interrupted. "Captain Seely is online."

"Thanks, Denise. Put him on bridgewide DTM."

"Sir."

"Captain Seely. Moore here."

"General. We are ready to go here," the clone said, very deadpan.

"Good. I just wanted to make sure and to tell you and your crew good luck."

"Thank you, sir," Captain Seely replied, with no change of expression. The lack of emotions from the clones really took some getting used to.

"Very good. Let's move out." Moore leaned back in his oversized seat. He was glad that Madira had designed the fleet ships so that they were armor-friendly. Alexander looked around at his armored-up crew and felt his gut turn over.

Abby, full Blue force map on and keep it there. Give me an overlay of all systems and fleet ship locations. Keep Buckley's AIC on an open channel just in case. And, get me a link open to Dee, mindvoice only, he thought.

Done, sir. You are connected to your daughter now. Abigail said.

Thanks, Abby. Moore sighed and thought carefully about what to say. Once again he was sending his daughter into combat and this time they had very little idea as to what the enemy would be like.

Daddy?

Hey, princess. I just needed to tell you that I love you.

I love you too, Daddy.

Sweetheart, you don't have to do this if you don't want to. You could snap back home right now and nobody would ever say anything about it, or I'd kick their ass if they did.

Daddy! You know I can't do that. I couldn't leave the Archangels missing a pilot and I wouldn't do that to the crew.

I know you wouldn't. But what kind of father would I be if I didn't at least try to get you to go home? You be careful and watch your six, okay?

Okay, Daddy.

And princess.

Yes.

I love you.

I love you too, Daddy.

"All hands, all hands, QMT jump in ten, nine, eight, seven, six, five, four, three, two, one. QMT commencing."

Moore braced for the jump. The circle of rippling light appeared in front of the ship and the fleet started disappearing through it one at a time. Over the past months all of the fleet ships had been retrofitted with QMT snap-back and sling-forward systems. Any ship in the fleet could perform jumps forward or backward to any location within three light-years. To jump very long distances, it took a connection between networked QMT facilities. The *Madira* was the only one of the Penzington fleet so equipped but there were two of the 61 UM fleet ships equipped with that capability.

Moore watched as the fleet around him flashed out of reality one by one until it was time for the *Madira* to go. The bridge and the rest of the ship flashed with white light and buzzed and crackled. And then Moore was looking at a different part of space.

"Nav?" he said as the crackling subsided.

"One minute, sir."

"Sir, I see a red star to the starboard." The COB pointed out the viewport.

"Got it, COB." Moore nodded. "XO, status of the fleet?"

"All ships are accounted for, sir. We're here and ready to kick ass."

"Good. Nav, what's the holdup?" Moore asked impatiently.

"Got a lock, sir. We are exactly where we planned to be, one light-year from the inner system. We're in the Oort Cloud," Commander Swain replied.

"STO, does it look the same as our intel?"

"Yes, sir. As far as my AIC can make out this system exactly fits the intel. We have uninhabited gas giants and Kuiper Belt objects from about ten astronomical units out. There is an inhabited system on an

Earthlike planet, fourth planet out from the star. There is also a gas giant, third out, with an inhabited moon much like Ares, sir." The STO described the system as he displayed it DTM for the bridge crew.

"CO, CDC?"

"Go, CDC," Moore replied to the Combat Direction Center.

"Sir, we have zero contacts within real-time sensor range. There are plenty of targets further in the system but, as you know due to light lag, aren't at these locations anymore."

"How many targets inward, CDC?"

"Thousands, sir."

"Roger that, CDC."

"Alright, let's get the plan started. Snap the bots to the asteroid belt." Moore pulled up the attack plan DTM and watched as thirty of the 61 UM ships flashed inward to the asteroid belt at about eight AUs from the star. The thirty ships were filled with buzzsaw and builder bots. Millions of them. That many bots could turn asteroids into more bots faster than anybody could attrit them. At least that was what Moore was hoping.

"Bots away, General," Firestorm announced. "Ready for step two."

"Right. Get me the *Thatche*r and the *Hillenkoetter*," Moore ordered.

"Sir. Vice Admiral Walker and Captain Penzington are online." the comm officer replied.

"Sharon, Nancy, I guess this is it. You two are up to bat," Moore said.

"Yes, sir," Nancy replied.

"Looking forward to it, Alexander." Walker showed him a big, toothy grin. Even through the viewscreen the woman was large and intimidating. Even to Moore.

"Great. Godspeed and good luck."

Chapter 43

June 13, 2407 AD
Alpha Lyncis
203 Light-years from the Sol System
Tuesday, 6:01 AM, Expeditionary Mission Standard Time

"You heard the man, Nav," Captain Nancy Penzington ordered. "QMT to the fourth planet location now."

"Yes, ma'am," the clone navigation officer replied. Nancy would have preferred a fully human crew on her ship but there just hadn't been time to get that many humans out that far and up to speed. Besides, the clones were very proficient and there were billions of them available.

"Weapons Deck Officer, keep your finger on the gluonium missiles and fire as soon as you find targets." Nancy waited as the QMT flashes stopped, and blinked her eyes to clear them. There on the viewscreen was a big, pretty blue-and-green world. The planet was about twice the size of Earth but otherwise looked about the same. They were parked on the night side and could see lights covering almost every inch of land. About half of the planet appeared to be water and there were even lights scattered across the oceans.

"Finger on the trigger, ma'am," the Weapons Deck Officer clone replied.

"Davy, what is the status of my other four ships?"

"All four of the 61 UM 5 through 8 accounted for and ready, Captain," the lieutenant commander replied.

"Good. Tell them to target and fire at will. All barrier shields up and SIFs at maximum!"

"Roger that." Nancy watched as the SEAL did his job. He was proficient at whatever he did. She could see why Dee liked him.

"CO, CDC!"

"Go, CDC." Nancy replied.

"Multiple bogies detected inbound. Contact range in thirty seconds."

"Roger that, CDC." Nancy flashed her DTM battlescape view up to see the threats. There were about ten supercarrier-sized craft headed their way and each of those was being swarmed by smaller mecha-sized vehicles.

"Get ready to deploy the fighters, Air Boss."

"Ma'am, I have multiple ground locations locked."

"Don't wait on my command, fire!" Nancy ordered the Weapons Deck Officer.

"Firing!" The clone operated several controls on the console and then turned to back to her. "All one thousand missiles are away, Captain Penzington."

"XO, keep me posted on damage assessments."

"Roger that. Bringing the missile tracks on the screen now." Davy looked up at the viewscreen. "All ships report the complete complement of gluonium missiles have been fired."

The blue tracks for the missiles zipped across the viewscreen and slammed into the planet's surface. The gluonium bombs detonated, turning the entire night side of the planet into flashing reds and whites. Large sections of lit population centers bigger than Mons City vanished with each detonation.

A brilliant flash of blue tracked across the sky from the lead enemy ship approaching them at high speed. The blue beam looked as if it wasn't even pointed in the direction of her ships, and then in midspace the beam turned a complete ninety-degree turn twice, and then hit one of her ships. The supercarrier was surrounded briefly by a cloud of ionized material but it appeared that the Buckley-Freeman Barrier Shield was holding.

"How are they seeing us?" Nancy turned to Davy. "XO? The Buckley Switch is on, right?"

"Yes, ma'am. If the Buckley Switch wasn't on the shields wouldn't be up," Davy replied.

"Shit! That means they can see through the cloaking system." Nancy didn't like that. Part of their advantage was gone.

Another one of the crazy blue beams zipped from one of the enemy ships, hammering the ship 61 UM 7 again. The ship was covered by the ionized ball again and this time it appeared to have some fires venting from several locations.

"Captain, UM 7 is reporting casualties and has multiple SIF generator failures. I don't think she can take another hit like that," Rackman said. "Ma'am, we need to disperse or get in closer to the enemy so they can't use that blue beam on us."

"Good call, XO."

Allison, open me a channel to all my ship captains, Nancy thought. It was quicker to think than to talk. And besides, those captains were AIC-driven clones anyway. They'd probably prefer it.

Channel open.

All ships, spread out and take rapid evasive maneuvers. Get in as close to the enemy ships as you can and hopefully we can keep them from using that beam on us.

Roger that, Captain. The answer came from the four captains simultaneously—an eerie effect in her mindvoice. Nancy noted that she'd have to get used to that.

"Take us to hyperspace jaunt and get us on top of those enemy ships!" Nancy ordered the navigation officer. The ship lurched hard as if they'd hit an asteroid. "What the hell!"

"Shield generators down to fifty percent power, Captain!" the STO clone said emotionlessly. "I estimate we can take two more hits like that before they fail completely."

"Move us, Nav!"

Three of the blue beams converged on 61 UM 7 and the ship exploded. The Blue force tracking dot in Nancy's mind vanished. Over twenty thousand clones had just died. Clones or not, they were under her command and she wasn't moving fast enough to keep them alive.

"Goddamn it! I want every missile and DEG battery firing at those ships continuously! STO, keep me a constant shield status bar in my DTM!" Nancy looked at her ship and the remaining three. They were popping out of hyperspace jaunt right on top of the incoming enemy ships. The purple vortex of hyperspace appeared and disappeared in less than a couple of seconds. They didn't have far to jump.

The vortex vanished and immediately they were between two of the Chiata battleships. Directed-energy weapons poured out energy beams across the ship's surface and some sort of energy balls continued to slam into the hull. The ship rocked and lurched and bounced.

"We've got mecha everywhere, Captain!" the XO said.

"Air Boss! Deploy the fighters!"

"Yes, Captain."

"Well, at least the blue beams have stopped, right?" Nancy looked around the bridge for reassurance. "Anyone?"

"None have fired in the last few seconds as far as I can tell," the STO acknowledged.

Nancy looked at the shield status bar in her DTM and it was hovering around thirty percent. They could turn and run now but she wasn't sure the enemy would take the bait. And she had to give Fullback time to hit the planet farther in. The plan was to hold out for three minutes. That was a very long minute and a half away.

"UM 5 just collided with one of the enemy ships, Captain!" Rackman shouted. The shield system was deflecting the bombardment but the effect was that the ship felt and sounded like the inside of a bass drum.

"Order them to snap back to the Oort position!" Nancy looked at the location of the enemy ships surrounding them and her ships in her DTM. The enemy had them surrounded. They swarmed in and around them in a three-dimensional ball. They couldn't hyperspace jaunt out or even fly out under main propulsion. There was only one way out and they were still fifty seconds away from that.

"Alright, we will not survive this for fifty seconds more," Nancy said just as UM 5 vanished. As it did it left a gaping hole in the enemy ship it had collided into after popping out of hyperspace. Orange and white flames filled the port bow of the ship, and secondary explosions threw debris and vents of smoke jetting in all directions.

"Fire all weapons on that ship!" Nancy pointed at the damaged Chiata vessel.

"Roger that," the Weapons Deck Officer acknowledged.

"Captain, we are losing mecha fast. The fighter wing is down to seventy percent," the Air Boss said in a flat voice.

"Order all the fighters to go deathblossom, and then snap back to Kill Box One!" Nancy ordered. "That might buy us a few seconds."

"CO, CDC."

"Go, CDC!"

"CO, we are detecting three different clouds of movement headed our way."

"What does that mean, CDC?"

"Each cloud represents multiple ships. There are thirty-nine supercarrier-sized ships in the nearest and smallest one, and there are many other smaller vessels ranging from frigate class to fighter class. ETA one minute."

"Roger that, CDC!"

We better not be here in one minute, Nancy thought.

I agree, Allison replied in her mind. *The plan is working. They are taking the bait.*

Let's hope it is a plan we can survive.

The red beams from the forward directed-energy guns on the *Hillenkoetter* splashed across the front of the damaged enemy vessel, tearing into the interior of the alien ship. The DEG beams cut the alien ship as well as they did any other. Nancy was proud of that fact.

As smoke and debris jetted out of the Chiata ship, it continued to fire the energy balls from side-mounted cannons. The energy balls slammed into the shields and jarred Nancy to the bone with each impact. Several standard missiles twisted through the hailstorm of enemy fighters and antispacecraft fire. Two of them managed to make it to target, detonating inside the enemy ship. The bow of the ship blew open like an exploding cigar. Then a blue beam tore through the center of the damaged ship and hit dead center of the *Hillenkoetter*.

"Shit!" Nancy grabbed at her chair and toggled the armor restraints. "That does it! Shields are down to fifteen percent. We can't continue this. Nav! Snap-back to rendezvous at Kill Box One!"

"Yes, ma'am."

"Comm, see if you can get me a status from the Thatcher as soon as we materialize!"

"Yes, Captain."

"QMT commencing in three, two, one," the nav announced.

Chapter 44

June 13, 2407 AD
Alpha Lyncis
203 Light-years from the Sol System
Tuesday, 6:21 AM, Expeditionary Mission Standard Time

"Kill Box One, Captain." The clone navigation officer didn't even look up from his control panel as he talked. Nancy looked through the viewscreen as well as her DTM view and could see the red giant star, now almost ten astronomical units away. They were in an asteroid field that seemed to stretch as far as she could see in every direction.

"Captain, Blue force trackers are online and we have the bot ships tagged," Rackman said. "No sign of Vice Admiral Walker's fleet yet. The CHENG reports that repairs are under way on the SIF generators as well as the barrier shield system."

"The admiral will do her job. She'll show," Nancy said. She flashed through the fleet's locations in her DTM. The bot ships were arranged very two-dimensionally. "XO, have the bot ships move into more of a sphere using the asteroids as cover. The way the Chiata fought us just now was very three-dimensional and swarmlike."

"Yes, ma'am."

"Captain, I estimate the Chiata ships have located us by now and at estimated top hyperspace jaunt speeds will be here in ten to twenty seconds," the STO clone said. Nancy knew and could see in her DTM that all the clones had name designations, but it didn't seem to bother them that she only called them by rank or position. It was all a little weird to her.

If we survive this, I'm going to have to learn all the bridge crew by name and face, she thought.

That will be difficult with over eighty percent of the crew being clones. Each of the bridge crew has multiple twins somewhere else aboard the ship, Allison replied.

"Roger that, STO. Keep me apprised of their movement if you detect anything. CDC could miss it." Nancy pulled up the ship's status reports. The clones, humans, builder, and repair bots were working like mad to fix the damage to the hull as well as the shield generator systems. They had all of twenty seconds to get them back up to full power.

"Nav—move us back behind the bot fleet and get us cover behind an asteroid. I'd prefer to have cover from as many angles as possible. Let's let stay back as long as we can to get some repairs done." Nancy hoped there were enough bots and other ships to make a dent in the oncoming enemy onslaught. There were likely more than a hundred enemy ships following her. She suspected there would be just as many behind Vice Admiral Walker.

"Captain, the *Thatcher* and UM 3 and 4 just appeared," the STO said. "It looks like the *Thatcher* is in pretty bad shape."

"Patch me through, comm."

"Channel open, Captain."

Walker's face popped up on the screen. "Admiral Walker, I see you did about as badly as we did. Are you okay, ma'am?" Nancy asked.

"We'll make do, Captain Penzington. You're not in much better shape, it appears." Walker noted. "Be advised that over three hundred enemy ships are headed our way. Details of our engagement are being transmitted to your CDC for analysis."

"Yes, ma'am. I'll have our CDC return the favor. We believe that over one hundred are following us." Nancy choked down bile and butterflies. The odds were overwhelming. "Admiral, any suggestions ma'am? We are severely outgunned and outnumbered."

"Stick to the plan, Nancy. If it gets too hot, we snap back. I'm giving you this order now and you better adhere to it. We do not lose any human ships at this location. We *will* snap to the Oort and lick our wounds before we do. Do you understand me?"

"Yes, Admiral."

"CO, CDC."

"Go, CDC." Nancy said. "Looks like we're on, Admiral. Good hunting."

"Walker out."

"Captain, we just had over a hundred ships just materialize out of hyperspace jaunt."

"Roger that, CDC. Keep an eye out for three hundred more.

"Nav, get us under cover for now. We'll watch how they engage the bots before we make a move. I want us hugging one of these asteroids. Get me recon birds on vantage points to keep me in the loop on what is going on."

Allison, send the same orders to UM 6 and 8.

Done.

"Aye, ma'am."

As the Hillenkoetter and UM 6 and 8 placed small asteroids in the belt between the bot fleet and the Chiata, the blue beams started tearing across the asteroid field and pounding into the thirty ships of the bot fleet. The bot ships fired red DEG and nuclear-tipped missiles back at the oncoming enemy swarm. The Chiata ships moved in a cloud formation with each of the individual particles of the cloud moving in what appeared to be random fashion. Nancy had asked Allison to model the motion and found that they were moving using Kolmogorov statistics and a von Karmen spectra almost identical to how atmospheric molecules bounce around in a turbulent flow. While even the best AIC could predict the general nature of the turbulent flow, there was no way to predict the location of individual components of the field of ships. Like the randomness of the atmosphere, the Chiata swarm was just as unpredictable.

The Chiata ships closed the gap on the bot fleet and several of the zig-zagging blue beams turned and danced across space before they hit a target. In less than thirty seconds, five of the bot fleet ships had been totally destroyed. Fortunately, the thirty ships that had been deployed in the asteroid field, other than Walker's fleet and Nancy's, were completely bot controlled. There were no humans or clones aboard them. Moore's and Madira's plan had been to infect as many of the Chiata with buzzsaw replicator bots as they could. But that meant they had to get the bot ships close enough to latch some builder bots on.

"Captain, we need to find a way to hit that swarm all at once. While the cloud confuses our guns and missiles they are all still close in on each other," Rackman said. "I recall taking out some killer bees once with a can of spray lubricant and a torch. The bees swarmed right into my makeshift flamethrower."

"We'd need a big-ass flamethrower, XO."

"Yes, ma'am, or a bunch of nukes," Rackman agreed. "And while we have used most of ours, I'm sure some of these ships here still have them."

"Good call, XO."

"CO, CDC."

"Go, CDC."

"Three hundred more ships just materialized in five clouds of sixty supercarrier-sized vessels. They are flanking our position."

"Roger that, CDC." Nancy looked at the situation in her DTM view. The Kill Box One zone was at the origin of a sphere, whereas the surface of the sphere was now covered with alien ships bringing blue beams of death. And the sphere was collapsing and crushing inward.

Allison, get me a direct link to Vice Admiral Walker.

Done.

Admiral, my XO had a great idea.

Go.

We need to detonate multiple nukes at the heart of each of these enemy clouds simultaneously. Nancy explained further and uploaded the sim Allison just finished to her.

Got it, Captain. Good idea. You take care of it. I'll direct the bots.

Yes, ma'am.

"XO, we have seven major clouds hammering us from outside, trapping us in our own goddamned kill box. Identify seven bot ships with the most nukes still available and implement your plan ASAP!" Nancy ordered Rackman.

"I'm on it, Captain."

Nancy watched the battle continue to unfold as the bot fleet was getting hammered and the enemy fleet was still too far outside the kill box to let the buzzsaw bots loose. There were too many enemy ships just to kamikaze the bots and have them QMT into them. The idea was to infect as many of the enemy as possible. And that meant that they had to lure the enemy into the trap.

She hoped that dropping nukes into the heart of the clouds would disperse the aliens and drive them to come closer in. Once the battle bots were able to engage the enemy ships they would attach, dig in, and start multiplying. Going to hyperspace wouldn't help the Chiata at that point because they would be infected. Nancy hoped they'd suffer the same fate as the original *Madira* had and be eaten from the inside out and destroyed.

"Ships identified and calculating QMT coordinates, Captain," Rackman said. "They will be ready to engage in seconds."

"Davy, they must all go simultaneously. Have them QMT in, drop their missiles, and QMT out. Got it?" Nancy asked. Even though they were bot ships there was no need to lose them if they didn't have to.

"Understood, Captain. QMTs commencing!"

Nancy watched in her mindview as the blue dots of seven ships vanished from their current Kill Box One location and then reappeared inside the middle of a red cloud. Almost as soon as the blue dots appeared in the red clouds they disappeared again and reappeared back in formation with the rest of the fleet. There were bright flashes and multiple explosions covering the interior of the large enemy clouds. Several secondary explosions followed and the swarms fell apart into random vectors.

"That's what happens when you put all your eggs in one basket," Nancy said. She was very pleased to see that they had managed to damage several of the large Chiata vessels and totally wiped out many of the smaller ships and fighters.

"It's working!" Rackman shouted as he pounded his right fist against his left palm. "Now if they will just dig in closer."

"I suspect we've managed to really piss them off," Nancy told her only non-clone bridge crewman.

Blue beams rampaged through the bot fleet. The bots were doing a good job at moving around through the asteroids for cover, but the blue beams of death were hard to avoid. Of the thirty ships they started with, they were now down to nineteen. And in order to lure the Chiata in closer, the remaining ships were pulling in close to each other and nearer to asteroids. The *Hillenkoetter* and the *Thatcher* were right in the middle of it.

The disrupted swarms filled the empty space between the asteroids surrounding the human and bot fleet ships. They were in range. Nancy was tired of seeing humanity's assets continually blasted away. The attrition rate of the human ships was ten times that of the Chiata fleet. It was time to do more damage.

"Come on, Admiral, they're in close enough," Nancy said through clenched teeth as one of the blue beams zigged around the edge of the asteroid and pounded into the shields of her ship. "Come on."

"Captain, the bots have been deployed," the STO announced.

"I see them," Davy added as he pointed out the viewport. "Let's hope they can get inside the enemy ships and cause them the same kind of problems we had."

A second blue beam tore through the asteroid near the aft section of the ship. Large chunks of molten rock slammed into the shields. Nancy watched as the shield status bar dropped to single-digit percentage. Internal fire alarms popped up on the ship status map in her DTM view.

Nancy, we can't take another hit like that, Allison warned her.

I know.

"XO! Can we confirm that the bots have engaged the enemy?"

"Yes, Captain! The bots are swarming like mad."

"Nav! Get us the hell out of here."

"Yes, ma'am," the navigation officer replied calmly and in a monotone.

Chapter 45

June 13, 2407 AD
Alpha Lyncis
203 Light-years from the Sol System
Tuesday, 7:33 AM, Expeditionary Mission Standard Time

"Vice Admiral Walker and Captain Penzington took extensive damage, General," Firestorm reported to Alexander. Their mission reports started filtering into his mind almost as soon as they had re-entered local space at the Oort Cloud muster point.

"Understood, XO. Get them parked and get them whatever help they need from the rest of the fleet. It's time for attack wave two." Moore nodded at his second in command.

"Yes, sir."

The plan was simple. Keep the main part of the fleet parked in the Oort Cloud, which was more than five days away from the Chiata at high speed. For several days they would hammer the interior of the Alpha Lyncis system with wave after wave of fast attacks while at the same time making no attempt to hide their position. If the Chiata found them and sent the majority of their fleet out to the Oort to face them, then Moore had Kill Box Two all set up for them. And he still had over forty ships at his disposal. Captain Seeley had seventy fully manned with clones. The goal was to chip away at the stone until there was one big last stand.

"Get me Captain Seeley," Moore ordered his communications officer.

"Captain Seeley is online, sir," the young lieutenant said nervously. While they had been fighting for almost two years, his crew were battle hardened, but the fight had been more mopping-up activities with few casualties. This engagement was different. This was all-out war. Moore's crew knew the odds of survival were very small. He could understand his young communications officer's fear. Moore stood and slowly clanked across the bridge and stood over her. He put an armored hand on her armored shoulder.

"Good job, Denise."

"Thank you, sir. Captain Seeley," she said as the clone fleet's captain appeared on the viewscreen.

"General, we are ready and awaiting your order, sir," the clone of one of Moore's old Marine buddies from the Martian Wars said calmly. While he looked the same, he sounded very different. It was a bit haunting to Alexander.

"Alright, Captain Seeley, commence your jump, and good hunting." Moore nodded. "Minimize your losses as best you can and still maximize Chiata damage. If it gets too overwhelming, snap out of there. Understood?"

"Yes, sir. Good hunting to you too, sir." The clone captain's face disappeared and then the viewscreen changed back to the forward view.

"Nav, take us in. XO, sound the alarm." Moore watched the Blue force tracker in his DTM and highlighted the four ships going with him. He would have five of the Penzington Fleet ships with him all crewed by bots. Seeley would have five of his own fleet with him likewise filled with bots. "Let's go start the ground war."

"All hands, all hands, prepare for QMT in ten, nine, eight, seven, six, five, four, three, two, one. QMT commencing."

The Earthlike planet popped up on the viewscreen almost as soon as the QMT flashes stopped. As the sizzling subsided in Alexander's ears he could immediately hear the proximity alarms kick in.

"General, we've got multiple contacts scattered about. Several of them have turned toward us," the STO reported. "They'll be on us soon, sir."

"Nav! You have full evasive maneuver authority," Moore ordered.

"STO, find me some population centers not hit by Penzington's bombing run."

"Aye, sir! Already got them. Coordinates are in the battleview now."

"CO, CDC!"

"Go, CDC!"

"Sir, according to the analysis from wave-one data we will be in range of the blue beams in thirty seconds."

"Understood, CDC."

"XO, order the bot ships QMTed over the target coordinates and immediately deploy. Then have them fire nukes on targets of opportunity."

"Aye, sir!" Firestorm turned to her console and tapped a few commands. "Air Boss, Ground Boss, you heard the general. I want bot mecha flying and on the surface ASAP. Release the buzzsaws."

"As soon as we gauge the threat we'll determine how to deploy our mecha," Moore said out loud as a general information order to the bridge crew. "Gunnery officer!"

"Sir," Lieutenant Commander Marcus St. James looked up from his console. The gunner was another youngster in Moore's crew. Nearly two years fighting bots could barely prepare him for what he was facing now. Moore had to encourage him.

"I don't hear the guns or the DEGs, lieutenant commander. Find targets and start hitting them!" Moore ordered. That was encouragement enough as far as he was concerned.

"Aye, sir!"

Almost instantly Alexander could feel the long-range plasma cannons and missile tubes popping. Beams from the portside bow DEGs cut across the sky into the oncoming swarm of Chiata ships. They were in range of the *Madira*'s guns. That meant that the *Madira* was in range of theirs. Then huge balls of plasma from the Chiata cannons started slamming into the ship's barrier shield.

Abby, how many Chiata supercarriers are engaging us? The red dots were too numerous to count quickly.

Two-hundred eighty-seven, sir. There are many other smaller vessels and fighter-sized vehicles. The total target number is on the order of four hundred, his AIC answered.

Holy shit. We're vastly outnumbered.

Yes, sir.

What do Marines do when they are outnumbered, Abby?

Attack, sir.

Goddamned right. Be ready to take the QMT controls at any instant. And keep me posted on the shield status.

Yes, sir.

"Incoming fire, General!" Firestorm announced. "Ships three and five have taken direct hits from surface-to-space weapons."

"Find the source, XO!" Moore said just as the *Madira* felt as if something grabbed it and pushed it backwards and then hit it with a giant sledgehammer. "What the hell was that!"

"Surface-to-space fire, sir!" the XO shouted over the hull rattling and the alarm klaxons.

"Those things pack a hell of a wallop," the Chief of the Boat added. "Sir, I'm getting damage and casualty reports on lower decks."

"General! I've got a fix on that fire," the STO said excitedly.

"Is it in range of the DEGs?"

"Yes sir!"

"Then feed the coordinates to the gunner. Gunnery Officer, hit that fucking thing!" Moore ordered. "Ground Boss, if we have any of the automated ground troops nearby, alert them that hell is about to rain on top of them. Then tell them to look at whatever it is and find and destroy anything else that looks like it. Air Boss, give them air support."

"Roger that, General," Hailstorm and Commander Wiggington replied simultaneously.

"General," the XO added. "All ground and air forces have been deployed and are fully engaged with the enemy on the surface. The buzzsaw bots are on the ground buzzing and sawing, sir. We're getting video feeds from them if you want to see it."

"Understood, Firestorm." Moore pulled up the ground view in his DTM. The bot mecha seemed to be doing a decent job at wreaking havoc on the Chiata planet's surface. He randomly picked an autotank from the blue dots and turned its video feed on in his mind.

Abby, put this on the screen for everybody.

Yes, General.

The screen view changed instantly and the bridge crew had the view from the front end of an automated hovertank. The tank was tearing through a city with some of the strangest architecture Alexander had ever seen. The buildings looked like they had been molded from molten metal. There were energy beams and plasma balls zipping by as the video bounced and jumped. The audio was an earsplitting mixture of metal screeching, cannons firing, and energy balls exploding. Had there been a pilot there would have been guttural shouts and grunts added to the mix.

At one point it was clear that the hovertank reconfigured to bot mode as the viewpoint shifted a few meters higher and bounced up and down with each giant mechanized step. The giant armored behemoth smashed and trashed and fired its weapons nonstop. It was inflicting a good bit of damage.

The hovertank turned a corner around what appeared to be a building and then it was overwhelmed by a blur of motion. Large glowing red and green objects moving at very high speeds began pounding into the tank. Very high-pitched and very eerie screeching sounds saturated the audio to the point it was beyond earsplitting. Then it was clear that one of the bot tank's mechanized arms had been ripped free and one of the red and green blurs was using it as a war club. Then the tank went down and the video was out.

"My God!" Firestorm gasped. "Were those things civilians?"

"We'll analyze them later, XO." Moore had his AIC toggle the screen back to forward view of the *Madira*. The planet beneath was close and they could see fireballs erupting on the surface below as the bot ships made bombing runs.

Then the supercarrier lurched again and a deafening twang rang through the hull like it was a bell that had been rung. This time the lurching was in a different direction. The shield status alert popped up in his DTM view as down to seventy percent. Then Alexander saw several of the zigzagging blue beams of death cut into ship Two of his attack fleet. The ship's barrier shield flashed with blue ionization all around it and then Moore could see smoke and fireballs shooting from the aft section.

"Sir, number Two reports main guns and propulsion are offline. She's dead in the water, General!" the XO reported.

"Have them fire all their nukes and QMT out now!" Moore ordered. The ship was bot-controlled, but they could repair it and use it again on the next wave. That is, if they could get it out before it was destroyed. "Nav, hyperspace jaunt us between the Chiata swarm attacking Two and let's give her some cover."

"Jaunting now, General!"

The purple whirling hyperspace conduit spun up in front of them for a brief instant and then it died away. They were between the wounded Number Two ship and about thirty Chiata ships.

"Find targets!" Moore shouted. "Take us into the enemy swarm at close quarters. Let's see if we can get too close for them to use those beams."

"Yes, sir."

The navigation officer took the ship at top sublight speeds into the swarm and aimed directly at one of the Chiata supercarrier-sized ships. The enemy ship was at least as long as a supercarrier and maybe wider. The surface was covered with shiny silver tall, pointed spires that looked something like a cross between a stalagmite and the tip of a spear. The rest of the ship was a dull metal gray with red and green earthy tones mixed in here and there. The ship looked less like a vessel and more like some sort of animal. If Alexander had to describe the thing he would say it looked like a porcupine—a huge, deadly porcupine. Then several of the spires glowed red and the giant plasma balls poured out of them at the *Madira*.

"Return fire, gunner!" he shouted as the energy balls pounded the barrier shield. The shield status bar went from green to yellow and showed forty-five percent.

"At least we're too close for those damned blue beams, sir," the XO grunted. Then a blue beam zigged up from a ship on the other side of the closest ship. The beam tracked around the bow of the Chiata ship, turned right, traveled within meters of the bridge of the *Madira*, and made a final turn past them, making a direct hit on the unprotected Number Two. Number Two cracked in the midsection and then exploded. SIF generators blew out followed by the hyperspace projector core. Then there was nothing but a giant fireball where Number Two had been. Shrapnel from the explosion pounded the aft end of the *Madira*. The supercarrier continued to shake violently. The shield status bar dropped to forty percent.

"Holy shit!" the COB shouted. "Sir, we're taking damage pretty quickly. I'm getting casualty reports flooding in. The aft hangar SIFs are down and it is vented to space."

"Understood, COB. I'm open for suggestions." Moore turned to the gunner and then back to the viewscreen. Then he saw another of the blue beams originate from an oversized tuning-fork-shaped spire at the front of the nearest ship. The beam only had to zig once before it tore across the Chiata ship in front of them. It was so close that it ripped right through several of the porcupine spires and then directly into the *Madira*'s starboard side at midsection. Alexander's teeth rattled and he bit his tongue until it bled.

The shield status bar dropped into the red, showing twenty-seven percent.

"CHENG to CO!"

"Go, CHENG!"

"General, we can't take another hit like that! The shield generators are overheating and I've got more relays throwing sparks down here than you can count!" Buckley sounded shaken. Moore knew the CHENG had been through some very serious shit during the wars and could handle pressure. *The situation must be critical down there,* he thought.

Yes, sir, I am detecting nearly sixty percent of the electrical system is overloaded, Abigail replied. *There are multiple high-energy gamma ray detectors sounding alarms. It is ugly down there, sir.*

"I know, Joe! Work harder or we die! I'm busy right now. Just keep the QMT system functioning and ready to snap out of here. And get more power to the shields. I don't care where it comes from."

"Aye, sir."

"Gunner! I want all weapons targeting those Goddamned tuning-fork spires. We need to stop those blue beams." Moore ordered. "Nav! Get us in closer to the enemy ship. I don't care if we rub up against it and spoon with the Goddamned thing!"

"Aye, sir!"

The red beams from the DEGs tracked across the hull of the nearest Chiata porcupine, leaving an ionizing trail behind it. As far as Moore could tell the Chiata ships didn't have shields, but the armor plating barely was affected. The beam tracked across a chink in the armor where the blue beam had blown several of the spires away and there, suddenly, secondary explosions occurred. Moore's eyebrows raised and he slammed a fist down.

"Right there!" he shouted. "Gunner! Hit the spot where the secondary explosions are happening. Fire everything there! Missiles and DEGs!"

"Aye, sir!"

The beam slewed back into the damaged area and chunks of the armor began to crack and bulge. Then missiles tracked into the same spot. Several of the spires spewing the plasma balls looked as if they had been stopped up and began to bulge at the center. One of them exploded, sending the top half of the stalagmite careening into an adjacent one. Another missile exploded in the vicinity. The exploding missile set off several secondary explosions and the DEGs then had a serious soft spot to hammer.

The red beams tore deeper and deeper into the interior. More of the spires bulged and exploded. A large crack began to form across the hull of the enemy ship, which looked like earth cracking during an earthquake with a volcanic eruption pouring out from the crack at the same time. The crack glowed red as the surfaces on either side separated from each other. Sparks, fire, debris, and atmosphere poured from the crack.

"Keep hammering that son of a bitch!" Moore growled. Then the *Madira* was hit so hard that he was nearly knocked unconscious as his head pounded against the helmet seal of his armored suit. Had he been wearing his helmet that wouldn't have happened. His ears rang and his head hurt badly.

"Nav! Get us the hell out of here!" he shouted. The ship didn't move. "Nav!"

Alexander tied to shake his head but it hurt too much. He blinked several times to clear the stars in his eyes and to keep from tunneling in from the pain in his back and neck. There were sparks flying from consoles and as he turned to the navigation officer's station he could see her suit sitting upright while her head was twisted sideways. Her neck was broken. Commander Penny Swain was dead, and from the looks of it so was the COB.

He grabbed his helmet box from his right shoulder and instinctively slapped the patch against his neck. The box unfolded and wrapped around his neck, connecting to the seal as it deployed the head cover and then the visor. The helmet was fully deployed in seconds. He instinctively bit at the water tube and triggered stimulants and pain meds to be filtered in. Moore believed he could stand. His neck was likely fractured but the suit would administer some immunoboost if he needed it and he'd be fine.

Sir! The shields are down! Abigail warned him.

Abby! Sound the order to the fleet and QMT us out of here now!

Roger that! The AIC said. *Sir! General Moore! General Alexander Moore?*

Just as the QMT lights flashed and the sizzling began, Alexander could see the Chiata ship crack completely in two. Explosions followed one after the other in a chain reaction from the center of the ship toward the bow and the stern. He could hear Abigail shouting at him in his mind but he couldn't respond. He felt as if his mind was suddenly forced to lose focus. Then he lost control of his suit and he fell hard backwards into his chair. He could see Firestorm out of the corner of his eye leaning over her console. He couldn't tell if she was still alive or not. Fire started to engulf the bridge on the forward port side right up until the viewport on the same side cracked all over like a spider web and then gave way. Atmosphere rushed into space, pulling anything that wasn't tied down with it. At least it blew out the flames. Moore tried one more time to stand but his body didn't respond. He could see the Oort Cloud out the broken window as he passed out.

Chapter 46

June 13, 2407 AD
Alpha Lyncis
203 Light-years from the Sol System
Tuesday, 9:43 AM, Expeditionary Mission Standard Time

"Is Dee okay?" Moore started awake. His vision was blurred and there was a bright light shining in his face that was annoying as hell. The worst of it was that he couldn't move anything.

Your daughter is fine, sir, Abigail said into his mind. *She was safely restrained in her mecha when we were hit. I'm very happy to hear your voice.*

Abby? What the hell is going on? Why can't I move?

Your neck was fractured, sir. Medics are here now. Stay calm, sir.

Where is Sehera?

She is here.

"Sehera?"

"Alexander. I'm here."

Moore could see his wife lean in over him briefly, but he couldn't turn toward her. He felt no pain anywhere in his body. He figured the suit was taking care of that.

"Sehera, what is wrong with me?"

"Alexander, your neck is broken. You have to give the immunoboost time to fix it. You had extensive spinal-cord damage. It may take a day or two after the repairs before you will walk again."

"Where am I?" Moore couldn't see anything but his wife's face and the motion of doctors in his peripheral view.

"You are in the med bay. We are safe at the outer system muster point," Sehera assured him. "You need to stay calm and heal."

"How bad was it?" He almost whispered. "How many dead?"

"I don't know. But you were the only one alive on the bridge when they got there. The air had vented to space and you and Firestorm were the only crew with your helmets on. Sally was revived. I think she's going to make it," Sehera said.

Abby, DTM me a casualty list.

Sir, are you sure you want to do that right now? the AIC sounded reluctant.

Abby! Now.

Yes, sir.

"How are you okay? Were you wearing your helmet?" he asked his wife.

"I was, but I was here in the med bay helping. The most damage was on the bridge spire. They knew where to hit us," Sehera told him. Moore was scrolling the casualty list. There were more than one hundred neck injuries. More than seventy of them were dead and couldn't be revived. He'd have to implement a new order for either the suit neck brace to be deployed or the helmets to be on. Not including that in the original order was a stupid mistake on his part. Those lives were on his head.

"Sehera, I'm sorry."

"For what, Alexander?" Sehera asked him with almost a scolding tone in her voice. "For trying to stop an impending invasion of humanity? For putting soldiers in harm's way? For tracking this trail of evil we've been on for so long with the hopes to once and for all put an end to the wars? We will survive this and keep moving forward."

"I'm sorry for putting you in the middle of it. You should snap home to safety." Moore could feel his face at least. There were tears running down his cheeks. Sehera leaned in and kissed him through his open helmet visor. It reminded him of a time she had done that on Mars so long ago. He had been injured badly then too.

"That is a hell of a thing for you to say to me!"

"I love you."

"Dee is here," she whispered to him. "I love you too."

"In the meantime, sir," Chief Medical Officer USN Commander

Angela Muniz scanned Alexander once again with the handheld quantum imaging device. She frowned almost imperceptibly. "You *are* sidelined until I can release you. You either stay in your suit with the helmet on or you are in a full body exosuit."

"How long, Doc?" Moore was beginning to get bursts of feeling in his toes and legs. That had to be a good sign.

"At least two days," the doctor reluctantly told him. "I'm sorry, General. It will take that long for the spinal cord to heal."

"I can't be sidelined here. Not now." Alexander thought of the attack plan and how he had to be there to implement it. Nobody else would have the wherewithal to see this horrible thing through.

"Sir, you will have to stand down. If I have to, I'll do a medical override on your suit controls to keep you from moving."

"Are you telling me I can't move?"

"No, I'm telling you not to move until we are certain you will not reinjure your spinal cord. You could possibly make things worse by walking about," Doctor Muniz explained. Moore had already suspected as much.

"Very well, I will stay put. But I can work from my suit mentally at least. Right?" There was no way Moore wasn't going to stay on top of the plan even if he couldn't get up and walk around.

"I see no harm in that. I suspect General Rheims will want to do the same. She has regained consciousness and I *did* have to lock her suit out to keep her still. Now if you'll excuse me, General. I have thirty other injuries just like yours to deal with."

"Understood. Thank you, Doctor."

Abby, note for the record that I'm putting Captain Jack Boland as acting ship's captain U.S.S. Sienna Madira II. With the loss of the Air Boss and the rest of the bridge crew there was nobody else to choose from. Boland could handle it.

Understood, General. I'll have him report to you ASAP.

"So, Captain Seeley, I'm sorry that your losses were as severe as mine," Moore said to the clone captain. Moore sat upright in an oversized wheelchair that was designed for moving downed AEMs.

He had been moved to the captain's lounge of the *Madira*. It had become his own personal war room over the past couple years. Now that he couldn't be on the bridge, he decided to make it his new place of operations. It had only taken him a couple of hours on the immunoboost before he could feel his lower extremities well enough to control them and for the meds to make the pain of healing bearable enough to go back to work.

The suit wouldn't let him get hurt as long as he didn't move around, so he had himself wheeled to the lounge and stayed put. Sehera had originally insisted he go to their quarters, but Alexander wouldn't have it. He needed space to be able to brief with his remaining war planners and the lounge was ideally suited.

"Thank you, General," Seeley replied. "The Chiata were considerably more effective than we had expected them to be."

"Considerably," Moore agreed.

Sehera, Deanna, Lieutenant Commander, Lieutenant Colonel Jones, and Gunny Suez sat in chairs against the wall while Captain Boland, Captain Penzington, Captain Seely, General Warboys, and Vice Admiral Walker sat at the table. There was plenty of room for them all to sit at the table, but there was protocol to consider, and Moore couldn't turn his head yet as his helmet was locked in place. Therefore, he'd had them all sit at the far end of the table from him and at the end wall. That way he would be able to see all of their faces. It had taken a few minutes to get past the small talk and well wishes until they finally got down to business.

"Sir, we are getting our asses handed to us," DeathRay said. "From all the data we've got from the first two waves, simulations show that we are not doing near as much damage as we had hoped and we are taking on many more casualties than expected."

"After looking at the video from the autotanks and bots, General, there is no way in hell I'd suggest sending in the Warlords or the AEMs," General Warboys added. "I'm sure Lieutenant Colonel Jones and Top will agree with me."

"Our losses were ninety-three percent greater than we had anticipated in our engagement at the gas giant," Captain Seely said. The clone captain made almost no facial expression as he said it. "On the upside, General, we did learn how to destroy one of the blue-beam guns. From a review of your mission it would appear that you also found a way through their armor."

"No, Captain Seeley," Moore replied. "We didn't. The bastards shot themselves to shoot us. We just seized the opportunity."

"Yes, General, I did gather that," the clone said. "However, sir, it does show us that force concentration on weakened structures is the key. We now just must determine how to create such weakened structures."

"Famous last words," Nancy said.

"You have something to add, Nancy?" Moore asked.

"Yes, sir." Nancy looked back and forth at the others in the room. Moore guessed she was gauging them all. He noted that Vice Admiral Walker remained expressionless and quiet.

"Well, then, let's hear it."

"We can't keep up the asymmetric terror approach. I know it was partly my idea, but it isn't going to see us through to the end, sir." Nancy pulled up a DTM battlescape with a numbers projection analysis on it. "Allison has run the numbers based on our first two attack waves. The data back from the recon bots at Kill Box One shows that we only managed to infect thirty percent of the ships with the builder bots. And as soon as they managed to get inside the ships, the other Chiata ships turned those blue beams on themselves and destroyed the infected one."

Moore listened to Nancy's analysis. She was the expert in the fleet on developing analyses from intelligence and then determining courses of action. She had been trained to do it and had lived her life as a spy doing it for decades. Alexander hoped she'd figured something out—some course of action where they all didn't end up dead.

"In the first attack wave the only positive was in determining the strength of the Chiata weapons and capabilities of their vessels. The automated mecha managed to hold their own against the fighter-class Chiata longer than any other matchups. You can see this chart here shows that although there were superior numbers of enemy fighters, the kill-to-attrition ratio was almost one to one. This graph here shows that the automated ground troops were wiped out quickly—but there is one interesting piece of data." Nancy paused and zoomed in on the geographic area nearest the surface-to-space weapon of Moore's engagement.

"Sir, here is where your fleet engaged the surface. The autotanks and buzzsaws were deployed here. They were not doing well except for a few seconds following the DEG attack on the surface-to-space weapon."

"So, what happened? The DEGs disrupted them somehow?" he asked.

"Uh, no, sir, I don't think so. I think the DEG engagement was likely a coincidence." Nancy turned to DeathRay. "It comes down to mecha jocks again, sir. At this precise moment seven of the autoGnat-Ts went into pukin' deathblossom maneuvers. DeathRay and Apple One here can both express to you how difficult these maneuvers are but they can also attest to how effective they can be. What was different here was that the bot-controlled mecha targeted differently than ours do."

"How so?" Alexander was intrigued.

"They targeted any Red force target in range and not just flying ones," Nancy pointed at one of the autoGnat-Ts and replayed the three-dimensional simulation of its engagement from ten seconds before deathblossom to ten seconds after where it was destroyed. "During the engagement, several ground and aerial targets were taken out and the effectiveness of the ground forces increased as well. It is the only twenty seconds or so where the autotanks were playing offense instead of defense."

"Twenty seconds!" Warboys gasped. "That is *not* a very long window, Captain Penzington."

"With all due respect, General," Nancy turned and gave the legendary tank commander a raised eyebrow, "it might be enough."

"Enough for what?" Warboys shook his head side to side.

"Major Moore, would you take it from here?" Nancy nodded at Dee. Alexander could see the slight evidence of a smile between the two.

"Yes, Captain. Be glad to." Dee stood up and stepped a bit forward. Moore was certain she moved so he could look her in the eye. "I've already been discussing this with the CHENG for some time now and he agrees that he could fix this in a matter of minutes with a simple software fix."

"The CHENG? Fix what?" Alexander would have shrugged and held his hands up if he could move.

"Time, General, is our biggest problem. Most people believe that the pukin' deathblossom can only last about eighteen seconds because the pilots can't take any more of the stress. That isn't entirely true. I've been watching the bot planes and the clone pilots, and their deathblossoms are only a few seconds longer. My AIC and the CHENG's have decided that the targeting algorithm simply cannot keep up much longer than this amount of time. It is like predicting the weather longer than a month. There are just too many variables for the model to continue to track accurately. So, we stop the deathblossom at this point, not just because the pilots can't take it longer."

"Okay, so where are we going with this, Major?" Warboys asked her.

"General, the problem is that after the deathblossom maneuver there is a second or two that the computer's targeting system is sluggish. The pilots are definitely sluggish. So they need a break. I would suspect that the tank drivers on the ground would have been much more effective if they knew when they could go to offense and when to circle the wagons more precisely," Deanna explained. Alexander understood what she was saying but didn't quite see how it could be implemented. There was no way the pilots could be expected to do deathblossom after deathblossom. It would be too physically demanding.

"Major," Vice Admiral Walker finally spoke up. "You said you have been working with the CHENG on something. I suspect it is more than just an understanding of the deathblossom targeting. A software fix, I think you said?"

"Yes, Admiral." Deanna nodded her head. Her helmet was not deployed, but the neck brace was in place. "It is within the capabilities of the technology already installed on all of our mecha and suits to conduct snap-back and sling-forward teleportations at our individual AIC's discretion."

"What? You mean we could teleport right now to wherever we wanted to?" Warboys asked.

"Well, no, sir. That isn't what I said." Deanna held up her armored hand. "I said the suits and mecha have the capability. They do not have the authority."

"Don't have the authority?" Alexander looked at his daughter. "Who does?"

"Right now, according to the CHENG, the safety protocols are controlled by the QMT contingent of the CDC and the medical emergency response software," Deanna explained. "Sir, it is just a software fix according to the CHENG. The AICs of the mecha pilots and the AEMs could teleport whenever they needed to and to wherever they needed to. Commander Buckley says the protocol can be implemented in minutes following your approval, sir."

"My approval," Alexander said dryly. "Okay, you have the fish on the hook, Major Moore. Reel me the rest of the way in."

"Okay, sir." Deanna smiled at him. Alexander wanted to give her a hug, but for now, he'd just smile back at her. "Well, we set up waves of attack. There need to be enough mecha in the engagement so that we can always have a squadron conducting a deathblossom. As soon as the maneuver is complete, they QMT out to a safe location to recover. The tankheads and AEMs can stay on the offensive. And they can QMT their positions to maximize tactical advantage. This is very similar to the tactics being implemented with the supercarriers."

"Okay, I've heard enough," Alexander stopped his daughter. "This is a tool we can use as a tactic. It is not a tactic yet. I'd like to suggest that we freeze the current battleplan and develop a better one based on the engagement assessment and this new concept that Captain Penzington and Major Moore have come up with. This is just a suggestion, mind you. Until Doc Muniz releases me, Vice Admiral Walker is in charge out here."

"General Moore," Walker looked Alexander in the eyes and gave him a toothy grin. "Sir, before I heard this briefing I had planned to suggest we snap back to 61 Ursae Majoris and regroup and rethink what we were going to do. But having heard this idea, I believe we can devise a battle plan that would enable us to take this system."

"Take the system?" Alexander wasn't so certain they could take the system. He was even less certain they could hold it. "And hold it?"

"We can start with taking it," Walker said.

"I'd love to hear that plan, Admiral." Warboys sounded eager.

"Me too, Mason," Alexander agreed.

Chapter 47

June 16, 2407 AD
Alpha Lyncis
203 Light-years from the Sol System
Friday, 7:23 AM, Expeditionary Mission Standard Time

It had only taken the rest of the day for the seniors to hammer out a plan. DeathRay had actually had to approve the CHENG to fix the software, as he was acting captain of the *Madira*. Vice Admiral Walker, being the ranking senior, took command of the fleet. She had to give the order to the rest of the fleet to make the software mods to the emergency QMT system developed by Buckley. For several more hours they all sat in the lounge using it as a makeshift loony bin to conduct virtual simulations and wargaming. Finally, they had a plan.

It had taken another full two days to prepare for the new battle plan and to make repairs to all the ships. The builder bots made repairs much more quickly than any human crews could have. In fact, without the bots, the *Madira* would not have been fightworthy in time. Having that time had allowed the mecha jocks and the AEMs to practice implementing the QMT system via their AICs. Unless the teleportation capability changed battle tactics and strategies completely. Simulations and statistics even showed a few scenarios where they could take and hold the system. The problem with all the models was that everyone knew that there were lies, damned lies, and then statistics.

Recon bots had been QMTing in and out of the inner system and keeping a watch on the Chiata movement. The location of the fleet must have been discovered, as it appeared that the Chiata had dispatched several hundred ships toward the Oort Cloud. The bots had detected cosmic ray trails and hyperspace distortions projecting faster than light vortexes pointed in their direction. The recon on the speeds the Chiata traveled enabled estimates that they would arrive in another day. There would be bot booby traps left behind for them when they popped out of hyperspace, but the entire fleet would be long gone by then.

Alexander was feeling much better and had all the feeling back in his body. If asked he'd say he never felt better. Hell, he knew that he had felt worse after being tortured by Elle Ahmi and brought back from death several times for more torture. At that time, he had forced himself up, and with the help of Sehera, he had escaped. After hiding out for thirty days with no immunoboost, he had managed to heal enough to come back and kill an entire squad of Separatist soldiers. He could manage sitting in a chair and giving orders, of this he was certain.

Firestorm was on the way to recovery as well. While she was still in a wheelchair with her suit locked out, she was at least participating in the loony bin activities. Moore had been given the go-ahead for active duty just in time before the attack began. Unfortunately, Moore wouldn't have his XO back in time. DeathRay had managed to find a suitable stand-in from the CDC teams—a Navy lieutenant commander. Moore hoped she'd be able to fill Firestorm's shoes.

Alexander stepped onto the bridge carefully. He scanned the room and surveyed the repair job the bots had done. There was a completely new crew that Alexander didn't really know. They were all human, though.

"Captain Boland," he said. "If I hadn't been here when it happened, I wouldn't think the bridge had ever been damaged."

"Aye, sir. The damned bots did a good job," DeathRay said. "You want to sit in the chair, General?"

"I've been sitting in a chair enough lately," Moore said with a smile. "However, I will relieve you of command and return you to your position as CAG of the flight wing."

"I stand relieved, sir. Honestly, you were never not in charge as far as I was concerned." Jack saluted him. Alexander returned the salute and then shook DeathRay's armored hand.

"Thanks, Jack. Now, you stay on my daughter's wing and watch her ass, you hear me?"

"Yes, sir."

"And Jack," Moore added. "Watch your ass too."

"Always do, sir."

Moore waited for DeathRay to exit the bridge before he did his walk-around to get to know his new bridge crew. He had met them all before at some point and time aboard the ship, but now he had to really work with them and depend on them to help him do his job.

"Lieutenant Commander Julie Turner," he addressed his new XO. The female sailor was no more than five foot six, with brown hair and big brown eyes. She looked younger than Dee. From records Abby flashed into his DTM, he could see that she had been through a rejuv just before the expeditionary mission left the Sol System. She was really almost as old as DeathRay.

"Executive Officer reporting for duty, sir!" she said, a bit overzealously.

"At ease, XO." Moore held his armored hand out to shake hers. "Thanks for stepping up, Julie."

"Hooyay, sir." She gave the standard Navy response. Moore just nodded her to her post.

"Communications Officer!" He turned to the comm console.

"Aye, sir!" a young, dark-haired lieutenant junior grade Abby identified as Kellie Miltion replied. Moore would have to keep a running tab of the names in his DTM on the top layer until he learned them. For now, he'd likely just stick to the position titles.

"Get me Vice Admiral Walker online."

"Aye, sir."

"Nav!" Again another new name popped up into his mindview. There were so many lives he had known that had just been extinguished on the last run. There was some payback coming.

"Aye sir?"

"Open battle plan package titled 'Last Stand' in your DTM and load the coordinates for QMT," Moore ordered.

"Aye, sir!" his new navigation officer replied eagerly.

"Sir, Vice Admiral Walker is online," the communications officer announced. "Main viewscreen, sir?"

"Main screen." Moore nodded. Walker's face appeared on the main viewer. "Fullback, you ready to rock and roll?"

"General, it would be my pleasure. I'm getting tired of all this sitting around anyway. I just spoke with Captain Seeley and the clone fleet is ready to go," Walker replied.

"Very well then, let's go kick some Chiata ass!" Moore said. "I owe them some payback."

"Yes, sir, we all do. The *Thatcher* subfleet is ready when you are."

"See you at the rendezvous then, and good hunting. Moore out."

"All hands, all hands, battle stations. All hands, all hands, battle stations. QMT in ten seconds, nine . . ."

Chapter 48

June 16, 2407 AD
Alpha Lyncis
203 Light-years from the Sol System
Friday, 7:39 AM, Expeditionary Mission Standard Time

"The more you use the fewer you lose!" the lieutenant commander said eagerly to the bridge crew. The clones didn't seem to care one way or the other about his enthusiasm. "Captain, the shields appear to be holding, but we do have fires in the forward hangar. Fire crews have been dispatched, ma'am."

The *Hillenkoetter* rang like a bell and the impact of cannon fire bounced the bridge crew around again. They were all in full armor, and at least they were far enough back in the mix that they were presently safe from the surface-to-space fire.

Since all sixty-five or so of the remaining combined fleets QMTed directly into space around the third planetary system the numbers were a little more even. As it currently stood, Nancy's DTM battleview showed only two hundred thirty-one red dots of battleship or carrier size in range. The blue dots all popped into reality, space-guns ablazing and missiles firing, and this time with a better understanding of where to hit.

"Focus all DEG batteries on those tuning fork-shaped spires. Go for the blue beams first. Then we'll worry about the cannons," Nancy ordered the Weapons Deck Officer.

"Ma'am, all the tanks and AEMs have been deployed," the clone Ground Boss announced.

"Fighters have been deployed and are in position," the Air Boss added.

"Well, let's hope the plan works." Nancy thought of Jack and Dee for a brief moment. "Alright, Nav, be ready to bounce us about randomly. I want a QMT every thirty seconds. We pop into a swarm and hit and then pop out of that one and into a different one. We don't give them time to find us and target us with the blue beams. Got it?"

"Aye, ma'am." The navigation officer continued to tap furiously at the helm controls.

"Captain, the Chiata fleet is split up into roughly seven swarms," the STO said. "Each swarm has roughly thirty big ships in it. I'm tracking the centroid coordinates of them and passing them directly to the Nav."

"Good call, STO." Nancy said. "Nav, how about that first jump?"

"Aye, ma'am."

The ship was surrounded by white rippling spacetime and the interior buzzed and crackled. Then they were slightly farther from the Jovian planet's inhabited moon, but were smack in the middle of a Chiata swarm.

"Weapons Deck Officer, hit the tuning forks of the nearest-in-line ship with the DEGs and missiles." Nancy gripped the armrest of the chair a little too hard with her armored hand and could feel it start to give a bit. She eased her grip prematurely as cannon fire from the nearest porcupine started pounding them immediately.

"Seventeen seconds until they lock us up, Captain," Rackman alerted her.

"Keep firing on that ship!" Nancy shouted over the violent ringing and thudding of the cannon fire against the barrier shield.

"Stay on that lead ship's tuning fork!" she shouted.

"Ten seconds," Rackman warned.

"Don't let up, gunner! Nav, be ready on my command." Nancy held the chair arm tightly and did her best not to bite her lip. "Wait! Wait!"

An orange crack formed across the base of the tuning fork and began to vent debris and plasma. Arcs began to form across the tines of the fork and it looked as if it were about to fire.

"Five seconds!"

"Keep firing!"

"Three seconds, Captain!"

"Go, Nav!" Nancy shouted. The ship popped and crackled and vanished from reality space and then popped right back into a different swarm. "Pass along the previous target coordinates to the fleet and start hitting the lead ship!"

"Twenty-seven seconds, Captain!" Rackman started his countdown.

"We have got to take out some of these blue beams!" Nancy slammed her fist down. "Hit it faster, Gunner!"

"Aye, ma'am."

"Air Boss, tell me that the mecha jocks are doing better than we are!"

Chapter 49

June 16, 2407 AD
Alpha Lyncis
203 Light-years from the Sol System
Friday, 7:49 AM, Expeditionary Mission Standard Time

"Oh shit!" Dee shouted to DeathRay over the tac-net. "I hope the fleet is doing better than we are!"

"Stay frosty, Apple One," DeathRay ordered. "Keep cover fire going for the Maniacs while they're puking. We're up in a few minutes following the *Hillenkoetter's* Gnat squads, then the Dawgs."

"Roger that!" Apple One replied.

Jack was going at it all guns blazing. He'd never fought anything like this before. Usually humans in a fight tend to want to survive. But these things, these creatures, they didn't seem to care if they died or not, as long as they took out one of the pilots when they did—as long as they took out one of the members of *his* fighter squadron. And that just pissed DeathRay off.

"Guns, guns, guns!" DeathRay shouted as he rolled over his Gnat-T fighter end over end and toggled the switch to transform into bot mode. As he stood on his head looking backwards at the oncoming barrage of blue shimmering cannon fire, he lowered his weapons in the front to full blast from the DEGs. The enemy rounds hit the new Buckley-Freeman barrier shields and then disappeared off into some other spacetime coordinates. The shield generators were holding strong.

DeathRay stomped hard on the right outside pedal, yawing the bot about its center torso in order to track the alien fighter. The damned thing looked like smaller version of the porcupine-shaped supercarriers. His shoulder cannons fired behind him in a wide spread and he loosed missiles.

"Fox Three! Fox Three! Fox Three!" All in QM sensor mode and quantum mechanically locked onto targets. Without some sort of miracle or alien magic the laws of physics had the alien Gomer motherfuckers dead to rights.

Although DeathRay was seemingly surrounded by four different porcupines, they now had hell raining on them as best he could manage. Jack shot his leg thrusters at full speed, forcing him straight downward into the bowl at top speed.

"Archangels! This is DeathRay! Take the fight to the bottom of the bowl! Take the fight to the bottom of the bowl! We've gotta get these things close to the surface and see if we can't make them spread out!" DeathRay shouted.

Jack, Gomers 2 and 3 are breaking off. They're going after Dee.

Roger that, Candis. Jack rolled over and toggled his bot back to fighter mode as he nosed closer and closer to the surface of the inhabited Jovian moon. He tore through the atmosphere as it thickened around him and created hot, glowing red plasma contrails about his wingtips. The alien cityscape spires below were approaching fast. He could see the tankheads, AEMs, and the bots bouncing around like mad fleas on a dog.

He'd hoped the thicker atmosphere would bleed off his speed better, but he realized he was going to have to kick in some extra propulsion. He pulled back on the HOTAS hard and pulled up just in time to miss one of the-law-of-physics-breaking skyscraper spires just beneath him. He was so close that when he veered up, he had to scream, with a guttural, jaw-clenching, stomach-compressing roar, to force the blood from his thighs back into his head. He rolled upside-down slightly and toggled the fighter mode switch. The rapid shift made blood jump to his head almost instantly.

"Whooooo, shit!" he grunted. "Stay fast, Apple One. These goddamned porcupines can corner hard!"

Jack rolled the fighter mode Gnat over so he could see how close he was to the surface, and he could see glass and debris flying from the skyscraper. His shockwave had likely burst some of the structure. The

Chiata were at least going to need a shitload of screen doors for that building.

Cannon fire pinged the shields all around him and in front of him as his speed continued to take him toward the surface. He could see that the Marines on the surface were having just as tough a time as his squadron. Jack pulled the throttle back, did a complete one-hundred-eighty-degree yaw, flipping his nose into the rearward direction and going to guns.

"Guns, guns, guns!" he shouted. "Scratch one more porcupine!" Jack said as he yawed his fighter back over and back into bot mode—just as his mecha nearly scraped the ground. It looked as though he was running across the surface at over two thousand meters per second, jumping alien structures and the occasional AEM or hovertank. He fired the leg thrusters, pushing him upward, away from the surface, and then back into fighter mode, screaming upward enough to clear the oncoming buildings that were covered with the red and green glowing ground-combat creatures.

What are these things? he thought.

They're certainly not easy to kill, Candis responded in his mind.

Where's Dee, Candis?

Jack threw the ball up into his DTM and he zoomed around looking for Blue forces. His wingman popped up off his four o'clock just where she was supposed to be. Dee was covering his ass but she was taking on heavy fire. She had managed to bleed off her speed on a higher arc than he had, unfortunately placing too much distance between them. Jack went full throttle toward his wingman. How had he gotten separated after all these years when he'd beat into all of his squadron to *never* get separated from your wingman? But these alien things understood that. These things knew somehow how to drive a wedge, just like a maul through a stump, to split their wingmen apart and then pick them off. Jack had to rethink his way of fighting because this was an enemy he'd never thought of before. As Jack closed in on Dee, she shouted over the QMs and the tac-net.

"DeathRay, DeathRay, where the hell are you?! These motherfuckers are all over me and I can't shake 'em!"

"Hang in there, Apple One! I'm coming as fast as I can! Keep switching modes on 'em! That seems to create some amount of confusion! And take it to the ground, Dee, take it to the ground!"

Jack watched as Dee pulled off a perfect Fokker's feint, rolling over onto her head just as he had done, and firing her thrusters right through the ball that her assailants had her trapped in. At least it wasn't a death wheel she was trapped in. She poked through the bottom of the ball, reached out with a hand and literally smashed through a spire cannon of one of the enemy fighters, at the same time firing her shoulder cannons at the enemy fighter behind her.

"Take that, you fucking Gomers!" she screamed.

As soon as she passed through the small ball that she was trapped in, she toggled over into fighter mode at full throttle toward the surface. Jack swiftly calculated in his direct mind link several plots that would get him there through the enemy fire, and quickly. He watched the lines veer together, and he found the one that he liked, took it, and improvised along the way.

"Fox Three!" He fired a missile into the mix. The missile shot out, leaving a slight purple ion glow behind it as it left, trailing into the rear section of one of her pursuers. "Scratch three," Jack said.

About that time, his ship rocked, the armor plating of the hull shook and his sif generator warning light came on. The barrier shield was weakened by the impact.

Barrier shield at seventy-three percent, Candis warned him.

"Ding! Ding! Ding!" the Bitchin' Betty chimed. "Warning! Radar lock detected. Warning! Radar lock detected."

Jack looked at the bowl in his mind and zoomed out. He noticed there was a Gomer on his tail and it was closing in fast.

I'm not leaving my wingman, he thought. *I've gotta get to Dee.*

She's breaking through, Jack, Candis said. *She's getting close to the surface with only two pursuers now. She can handle 'em. You're going to have to take evasives.*

Jack thought about that for a second.

That's exactly how they want us to play this game. I'm not *leaving my wingman. We're going to stick to the tactics that work. And maybe add some new ones.*

Jack rolled his fighter onto the track that he'd planned to meet Dee. He was constantly changing as she was juking and jinking and weaving in and out of the enemy fire. He could see gusts of debris flying up as she approached the surface of the alien city. He went to full throttle and afterburners, with the g-load throwing him into the back of the seat as hard as it could. He went into a corkscrew to hopefully throw off the radar track. His pursuer came in even closer.

"Apple One, DeathRay."

"Go, DeathRay."

"I've got one locked. I'm trying to shake him. But I'm not coming off your tail. Gimme five seconds. When I get on your tail we're gonna do a little shake an' bake on this guy."

"Roger that, DeathRay. Fox Three! Fox Three!" he heard Dee shout as he approached.

But this guy was serious. He stayed on DeathRay's six in the same deadly dance, corkscrew spirals, and jukes and jinks, all the way to the surface. Going into bot mode would slow him down too much at this point, and this guy was stuck on his tail. He could now see Dee's pursuer hot on her tail and firing, lighting her up—but he was in range.

Candis, feed Apple One's AIC jump coordinates and time both jumps simultaneously now!

Got it, Jack! QMT in three, two, one!

Jack could see the fighter on Dee's tail letting loose blue fireballs that were tracking dead on, but then there was a white flash and the crackling sound and both of them were behind the Gomer on Jack's six o'clock and still carrying their momentum.

"Guns, guns, guns!" He plowed through the tailpipe of the porcupine in front of him and it exploded in a ball of orange-red flames, throwing pieces of the alien craft everywhere. There was nothing left of whatever the pilot was.

This startled the second pursuer that had been on Dee's tail. Jack could just imagine what the thing must have thought having her dead in its sights one instant and then her vanishing and reappearing on its six the next. Dee was still in bot mode and pointed in the wrong direction to fire, but the startled and confused alien fighter was giving her plenty of time to correct that issue. Dee did a feint and loaded the alien's ass end full of cannon fire from her guns, taking it out.

Jack winced as some of Dee's plasma rounds, glowing the size of grapefruits and traveling at near the speed of light, zipped past several tankheads below, but fortunately they missed.

As for the third Gomer that had been on them, Dee was still tracking it. She pitched over again, going back to fighter mode, and let loose another volley of cannon fire. Jack followed it up with his rear DEGs.

An array of flaming balls zipped out across the sky into the nose shields of his pursuer. The QMT tactic worked like a charm. They had managed to catch the aliens unaware and took them out.

DeathRay flew through the fiery ball of the fighter Dee had just taken out in front of them and closed in on Dee's wing.

"Jesus, DeathRay, I've got seven more porcupines DTM inbound fast."

"Roger that," he said. "We've got to do something to bring these things down. It's time to surprise these bastards continuously."

"I agree!" Apple One replied.

"Get ready for another QMT bait and switch!" he told her.

"Ooh-fuckin'-rah!" Dee replied. DeathRay knew that Marines just couldn't help themselves sometimes.

Chapter 50

June 16, 2407 AD
Alpha Lyncis
203 Light-years from the Sol System
Friday, 8:19 AM, Expeditionary Mission Standard Time

"Look out, Warlord One, you've got two of those blurs up your ass!" Warlord Three shouted over the tankhead's tac-net.

"I've got him, Three!" General Mason Warboys pulled his hovertank from tank mode into to bot mode and flipped over head first, bringing the cannon up like a club and swatting at one of the red and green blurs that was bouncing around him. The cannon caught the blur midsection and sent it careening in the opposite direction. The second blur was too fast for him and it was pounding away at the bot mode tank's armored torso.

Warboys bearhugged the blur with the full strength of his mechanized grip until he thought his arms were going to pop out of the sockets. He could hear metal screeching, and system alerts were sounding inside the cockpit. Then something felt as if it gave way. Red and green glowing liquid squirted in every direction like a bursting water balloon filled with paints. The glowing liquid oozed over his tank, but the whirling dervish of a creature he had been holding had stopped fighting him.

"That's two!" he said to himself.

"Warning, enemy targeting system detected!" his Bitchin' Betty chimed in. It was too late. A blue beam similar to the ones fired from the large ships zigged across in front of him then turned a full ninety-degree turn and hit him directly on the chest section of the tank. The impact knocked him backwards several tens of meters.

Sir, shields are at fifty percent! his AIC said into his mind.

"Warlord One is down!" he heard Two shout over the net.

"I'm up," Warboys rebutted. "I'm not dead yet, Two. Where the hell did that come from?"

"I didn't see it!" Two replied. "We need to get out of here."

"Warlords! QMT to next set of coordinates and stay at it." Mason triggered his QMT random jump and repositioned himself as he reappeared in reality space.

He quickly scanned the battlescape view in his DTM. The Maniacs were currently doing their pukin' deathblossom thing and were alleviating some of the ground stress. The Archangels and three clone squadrons were also mixing it up above and on the surface. The fighters helped. But as far as Mason could tell both the tankheads and the AEMs were getting their teeth kicked in.

"Alright, Warlords, let's take out a that nearest cannon spire a quarter klick at the following coordinates." He DTMed the location to the tank squad. "Stay in phalanx charge at full speed."

"Roger that, One!" the Warlords replied.

"Keep an eye out for whatever is firing those blue beams!" Warboys ordered. He pounded his tank at top speed across what could only be considered a street. There were vehicles that could have been considered cars. There was just no way of knowing as none of the oddly shaped things were moving. The only motion was from either the red-green blurs or the fighter porcupine-like things that were bouncing about overhead and strafing the shit out of them every chance the bastards got.

The street led in straight paths and made abrupt turns. There were no curved paths. The street was similar to that strange blue beam in that regard.

Find me a path to that spire, he told his AIC.

Got it, General. His AIC responded by highlighting a path in his DTM view.

Warboys took point in the phalanx charge down the street. The red-green blurry things were coming out of every nook and cranny in the cityscape.

"Guns, guns, guns!" he shouted as he fired his shoulder-mounted cannons into what he hoped was the torso of one of the aliens. The tracers tracked across the façade of one of the buildings, blowing holes and flinging shrapnel in every direction, and finally hit something that became another paint-balloon splatter effect.

"Look out, Six! One behind you!"

"He's on me like stink on shit!" Warlord Six shouted.

"Don't break ranks!" Mason ordered. "They're trying to scatter us and pick us off!"

"I've got him, Six!" Warlord Four replied. "Fox Three!"

Mason could see in his DTM that the missile hit home. Six was cleared, but then four more of the damned blurs dropped in right in the middle of them as if they'd just fallen from the sky.

"He's on my back," Two shouted.

"Shit, I've got two on my three-nine!" Five sounded terrified.

"Keep it together, Warlords!" Mason shouted over the net at his squad. "Guns, guns, guns!"

He turned and went to his cannons, bull's-eyeing the blur on Two's back. Five was already on the ground being pounded. One of the arms of his tank was being torn free. Mason reversed direction, throwing up chunks of whatever the street was made from as he fired his foot thrusters. He dove headfirst on top of Five, driving a metal fist the size of a refrigerator through a blur's midback. His fist went through the thing and he could hear a screech that was beyond anything he'd ever heard before. It was horrific, but Mason pulled the thing off of Five and staggered backwards. The blur seemed to turn itself around and tendrils of red and green wrapped around the cockpit dome of his bot mode tank.

The tank groaned against the stress of the thing's grip. Mason struggled and flailed wildly at the alien with his other mechanized arm, but the alien thing had little if any solid geometry.

"Hold still, you son of a bitch!" He continued to swat at it and push it back from his face.

"Three is down!"

"Shit, they're all over me!"

Then it began raining aliens—hundreds more began to fall from above. Mason could only assume that the aliens had managed to get reinforcements. Either that or they had just stumbled into the middle of a hive.

The Blue force tracker in his mindview flashed Three from yellow to red and then black. Then Seven went black. The Warlords were being devastated, and he was under a pile of alien blurs and could do very little to save himself.

"Evac out now! Warlords! I repeat! Evac QMT now!" Just as Mason started the QMT algorithm, his canopy was pulled free. Another alien tendril ripped precious technology from the torso of his tank.

"Warning, QMT system failure . . ." His Bitchin' Betty trailed off.

Mason reached over to tap the emergency personnel wrist band QMT snap-back system, and to his surprise, his left arm was not there. He looked at the sealed-off stump of his armor suit in horror. He had not even felt the injury. Then he was torn free from the tank and could only see a whirl of motion spinning about himself.

Son of a bitch! This is it, ain't it, Brenda? he thought to his AIC.

I think so, sir! It was an honor.

Detonate my suit, Brenda. Authorization Warboys One Warlord One, Mason thought. His mind was no longer able to keep up with what was happening to him. The world spun as the aliens tore him apart. Only the last bit of stims and immunoboost had kept him alive this long. He still wasn't sure why he had felt no pain.

Did any of the Warlords make it out?

I don't know. Suit detonation now.

Chapter 51

June 16, 2407 AD
Alpha Lyncis
203 Light-years from the Sol System
Friday, 8:19 AM, Expeditionary Mission Standard Time

"The QMT bait and switch is working, General!" his XO shouted over the thud of enemy missiles hitting the barrier shield. Moore kept a tally on the shields the same as he did the countdown clock to the blue beams. They had managed to avoid being hit a single time by the zigzagging menacing death beams so far.

"Keep hitting that tuning fork spire, Gunner!" he said.

"Aye, sir!"

"Thirteen seconds, General!" the XO shouted.

"Shit, there just isn't enough time to do enough damage!" He pounded his armored fist against his armored thigh. "We need to stay on that target longer."

"Ten seconds!"

Then jump, but to a place with the same target in range, Alexander. His AIC highlighted a location in space on the other side of the alien ship in his DTM battlescape view.

You are brilliant, Abigail! Pass the coordinates to the Nav now!

"Nav! Change the jump coordinates to the ones you are receiving now!"

"Got it, sir!"

"Five seconds, General!" the XO shouted.

"Go, Nav!" Moore gritted his teeth. The QMT jump flashed just in time. The *Madira* sling-forward maneuver placed them in reality space at almost the mirror-image location of where they had been.

"I've got the target acquired, General!" the Weapons Deck Officer shouted.

"Well, don't waste time telling me about it, Gunner! Fire, dammit!"

"Twenty-nine seconds, General!" the XO started the clock over.

"General, I'm picking up a huge EM buildup around the tuning fork spire!" the STO said.

"Zoom in on the screen!" Moore ordered. The spire was cracking all about the base and upward through the center between the tines. The blue arcs jumped from time to time like the thing was about to fire, but then orange and red plasma ejected out around it in all directions. The spire exploded in a mix of blue arcs and red and orange plasma with the force of a small tactical gluonium bomb. Secondary explosions raced longitudinally up the ship until there was one final huge blast, throwing pieces of the supercarrier-sized ship into a nearby swarm ship, breaking through parts of its exterior armor.

"Nineteen seconds!"

"Gunner! Target the damaged area of the second ship!"

"On it, General!"

The red and green beams from the DEGs tracked across into the open wound of the Chiata ship. The cannon spires on the side facing them were mostly wiped out by the explosion of the first one. The other fleet ships nearest the *Madira* were occupying the local swarm enough so that they were managing to minimize damage. The Buckley-Freeman shields were holding solid.

"Give me a missile in there!" Moore ordered.

"Aye, sir!" the gunner replied and toggled several other controls. A nuclear-tipped missile tracked out from the ship and corkscrewed about the DEG beams all the way to target. The missile vanished past the burned-through armor and then exploded in the interior of the alien ship. The Chiata vessel bulged in the center then popped from the overpressure. The ship was nearly torn in half even before secondary explosions began.

"Nine seconds!"

Then a blue beam zigged from out of nowhere and slammed into the aft barrier shield. Moore felt the jolt, but this time his crew was fully armored and strapped in.

"CO, CDC!"

"Where the hell did that come from, CDC?"

"Sir! I have two hundred more ships just dropped out of hyperspace jaunt right on top of us!" the CDC replied.

"I have them confirmed, General!" the STO replied.

"Communications Officer, sound the retreat call!"

"Aye, sir!"

"Nav, get us out of here now!"

A second blue beam zigged across the sky in front of them into one of the *Thatcher* fleet ships. Then another. The ship exploded before it could QMT. From the looks of it, Captain Seeley's ships were getting hammered as well. The *Madira* was slammed just as the sling-forward algorithm kicked in.

"Shields are down to forty percent, General! It looks like, oh my God," the XO paused in disbelief.

"What is it, XO?"

"General, seventeen fleet ships are lost, sir. The rest of the fleet managed to QMT out," the XO explained.

"Where are we, Nav?" Moore hoped that at least they were where they had planned to be. Seventeen ships. That was over three hundred thousand souls, assuming the clones had souls too. Moore hadn't expected, and nobody had known or could have known, that the damned Chiata could target while in hyperspace.

"We are at the planned evac point in the Oort Cloud on the opposite side of the star where we previously were, sir. At least another five days away from the alien fleet," the navigation officer replied.

"And the mecha and AEMs?" Moore held his breath for a moment.

"They are all accounted for, sir. The fighters are nearby waiting for the ground troops and mecha to clear the hangar decks," the XO said. "And several of the hangars are still on fire, sir. Fire crews are working the problem. Also, sir, with so many ships lost, we have mecha out there not knowing where to go. There are tanks and AEMs floating in free space."

"Okay, give me a moment to think." Moore took a deep breath and then pulled up the casualties list. Dee wasn't on it. He exhaled. "Start the emergency QMTs, wounded, then AEMs first, followed by tanks. The mecha jocks won't mind flying a holding pattern for a while."

"Yes, sir."

Abigail, give me the summary, he thought.

Yes sir. We lost twenty-seven percent of the ground forces, including General Warboys. Sixteen percent of the fighters were lost, a little heavier on the clone pilots, which is as planned and expected. Of the total sixty-five supercarrier class ships we started with on this attack wave, we lost seventeen. We are down to forty-eight ships, sir.

We can't keep sending in soldiers to the meat grinder like this, Alexander thought.

What else can we do, General?

We can go home and rethink our plans. Clearly, what we're doing ain't working.

Yes, sir.

How could I have thought we could hold this system? Moore wasn't sure if he was getting overly confident in his old age, or incompetent. This was as bad as the first Martian Desert Campaign that he had sworn never to let happen again.

Perhaps we continue to underestimate the Chiata strength? Abigail suggested.

Or overestimate our own.

Epilogue

June 18, 2407 AD
Alpha Lyncis
203 Light-years from the Sol System
Sunday, 7:19 PM, Expeditionary Mission Standard Time

It had taken most of two days to orchestrate a complete rescue. There was always the fear that somehow the relentless Chiata would find them and get to them before they could get further away. But in the end, that didn't happen and the Chiata were at least limited in technology to hyperspace jaunt propulsion. They were limited to speeds of about seventy-five times the speed of light. That was still way faster than human hyperspace technology. Had it not been for the QMT systems, things would have been a lot worse.

"XO to CO."

"Go, Firestorm." Deanna listened as her father talked to the bridge crew. The XO was finally out of the wheelchair and was back on active duty.

"That is the last of the survivors, sir. All the ships report loaded and ready to snap back to Alpha Ursae Majoris."

"Understood, XO. Hopefully, the bots are finished building a big pad so we can leap all the way back home. Otherwise it will be a long seventy-two hours," Moore said.

"Yes, sir. Any other orders, sir?"

"Are the bots in place here?"

"The busy bastards are already turning a nearby comet into thousands of other bots, sir."

"Good. I'd hate to leave without giving the Chiata a parting gift."

"Yes, sir."

"Sound the general retreat, XO. All ships to return to rendezvous at Alpha Ursae Majoris as soon as their Nav is ready."

"Ready to go, Daddy?"

"Looks like it, Princess." Deanna cringed when he called her that. But with a bit of thought she knew she didn't mind. In fact, it helped her feel that she was safe and things were okay in the universe. The feeling of the safe little girl in her superhuman daddy's arms quickly vanished. The Chiata were right out there. The alien menace was only one light-year away from where she was standing. And there was nothing that humanity had been able to do so far to stop them. Maybe they slowed them down, but most likely, Dee figured, they'd just pissed them off.

Deanna looked out at the red star in the distance and thought she'd be glad to put as much distance between herself and it as soon as possible. She knew that she'd meet the Chiata again someday soon. But for now, she just wanted the hell away from them.

"They know we're out there now," she said to her father as they stood looking out the window of the lounge. "They'll be coming."

"They knew we were there all along." her father replied. "They were already coming. We just didn't know it."

"Grandmother did," Dee replied.

"So she did." Alexander agreed.

Dee turned and looked at her father. He had always been larger than life and bigger than any odds and as strong or stronger than any situation had ever required him to be. But this was different. They'd just gotten their asses kicked and the bully that did it was still coming after them.

"Daddy, what are we going to do?"

"We will do what any good Marine has always done since there have been Marines." Her father put his arm around her and looked her in the eyes. "We will improvise and adapt and we will overcome. We will fight."

"What if that isn't enough, Daddy?" Dee longed to get out of her armor and simply hug her father.

"Then we will die fighting." her father told her.

"Ooh-fuckin'-rah, Daddy." she whispered.

"Ooh-fuckin'-rah, Princess."